WHEEL OF FIRE

Recent Titles by Hilary Bonner

A David Vogel mystery

DEADLY DANCE *
WHEEL OF FIRE *

Novels

THE CRUELLEST GAME
FRIENDS TO DIE FOR
DEATH COMES FIRST

* *available from Severn House*

WHEEL OF FIRE

Hilary Bonner

This first world edition published 2018
in Great Britain and 2019 in the USA by
SEVERN HOUSE PUBLISHERS LTD of
Eardley House, 4 Uxbridge Street, London W8 7SY
Trade paperback edition first published
in Great Britain and the USA 2019 by
SEVERN HOUSE PUBLISHERS LTD

British Library Cataloguing in Publication Data
A CIP catalogue record for this title is available from the British Library.

ISBN-13: 978-0-7278-8828-0 (cased)
ISBN-13: 978-1-84751-954-2 (trade paper)
ISBN-13: 978-1-4483-0163-8 (e-book)

This is a work of fiction. Names, characters, places and incidents
are either the product of the author's imagination or are used fictitiously.
Except where actual historical events and characters are being described
for the storyline of this novel, all situations in this publication are
fictitious and any resemblance to actual persons, living or dead,
business establishments, events or locales is purely coincidental.

All Severn House titles are printed on acid-free paper.

Severn House Publishers support the Forest Stewardship Council™ [FSC™],
the leading international forest certification organisation.
All our titles that are printed on FSC certified paper carry the FSC logo.

Typeset by Palimpsest Book Production Ltd.,
Falkirk, Stirlingshire, Scotland.
Printed and bound in Great Britain by
TJ International, Padstow, Cornwall.

For
Jean and Louis

Always there

ACKNOWLEDGMENTS

With grateful thanks to Fire Officer Dave West and his colleagues at Wellington Fire Station; Wellington-based PC Hayden Smith of the Avon and Somerset Constabulary; Police Sergeant Andrew Pugh of the Brentford Safer Neighbourhood Team; Detective Constable Shane O'Neill of the Metropolitan Police Force; and Joe Coggins of the Canal and River Trust.

'I am bound upon a wheel of fire, that mine own tears do scald like molten lead.'

William Shakespeare, *King Lear*

PROLOGUE

The storm was over. The rain had stopped. The flames that engulfed the big old house raged unhindered. Later, some claimed that the glow in the sky could be seen as far away as Taunton or Tiverton, each fourteen or fifteen miles from Blackdown Manor as the crow flies.

Tom Withey was a trainee fire officer. He'd celebrated his twentieth birthday only a week earlier. He had never seen anything like it before, and he hoped he never would again.

There were people inside that house. Either dead or dying. Nobody was likely to get out alive, that was for sure.

Tom was the newest member of the five-man Wellington crew aboard the first fire appliance to arrive at the scene. Tom checked his watch. It was 2.03 a.m. They had left the fire station just three and a half minutes after the emergency call, well below the maximum five-minute time limit set by the British Fire and Rescue Service, and, after a hair-raising high-speed dash through the winding country lanes of West Somerset, had arrived at the gates to the old manor within less than half an hour. Tom, unaware then of what lay ahead, had enjoyed that bit.

As they approached they'd at first seen little sign of fire, even though the sky had cleared, and a weak moon peeped through the clouds. Perhaps there was some smoke escaping from the front of the house. Tom and the boys weren't sure.

The electrically-operated iron double gates stood open. After all, they would presumably have been expected, along with other emergency services. Billy Prettyjohn, the driver, swung the engine, Wellington's biggest and best, carrying 18,000 litres of water in its own internal tank, expertly through the gateway. He prepared to accelerate.

It didn't look like a major incident, necessarily. Not then. And the crew were all aware that Wellington's second appliance was only four minutes behind them, and that two more were on the way, one from Taunton and one from Honiton. Four engines called out, as is standard with a house fire, and certainly when the house in question is a big old manor. But Billy was local, like all of them. He knew the drive leading to Blackdown Manor was a good quarter of a mile long. And he was an experienced fire officer, who had learned first-hand that just a few seconds could mean the difference between dealing with a fire that is easily containable and being faced with one already out of control.

Suddenly there was a shrieking noise as Billy braked hard, and the big engine jolted to a halt.

'Fuck,' said Billy.

'I don't fucking believe it,' said Bob Parsons, officer in charge and also Wellington's station manager, who was strapped into his designated front seat alongside Billy.

'What's happening?' called out Pete Biffin, one of the three firefighters riding in the back.

'There's a bloody great tree right across the drive,' Billy shouted back. 'Must have come down in the storm.'

Bob Parsons jumped out for a closer look. In the beam of his torch he could clearly see that a dense stretch of woodland, flanked by iron railings, lined either side of the drive, eliminating any possibility of manoeuvring the fire engine around the fallen tree.

Parsons whistled long and low, then turned back towards his crew.

'Right lads, everybody out,' he said. 'Let's see if we can shift this thing.'

The crew, apart from driver Billy Prettyjohn who stayed ready at the wheel, quickly joined their OIC. The closer they got to the fallen tree, the bigger and heavier it looked.

Pete Biffin stepped forward. Like all of the Wellington team he was a retained part-time fireman. His day job was farming.

'It's an oak, Bob,' he said. 'Look at the size of it. And damaged by lightning at some stage, I'd say. You can see the split in the trunk. That's why it came down.'

'Never mind why it came down,' countered Bob Parsons. 'How the heck can we get it out of the damned way?'

'We can't,' said Pete. 'Haven't got the gear. Not for that. We need specialist lifting equipment, Bob. Even a tractor with chains won't do it. We're going to have to call in USAR.'

Parsons grunted his irritation. Urban Search And Rescue are a specialist part of the fire service, equipped and trained to deal with a vast range of challenges including lifting and moving large heavy objects. They even have their own fork-lift trucks. Pete Biffin was not really telling Parsons anything he didn't already know. But Bob hadn't wanted to accept the necessity to call in USAR to move the oak, because that would mean an unspecified delay in getting through to the manor. By which time a fire which, so far, appeared to be only a minor incident, might have turned into something else. And the Devon and Somerset Fire Service's USAR team were based at Exeter, almost thirty miles away. Nonetheless, Parsons knew he had no choice.

'Right, Billy, you get on to it,' he instructed. 'Call 'em in. Meanwhile, does anyone know if there's another route to the house?'

There was a muttering, nobody was sure.

'There could be—' began Pete Biffin.

Tom Withey heard his own voice, interrupting.

'There's a light on in The Gatehouse, you can just see it through a chink in the upstairs curtains,' he said. 'Perhaps there's someone there, someone who might be able to help.'

'Well done, lad,' said Parsons, as he strode across to the house and knocked on the door.

There was no response.

'I thought I saw movement,' ventured Tom uncertainly. 'B-but it could have been a trick of the light.'

Bob Parsons hammered more loudly on the door. There was still no response.

He turned back to his crew. 'Any other ideas?'

'Look, I don't think this will help much, but I'm pretty sure there's a track from Blackdown Farm leading to the manor,' said Pete Biffin. 'It's meant for tractors, though. I don't reckon we'd stand much chance of getting this beast through.'

'I was on an engine once and the driver took it straight through a hedge,' muttered Parsons.

'I reckon we'd have to mow down hedges on either side, and a stretch or two of bank as well,' said Pete. 'No, the more I think about it, the more I can't see that it's worth even trying that track. We'd just get stuck.'

Parsons turned to stare at Blackdown Manor. The moon seemed to be growing increasingly brighter. There was still little sign of a fire, although he was fairly sure that he could see some smoke now.

'Anyone know if there's any water close to the house?' he asked.

It was Pete Biffin again who answered the question. As a boy he'd helped his father deliver eggs and vegetables to Blackdown Manor.

'There's a big ornamental pond, right in front of the place,' Pete volunteered, knowing exactly what his station manager was getting at. 'We should be able to pump from that.'

'Right,' said Parsons. 'Let's unload the LPP and get on up there to check the place out properly.'

Parsons was referring to the Light Portable Pump carried by all British fire appliances. Tom Withey – a big strong lad, who, along with all the other fire officers stationed at Wellington, trained at least three times a week – had already helped to carry one several times. He reckoned that most people would not regard an LPP as remotely light or portable. The pumps were basically adapted car engines, and weighed the best part of half a ton. Four fit men were needed to carry one of them. And the shorter the distance the better. On this occasion, the pump would have to be somehow or other lifted over the fallen tree, and then there was still a quarter of a mile of driveway to cover.

As, along with the rest of the crew, he turned to run back to the engine and unload the pump, Tom just hoped he was up to the task. Bob Parsons was still speaking.

'The way things are at the moment if there's anyone inside we should be able to get them out,' Parsons continued. 'And at least we can assess how serious the situation is. So, the quicker we get there the better.'

Within seconds the team had removed the portable pump from the fire engine and were attempting to lift it over the stricken oak, two men on top of the trunk pulling, and two with their feet still on the ground pushing.

Then it happened. Boom. A blast, like a major bomb going off, ripped through the night air and the rear part of Blackdown Manor exploded. This was followed within seconds by an eruption of flames shooting into the sky, twenty maybe thirty feet high. Along with the ever-brightening moon, the flames provided terrifying clear illumination of the scene now confronting the shocked

Wellington firefighters. It looked as if the top of the old house was simply no longer there, having been lifted by a force of unimaginable magnitude.

Tom felt numb. He couldn't move. He couldn't think. What the hell had caused that? He and the rest of the crew remained stricken, straddled across the fallen tree for several seconds, still carrying the heavy pump between them.

In the distance, Tom heard Bob Parsons's voice.

'She's blown,' said Parsons, shocked, but still in control, only the slightest tremor in his voice.

Like all of them, he was staring at the blazing manor house.

'Right lads,' he continued. 'We aren't going to be able to do anything with an LPP now. So, let's put the bugger down, shall we. Careful as you go.'

Only then did Tom become aware of the pain in his arms and legs from muscles straining under the weight of the so-called portable pump.

Once the pump had been safely lowered to the ground, Parsons spoke again. 'Gas,' he said. 'Gotta be. Either that or it's a terrorist attack. Which would be a first for these parts. Anyone know if they've got a gas tank out the back?'

He glanced towards Pete Biffin.

The younger man shook his head. 'I dunno, Bob, but I shouldn't be surprised. They must have something for heating, and there's no natural gas out here. Either a gas tank or oil, and oil wouldn't blow like that.'

'No. And neither does a gas tank as a rule. Not without some help in my experience. But that isn't our problem. Our job is to get help to those poor bastards—'

Parsons was interrupted by another loud bang from the other end of the drive. Some kind of secondary explosion, or perhaps just the crash of the grand old house tumbling down. None of the crew were too sure.

'Jesus,' said Parsons.

He spoke into his radio.

'Urgent assistance,' he demanded. 'We have a major incident. There's been a large explosion at Blackdown Manor, perhaps a double explosion, which seems to have lifted most of the roof, and we now have an out of control fire spreading rapidly throughout.

We believe there are people still inside the building, probably trapped. We have already requested USAR to shift an oak tree blocking the drive. This should now be top priority. Virtually the entire house seems to be on fire, and we can't get an engine near to it. Also, if they're not on their way already, we need medics—'

It was clear that Parsons had been interrupted by the co-ordinator. He listened for a few seconds.

'You've just heard what?' he said then, the surprise clear in his voice.

He listened for a few seconds more.

'Right,' he said. 'Got it.'

He turned back to his men.

'There's been a development,' he said. 'We're not going anywhere close to that burning house, boys. Even if we could find a way through. We have to back off.'

Tom Withey, in spite of his youth and his newness to the job, was already trained to continue to function under devastatingly horrific circumstances. But, now, not only was the way to the blazing Blackdown Manor at least temporarily impassable, but the boss was instructing his men to back off.

'It's been reported that there are armed intruders on the property,' Parsons continued. 'We can't take the risk . . .'

Tom listened in a near daze. So, all he and the rest of the crew were going to be able to do was to stand and watch. And Tom knew, beyond any reasonable doubt, that he was watching people burn to death. He thought it was probably the most difficult thing he'd had to do in his whole young life.

ONE

Saslow picked up Detective Inspector David Vogel from his home, at Sea Mills on the M5 side of Bristol, at 6.15 a.m. It was still dark on a cold, wet, early-October morning. Pretty typical of the west of England, Vogel thought. He wasn't looking forward to being driven halfway across Somerset on what could quite probably not be a police matter at all.

Then there was the very slight awkwardness he sometimes felt nowadays with Saslow. The two officers had been working together since soon after Vogel transferred from the Met to the Avon and Somerset Constabulary's Major Crime Investigation Team. In the beginning Dawn Saslow, small, dark, and clever, had been a uniformed constable. Vogel quickly formed a high opinion of her, and had been instrumental in her promotion to MCIT. But things hadn't been quite the same between them since their last big case. And neither had Saslow, in Vogel's opinion. She remained an exceptional officer, but had, he thought, lost more than a little of her raw, almost schoolgirl-like enthusiasm for the job.

He settled into the passenger seat and turned towards the young DC.

'How are you feeling then, Dawn?' he asked.

Saslow's eyes were focused on the steering wheel. Vogel cursed himself as soon as he had spoken. Not so long ago he wouldn't have bothered to enquire after her welfare, and Saslow would know that.

'I meant, with such an early start,' he added quickly.

She answered equably enough.

'I'm fine, sir,' she said. 'Could have done with a couple of hours more kip.'

'Me too,' said Vogel, with feeling.

'You think this could turn out to be a wild goose chase, don't you, boss?' Saslow continued, as she eased her pool vehicle away from the kerb.

Londoner Vogel, a true city boy, did not hold a driving licence.

Learning to drive had actually been a condition of his transfer to the Avon and Somerset from the Met. But somehow or other he'd still managed to avoid more than a couple of extremely unsatisfactory lessons.

'Something of the sort,' muttered Vogel.

'I thought so,' continued Saslow. 'I mean, I was a bit surprised to hear we'd been called out to a house fire. Even a major one.'

'No ordinary house, and no ordinary householder,' said Vogel.

He took off his thick-lensed spectacles and rubbed them inadequately against his sleeve.

'I assume you've heard of Sir John Fairbrother?'

'Vaguely, sir. One of the great and the good, isn't he?'

Vogel chuckled wryly.

'One of the greatly rich, that's for sure,' said the DI. 'Chairman and CEO of Fairbrother International. His family still own Fairbrother's Bank, the second oldest private bank in the UK and the sixth oldest in the world. Sir John is in his early sixties now, but apparently has always continued to run the family business with a rod of iron. And he has a reputation for being something of a maverick. There's been a rumour that he's had to step back a bit in recent months because he hasn't been well. Unsubstantiated, though, and officially denied. But the city seemed to believe it. The shares in Fairbrother International keep dropping.'

'So how ill do we think he is, boss?' asked Saslow.

'Very ill indeed now, Saslow. In fact, it would seem that he's dead. I thought you knew that?'

'I knew two people were suspected of having died in this fire, but I wasn't told who they were, or even if they'd been identified,' responded Saslow.

'No, well, of course there's no question of them having been identified yet,' said Vogel. 'And, as we all know, in the case of a fire sometimes formal identification is never possible. But there's not much doubt that in this case the two casualties are Sir John and his Filipino nurse. It was the nurse who called 999, from inside the house, Blackdown Manor.'

He reached into a pocket for his notebook, and glanced at it before continuing.

'The call was logged at 1.31am this morning. The 999 operator reported that the woman, who gave her name as Sophia Santos, sounded anxious but in control. Her English was not perfect, but good enough not to be a problem.

'She indicated that she was with her employer, Sir John, in his bedroom, and that they had both smelt smoke. The operator asked if Sophia thought they could safely leave the house, and the nurse replied that Sir John was unwell, and that she believed it would be safer to stay in the bedroom which had a fire door. She also said she had spoken to someone called George, whom she described as Sir John's driver, and that he had said they should stay where they were and he would come to assist them. The operator had begun to ask other questions when Sophia apparently ended the call, in spite of the operator's request for her to stay on the line, saying that her employer needed her. Repeated attempts by the 999 operator to call her back failed.

'Then, at 2.05 a.m., Sophia called again. By then she was panicking. The operator tried to calm her down and told her that firefighters had arrived at Blackdown Manor, and she was sure they would soon get to her and her employer.

'The nurse then said they might be too late, and that the police were also needed because there were armed intruders on the property. "Bad men with guns", were her exact words apparently. The operator asked how she knew that, if she had seen these "bad men", and the nurse replied that she hadn't seen them, that George had told her. She also said she was afraid that these men intended to kill Sir John and her too. The operator asked if this George was now with her and Sir John, and she replied that he hadn't been able to get through yet, he too was afraid of the men with guns, and she'd only been able to talk to him on the phone. The operator then asked if she could speak to Sir John. The nurse replied that her employer's speech wasn't good, and he no longer used a phone.'

Vogel put his notebook down and turned towards Saslow.

'Apparently, this time the 999 operator managed to keep Sophia on the line for about four minutes, reassuring the nurse about the arrival of the emergency services and so on, until she heard a loud bang down the phone line and Sophia began to scream uncontrollably. The operator tried to calm her and find out what had happened, but Sophia just carried on screaming until the line went dead.'

Vogel closed his notebook and put it back in his pocket. For a moment there was silence in the car. Neither Saslow nor Vogel had any words.

Saslow spoke first. 'Jesus boss, seems like that 999 operator heard that poor woman dying.'

'Yes, I think she probably did, Saslow,' said Vogel quietly.

'That's just so terrible,' said Saslow. 'I wonder how often that happens, boss?'

'In the age we live in, where almost everyone has a mobile phone, I suspect it's not that unusual.'

'I wouldn't like that job, boss,' commented Saslow.

'No, at least we're not always totally helpless in the face of death and destruction, eh Saslow?'

Saslow glanced sideways at her senior officer. He did have a disconcerting turn of phrase at times. She decided to take him at face value and made no comment.

'And that was the last call from anyone in the house,' Vogel continued. 'As might be expected. All further attempts to regain contact failed.'

There was another short silence, interrupted again by Saslow.

'But I presume the reason we are on our way there is because of the armed intruders, not the fire.'

'Well, yes. That's the primary reason, at this stage. If there ever were any armed intruders, of course.'

Saslow frowned.

'So that's why you said we might be on a wild goose chase, is it, boss? You don't really believe there were armed men at Blackdown Manor, is that it?'

'Well, not any longer, that's for sure,' Vogel muttered. 'Of course, once the 999 operator was told there were people with guns on the premises she reported it immediately, and the fire boys were held back until armed response got there. They couldn't get their engines through anyway because there was a bloody great fallen tree blocking the drive leading to the house, and they had to call USAR out. I don't know the exact timing yet, but I under-stand it was gone four a.m., almost three hours after the first 999 call, before armed response declared the area clear. Only then were the emergency services allowed through. They couldn't get into the house, of course, but, largely because of the explosion, the fire had taken hold so quickly that the place was already pretty damn near burned down and it was accepted that nobody inside, victim or intruder, could have survived. Since then, Saslow, half the available firefighters and appliances in the area have been trampling all over the place fighting the blaze. If there ever were any armed intruders, they are either well gone or well dead.'

'Right, but you said primary reason, boss. It's not usual procedure for MCIT be called out of Bristol for a house fire, even when there are fatalities, is it?'

'No, Saslow. Unless the fire was started deliberately, of course.'

'And do we believe that is what happened in this case?'

'I've not been told that. Not yet, anyway. There is another reason, though.'

'Is there, sir?'

'Think about it, Saslow. Sir John Fairbrother. Friends with the county set, and every darned bigwig in the west of England. This whole thing already stinks of something, though God knows what. Tales of a gang of armed men tramping through the Blackdown Hills in the middle of the night? I mean, for God's sake. We're in the heart of twenty-first-century rural Somerset, not Al Capone's Chicago. The nurse could well have been off her trolley. Or maybe Fairbrother himself. But the chief constable wants nothing left to chance. I'd say they were in the same flippin' lodge, but I think Sir John may have been above and beyond that sort of thing.'

'Really, sir?'

Vogel could not fail to detect the note of interest in the DC's voice.

'I didn't say that, Saslow,' he told her.

Vogel disliked Freemasonry. And he particularly disliked even the idea of senior police officers being Masons. Not so many as had once undoubtedly been the case, but he suspected there remained far more police Masons than might actually admit it. He thought it unhealthy for police officers to be members of a secret society known to protect its own regardless. And he saw no place for Masonry, its funny handshakes and its clandestine medieval rituals, within a modern police service. But neither did he have a scrap of proof that his own chief constable was a Mason. He was merely repeating a rumour, and he should know better.

'Of course not, sir,' said Saslow, with only the merest hint of a smile.

The drive to Blackdown Manor took just over an hour and a quarter. Two uniforms were on sentry duty. Vogel flashed his warrant card, and he and Saslow were ushered past. Both officers let out an involuntary gasp as Saslow steered their vehicle through the big iron gates and on to the drive. She drove slowly past the fallen tree that had been cleared to one side by USAR, and Vogel was sure she was as transfixed by the sight which lay before them as he was. Neither Vogel nor Saslow had ever seen the house before the fire. But the horror of what had happened was starkly apparent. The building had been almost totally destroyed. The roof was entirely gone. Only a few sections of wall still stood, in ragged defiance, silhouetted against the morning sky. There were no longer any visible flames, but the building was clearly still burning. Smoke continued to drift above the ruins, creating a haze over the entire scene ahead. Several fire appliances were still in action, pouring huge arcs of gushing water onto the remains of the old house. Vogel counted at least five in attendance. And he could see two ambulances standing by. He did not think there was going to be much call for the attentions of any of the medics who had been summoned to the scene. As he had already told Saslow, it was not believed possible for there to be any survivors of the terrible fire which had engulfed the old manor house. But saying it, and seeing it, were two different things. Vogel felt a cold shiver run up and down his spine. His chosen career demanded frequent, and all too close, confrontation with death and destruction. He would never get used to it, not for as long as he lived.

He fleetingly reflected on the other consequences of the fire, in addition to the loss of human life. Vogel loved dogs. He wondered if there had been any dogs in the house, or any other animals, cats perhaps, and whether or not they had managed to escape, or if they too had suffered the unspeakable horror of burning to death. Vogel also had a love of beautiful things. He wondered what treasures might have been lost that night in the old house, which had apparently been in the Fairbrother family for centuries. Almost certainly there would have been irreplaceable antique furniture, fine paintings and other works of art, that had been handed down from generation to generation.

Saslow drove as near as she was allowed to the burned down house. The ambulances, one of the fire appliances, and a smattering of other less immediately identifiable vehicles, effectively blocked the latter part of the driveway. The two officers still had to walk a hundred yards or so over a lawn turned into a bog by the earlier rain and the attentions of the fire service, which had doubtless already pumped thousands of gallons of water onto the house and the area immediately surrounding it.

Vogel picked his way carefully, his feet inadequately clad as usual. Saslow, wearing suitably protective clothing and footwear, of course, was striding ahead. Vogel found himself having to hurry to keep up with her.

The fire, although still burning, seemed to be just about under control. But, close up, the destruction of the old house appeared even more devastating. Glassless windows, in those portions of wall which remained precariously upright, revealed nothing behind, as if the mighty old house were a flimsy film set.

Vogel had been told that a detective constable from Taunton and a local police community support officer were already in attendance, in addition to the uniforms by the gate. He could see no sign of an armed response team, and assumed they had probably left having declared the scene clear.

Vogel looked around for whoever might be the senior fire officer.

'Where's your gaffer?' asked Vogel of the nearest firefighter.

'That's him,' replied the firefighter, pointing towards a tall man, wearing the distinctive white helmet of a Fire and Rescue Service station manager, standing a little apart, staring at the ruins of the old house.

'Hey, Bob,' he called out. 'You're wanted.'

Bob Parsons turned at once and walked over.

Vogel introduced himself and Saslow.

'I understand there are at least two dead, is that right?' Vogel asked.

'Must be, from what we've been told,' replied Parsons. 'The woman who called in the fire, and her employer, Sir John Fairbrother. Both trapped in his bedroom, we understand. But we've no way of telling for sure, obviously, and won't for some time.'

He waved an arm at the still burning house.

'Twenty-four hours at least before even my men will stand a chance of getting in there,' he continued. 'There's also talk of the possibility of armed intruders having been trapped inside. But I expect you know that?'

Vogel nodded his assent.

'How long after the first call to the emergency services did you guys arrive here?' asked Vogel.

'We were here within just over half an hour. We're based in Wellington, pretty close and we weren't out on another call. So we came straight away. Only problem was, we couldn't get our vehicle through because of the fallen tree across the drive. Then, after the second 999 call, we were told to stand down as there might be armed intruders on the premises. In any case, by then there'd been that huge explosion . . .'

Bob Parsons stopped abruptly, turning away slightly to stare at the remains of the old house again. Vogel prompted him to continue.

'So what actually happened? What did you see?'

'Well, when we arrived the house was barely ablaze. We could see smoke, but that was all. We'd been told that Sir John and his nurse were still inside, and, from what we could see, we couldn't work out why they didn't just walk out, when they had the chance. We didn't know at that stage about the possibility of armed intruders, of course. My lads are used to danger, but they're not trained to face guns. And they'd have told me and headquarters where to go if they'd been asked to. But as it was, well, we decided to go ahead on foot, to at least see if we could get the people we'd been told were inside to safety. We were lugging our portable pump over the tree trunk when the whole shooting match went up. One minute barely any sign of a fire, then this huge explosion and an eruption of flames. Almost certainly a BLEVY. And quite a sight I can tell you—'

'What's a BLEVY?' interrupted Vogel.

'Boiling Liquid Expanding Vapour Explosion,' replied Parsons. 'Goes off like a bloody great bomb. The propane gas tank out the back went up, no longer much doubt about that. We were nearly a quarter of a mile away, but I swear you could feel the force of it in the air.'

Parsons wiped a gloved hand across his face, leaving a broad stroke of soot. Vogel noticed how drawn he looked, and could see the pain in his eyes.

'There was nothing we could do,' Parsons continued. 'Absolutely nothing. If only our path hadn't been blocked, we may have got there just in time to prevent the explosion. As long as we hadn't been confronted by any armed intruders, of course. There's no way of telling now. As it was, we were helpless. We could do nothing for those poor people. Then we were told to stand down, and in any case, after the place blew I don't think we would have had a hope in hell of getting anyone out. As it was, all we could do was watch.'

'That must have been tough,' said Vogel, whose heart went out to the man.

'It never gets any easier,' said Parsons.

Then he almost visually shook himself out of his reverie.

'There's something else you should know.'

'Yes?' enquired Vogel.

'We can't be sure, of course.' Parsons continued, slightly hesitantly. 'But we do already have reason to suspect this fire may have been started deliberately.'

Vogel pursed his lips together and breathed slowly out in a silent whistle.

'You suspect arson?' he queried. 'This soon?'

'Two seats of fire,' responded Parsons. 'Classic first indication. Like I told you, we could see smoke coming from the front of the house when we arrived. Big house though. Nowhere near the gas tank at the back which exploded a few minutes later causing a second and calamitous fire. As I said, boy, did it blow, and you got a job to make one of those tanks go off, particularly if its properly situated away from the house, as this one was. You'd generally need there to be a leak, and for the gas leaking to come directly in contact with flame. In view, like I said, of there being two seats of fire, I'd guess that the tank had been tampered with. It's only a hunch. So far. However, what we clearly do already know pretty much for sure is that there were two separate sources of fire. One from somewhere near the tank causing it to explode, combined with a probable leak, which may have been a coincidence but because of the other, and almost certainly the initial, source of fire, we're inclined to think it isn't. That was somewhere near the front door, effectively blocking what would be the natural exit path if you were trying to get out of the house. We'll have to wait for the fire investigators to finish their work to be sure, and that could take several days but, if you want my opinion, it's all highly suspicious, at the very least.'

'Does that lead us back to those mysterious armed intruders?' asked Vogel.

'I really don't know. Possibly. Although we never saw any signs of intruders, and neither did the armed response boys. They came back in with us when they allowed us through and stayed until after daybreak when they double-checked the area. You only just missed them actually. All the same, and although it's just guesswork so far, it has to be a possibility, doesn't it?'

'Yes, like you said, there could be intruders dead in there as well as the two victims we know about,' said Vogel. 'And you can't search the place yet?'

'No way,' said Bob Parsons. 'The house is still burning as you can see, and the few bits of it that remain standing are likely to collapse at any moment. All we can do is pour water on it. But, bizarrely, because of the size of the explosion, the speed with which the fire took hold and its ferocity, we may be able to put the fire out sufficiently to gain entry more quickly than is often the case when a big old place like this goes up—'

Parsons was interrupted by a fire officer calling out from closer to the house.

'Bob, sorry, but you're needed round the back.'

'You'll have to excuse me,' said Parsons to Vogel.

'Of course, you get on,' Vogel responded. 'Thank you for your time.'

Parsons began to walk towards the house. After a few steps he stopped and turned back to face Vogel.

'Just one more thing I should tell you,' he said. 'Do you know about this gardener, odd-job-man, driver chap?'

'I was going to ask about him,' replied Vogel. 'George something, isn't it? All I know is that he's the one who apparently started this armed intruder business. Obviously, we need to speak to him. Is he here?'

'Not any more. We and the medics found him outside the house when we were finally allowed through. Armed response had already helped him to relative safety and made him as comfortable as they could, but he was in quite a state. Bleeding from wounds to his shoulder and one leg. Couldn't stop sobbing, either. Kept saying this wasn't meant to happen.'

'I see,' said Vogel. 'Do you know how he sustained his injuries? Was he caught up in the fire? Was he burned? I thought nobody else was supposed to be in the house.'

'That's quite right,' said Bob Parsons. 'Though Grey claimed he tried to get into the house, but was too late. No. He said he'd been attacked by the armed men he'd alerted Sir John and his nurse to. Didn't look like anything to do with the fire, actually. Not burns anyway. More like stab wounds, though I was too busy tackling the fire to take a lot of notice. You'll have to ask the medics. They've taken him to hospital, the Musgrove in Taunton.'

'Well, that complicates the issue a bit doesn't it,' murmured Vogel.

He shivered. It really was a horrible morning. His feet were like blocks of ice. He looked down. His suede slip-ons were sodden already and caked in mud. He had a penchant for Hush Puppies, and this, he suspected, would be the ruination of yet another pair. His wife, Mary, would not be pleased. He did now possess a pair of wellington boots – purchased for him by Mary, of course, within the first few weeks of his transfer to the Avon and Somerset Constabulary – but he had a terrible habit of forgetting to take them with him. After all, he was a police officer, not a farm worker. Although sometimes nowadays he was beginning to wonder.

He turned up the collar of his honourable old corduroy jacket and wrapped his arms around his body. He was aware of Saslow shaking her head, almost imperceptibly. And probably disapprovingly. Rather like Mary. She was always trying to get him into all-weather gear, or at least to persuade him to buy himself a heavy-duty country coat. Something suitable for the rural areas and moorland which covered a hefty slice of the Avon and Somerset Constabulary's territory.

Vogel sniffed. He hoped he wasn't catching another cold. And if he were, he would get little sympathy from Mary. She seemed to think he developed them deliberately since moving out of the capital, as if to demonstrate how unsuited he was to life away from inner-city London – even though he'd been absolutely in agreement with his wife that it was worth making such a move, for the sake of their daughter. Vogel would do anything for Rosamund.

'Sir, would you like my scarf?' asked Saslow, interrupting his thoughts.

Vogel blinked rapidly behind his thick spectacles. This was extremely embarrassing. Was the DC taking the mickey? Or had he reached the stage in life where a young woman offered him part of her clothing merely to keep him warm? Vogel had never been a lady's man, there'd not really been anyone in his life other than Mary. But he did have his pride.

'No thank you, Saslow,' he said, his manner mild, as usual, and his voice giving nothing away. He hoped.

'I don't need it, sir,' said Saslow.

She didn't either. Her coat was a hooded puffer jacket of some sort, or Vogel thought that's what they were called, and she'd changed out of her shoes upon arrival at Blackdown Manor into the wellington boots she somehow always seemed to manage to have with her. Unlike Vogel.

'It's fine, Saslow,' said Vogel, trying to look as if it was.

He was rescued somewhat by the arrival at his side of a tall lean man, with thinning grey-brown hair, who swiftly introduced himself as Detective Constable Ted Dawson from Taunton nick.

'Sorry sir, I was on the phone to my sarge when you arrived,' Dawson apologised.

Vogel muttered a good morning and shook the man's hand.

'Fill me in then, Dawson,' he said. 'If the fire boys are right, and my guess is they probably are, then we might have a case of arson here.'

'Looks like it, sir,' replied Dawson.

'And at least two people have died,' Vogel continued. 'So, if it is arson we are looking at double murder. Question is, did the arsonist intend to kill?'

'Well, whether he did or not, he made a pretty good job of it, didn't he, sir?' commented Dawson.

'You could say that, Dawson. I've just been hearing about this driver gardener character. George something?'

'Yes sir. George Grey. Lives in The Gatehouse with his wife.'

'Did you see him before he was carted off to hospital?' asked Vogel.

'No sir, the paramedics took him away as soon as they were allowed through. I only got here an hour or so before you. Sounds like he'd have been in no condition to talk, anyway. They called me out to assist you with local knowledge, boss. I live in Wellington, you see. That's the market town ten miles or so away.'

Vogel nodded.

'I know,' he said confidently.

Although, in fact, the only knowledge he had of this part of the world had come from going online that morning.

'We're expecting a fire investigator later today, and CSI are here, boss, if you want to talk to them,' Dawson continued. 'They've had a snoop around the grounds, I understand, but, of course, they haven't been able to get near the house, and it's going to be a while before it's cooled down enough for anybody to do much. The structure will need checking, too.'

Vogel nodded. He had noticed a Crime Scene Investigators van parked just back from the fire appliances and a few officers milling around, a couple leaning against the van smoking.

'What about pathology?'

'Karen Crow was called first thing and arrived about half an hour before you, boss,' said Dawson, referring to the District Home Office Pathologist, a woman Vogel had already worked with several times since his move to the West Country.

'It was really just protocol at this stage, though. She left pretty much straightaway when she had ascertained that there was nothing she could do yet. And to tell the truth, it's doubtful she will be able to do an awful lot at any stage. You know how hard it is with fire cases, certainly a blaze as major as this. You're lucky to find anything much at all resembling a human body.'

Vogel tried not to visibly wince.

'Yes, of course,' he muttered thoughtfully.

Dawson was also appropriately dressed, in a cap, Barbour jacket, and the obligatory wellington boots. But then he would be. Vogel had guessed at once, just from his appearance and his manner, that this was the sort of career DC you didn't come across much anymore; approaching retirement, diligent, but content with his lot and unwilling to seek promotion, as that would mean change. Almost certainly Dawson had rarely allowed his police career to get in the way of his lifestyle. And so he had stayed put in the place where he'd been born and brought up, choosing a settled family life over career prospects.

Vogel didn't know any of that, of course. It was just guesswork. All he really knew was that Dawson had been co-opted to work with MCIT because of his local knowledge. He decided to make the most of it.

'All right, DC Dawson, I'm going to pick your brains,' he said. 'Any idea who might want to kill Sir John Fairbrother? I've done a bit of homework this morning. Surprisingly little about him online. Nothing derogatory. A rumour that he might have been unwell, which seems to have now been backed up by the 999 calls from a woman who said she was his nurse, a woman who appears to have died with him. One or two question marks about how well the family bank is doing, but that would almost be expected in the present climate, I should imagine. He was a bit of a philanthropist too, wasn't he? Known for helping with local causes around here? Is that right?'

'Well yes, he put up the rest of the money last year so that the restoration of the Wellington Monument could begin.'

'Ah yes,' said Vogel. 'I saw an item on the regional news a while back. Been fenced off amid rumours it might have to come down for safety reasons for years, hasn't it?'

Dawson nodded, and, although it was clear the question was rhetorical, replied.

'Yes. Work is now supposed to start next year. Though I'll believe it when I see it myself.'

Dawson smiled wryly.

A cynic, eh, thought Vogel. But he didn't object to that in a police officer, because it generally indicated a questioning mind.

'So, do I assume that Sir John was popular locally, then?'

'Well, he certainly used to be,' said Dawson in a non-committal sort of way.

'Come on, Dawson, is there any background you can give me that Google doesn't know?' Vogel persisted. 'That's what I want.'

'I can tell you what they say down the Culm Valley and up the Blue Ball, boss. I doubt Google's ever reached those two boozers.'

Dawson smiled.

So, the DC also showed signs, however limp, of a sense of humour. That was promising. Vogel and Saslow had been through a lot together the last year or so. The need for a copper who took his work seriously but not himself was greater than ever.

'Born and bred in the place, there's not much goes on in this neck of the woods I don't know about,' Dawson continued chattily, just as Vogel had already surmised.

'Right, spit it out then, man,' said Vogel.

'Well, boss, one of Sir John's ancestors, Edwin Fairbrother, acquired the place in seventeen something or other. He allegedly won it in a game of cards. Quite a swashbuckler, it seems. Not quite what you expect from a banker. But I suppose banking was different in those days. It's been the principal Fairbrother home ever since, and the family have always considered themselves to be proper Somerset people, involved in the community and so on. Sir John was known for that, even when he was away in London most of the time.

'Anything going on locally, particularly the Wellesley Theatre in Wellington, and even the little panto they put on in Culmstock every year, Sir John would turn up now and again. There was always a big donation for any local charitable cause, and he was a fair employer locally. Used to boast about always employing local people. The Kivel family, from over Wrangway, they were in his employ for generations. Jack and Martha lived in. Or in The Gatehouse to be precise, where the Greys were put. They looked after the whole manor, Martha was housekeeper, Jack was Sir John's right-hand man, did the garden and drove Sir John everywhere. Sir John used local builders and other tradesmen when he needed any work done. Simon Crockett always did the roofing, said it was like the flippin' Forth Bridge. Half of Wellie was in and out of Blackdown Manor doing jobs. Big old house. Lot of work.

'Then about a year ago everything changed. Sir John seemed to step back from everything locally. He'd had racehorses in training with the Pipes up at Nicholashayne for decades; out of the blue, David Pipe was told to sell the lot of 'em. The tradesmen Sir John had always relied on stopped getting called out. He no longer wanted goose eggs from Barry Byrant and Colin Sully; gardening help from Rob and David Crow; and suddenly he was never in for neighbours he had always made welcome, like John McCarten, the Childs or the Flahertys. He just didn't seem to be around much, or even very interested in the manor any more. Or so it was said.

Then Jack and Martha were given notice to quit. Just like that after nearly thirty years. And not personally, either. Sir John's solicitor did the deed, apparently. Word is severance pay was typically generous. But that was all that was typical. Sir John was away somewhere when the Kivels were sacked, and neither Jack nor Martha ever saw him again, they say. That upset the whole Kivel clan. They'd thought of themselves as extended family, and believed that Sir John felt the same. So the whole thing was a terrible shock. Especially when almost immediately Sir John brought in George and Janice Grey from London and installed them in The Gatehouse to take over the roles of Jack and Martha.'

Vogel thought for a moment, considering what Ted Dawson had said. Then he swung on his heels to face the older man.

'Do you have any theories about what may have caused John Fairbrother to have changed so dramatically, sacked all his local staff and so on? You must have, surely. C'mon man. Not much happens around these parts that you don't know about, you said.'

'There's been a lot of talk, but probably not a lot of substance. More about Sir John's health than anything else—'

'We know pretty much for certain that the man wasn't well,' Vogel interrupted. 'He employed a nurse. At least one nurse. Possibly more. Do you have any idea what was wrong with him?'

'I know what the rumour was . . .'

Vogel waited. Ted Dawson remained silent.

'Get on with it,' the DI prompted.

'Folk said he had Parkinson's.'

'Really?'

There'd been no mention of that online. Vogel had a basic knowledge of Parkinson's, of course, and was aware that it was a degenerative disease which ultimately destroyed the human nervous system, but he had never had personal experience of the condition. He knew enough to realise, however, that if it became public knowledge that the chairman and chief executive of an international company and a major private bank was suffering from the condition, the results in the world of business could be disastrous. Way beyond just a bit of a fall in the share prices. He addressed both Dawson and Saslow.

'The nurse, Sophia, told the emergency services that Sir John had difficulties with speaking, and indicated that he certainly couldn't talk on the phone,' he said. 'Do either of you know if that might be a symptom of Parkinson's?'

It was Saslow who answered, and straight away Vogel got the impression that she knew what she was talking about.

'It can do, boss,' she said. 'But usually not until the latter stages. The voice can become very soft and a bit shaky. Also, sometimes people get so they can't find the right words any more. My grandfather had Parkinson's, and that happened to him. It was awful to watch it happen. It's a cruel, cruel disease. My grandad, he'd always talked the hind leg off a donkey, you see . . .'

Saslow stopped abruptly.

'Thank you, Dawn,' responded Vogel gently. He turned again to Ted Dawson.

'Anything else you can tell us?' the DI enquired.

'Not a lot, really, boss,' said Dawson. 'It's all gossip, anyway. The gossip capital of the world, this corner of England. Specially the pubs. But that's what they're for, isn't it? Fiona up at the Blue Ball heard that the old man had got Parkinson's before anybody else. Always got her ear to the ground, that one. And Sir John used to be an occasional regular at the Blue Ball. Would even have a game of pool with the lads now and then. But it didn't explain why he cut himself off from everybody round here, not to me anyways. And as for sacking the Kivels! Well, you'd think he'd want a couple like that – who'd been with him for so long, living at his home – all the more once he was ill.'

'Yes, but he was Chair and CEO of Fairbrother International, for God's sake, so he had good reason to try to hide his illness for as long as possible, didn't he? Perhaps Jack and Martha got a little too close, do you think? Started to take things for granted, maybe?'

'I don't know about that,' replied Dawson. 'But it was always said they more or less ran the manor, and that nothing went on there without their say so.'

'Is it possible that maybe Sir John got rid of them because he didn't want anybody knowing so much about his affairs?' asked Saslow.

'If that's so then it's odd that it seemed to suit him so well for so long, isn't it?' commented Dawson. 'The Kivels and the Fairbrothers were always considered to be joined at the hip.

The kids grew up together. I can only think that something must have happened. Something to make Sir John no longer want that. Something more than being ill, I reckon. You see, from what I know of the set up with the two families, Sir John would have trusted the Kivels to keep his illness a secret. None more, I'd have thought.'

'So, we have a bit of a mystery then, don't we,' remarked Vogel. 'A mystery that's been the subject of local gossip in the pubs of this corner of Devon and Somerset for the best part of a year now.'

'Yes, that's about the size of it,' agreed Dawson. 'But everyone likes a nice conspiracy theory, don't they?'

Vogel walked a little closer to the still burning house, his inadequate footwear making squelching noises in the sodden ground. Dawson and Saslow followed.

'Anything of any substance other than the rumours about Sir John's health?' he asked over his shoulder.

'Well, there was always the inevitable theory that financial skulduggery is at the root of it all. But that wouldn't explain why Sir John cut himself off from the community here, and everyone who had previously been close to him, would it?'

'Did he no longer have contact with anybody locally?'

'Only the absolute minimum. From the moment he got rid of the Kivels and moved in the Greys. That's when everything changed. He was seen every so often being driven about by George Grey. And there were still one or two indispensables who were required for occasional visits. So he did have some contact.'

Dawson glanced towards the ruined house with a sorrowful shake of his head.

'Or he did, until the early hours of this morning. But apparently, he did his best to avoid it. Paul the Pool, as he's known around here, Paul Preston Evans, was one of the last to see him alive. He goes there every month to look after the swimming pool . . .' Dawson paused. 'Used to go there, I should say. The pool was in the basement. Ton of charcoal in it now, I should think. Anyway, Paul likes nothing better than passing on a good yarn. Sir John was in the pool when Paul arrived. Paul got a bollocking from Janice Grey. Apparently neither of them knew he was in the house. He'd just walked in through the back door, like he always did, he told 'em up the Blue Ball. And Mrs Grey sent him packing so she could help Sir John out of the pool room. But Paul said he'd been shocked to see how frail Sir John had looked. And it backed up the rumours. He was a proud man, of course, he wouldn't have wanted people to see him looking infirm. Everyone understood that, but nobody understood why he got rid of the Kivels. They would have protected him with their lives, would Jack and Martha.'

'What about Sir John's family? There are children, aren't there? Maybe he planned to rely on them for help as his condition deteriorated.'

'I doubt it,' responded Dawson. 'He had two kids, girl and a boy, who grew up here at Blackdown Manor, alongside Jack and Martha's boys, like I said, but the word is Sir John was estranged from both of them. The lad was a bit on the wild side and buggered off abroad years ago. Not been seen around these parts since. The daughter and her father used to be close, I understand, but not anymore, allegedly.'

The DI looked around him, again taking in the whole dreadful scene. Just a skeleton of the outer structure of the house remained. It was impossible to imagine that it would ever be rebuilt. He may not have visited Blackdown Manor before, but he had that morning looked at pictures of the place. It had been a stunningly beautiful old house, steeped in history, one of the finest examples in the country of a medieval manor, dating back to the fifteenth century and the reign of Henry VII, the first Tudor king of England. An even greater loss, of course, was that of two lives. Two people who had no doubt suffered awful deaths.

Vogel didn't like to think about that, but couldn't help himself. He glanced up at the sky, seeking diversion. The storm might be over, but it remained a thoroughly unpleasant morning. He felt sure he'd just felt a drop of rain. Unless he'd attracted the attention of a passing bird. All those years in central London, mostly based in a police station adjacent to Trafalgar Square, and he didn't remember once being hit by the excrement of a pigeon. In the country, and to Vogel even the thoroughly modern and cosmopolitan city of Bristol counted as country because it wasn't London, he seemed to be regularly wiping chalky droppings from his head and shoulders. That's how it seemed to him, anyway.

He took his phone from his pocket and called his senior officer, Detective Superintendent Reg Hemmings, the head of the Brunel MCIT.

'We almost certainly have a case of arson on our hands,' said Vogel, before giving Hemmings a brief rundown of everything he had so far learned concerning the fire.

Hemmings listened carefully.

'There's little doubt then, we need to set up a murder inquiry,' he said eventually.

'Yes boss,' responded Vogel. 'And we need a full rundown on the Fairbrother family and the family business, as soon as possible; everything that's known about Sir John's children, and everything we can find out about the bank, its financial history, its status today, and so on. Can we get a team to give this top priority? Two people have died in mysterious circumstances, boss. If we can work out why they were killed, then, with a bit of luck, we'll be well on the way towards identifying those responsible.'

Only when the call ended did Vogel realise how much more confident he must have sounded than he felt. This was not going to be a straightforward investigation. All he could do was take it stage by stage.

He turned to Saslow.

'Right, Dawn,' he said. 'We'd better get ourselves over to the Musgrove and see if we can have a word with George Grey.'

TWO

Grey was awake and sitting propped up against the pillows of his curtained hospital bed when Vogel and Saslow were shown into his ward at Taunton's Musgrove Park hospital. His eyes were red rimmed, and his distress obvious. His right shoulder bore a heavy dressing and there was a cradle keeping the bedding from resting on his left leg.

But Grey was in a far better condition than Vogel had expected, given the description of his condition by senior fire officer Bob Parsons, a man obviously not unfamiliar with serious injury.

The ward sister who escorted Vogel and Saslow to Grey's bed had confirmed that his injuries were stab wounds of some sort, but that they had not turned out to be as severe as at first feared.

She also promised to find the casualty doctor who had treated Grey. He might, she suggested, be able to explain further.

Vogel introduced himself to the injured man and sat down on a chair to the left of his bed. Saslow remained standing, to the right.

George Grey was probably in his early forties, Vogel judged. He had dark curly hair, vibrant blue eyes, and full sensual lips – an unusual looking man who might have been considered classically handsome were it not for a somewhat sallow complexion and a crooked nose that had probably been rather badly broken at some stage.

'The old man, he's dead, isn't he?' queried Grey at once.

Vogel nodded. 'We believe so,' he said. 'His body has yet to be retrieved, but we know that both Sir John and his nurse were inside the house when the fire broke out, and that there have not been any survivors.'

Grey's narrow shoulders slumped. His full lower lip trembled.

'That wasn't supposed to happen,' he muttered.

'I'm sorry, Mr Grey?' queried Vogel.

Grey said nothing more, his expression indicating that he might regret what he'd already said.

'What wasn't supposed to happen, Mr Grey?' Vogel persisted.

'I'm just sorry, that's all,' said Grey. 'I tried to help, you see. I tried to get to him. But I couldn't do nothing. I couldn't get through.'

'Mr Grey, I need you to tell me exactly what happened, and what you witnessed in the early hours of this morning,' Vogel began.

'Yeah, sure,' responded Grey, in what Vogel, himself a Londoner, considered to be an unusually strong Cockney accent nowadays.

Vogel waited. But Grey failed to continue. Instead he slumped further back against his pillows and closed his eyes. Clearly, he was not going to volunteer any information if he could help it.

'Mr Grey,' Vogel prompted, raising his voice. 'I realise you must be feeling unwell, but I am conducting a murder inquiry. You can either answer my questions here or at Taunton police station. But you really have to cooperate.'

There was no way, of course, that Vogel could insist on taking George Grey anywhere in his present condition. However, his empty threat seemed to do the trick.

Very slowly, Grey opened his eyes. 'A-all right,' he muttered falteringly. 'What do you want to know?'

'For a start, when were you first aware that fire had broken out at the manor?' asked Vogel.

'Not until Sophia, the nurse, phoned me,' Grey replied. 'I had no idea until then. It was the middle of the night, or it felt like it anyway. I was at home, in bed with the wife. Anyway, there wasn't much to see before the gas tank blew.'

'And I understand you told Sophia that she and Sir John should stay where they were, in his bedroom, because it was fire proofed. Is that so?'

Grey nodded. 'Yes. And Sir John wasn't good on his feet. I thought they would be safer.'

'You also told her that you would try to get to them, to assist them?'

'I did.'

'But you didn't dial 999, did you?' Vogel enquired.

'Well no, I knew Sophia was going to do that.'

'And did you set off immediately to go to their rescue?'

'Pretty much, yes.'

'Yet, there is another 999 call from Sophia, logged thirty-four minutes later, at 2.05, in which she says you had yet to get to them.'

'Well, I couldn't get through, could I? There were intruders, with guns I'm almost sure, proper big guns, rifles, or maybe shotguns. I told Sophia that.'

'When she called you a second time?'

'Yes.'

'But, why didn't you call her as soon as you thought there were armed intruders on the premises?'

'I was watching, wasn't I, waiting for an opportunity to get into the house. I hid in that clump of rhododendrons by the side of the pond.'

'How many intruders were there?'

'I don't know, I saw at least three. Maybe four.'

'The manor is protected by large electrically operated gates, Mr Grey. How did these people get in?'

'The storm, it damaged the electrics. I managed to open the gates yesterday, but I couldn't close them again. In any case, there was a bloody great oak tree across the drive, nobody could drive in. They must have been on foot.'

'But you didn't notice the arrival of these intruders, even though you say you were at home in The Gatehouse at the time we can assume they arrived at the manor. Is that right?'

'I told you, I was in bed asleep. With my wife.'

Vogel glanced at Saslow. It was her invitation to join in.

'You are in hospital suffering from what appear to be quite serious injuries, Mr Grey,' she said. 'Would you please tell us how you came by these injuries?'

'Yes, I was attacked, by the men with guns I told you about. The armed intruders, as you call them.'

'And would that have been before or after you received the second call from Sophia, Mr Grey?' asked Saslow.

'After. I wasn't in no condition to be having telephone conversations afterwards, I can tell you. In fact, even though I had my phone on silent, and I barely spoke above a whisper, I think it might have been that call that alerted them to me being close by.'

'It would seem that, during that last call, you still told Sophia that she and Sir John shouldn't move, this time because there were armed intruders on the property. Is that correct?'

'Yes, he's an important man, Sir John. I mean was. His sort always has enemies. He always said he felt secure at Blackdown. But I was afraid they may be after him. That they'd started the fire in order to smoke him out so that they could kill him. That's what I thought, anyway . . .'

Greys voice tailed away.

'Any idea who they might have been, Mr Grey?'

The injured man shook his head.

'Right. So you continued to advise Sir John's nurse that they should both stay where they were, in his bedroom, knowing, surely, there was a fair chance the fire would kill them. Is that it?'

'No,' said Grey. 'No. Of course not. Like I said, the fire still didn't look like much. I said they should stay where they were until either I or the emergency services got through. And I was hoping they'd get here pretty quick after what I'd seen, I can tell you.'

'But you didn't even dial 999 then?'

'No. I didn't get the chance, to tell the truth. I was attacked almost straightaway. Two, or maybe three of them, I think. Overpowered me and stabbed me. After that I didn't have any hope at all of getting through to Sir John. Then the tank blew. It was awful. Horrible. But I couldn't do nothing about it.'

'Look,' Vogel interjected. 'You realise none of this seems quite right, don't you?'

'Well, I can't help that, it's what happened,' said Grey stubbornly.

'After you were attacked, what did your attackers do next?'

'They ran off.'

'Did they speak to you at all?'

'No.'

'Not a word?'

'No. Nothing.'

'Do you think they knew who you were?'

'No. Why should they?'

'I have no idea, Mr Grey,' said Vogel. 'But you are telling me that they didn't know you and you didn't know them, is that it?'

'Yes. Anyway, like I said, it was dark.'

'You feel you were attacked simply because you were getting in the way, is that it?'

'Yes. Yes. That's it.'

At that moment a nurse arrived. Vogel turned to face her, enquiringly.

'Dr Carlisle will speak to you now, detective inspector,' she said.

'Right,' said Vogel. He turned back to the man in bed. 'We will need you to give a formal statement, and we will want to talk to you again, very soon,' he said.

Grey nodded. His complexion seemed to have grown even more pallid.

'And we will need to speak to your wife too, I understand she has visited you here already?'

'Yes,' said Grey. 'She came as soon as she realised I'd been hurt and brought here. But she's gone back home now . . . She can't tell you nothing, anyway.'

'I'll be the judge of that,' said Vogel.

As they left the ward, following in the wake of the nurse, Vogel spoke quietly to Saslow. 'Did you notice his hands?' he asked.

Saslow shook her head, surprised.

'Smoother than yours, I shouldn't wonder,' said the DI smiling. 'God knows, I don't know a lot about gardening, but I've never seen a gardener with hands like that.'

Dr Carlisle was young, thin, and bespectacled. He wore a white coat and a harassed expression. He was a stereotypical junior hospital doctor. Straight out of central casting, thought Vogel, who had met a number of junior hospital doctors in his time but didn't think he had ever encountered one who so fitted the part.

'Phillip Carlisle,' said the young man thrusting out a bony, long-fingered hand. 'How can I help?'

'I'd appreciate your professional opinion on Mr Grey's injuries,' said Vogel, taking the doctor's hand in his. He noticed that, in spite of his harassed air, the young man's skin was cool and his handshake firm.

'Well, he has suffered multiple wounds, incisions, to different parts of his body, four to his right shoulder and upper arm, and three to his left thigh,' replied Dr Carlisle. 'They are clearly consistent with stab wounds, probably inflicted by a knife of some sort.'

'And how serious are these wounds?'

'Not nearly as serious as we thought at first. Mr Grey was bleeding profusely when he was brought in. But he was extremely lucky. The wounds were not that deep, they may have been inflicted by a knife with a short blade, like a penknife, or even a Stanley knife, and certainly none of them were in any way life threatening. They had to be stitched, of course, and I'm sure are painful and debilitating. But they were all in areas of the body where there are no vital organs. Nonetheless, with as many stab wounds as were sustained, I would have expected at least one of them to have hit a major artery. They didn't. They missed.'

'So your prognosis is that Mr Grey will make a full recovery?'

'Oh yes. We will keep him in tonight, but he will probably be discharged tomorrow.'

Vogel was thoughtful as he left the hospital with Saslow.

'We need to check out the Greys, Saslow. See if you can get hold of Micky Palmer, will you? Never misses anything, Micky. I want to know all we can about them before we talk to Grey's missus, and before we take a formal statement from George Grey.'

'Right, boss,' said Saslow.

'Meanwhile I'll call Taunton nick and get them to send somebody here to stand guard over George. As a matter of urgency. I don't trust that man.'

'I know what you mean, boss. What will our next move be?'

'Looks like it might be a bit of a pub crawl, Dawn,' Vogel replied.

The DC smiled. These were words she never expected to hear from DI David Vogel. After all, everyone knew that Vogel never touched alcohol.

'Shall we start with lunch at the Blue Ball?' the DI asked.

As soon as the two police officers had left his bedside, Grey reached for his mobile phone, which was on the bedside cabinet, alongside his wallet. He dialled the number of a pay-as-you-go mobile.

'Look, I don't know what your plan is now, but this isn't what I signed up for,' he said. 'Nobody was supposed to die.'

The voice at the other end of the phone was cool and assured.

'He wouldn't have lived long anyway,' said the voice. 'The Parkinson's would have got him sooner or later. We probably did him a favour. Saved him a lot of suffering.'

'Oh yeah, that makes it all right, does it? What about that poor cow of a nurse?'

'She was trouble from the beginning. Asked too many questions. And she couldn't be trusted. We got lucky there.'

'She didn't seem like trouble to me. In any case, what the hell do you mean "lucky"?'

Involuntarily Grey raised his voice. He realised he had more or less shouted the word. He hunched himself even more closely over his phone and lowered his voice to little more than a whisper. 'Is that what you call it?' he hissed.

'In this case, yes,' said the voice.

'Look, I'm fucking furious,' said George, trying hard not to raise his voice again. 'I could get done for fucking murder.'

'No.' The voice was still cool, controlled. 'You'll be fine as long as you keep your head. You didn't do anything wrong, after all, did you? That fire was down to our mysterious intruders, wasn't it?'

George grunted. 'You know what,' he said. 'I've just had the filth round. Two of the Avon and Somerset's finest. And I don't think they believe a word of my story about armed intruders. Not a word of it.'

'Maybe not, but not believing you and proving you are lying are two different things. Just keep calm, George, and everything will be fine.'

'Will it?' snapped George. 'I don't think so. This is murder. And the cops never let go when they're investigating a murder. This DI Vogel, he wants to see me again, take a formal statement. I just don't know what I'm going to say . . .'

He felt as if every nerve in his body was jangling. He'd been in a few scrapes in his life, lived near the edge, always taken chances, but George Grey had probably never really experienced true fear before. So, this is how it is, he thought. This is how it is to fear life almost more than death.

The voice was speaking again.

'Look, how long are you being kept in hospital?'

'I don't know. Not long, I shouldn't think.'

'You're all right, then?'

'Oh yes, great! No, I'm OK. Just about. So they say. Hurts like fuck though.'

'Well, as long as there's no permanent damage. We need to meet, don't we? Soon. But I can't come to you.'

'I'm in hospital.'

'Not for long, you said so. We have to talk. I will look after you, you know, and that missus of yours. I said I would, didn't I? Whatever happened, I would make sure you were looked after.'

'Yeah well, it doesn't feel like it right now. I'm in fucking agony and I've got the filth all over me.'

'I can sort it. But we need to meet. And you need to keep out of the way of that DI Vogel until you feel more up to dealing with him. I will guide you, you know that.'

'All right.'

George realised he had little choice. He was already in too deep.

'OK,' he continued. 'Straightaway, after I'm discharged.'

'And when will that be?'

'I don't know. Tomorrow probably. Or maybe the next day. They haven't told me.'

'We haven't got time to waste. If you're OK, why don't you discharge yourself? Just get out of the hospital, and out of Somerset. We could meet today. I owe you, don't I?'

'In more ways than one,' said George.

'I was thinking of the practical way,' said the voice. 'You have completed a service. I owe you a substantial payment. And, yes, probably an explanation.'

'Yeah, both.'

'Both will be forthcoming. And a new plan. Just get on a train. Yes?'

'Yeah. I suppose so. Are you still in the same place?'

'I am. Let's meet in the pub. You'll need a drink by the time you get here.'

'All right.'

'But make sure you don't leave a paper trail. And ditch your phone. Get yourself a pay-as-you-go.'

'All right,' said George again.

The call ended. George Grey leaned back on his pillows and closed his eyes, shutting out the world. Just for a few seconds. He was worried. Very worried indeed.

THREE

I t was quiet in the pub. Monday lunchtime. Vogel decided not to make himself known at this stage, not to the landlady or any of the other customers. He preferred to observe.

The food was good, with a reasonable vegetarian selection. Vogel noticed that there were even vegan dishes on offer. He pondered momentarily on how times had changed. Vogel had become a vegetarian as a teenager after watching a TV documentary on abattoirs. In those days UK pubs and restaurants made scant concession to what was regarded as little more than an inconvenient dietary peculiarity. And his parents had dismissed Vogel's vegetarianism as a phase. But Vogel never touched meat again. He didn't do phases. Not even as a boy.

They'd just ordered; crab sandwiches for Saslow and grilled goat's cheese salad for Vogel, when Vogel's phone rang.

It was Micky Palmer with a progress report.

'We've been looking into the Fairbrother family like you asked, boss, and Sir John may have been popular in the Blackdown area, but not with his own family, it seems,' Micky began, at once backing up what Ted Dawson had said earlier. 'He's been estranged from his son, Freddie, for almost twenty years apparently. His daughter, Christabella, known to everyone as Bella, is a city high flier and used to be deputy chair of Fairbrother International, number two to her father. Always regarded as a chip off the old block. But a little over a year ago now there was some sort of blazing row between them. It's a matter of record in the press, boss. Not a huge story, but it's there. Nobody ever knew what the row was about. She simply quit, then she joined a rival bank. That went down like a ton of bricks, as you can imagine.'

'She's been told of her father's death, I presume?'

'Yep, the Met sent a couple of wooden tops round in the early hours, got to her just before news of the fire hit the media.'

'Have we made contact with her yet? We'll need to talk to her as soon as possible.'

'Of course, boss,' replied Palmer. 'I'll get Polly Jenkins on to it.'

Vogel grunted his approval. Polly Jenkins was one of the brightest young coppers he knew.

'What about the Greys?' he asked. 'Got anything on them yet?'

'Well, George Grey is a Londoner, proper East Ender apparently,' replied Micky. 'Not many of them about now, Hackney's very nearly the new Mayfair—'

'Get on with it, Micky,' interrupted Vogel, who had already gleaned what Grey's background was, just from meeting him the once.

Everybody knew that Micky Palmer was inclined to ramble. In Vogel's opinion it was the man's only fault. All the same, there was a great deal of work to be done in that brief golden period following a major crime.

'Sorry boss,' replied Palmer, who was well aware of how much Vogel respected him, and wasn't in the slightest offended. 'OK, he's known to the Met. All pretty petty stuff though. Minor robbery, handling stolen goods, that sort of thing. There was a GBH charge too, brawl in a pub. He lost it and used a glass. Did time for that. Been inside more than once. But nothing serious, and nothing lately. Latterly he ran a market stall, probably dodgy, but no evidence of that.'

'I see. Anything on Janice Grey? Has she got any sort of record?'

'Not that I've discovered so far,' said Micky. 'But I suspect there's something not right there. She and George were married eight years ago, and so far I can't find out anything about Janice before that. Almost like she didn't exist. I'm on to it, though, boss, big time.'

Vogel smiled as he ended the call. If there was anything of relevance, anything at all in Janice Grey's past, his money was on Micky Palmer unearthing it. Meanwhile, the DI quickly filled Saslow in on what he had just learned.

'It's all very interesting, isn't it?' remarked Vogel. 'Why would a man like Sir John Fairbrother hire a dubious character like George Grey and his wife to take over from an apparently thoroughly respectable couple whom he'd employed for years and – if Ted Dawson's got it right, which he probably has – trusted to damn near run his Somerset life for him?'

The food arrived. Saslow began to eat at once. She was

ravenous. Vogel sat back in his seat staring unseeingly at his goat's cheese salad.

'It's unthinkable that Fairbrother didn't know the sort of man he was hiring,' the DI mused. 'You would expect him to have had people who checked out anyone he might be considering taking into his employ, particularly people who are going to be as close to him as the Greys were, living on his property, presumably seeing him every day when he was at the manor.'

'I thought that,' said Saslow through a mouthful of sandwich. 'Doesn't make sense, does it?'

'No. And not the only mystery, either. There's also the matter of George Grey's possibly rather mysterious wife.'

'Maybe, but if there's anything about her we should know, Micky will find it, boss,' said Saslow, echoing Vogel's own thoughts.

She began to turn her full attention to her crab sandwiches, but had taken only a few bites more when her phone rang. She listened for several seconds before holding the phone away from her mouth.

'It's Taunton nick,' she said. 'Boss, you're not going to like this.'

'Oh, get on with it, Saslow,' said Vogel. 'You're as bad as Micky.'

'Grey's walked out of the hospital.'

'He's done what?'

'He's walked.'

'I thought I asked for someone to be put on duty outside his room?'

'Yes, boss. Taunton said they didn't have anyone available. They were working on it. But they hadn't yet got anyone over there. The cuts and all that.'

'The cuts?' queried Vogel, a note of bewilderment in his voice. 'Haven't they heard about prioritising? How often does Taunton nick have to deal with double death in a fire that's almost certainly arson?'

Saslow shrugged. 'What shall I say, boss?' she asked.

'Tell 'em as it's too damned late now, they can go back to concentrating on litter and parking,' growled Vogel.

Saslow tried not to smile.

'Oh, never mind, ask them if they have any idea where he is. Could he just have gone home?'

Saslow spoke into her phone again.

'They say not, boss,' she said. 'They've phoned his missus. He's not there apparently and she's not heard from him. Sounded genuinely surprised, they say.'

'Right, tell 'em to put Grey on missing persons straight away. We need to find him fast. If anyone knows what's been going on, it's this feller. He could well be the arsonist, too, I reckon.'

Saslow did as she was bid.

By the time she ended the call, Vogel was on his feet and heading towards the door, abandoning the rest of his goat's cheese salad without a backward glance.

'C'mon, Dawn,' he said over his shoulder. 'I think we need to pay Mrs Grey a visit sooner rather than later. Now her husband's gone missing that changes everything.'

Saslow was only halfway through her crab sandwiches. She was still hungry. She quickly wrapped her napkin around the remaining half and took it with her as she followed Vogel to the car park.

FOUR

At first nobody answered the door at The Gatehouse.
Vogel knocked loudly three times.
'She might be out, boss,' said Saslow.
Vogel glanced upwards at the bedroom window which overlooked the front door. The curtains were drawn. But there was a little chink open in the middle. He noticed, as had Tom Withey when he and the other Wellington firefighters had arrived at Blackdown Manor in the early hours, that one of the curtains seemed to move slightly.

'I don't think so, Saslow,' replied Vogel. 'I think she's watching us from upstairs.'

He opened the letterbox, bent forwards and shouted through it at the top of his voice. 'Mrs Grey, I am DI David Vogel of the Avon and Somerset Constabulary, and I need to speak to you urgently regarding your husband.'

Vogel stood back and waited. There was still no response from inside. He waited a minute or so, then stepped forwards again and once more shouted through the letterbox. 'Mrs Grey, please open the door. I really have to speak to you.'

Again, there was no response. Again, Vogel waited for a minute or so.

Then he called through the letterbox for the third time. This time he meant business. 'Mrs Grey, if you don't open this door I shall obtain a warrant to enter and search your property. Then I shall return with uniformed officers, and, your husband having alleged there were armed intruders on the premises last night, possibly an armed response unit. If you do not open this door I shall be compelled to follow these procedures, not least out of concern for your safety.'

Vogel stepped back again. This time the door opened.

A small bird-like woman stood in the doorway. Vogel thought she was probably in her early forties, about the same age as her husband, but she looked older. Her hair was grey and unkempt.

Vogel reflected obliquely on how unusual it had become for women to allow their hair to go naturally grey, even when they were in their seventies and eighties. His Mary was not a vain woman, nor in any way preoccupied with physical appearance, but she had immediately chosen to have her hair highlighted as soon as the first streaks of grey began to show in her natural light brown.

Janice Grey's opening remark was not promising.

'I can't help you,' she said, standing full square in the middle of the doorway, her body language making it quite clear she had no intention of inviting the two officers in. Vogel thought she looked as if she may have been crying. Which he supposed was not surprising. In spite of that, and her small stature, she was clearly no pushover.

'I don't know where my George is,' Janice Grey continued. 'I have no idea why he walked out of hospital or where he's gone to. So, it's no good asking me. I didn't know nothing about it until this woman copper from Taunton phoned me. I told her that then, and now I am telling you.'

She made a move to shut the front door. Vogel stepped forward and thrust his foot in the doorjamb. He couldn't remember the last time he'd done that, and found he rather enjoyed it.

He pushed against the door forcing Janice Grey back into the hall.

'We need to come in, Mrs Grey,' said Vogel authoritatively, stepping forward as he spoke.

With an air of resignation, the woman made way for him and Saslow to enter, and led them into the sitting room. It was a predominantly pink room, and chintzy, the soft furnishings and the floral curtains distinctly cottagey in style. Vogel wondered whether the Greys had been responsible for the décor, or the Kivels. He somehow suspected the latter. Nonetheless the place remained well cared for. Everything was neat and tidy. The restful, homely atmosphere thus created at once seemed incongruous considering the recent events at Blackdown Manor; which included arson leading to two violent deaths, a possible invasion of armed intruders, and now the disappearance of the principal witness who was also the prime suspect.

'Look, Mrs Grey,' Vogel began. 'What I would like to know from you first, before we move on to the events of the last twenty-four hours, is how you and your husband came to be in the employment of Sir John Fairbrother in the first place?'

The woman sat down abruptly on an upright chair by the fire-place. She did not ask Saslow and Vogel to sit. Saslow did so anyway, perching herself on the edge of the chintzy sofa. Vogel kept standing. If he had sat on any other of the available chairs in the room he would have found himself at a lower level than Janice Grey. And Vogel would never allow that. When he was working, and particularly when conducting something as serious as a murder inquiry, Vogel was always conscious of the necessity of preventing almost anyone he encountered from taking even the hint of psychological advantage – and of never inadvertently putting himself at a disadvantage.

'George arranged everything, I don't know nothing about it,' Janice Grey replied.

'Oh, come on, Mrs Grey, I don't believe that,' persisted Vogel. 'You don't seem to me to be the sort of woman who would meekly uproot herself and move halfways across the country on the say so of her husband. Or any man, come to that. You and George are Londoners, city people. Not likely candidates at all. Leaving aside any other considerations, how did you both get this job?'

'We applied for it,' said Mrs Grey abruptly.

'I think I need a little more detail than that,' said Vogel. 'How did you apply for it? Did you go through an agency?'

'No, my Georgie saw an ad in the paper.'

'Which paper?'

'I dunno. The *Standard* I expect. He always used to get the *Standard*, did my Georgie.'

'So, why did he apply for this job?'

'Sorry?'

'Mrs Grey, I'll say it again, you and your husband are Londoners, through and through. What made George apply for a job which involved looking after a country house, miles from anywhere?'

Janice Grey shrugged. 'We both wanted a change, didn't we?' she said.

Vogel assumed it was a rhetorical question.

'And what on earth does your Georgie know about gardening?' he continued.

Janice Grey shrugged again. ''E only has to mow the lawns,

more or less. 'E 'as one of those bloody great mowers you sit on, don't he? He likes that. Otherwise, he would just drive the boss about, not that he ever went out much, and do little jobs around the house when he could.'

She paused.

'He's quite handy about the house, my George you know,' she said somewhat defensively.

I'll bet he is, thought Vogel, particularly when it comes to breaking into them.

'Mrs Grey, your husband has a criminal record,' he continued. 'Was Sir John aware of that?'

Janice Grey frowned. 'Might 'ave known you'd get onto that,' she muttered.

'Well yes, Mrs Grey, obviously we are checking out everyone close to Sir John. Two people have died and now your husband appears to have gone missing. Doesn't look very good, does it?'

'Not to you, I don't suppose,' said the woman, still muttering.

'I'm going to ask you again, Mrs Grey,' said Vogel. 'Was Sir John Fairbrother aware of your husband's criminal record?'

'I dunno,' replied the woman, this time a tad belligerently. 'I told you, my Georgie dealt with all that sort of stuff.'

'All right, Mrs Grey, moving on to last night, when were you first aware that there was a fire at the manor?'

'When Sophia called George. Woke us both up. He told me straight away, before he went over to try to help.'

'And you just stayed here, in The Gatehouse, is that correct?'

'Yes. Until the explosion. Frightened the life out of me, I can tell you. I went outside then, and what a terrible sight it was. That beautiful house, just a ball of fire. One of the fireman said I should get back in, so I did. And I stayed here until a policeman came and said my George had been injured and they were taking him to hospital.'

'But that would have been more than three hours later, wasn't it, Mrs Grey? You've just told us about the explosion. Weren't you worried about your husband, when he didn't come back?'

'Of course I was. But there was nothing I could do.'

Vogel was considering whether or not to press Janice Grey further on her somewhat questionable account of the night's events, when Saslow's phone rang and she left the room to take the call.

He decided he might learn more from a more indirect line of questioning.

'You were both in Sir John's employ, Mrs Grey, not just your husband, is that right?' Vogel continued, in Saslow's absence.

'Yes.'

'So, what exactly were your duties?'

'I was sort of housekeeper. We had a girl from the village come in two mornings a week to do the heavy cleaning, she wasn't allowed in Sir John's bedroom though, and he used to stay in his room when she was in the house. I did that, and made sure everything was how Sir John liked it. He was only living in part of the house anyway.'

'Did you do anything else?'

'Well, I helped look after him. Sophia was live-in, of course. I used to do shifts to relieve her, and occasionally we had an agency nurse from Exeter.'

'You did nursing shifts? I've been told Sir John was suffering from Parkinson's. Is that correct?'

'Yes, he was.'

'Well, Parkinson's is a very serious condition. Are you a qualified nurse, Mrs Grey?'

'Uh, well, um . . .' She seemed unable to find appropriate words.

'C'mon, Mrs Grey,' Vogel persisted. 'It's a simple enough question. Are you a nurse?'

The woman looked curiously alarmed.

She was ultimately saved from answering the question by the return of Saslow, who held out her phone to Vogel saying, 'It's Micky Palmer. You'd better hear this, boss.'

Vogel took the phone and, in turn, left the room, listening intently.

Saslow sat down on the sofa again. Janice Grey stared at her for a moment or two then glanced away. Neither woman spoke.

Vogel was not out of the room for long. Upon his return he got straight to the point. 'You were a nurse, weren't you, Mrs Grey?' he enquired.

That same expression of resignation which had appeared on her face when she had allowed the two officers into her home reappeared.

'Yes, I was,' she replied finally. 'Well, an auxiliary nurse.'

'At the East London Infirmary?'

'Yes. And I was as good as any SRN too. Better, probably. The rest of them didn't like me, did they? They ganged up on me. I wasn't to blame for nothing. I didn't do nothing. Look, it happened nearly ten years ago, but I'm never going to be allowed to move on, am I? Never. It's pretty obvious you know all about it now.'

'I know that you stood trial for the murder of three elderly patients in the geriatric ward of the East London Infirmary,' said Vogel. 'And that you were cleared of all charges. It was the end of any hope of a nursing career for you though, wasn't it?'

'It was. I lost the chance to do the only thing I've ever been any good at.'

'You were Jane Farley then, weren't you?'

'Why are you asking? You know very well.'

'So, you married George, got a new name and a new life. He might have been a petty criminal, but his name was certainly better than yours.'

'It wasn't fair,' said Janice Grey. 'I was found not guilty. They still hounded me. The press. The families of the people who died. It wasn't my fault. I didn't hurt nobody. But it just went on and on. Even after I married George somebody would always find out. And then, more recently, there was internet trolling too. I couldn't work at anything, let alone nursing. In my other life, me and my first husband, Jim, we had our own house, and we had two children. I lost it all, Jim, the house, even my kids. He chucked me out on my ear right after the trial, and poisoned the kids against me. They're grown up now, near enough, and they don't want anything to do with me. I haven't seen 'em in years. And I had nothing to fight back with, did I? No money and a ruined reputation. There wasn't nothing I could do. I was just lucky Georgie took up with me, to tell the truth, and he's stood by me too. But we were pretty much at the end of our tether when this job turned up. He'd lost his market stall. I didn't have any work. We were living hand to mouth in one room. All we wanted was a fresh start. Then Sir John came into our lives, and it was like a miracle. This was our fresh start. Or it was supposed to be.'

'Did Sir John know about your past?' Vogel asked.

'I left that to George,' said Mrs Grey again. 'George looked after all that sort of thing.'

'Well, it's hard to believe that a man like Sir John would have hired people for jobs like yours without checking them out thoroughly, isn't it?' Vogel persisted.

'I wouldn't know.'

'You must know, surely, why he suddenly decided to sack a couple he had employed for many years and take on you and your husband in their place?'

'I've no idea,' said Janice Grey. 'You'd have to ask him. Only you can't, can you?'

She uttered a short dry chuckle.

'Is that supposed to be a joke, Mrs Grey?' asked Vogel.

The woman looked down at her hands, clasped on her lap.

'No. I'm sorry. We were both very fond of Sir John. He was good to us. Gave us a chance, didn't he? Or, at least, he tried to.'

'Do you think he trusted you?'

'Yes. I'm sure he did. We never gave him no reason not to. Whatever you might think.'

'And you say he even trusted you to nurse him?' Vogel was watching the woman carefully, assessing her every reaction.

She looked up at him directly, eye to eye, and her answer was almost aggressive. 'Yes, he did, and, why wouldn't he? I am a good nurse.'

'Not everyone would trust someone with your past.'

'I told you, I don't even know if he knew about it. If he did, then obviously he accepted the "not guilty" verdict. Even if nobody else did. Actually, he used to say I was his favourite. That I had the touch. I always did, you know . . .'

Janice Grey's voice tailed off.

'I'm sorry he's gone. You can believe what you like of me and George, Mr Vogel. But Sir John Fairbrother was a kind man. A nice gentle man. He didn't behave posh, the way you might expect from someone in his position, and with all that money. I liked him. He was good to us. I would never have done anything that might hurt him, and I don't believe my Georgie would have done, either. Not knowingly, anyway.'

'What do you mean by "not knowingly", Mrs Grey?' asked Vogel.

'Nothing, I don't mean nothing,' Janice Grey replied quickly.

Too quickly, Vogel wondered? None the less he thought he could detect the sign of tears in the corner of each of the woman's eyes.

She was either an extremely good actress, or she was telling the truth, thought Vogel.

'And what are we going to do now, Georgie and me? Sir John gave us a home as well as jobs,' Janice continued, the desperation clear in her voice. 'God knows what will happen to us now.'

Against his better judgement Vogel found himself feeling some sympathy for Janice Grey. He made himself consider again what he'd just learned on the phone from Micky Palmer about the woman's Old Bailey trial eight years previously. The case against her had seemed overwhelming. The Crown Prosecution Service and the officers who'd put together the case against her had been convinced she would be found guilty and spend most of the rest of her life in jail.

But she'd convinced a jury of her innocence. And apparently the way in which she had conducted herself, when called by her barrister to give evidence in her own defence, had evoked grudging admiration even from the prosecution counsel.

Vogel made a mental note not to underestimate this woman.

FIVE

Vogel and Saslow drove back to Bristol later that afternoon and headed for Kenneth Steele House, home of the MCIT unit. The DI wanted to catch up with all that was happening across the board, and collate in his own head the various strands of the murder inquiry which would now occupy his every waking hour. He also needed to see his boss.

Detective Superintendent Reg Hemmings had appointed himself Senior Investigating Officer, as usual, with Vogel and DI Margot Hartley as his joint deputy SIOs. Hartley, one of the best organisers in British policing, Vogel thought, was, again as usual, office manager. Vogel would take the hands-on-role to which he was invariably considered best suited.

'The temporary Incident Room we're setting up near the crime scene, at Wellington police station, should be fully operational by tomorrow morning, and I suggest you work out of there until we've completed the obvious investigations locally,' Hemmings told Vogel. 'I'm hoping to have about fifty officers on board. There won't be room for them all at Wellington, of course. I'll keep Micky Palmer and his team here, where they have access to HOLMES, if that suits you.'

Vogel knew the importance of that. HOLMES was the Home Office Large Major Enquiry System, used for sharing and collating information throughout the country by all forty-three British police forces, but installed only in selected police and specialist unit stations.

He nodded his agreement, gave Hemmings a brief report of his own investigations so far, in particular his interviews with the Greys, and then headed for the MCIT's permanent incident room.

Micky, whom Hemmings had poached from Gloucestershire police a few months earlier, convincing the detective constable to make the move on the grounds that MCIT would make far better use of his considerable talents, and of him, was engrossed in his computer. He was a quiet man, with deceptively sleepy eyes and a mischievous sense of humour which lurked just below the surface, who liked to work independently and could only function when permitted to do things his way. He'd been immersed in a destructive personality clash with Gloucester's head of CID, and had jumped at the chance of joining Hemmings' team. Brain like a bacon slicer, Hemmings had murmured when he'd introduced Vogel to Micky Palmer several months earlier. And in the time Palmer had been on board Vogel had already seen plenty of evidence to back up his superior's assessment.

DC Polly Jenkins, recently promoted from uniform, and a young officer for whom Vogel had gained considerable respect when they had worked together the previous year on what had turned out to be one of the biggest and, arguably, the most disturbing murder enquiries of his career, was also one of the newer members of MCIT.

She made a beeline for Vogel as soon as he entered the incident room.

'I've tracked down Bella Fairbrother,' said Polly. 'She's on her way down here. I spoke to her on her mobile. But only briefly. She said she was on the motorway and would call us when she arrived.'

'Do we know where she's staying?'

'Uh no, she didn't want to talk because she was driving . . .' Polly sounded apologetic.

'It's OK, Polly,' said Vogel quickly. 'Just get back to her and ask her. Tell her we need to meet her as soon as she reaches her destination.'

Micky Palmer had by then looked up from his computer and noticed Vogel's presence. The DI walked across to his desk.

'Anything more?' Vogel asked.

Micky nodded. 'Just been checking out the errant eldest boy. Typical spoiled rich kid, apparently. He was a bit of a lad and regarded by his father as a wastrel. Unlike his kid sister, no work ethic at all. Played at being an actor, and was allegedly quite talented, but made little effort. In his teens and into his early twenties he was known to us as trouble. Had a community service order against him, spent a couple of nights in jail when he got in a pub brawl, done for drink driving, cautioned for possession of marijuana, that sort of thing. When he was twenty-two he took off on some sort of round-the-world trip. Word is his father was glad to see the back of him. And apparently, he's never been back. Supposed to be in Australia, sir. We're trying to get in touch, and I've been on to our friends down under. But he seems to have cleaned up his act, certainly no record of him being in any trouble.'

'Do we know who inherits?'

'I've been on to the company secretary and Fairbrother's lawyers, but everyone's being a bit cagey, boss,' said Micky. 'I suppose you can understand it up to a point. Solicitors are conditioned to be secretive about things like wills. But I've certainly learned that this is going to be a very complicated matter. Pretty obviously with one of the most famous banks in the world involved, I suppose. Traditionally, ever since the bank was founded in the seventeenth century it's been handed down from son to son. Seems unlikely Sir John's son is going to be involved, though neither would he want to be, from all accounts, and the daughter walked out of the place for reasons yet to be learned. Plus, she's a woman. And a mother. A single mother, it seems, just to make matters worse.'

'Come on, Micky, you sound like some terrible old chauvinist.'

'Not me, boss, them. There's never been a woman at the top of Fairbrother's and it seems unlikely the board would accept one.'

'Not even Sir John's clearly extremely able daughter?' queried Vogel.

'Well, the word is a lot of the old guard weren't happy having her on the board at all, let alone as deputy chair. There have been one or two women in the past. Sir John's first wife, Bella's mother, before he divorced her and kicked her out; and his mother, I think. But it seems they were regarded only as token women really, and not allowed to take much of an active part in anything. Whenever they were given opportunity to vote, which was not often, it would have been only to support the family position. They were always expected to vote with the chair – that is Sir John and his father before him.'

'So aren't there any other women on the board now? Was Bella Fairbrother the only one?'

'Apparently so.'

'Sounds like quite a can of worms,' commented Vogel.

'It certainly is, boss,' said Micky.

Polly approached Vogel again. She was of West Indian descent, dressed streetwise, and had an enviable knack of getting on with almost everyone she encountered. Vogel was glad she was now permanently part of MCIT.

'I spoke to Bella Fairbrother again,' said Polly. 'She's staying at the Mount Somerset, just outside Taunton. Says she'll be there in half an hour.'

'Right.'

Vogel turned to Saslow.

'C'mon then, Dawn, what are you waiting for?' he asked. 'Let's get over there.'

'But boss, we've only just come from Taunton . . .' began Saslow lamely.

'The goal posts have moved,' said Vogel. 'Now we are going back.'

SIX

Bella Fairbrother was elegant, assured, well dressed, and bristled with self-confidence. Vogel knew her to be thirty-nine years old. He thought she probably looked younger, and in some ways behaved as if she was older. She had only very recently heard of her father's violent death in a fire, but was certainly displaying little or no sign of distress. Her expression was entirely non-committal. Everything about her indicated cool containment. Almost certainly she was accustomed to giving little away of her inner feelings. Superficially, her manner reminded Vogel of his old boss when he'd been in the Met. Only, the preposterously named Nobby Clarke was a tall blonde woman. Bella Fairbrother was of average height, with a full head of tumbling brunette hair which fell over her shoulders in a style Vogel thought would probably be considered rather old fashioned. It suited her though, and Vogel felt sure it would prove to be the only remotely old-fashioned thing about the thoroughly modern Miss Fairbrother.

'Very pleased to meet you, detective inspector,' said Bella, offering a perfectly manicured hand, in a manner which seemed almost to suggest that he should kiss it. Now that would be old fashioned, thought Vogel. And in the current climate could land him in jail, too.

'I am sorry for your loss,' said Vogel, taking the extended hand in his firmest handshake.

'Don't be, detective inspector,' responded Bella. 'As far as I am concerned, my father was a bigot and totally set in his ways. He and I have always had a difficult relationship, and for some time now, since I resigned as his deputy at Fairbrother International, we've had hardly any contact at all, which has suited both of us.'

Vogel was surprised, both by her frankness and her vehement manner.

'That sounds quite harsh, Miss Fairbrother,' Vogel responded mildly.

'Does it? Yes, well, nothing to how harsh he could be.

Nonetheless, I am, of course, shocked by what happened. I wouldn't wish death in a fire on anyone. Obviously.'

'Obviously,' replied Vogel. 'Could I ask you please when you last saw your father?'

'Of course. It must have been a couple of months after I resigned. We were both invited to the same drinks reception in the City. We passed the time of day in a civilised manner; you have to keep appearances up if you're a Fairbrother. But that was all. In effect, we barely spoke.'

'Might I also ask what caused your estrangement from your father, Miss Fairbrother, and why you quit the family bank.'

'I'm sorry, DI Vogel, I really don't see what that has to do with the matter in hand.'

'Miss Fairbrother,' said Vogel firmly, 'the fire officers called to Blackdown Manor last night strongly suspect that the blaze which destroyed the house and killed your father was started deliberately. Arson is being investigated. Therefore, I am conducting a murder inquiry. Actually, an inquiry into a double murder. As far as I am concerned at the moment, everything concerning anybody close to or related to either of the deceased could have a bearing on the case. Now, will you please answer the question.'

Bella Fairbrother looked genuinely shocked. 'Murder?' she said, turning the one word into a question. 'The two officers who came to tell me the news this morning did say that investigations into the cause of the fire were on-going. But well, I suppose I didn't take it in really. I mean, arson? Oh my God. I guess I just thought that was procedure in the event of deaths in a fire. I didn't realise . . .'

She didn't finish the sentence.

'Miss Fairbrother, will you please answer my question,' Vogel repeated.

He had already realised that this woman was never going to be easy to deal with. She was independent, feisty, and clearly a real handful. But none of that indicated that she might have any involvement with the fire at Blackdown Manor, nor indeed necessarily any relevant information to supply. But Vogel intended to make absolutely sure.

'Of course,' said Bella Fairbrother, although she still sounded a tad reluctant. 'It was business really. Well, everything with my

father was business. That was what he lived for. He made me
deputy chair but expected me just to follow his lead and do what
he said. He wanted me to be like all the other Fairbrother women
throughout history, subservient and totally obedient to their men.
He was never interested in my ideas, and rarely inclined to share
his. Neither did he allow me to become fully aware of everything
that he was doing, and what was being done in the name of
Fairbrother International. I found out about certain of our banking
investments in Third World countries that made Barclays look
like philanthropists. There was also some extremely dubious
hedge fund investment. My father wouldn't discuss anything with
me. I was beginning to feel like a puppet. The final straw came
when he took it upon himself to make it clear that he had no
intention of ever handing Fairbrother's over to me. I would never
get to run the company. It transpired he had drawn up a plan for
succession which barely included me. And he told me he didn't
see why I should mind, after all I was a girl, and girls wouldn't ever
be proper bankers.'

Bella Fairbrother paused and took a deep breath.

'My father was a dinosaur, Mr Vogel,' she continued. 'A very
ruthless one. Perhaps you understand now why I distanced myself
from him, and why I shall not be crying at his funeral.'

'I couldn't comment on that, Miss Fairbrother,' said Vogel. 'But,
may I say, even now after his death, you do seem very angry.'

'I am angry, Mr Vogel,' said Bella. 'My father kept such a tight
rein on the affairs of the bank, it wasn't just me who was kept in
the dark half the time. He never trusted his own board fully. They
are now frantically trying to sort out the numerous complex financial arrangements he had unilaterally executed. And if my father
were still alive, Mr Vogel, he would tell you that is the way he
would always work.'

'I see,' said Vogel.

'Do you?' queried Bella Fairbrother. 'Look, Mr Vogel, I am
going to take you into my confidence here. I may as well because,
unless there's a miracle, all this is going to come out sooner or
later. I had a meeting with Ben Travis, the company secretary and
Jimmy Martins, the deputy chairman, this afternoon. That's why
I didn't get here until now. Fairbrother's is a huge and historic
business. Millions of people's livelihoods worldwide depend on

our family company, both directly and indirectly. I realise it must be difficult for someone like you to comprehend a concept of this magnitude, but if Fairbrother's were to go under the repercussions would be catastrophic.'

Bella Fairbrother paused. Vogel blinked rapidly behind his spectacles. He always did when he felt uncomfortable. But he was actually far more embarrassed for the young woman addressing him, who obviously had no idea how she appeared to others, than he was for himself. Vogel knew well enough when he was being patronised, and he didn't take to it kindly. Nonetheless, Bella Fairbrother was correct in her clear assumption that he was unfamiliar with international finance, and indeed had little grasp of how the possible collapse of the Fairbrother family bank might affect businesses and individuals across the globe. He was however extremely familiar with the consequences of greed and of misuse of power at all levels of society. Therefore, he did his best to appear both dispassionate and expressionless, apart from the rapid blinking which he felt confident Miss Bella Fairbrother was far too self-obsessed to notice, whilst continuing to concentrate his mind totally on everything she had to say.

'As soon as they heard the news of my father's death early this morning a board meeting was called,' Bella Fairbrother continued. 'Martins and Travis set about making provision for trade to continue as usual with Martins as temporary chair until someone could be appointed in the proper way. Jimmy Martins has already made it pretty clear he will not be prepared to take over as chairman on a permanent basis. And I don't blame him. Being deputy chair to my father was a bit like trying to co-pilot an aircraft whilst wearing a blindfold. It is going to be very difficult indeed for anyone to take over the running of the bank from my father. He wove a tangled web, Mr Vogel. There were accounts and investments worldwide to which only he had access. In some cases, only he knew of their existence. Half the time he didn't even follow proper Companies House procedure. Of course, most members of the board were aware of this, whatever they might say now, but if you wanted to remain in a senior position at Fairbrother's you simply did as you were told.

'When they learned that he was seriously ill, about five or six months ago, Travis and Martins and the board found themselves in a pretty pickle. And they still didn't know what to do about it. In name, at least, my father remained chairman and chief executive, and nobody quite had the balls to overthrow him. Although he eventually stopped coming into the office, he was on the phone all the time, conference calls and so on, making sure things were still done his way. And he continued to control all the fundamental data concerning the business. In spite of his illness, he always remained confident of his own ability to deal with any situation.

'But he was a maverick, Mr Vogel. And, now, well, without the sheer magnitude and extraordinary power of his personality, without his ability to juggle, when others would have no idea how to, nobody knows quite how to get out of the hole he seems to have dug for Fairbrother's. It is possible that the bank may have to cease trading, or at the very least be subjected to a hostile takeover.'

'You are being very frank, Miss Fairbrother,' said Vogel, who genuinely had not expected so much information to be so freely offered.

'I am afraid everything I have just shared with you will become public knowledge in the very near future unless I – and I really believe it is going to be down to me – can find a way of sorting out this mess and come up with a plan to save Fairbrother's,' responded Bella. 'And that is going to take some doing, I can tell you, detective inspector.'

'I see,' said Vogel.

Bella Fairbrother took in a deep intake of breath and let it out very slowly.

'It's all just so awful,' she said eventually, showing the first sign of any emotion since Vogel had met her. 'I can't believe that Blackdown Manor has gone. It was such a beautiful house, full of beautiful things. I grew up there, of course. And I had a very happy upbringing too, until my father decided to chuck my mother out and move in that tart he later married. After that it was sheer misery, probably why my brother turned out the way he did, too.'

Bella Fairbrother sounded bitter. And angry again.

'Miss Fairbrother, you are clearly not sorry that your father is dead, you have made no secret of that,' said Vogel. 'I wonder if you actually desired his death.'

Bella Fairbrother laughed briefly. It was a laugh without mirth.

'Not enough to kill him, or to have him killed, if that's what you are suggesting, detective inspector,' she said.

'I would not dream of suggesting any such thing without appropriate evidence,' said Vogel deadpan.

'No, well, in any case, I had known for some time what a mess he was going to leave behind him. And, I also knew that my father would die sooner rather than later of natural causes. Whether or not I wanted him dead is irrelevant. I only had to wait a few months. In any case, I am a senior executive of a major bank, Mr Vogel, and I have every reason to believe that when the present chief executive takes retirement within the next year or so I shall be offered that position. I am only stepping in to assist Fairbrother's at this stage because I have been asked to do so by the board, because I have a greater knowledge of how my father ran things than anyone else And I do not want Fairbrother's to go under, obviously. It is my family heritage.'

'Yes indeed,' murmured Vogel. 'I wonder, speaking of heritage. Have you been in touch with your brother at all? We need to speak to him too, of course.'

'I don't see why, he's not been near our father for years. Not even been in this country for years either, as far as I know.'

'Miss Fairbrother, I am not at all clear who or what is going to benefit from your father's death. You paint a picture of possible collapse as far as the bank is concerned. But as a rule, when a wealthy man is murdered, excepting crimes of passion, there is usually a financial motive. That is why I need to speak to your brother, and to any other surviving family members.'

Bella Fairbrother sighed.

'All I have is a mobile phone number for Freddie,' she said. 'He does call me occasionally, and me him. But at the moment it's just ringing out. I'll give you the number.'

Bella reached into her bag for her phone.

'Thank you,' said Vogel. 'Of course, your father's death, and the fact that it's a suspicious death, is already in the press and on the net. Your brother is bound to hear of it, so he will surely get in touch with you then. Or even the police.'

'I wouldn't bet on it,' said Bella Fairbrother. 'My brother is not like other men.'

SEVEN

George Grey arrived at London's Paddington station at about the same time Bella Fairbrother reached the Mount Somerset Hotel.

He'd bided his time at Musgrove Park hospital until a moment when there seemed to be little going on in his ward, and few medical staff around, before making his move.

His clothes, which were in a bag in his bedside locker, were steeped in blood and had been partially shredded during the repeated stabbing he had sustained. They were of little use to him. Not if he wished to be as inconspicuous as possible.

His shoes were also in the cabinet, spattered with blood, but otherwise undamaged. He had removed them and, carrying them in one hand behind his back, along with his wallet and phone, made his way along the central corridor dividing the rows of individual rooms which now made up the bulk of the patient accommodation at the Musgrove.

There was a nursing station at one end of the corridor, but the sole nurse sitting there had been busy at her computer, and in any case, even if she had seen George, he'd hoped she would merely assume he was on his way to the toilet.

The doors to most of the rooms stood open. George peered inside two or three before seeing what he wanted to see. The male patient inside was hooked up to a drip and to a PCA – a patient-controlled analgesia, probably morphine – pump, and he looked as if he'd been making good use of it. He lay on his back, eyes shut, mouth open, snoring heavily. George entered the room quietly, opened the patient's bedside cabinet as softly as he could, and inside found exactly what he was hoping for: the man's clothes, neatly folded. There was a pair of jeans, a polo shirt, a V-necked sweater and a lightweight jacket made of some kind of shiny beige material. George wrinkled his nose in distaste. He was, by nature and when he could afford it, quite a natty dresser. Normally he wouldn't be seen dead in a jacket like that. Under these circumstances, he was phenomenally grateful for it.

He'd bundled up the clothes, tucked them under his arm and continued along the corridor to the toilet. His luck held. The nurse he'd noticed earlier still did not look up. In any case, he reminded himself, she had no reason to be suspicious. He didn't think she'd been on duty for long. She probably had no idea that the police had just visited him, and that he didn't have any clothes of his own that were even remotely wearable.

Once in the toilet he had removed his hospital issue gown, which he stuffed into the waste bin, in case its early discovery might attract unwanted attention, and dressed in the other man's clothes. He'd discarded the underpants – he really couldn't wear another man's underpants – and pulled on the jeans carefully over his wounded and bandaged legs. George Grey was a small man. The patient whose clothes he had stolen was clearly much bigger. Better that way than the other, thought George. Fortuitously there was a belt in the jeans. George pulled it tight and then rolled up the bottoms. The shirt and the jumper were a good two sizes too big. The unattractive jacket hung loosely from his thin shoulders. George was grateful for anything. He put his wallet in the hip pockets of the jeans, and his phone in the top pocket of the jacket, and exited the toilet carefully, looking to the left and to the right, before concluding that the coast was clear, and heading for the stairs at the far end of the corridor to the nurse's station.

Two doctors, talking animatedly, had emerged from one of the rooms right in front of George, who had looked down at the floor, avoiding the slightest chance of eye contact. He needn't have worried. The doctors took no notice of him at all.

He'd left the hospital without a problem and picked up a taxi from the hospital rank to take him into Taunton town centre. He found a cash point and took out £400, which just about emptied his current account. He'd been given the obvious instruction not to leave a paper trail, so he wouldn't be able to use his credit cards for a bit. The police would know he had started off in Taunton, obviously, so he was giving nothing away by drawing cash there. He then bought a pay-as-you-go phone in the Vodafone shop. His injured leg and shoulder were throbbing consistently. He knew he wasn't well enough to be out and about, far from it, but he had no choice. There was a chemist in the high street, where he acquired co-codamol, the mixture of codeine and paracetamol which he thought was the strongest pain killer you could buy over the counter, and a bottle of Night Nurse, the knock-out cold remedy he reckoned would help him to sleep that night. If he got a chance to sleep.

There was a Marks and Spencer up the road, and he was just thinking about buying himself some clothes which fitted, when he spotted two police officers on the corner. He suddenly became convinced that one of them was staring at him. He was, of course, being paranoid, wasn't he? Surely it was unlikely that any sort of alert would have been put out for him yet. On the other hand, he must look bad enough to attract attention. He had noticed in the mirror in the hospital toilet that his face seemed drained of all colour, and, however hard he tried, he could not help walking with a limp.

He decided to forego the opportunity to buy some new clothes and to get out of Taunton as quickly as he could.

The journey had not been a comfortable one. Every jolt the train made reverberated right through George's body. From the buffet car he bought a bottle of water and a couple of miniature bottles of whisky with which he washed down the co-codamol. First two of the small white pills, then another two. He read the label. Mostly paracetamol. Just eight grams of codeine. The pills didn't touch the sides. He took a couple more, and, by the time he reached Paddington, wasn't entirely sure how many he'd taken. They still didn't seem to have helped much, though. As he stepped off the train he could feel the stitches in his thigh pulling and a sharp pain darted up and down his leg.

He winced as his feet hit the platform, then he made his way towards the underground still trying, without success, not to limp. He was sweating, even though it was a cool day, and he felt quite faint.

In spite of his continuing efforts not to draw attention to himself, he was sure people were staring at him. He could feel a wetness around the injured area of his leg. He glanced down. To his dismay there was a growing blackish-red patch on the pale blue jeans. His thigh was bleeding again.

As quickly as he could manage, he took the escalator down to the Tube station. He leaned against the wall next to the ticket office for a few seconds, struggling to maintain control and keep calm.

It wasn't just his physical discomfort and the combined effects of painkillers and alcohol which were causing George Grey to sweat. He was becoming more and more frightened by the minute. He could see no way out of the situation he had found himself in.

'This wasn't supposed to happen, nobody was supposed to die,' he repeated under his breath for the umpteenth time. 'Nobody was supposed to die.'

He shook his head in a desperate attempt to clear it, before approaching the ticket office, acquiring an Oyster card and putting twenty pounds on it. He didn't know how long he would be in London, nor how much he would need to use public transport.

He took the District line to Earls Court, then changed onto the Piccadilly line. He alighted at Boston Manor, the nearest Tube station to Brentford, a West London suburb he had only ever visited once before, for much the same purpose as on this occasion. As instructed, he made a call from his new pay-as-you-go phone.

'I've just got out of the Tube,' he said. 'I'm calling like you said. Look, I'm not feeling all that hot. Can you come and get me? Or send somebody.'

'What makes you think I have anyone to send,' said the voice at the other end of the phone sharply. 'No. Make your own way to the pub, like we said.'

'I can't walk very far,' said George. 'I should be in hospital, remember? I'm afraid I might pass out.'

'Try not to. There's a taxi office next to the Tube station. Get a cab.'

'I didn't want to draw attention to myself. I, uh, I think I'm bleeding.'

'For God's sake, George,' said the voice. 'Get a grip. It's dark. Don't be paranoid. As long as you hold yourself together no taxi driver is going to take any notice of you. You're just a fare.'

'Well, I don't know about that—'

The interruption was loud and authoritative. 'George. Have you got money?'

'Yes, well, some . . .'

'Right, that's OK then. And you're soon going to have an awful lot more. Just get in a cab.'

George was beginning to feel increasingly woozier. Nonetheless he wanted that money. He was owed it after all. And he needed reassurance and instructions. He needed to know what he should do next. George Grey had never been very good at making his own decisions in life. Most of the trouble he'd got into over the years had been down to unwisely following the lead of others. Even in severe pain and half out of his head on a cocktail of drugs and alcohol he was starkly aware of that. But, as ever, he was unable to do anything other than acquiesce to someone, almost anyone, stronger than himself.

'All right,' he said.

'Good. Uh, just one thing, George, you are sure you haven't been followed, aren't you?'

'Now you're being paranoid,' said George. 'Of course, I haven't been followed. The filth wouldn't even have known I'd left the hospital before I got the London train.'

'You can never be sure,' said the voice. 'Just be careful, George.'

'I was being careful,' muttered George into his phone. Then he realised nobody was listening any more.

EIGHT

'**R**ight, Saslow, I think we'd better interview the Kivels tomorrow, don't you,' said Vogel, as they were about to head back to Bristol after leaving Bella Fairbrother at the Mount Somerset.

'Yes, boss,' said Saslow.

'OK, get on to Kenneth Steele and ask someone to find a phone number for them. Arrange a meet for us as early as possible in the morning, will you?'

Saslow winced. She didn't fancy another early start.

'Don't you think we should stay over in the Blackdowns, boss?' she asked hopefully. 'I mean, the Wellington incident room will be fully operational by tomorrow. Shouldn't we be on the spot.'

'We are on the spot, Dawn, not much more than an hour's drive away anyway,' said Vogel.

Depending on the traffic, it could easily be an hour and a half in the holiday season and at peak times considerably more, thought Saslow. It had actually taken an hour and a quarter from Sea Mills that day, and only that because they'd left in the middle of the night. Or it had felt like the middle of night to her anyway. Saslow was not naturally an early riser, and in order to pick Vogel up at whatever time he decreed she had to rise considerably earlier than him. But she said nothing.

'Anyway, don't know about you, but I'd rather spend an hour less in my own bed any time than two hours more in a bed in some darned hotel,' Vogel continued.

'Yes, boss,' said Saslow resignedly.

Everybody knew that David Vogel was a devoted family man. His family was even more important to him than the job with which he was also obsessed, something Saslow suspected not to be the case with a number of the gnarled old detectives she had already encountered in her short career. Rumour even had it that Vogel had resigned from his top job as a senior officer with the Met's prestigious Major Investigation Team, and asked for a transfer to the Avon and Somerset Constabulary, entirely for the sake of his fourteen-year-old daughter Rosamund.

Rosamund, whom Saslow knew Vogel adored, had cerebral palsy. Swimming was her great love, and, Vogel had confided in Saslow, although he rarely spoke about his private life, that when his daughter was swimming she seemed able to forget the limits her condition inflicted on her body and revelled in the freedom of movement the support of water gave her. The otherwise very ordinary and quite small bungalow which was the Vogel home, had one rather extraordinary feature. The previous owner had built a fairly luxurious mini spa, equipped with an endless pool, in the overly large garage, and Rosamund was able to swim whenever she wanted. Vogel would never have been able to afford anything like that in the London area.

The two officers didn't speak much for the rest of the journey. Saslow could sense that Vogel was deep in thought. He was the kind of detective who believed that the solving of a crime lay as much inside the head as in the work done on the road. Evidence-, intelligence- and information-driven, of course; but then dependent on the dissection and analysis of the smallest detail of all collated material by the investigating officers.

Just as they were pulling up outside Vogel's bungalow his phone rang.

'The Kivels will see you at 8.30 in the morning,' said Polly Jenkins, who clearly was still at work at Kenneth Steele House. 'Martha Kivel says there'll be a decent breakfast if you want it.'

Polly chuckled.

'Thank you, Polly,' said Vogel. 'Never mind breakfast, what's the address?'

Polly chuckled again, then duly recited the address of the Kivel cottage in Wrangway.

'Thanks, Polly,' said Vogel. 'You should go home now. I think we've all had enough for one day. Get over to Wellington police station in the morning. We'll be running the investigation out of there for the next two or three days at least.'

'Yes, boss,' said Polly.

Saslow glanced across at her senior officer. His face was impassive. Vogel was by and large a quiet, self-contained man. He was also known for his powerful intellect. With his diffident manner, his thick-lensed spectacles, and his very slight stoop, he rather more resembled a university professor than a police detective at the cutting edge of major crime. In his spare time, he had played backgammon at the highest level and his principal hobby was compiling crosswords.

Saslow knew he would have at once memorised the Kivels' address and would have no need to write it down or tap it into his phone.

Vogel opened the passenger door, glanced sideways at Saslow, and said, 'Pick me up at 7.15 then, Dawn.'

Saslow muttered assent. She would have to leave her flat nearer to the centre of Bristol before seven. At least this was, however, an hour later than they had left that morning.

She watched Vogel walk up his garden path. The family dog started to bark, then whimper. The front door opened. Vogel's wife Mary appeared in the doorway, silhouetted against the bright light of the hallway behind her. Timmy the Border collie squeezed past in order to more quickly reach his master.

Vogel's pace seemed to quicken, his stride lengthen. Timmy bounded by his side as he hurried towards his wife. Saslow could only see the back of her senior officer's head, but she had no doubt that he was smiling.

Meanwhile, to the mild alarm of the landlord, George Grey had arrived at Brentford's Brewery Tap pub. George looked pale and wan. He was limping heavily, and his clothes were dishevelled and didn't seem to fit him. There was a suspicious looking dark stain on the left leg of his blue jeans.

He staggered very slightly on his way to the bar. Peter Forest wondered if he was already drunk, and also if he might be a vagrant.

But he sounded reasonably lucid when he ordered a large Scotch, so Forest served him. It was possible, thought Forest, that his customer was merely unwell. And, although he was definitely not a regular, there was something vaguely familiar about him, too.

George made his way to a table by the window, where he was almost immediately joined by a second man, heavily bearded and of indeterminate years, wearing a baseball hat and an expensive looking leather jacket. The landlord watched as the man put what seemed to be a solicitous arm around George's thin shoulders, before approaching the bar and ordering two more large whiskies.

Forest hesitated very slightly.

'Is your friend all right?' he asked. 'Looks a bit rough.'

'Bad trip to the dentist,' came the reply, accompanied by a reassuring smile.

Forest served the whiskies. The second man was certainly well capable of caring for the first, and the landlord considered that his presence absolved him of any responsibility. It was a busy time of day. There were other people in the pub waiting to be served. Forest proceeded to give them his full attention.

'This isn't what was supposed to have happened,' muttered George half to himself, for the umpteenth time that day, as his companion sat down beside him.

'Nobody was supposed to have got hurt. I was supposed to rescue them. Then everything was going to be all right. That's what you said.'

'We all make mistakes,' replied the man in the leather jacket calmly.

George downed the remains of his first double whisky, and started on the second.

'Some mistake. Two deaths, and I'm the one's going to get the blame. You told me to start the fire. You had it all arranged, you said. I was careful. I really was careful. Then that bloody tank exploded. Like a bomb, it was. How did that happen? It wasn't close to the house, and I started the fire at the front, like you told me to.'

George Grey began to cry. Leather jacket manoeuvred himself so that, should the landlord be watching still, his view would be at least partially obstructed. Then he again put an arm around one of George's shoulders. But it was not the caring sympathetic gesture which he hoped it would be taken for, if anyone noticed. Instead he dug hard fingers into George's flesh and hissed threateningly into his ear.

'Pull yourself together, George,' he said. 'If anybody gets it in the neck for this it's going to be you, like you said. If you keep your cool everything will be all right.'

'I don't see how, I'm a murderer now, aren't I? And it wasn't my fault. I walked out of hospital, too. I'm not sure I should have done that. Perhaps I should go to the police and explain. Tell them what happened. Tell them I didn't mean it.'

'Now, George, you don't want to do anything stupid, do you,' murmured leather jacket.

George continued to snivel. The man in the leather jacket glanced around the pub. There were several other drinkers propping up the bar, who seemed to be keeping the landlord busy. And they were all watching a football match on TV.

'Look, George, I want to help you,' he said, sounding suddenly encouraging, perhaps even caring. 'Why don't you have another drink – it will calm your nerves.'

He pushed his own whisky, which had stood untouched before him, along the table towards George.

'We need to perk you up,' leather jacket continued. 'I bet you've not eaten anything since you left the hospital, have you?'

George shook his head, as he reached out for the proffered whisky. It was his third in the pub, on top of the two he had consumed earlier on the train, and then there were the painkillers.

'Well, you should come back with me then. I'll feed you. And you need to get some rest, too. You can stay the night. And if you're still feeling rough, I've a tame doctor I could get over.'

George was beginning to feel very light headed indeed, but he hadn't forgotten the principal purpose of his journey to London.

'I want my money,' he said. 'Then I can get away. You said you would arrange that, if it came to it, and it has come to it. The police are after me for murder, for God's sake. I can't think of anything else to do. I need you to help me get away.'

'Of course,' said leather jacket soothingly. 'Of course, I will help you.'

George looked relieved. 'As long as you don't let me down,' he said,

'I won't, I promise you I won't.'

'All right, I believe you, but I want my money,' said George.

'Not here,' said leather jacket. 'I can't pass that amount of cash over to you here. I haven't even brought it with me. Come back with me, and I'll give it you. In cash. Straight away. Then we can plan what you are going to do next, you and Janice, of course.'

George sighed heavily, but he no longer had the strength to argue. In any case, this was an argument he clearly could not win. If leather jacket didn't have the cash with him, then George had to do what he said to get it. And neither did he have a hope of evading the forces of law and order without the assistance of the man he held responsible for the trouble he was in. It was Catch-22.

'I can't walk far,' said George. 'You must be able to see that. I've pretty much had it.'

'It's not far. You know that. Just a few steps. I'll get you another drink first. Do you good.'

George swallowed the rest of his third double, and accepted the fourth. He had hoped the whisky might make him feel better. But, like so much in his life, he hadn't thought it through at all. He felt worse than before. Considerably worse. His head was spinning uncontrollably.

He tried to stand up, but couldn't quite make it.

'You're going to have to help me,' he said.

Leather jacket glanced back at the bar again. This time he couldn't see the landlord at all. He stood up quickly and more or less lifted George out of his seat.

'I should never have left hoshpital,' muttered George, who had begun to seriously slur his words. 'Too shoon. I feel bad, real bad.'

'C'mon George, you can do it,' responded leather jacket, as he wrapped an arm around George's middle and half carried him out of the pub into the shadows of Catherine Wheel Road.

It was dark by then and there seemed to be nobody else around in the quiet cul de sac, off Brentford High Street, which led only to the Grand Union Canal, and on to the River Thames, via a network of paths and footbridges.

NINE

In the morning, it seemed Saslow was so anxious not to be late that she actually arrived at Vogel's house ten minutes early. Nonetheless, by the time Vogel and Saslow reached Taunton the local commuters were making their way to work in droves, and they hit heavy motorway traffic. But by and large they had a pretty good run and arrived at the Kivels' cottage, several miles closer than Blackdown Manor, at just gone quarter past eight.

Moorview Cottage was one of a pair tucked away at the foot of Sampford Moor just out of sight of the motorway. You could hear the steady hum of the M5, though, Vogel noticed as he stepped out of the car, but only just. The place still seemed very peaceful.

It was a cool morning, yet the sun shone brightly. In stark contrast to the previous day.

The cottage was tiny, but very pretty, the render freshly painted cream and the woodwork pale blue, the front garden neat and tidy.

Vogel suspected there would be a bigger garden at the back which would almost certainly contain a vegetable patch, and perhaps a chicken run in one corner. Vogel remained a city boy who had little interest in rural life, but as a committed vegetarian he did fantasise about the joys of growing his own vegetables; as long as he didn't have to do any digging, planting, or any of the other – to him totally mysterious – tasks that would presumably be necessary. He also liked the idea of being able to walk on to his own patch of land and gather free range eggs, but the thought of having to look after hens, feed them, clean up after them, and perhaps even touch them on occasions, appalled him.

Jack Kivel answered the door, smiling in welcome. He was of average height, but broad shouldered and fit looking, and with a decent head of dark brown hair; barely any grey to be seen in spite of almost certainly being nearer to sixty than fifty. And Vogel didn't think for one moment that he had been using colour.

He introduced himself and Saslow.

Kivel nodded by way of response. 'Happy to help any way we

can,' he said. 'Dreadful business. Sir John dead. That beautiful house gone. And there surely can't be a worse way to die than in a fire.'

He shook his head sorrowfully as he led Vogel and Saslow into a glowingly warm and unexpectedly spacious kitchen. It had a low-beamed ceiling, a flag-stoned floor, and a window almost right along the back wall with a wide ledge which doubled as a seat. Vogel's Mary would have said it was her idea of a storybook country kitchen. An Aga took pride of place. Martha Kivel was bending over it, attending to the open oven. She stood up and pushed the door shut.

'There's a tray of bacon in there,' she said almost by way of greeting. 'It'll be ready in five minutes. Bacon baps, I thought. Nice and quick, and you can take one with you if you like. I know you people, always in a hurry.'

'That would be lovely,' said Saslow, with genuine enthusiasm, shooting a glance at the strictly vegetarian Vogel.

'Thank you very much, Mrs Kivel,' said Vogel quickly. 'But I had breakfast before I left home.'

'You'm an early riser, then,' remarked Martha Kivel approvingly. She stepped forward towards the two officers, stretching out her right hand.

'I'm forgetting me manners. Martha Kivel, pleased to meet you.'

In turn Vogel and Saslow grasped her hand. Martha then gestured for the two officers to sit down at the scrubbed kitchen table. In this kitchen everything that should gleam did so obediently. Martha poured them tea from a brown earthenware pot without asking whether they wanted it or not, putting the milk in the cups first. There was a sugar bowl on the table next to what was quite clearly a home-made Victoria sponge cake. Vogel's favourite.

'You'll have a slice of my sponge, though, won't you, Mr Vogel?' enquired Martha. 'Only made yesterday.'

Vogel agreed that he would, and tried not to sound too eager. After all, he'd only grabbed a quick bowl of cereal earlier and was actually every bit as hungry as Saslow.

He took a hasty bite before beginning to speak. The sponge was quite delicious. Everything about the Kivels, man and wife, indicated that they would be the perfect people to look after a rich man, in dwindling health, and his home. Everything about them indicated that they were capable, honest and diligent.

'Obviously, you realise I want to ask you questions about the fire, and your relationship with Sir John,' Vogel began.

Jack and Martha Kivel nodded in unison.

'Us don't know ought about the fire to tell the truth,' said Martha Kivel. 'The manor be over t'other side of moor from here, as you'd know. Nothing to alert us yer. I suppose if us had stepped outside in the middle of the night we might have seen a glow in the sky from a blaze big enough to burn that house down. But we was asleep.'

She turned towards her husband. 'Sleep the sleep of the just, us do, don't us, Jack.'

Jack Kivel nodded in an abstracted sort of way.

Vogel allowed himself a small smile. 'So how did you both hear about the fire?' he asked.

'Our postman, Colin, he heard about it as soon as he started on his rounds. Called us on his mobile early yesterday morning, oh about a quarter to seven I think it was. Said he didn't want us to find out on the news or anything like that. He knew it would be a dreadful shock for Jack and me, seeing as how long we worked for the Fairbrothers. Jack, even before we were wed. And it was a dreadful shock too. It may have ended badly, but we still feel like part of the family really. Saw young Bella and Freddie Fairbrother grow up. They played with our kids. Sir John was like an uncle to our boys . . .'

Martha looked suddenly close to tears. She reached out and grasped her husband's hand tightly.

'How long exactly did you work for Sir John, Mrs Kivel?' enquired Vogel.

'Well, my Jack's always worked for him, really, one way and another. And funnily enough it was twenty-nine year ago last Sunday that he asked us if we'd like to live in, be his caretaker and housekeeper like. Well, us was living with Jack's parents at the time, couldn't afford nothing other, I was pregnant with our second lad, Andy, and there wasn't much room apart from anything else. It wasn't ideal that was for sure. Sir John offered us The Gatehouse as our home. It had three bedrooms, a lovely garden, and we was surrounded by all that wonderful countryside. We were thrilled, weren't we, Jack?'

'We were,' said Jack. 'And we had a good life up there too.

Busy, especially when Sir John was at home, Martha did a lot of the cooking and that. He liked to entertain at weekends. Sometimes he even got me serving the drinks. "C'mon, Jack," he used to say, "butler duties tonight."

'"On your head be it, Sir John," I'd say. We always had a bit of a laugh together, the boss and me. It's how Martha says, we felt more like family than staff.'

'So how did things go wrong?'

'They didn't really. Or didn't seem to. As far as we was concerned anyway. The boss went up to London, like he did most weeks. I drove him to the station as usual, Tiverton Parkway, in his Bentley. He had one of those old Bentleys, said the new ones weren't proper Bentleys at all. Typical of Sir John, that. Anyway, he seemed in good form. "You know what, Jack," he said, "I'm thinking of sending you on a course mixing cocktails, then you'll be a proper butler. What do you think of that?"

'I said, "Not bleddy likely, the only thing I'm any good at mixing is our Martha's Christmas puddings." He laughed, then climbed on board the train, still chuckling. I always went on to the platform to see him off. Like you would with family, you see. That's how it was. He leaned out the window and waved to me as the train pulled out of the station. Like he always did. And he was still chuckling. I can picture it now. That was the last time I ever saw him.'

'Really? You've never even caught a glimpse of him since?'

'A glimpse? Well yes, I suppose we both have.' Martha interrupted. 'Two or three times, but only in his car. Being driven by that George Grey.'

Martha spat the last words out.

'I was in Wellington one day in Tim Potter's, the butchers, the traffic was queued back from the lights, I happened to glance out, and I saw Sir John's car stopped in the street outside,' she continued in a more normal tone of voice. 'It was strange, really. There he was just a few feet away from me. And yet there was this huge distance between us, after all those years. I couldn't see him clearly, just his shape, because the Bentley's rear windows be tinted. I could see his white hair though. No mistaking that.'

'OK, so, Jack, what happened after you put him on the train that last time?' asked Vogel.

'Well, it was a Monday morning,' replied Jack Kivel. 'He didn't have a regular routine. He was his own boss after all. Sometimes he'd stay down for a week or two and not go back to London at all, and sometimes he'd stay in London and not make it back here for two or three weeks. But more often than not he spent the working week in London and his weekends here, so he'd travel up on an early train on Monday mornings. Anyway, two or three days later his secretary called and said Sir John wouldn't be coming back that weekend or the weekend after. Well, that wasn't particularly unusual, but I kept expecting to hear from him directly. He was always ringing me when he was away, asking me if I'd planted the new potatoes yet, or if the tree man had been, or some such thing. I didn't hear though, so eventually I thought I'd better give him a ring, find out what was going on, like. I had his mobile number, of course. He just didn't pick up.'

Jack paused. He seemed uncomfortable, perhaps both moved and saddened by the story he and his wife were telling. His hands lay lightly clasped on his lap now, and every so often he unclasped them and rubbed his palms together. It looked to Vogel like an involuntary nervous gesture. After a few seconds Jack continued to speak.

'Martha tried, too. He didn't answer her either. And that was strange, because he'd always picked up to us before. We kept leaving messages. But no response at all. In the end Martha called Bella to ask if her father was all right. It was then that Bella told her they'd had a bust up, she wasn't speaking to him and she didn't give a fuck whether he was all right or not—'

'Jack,' interrupted Martha reprovingly.

'I'm only saying what Bella said, dear, so they understand.' Jack turned to face his wife. 'Martha don't hold with language like that, do you, Martha?'

Martha shook her head.

'No, I don't,' she said emphatically. 'And Bella wasn't brought up to use it, neither.'

She switched her full attention to Vogel and Saslow again.

'Anyway, just as us was getting really worried and wondering what the heck was going on, the secretary phones again and says Sir John's solicitor would be down for the weekend.' Martha related. 'We was to get everything ready. Now, I could have sworn she said

Sir John and his solicitor were coming. But maybe I just assumed that. It didn't occur to either me or Jack that Sir John's solicitor would come without Sir John. But he did. He arrived alone. And as soon as he was settled in, he said he'd like a word with us. He sat us down in the sitting room, poured us drinks, white wine for me, and a whisky for Jack, and said he had some difficult news.

'Then he told us that, with great regret, Sir John had decided it was time for us to move on. Neither Jack nor I grasped exactly what he was saying at first. I didn't anyway. Time to move on? What the heck did that mean? "I am afraid Sir John feels that he no longer has need of your services," he went on, cool as you like. Jack looked at me and I looked at Jack. "You mean he's bleddy well giving us the sack, after all these years?" Jack said. "Well, Sir John wouldn't put it like that," he said. "I bet he bleddy wouldn't," Jack said. "But that's what it bleddy well amounts to, isn't it?"

'I know I started to cry. I couldn't take it in really. I remember saying, But we live here, this is our home. Where are we going to live? It was then that he told us about the settlement. Basically, this cottage, and one hundred thousand pounds. Afterwards everybody said how generous that was. But we were just in shock. Blackdown Manor was our home for nearly thirty years. And Jack had always been Sir John's right-hand man, from when he was only a lad, really. It was far more than a job, you see. Far more. For both of us. We looked after Sir John, and his family, proper looked after 'em. That's how we saw it anyway.'

For an awful moment Vogel thought Martha was going to burst into tears in front of him and Saslow. But she didn't.

'Us couldn't believe it really,' she continued. 'All that time. And The Gatehouse. Didn't matter that us was given another place. The Gatehouse was ours. Sir John let me do what I liked with it. Everything belonged to Sir John, of course. Even the furniture, although we were allowed to take what we liked when he chucked us out. But not a lot of it would fit in here anyway.'

Vogel thought about the floral curtains, the pink wallpaper, the big chintzy sofa. So, they had been Mrs Kivel's choice, just as he'd suspected. It somehow had never seemed likely that these would be the work of the Greys.

'Not that we're not happy here now,' Martha Kivel continued. 'Lovely little cottage. Sir John had it done up for us an' all.

And we only need the two bedrooms with the boys being married with their own families. But at the time, well, 'twas terrible. And then they tells us the settlement is conditional on us packing up and moving by the end of the month. We had sixteen days to get out. We agreed to it all, of course. Straightaway. Didn't have any choice. And with what he gave us and what we'd put away all them years we were living rent free, well we'm not badly off. Jack still does a bit of gardening and a few odd jobs here and there, and I have a couple of ladies I clean for, and I makes cakes and puddings that they sell in the Cheese and Wine Shop down in Wellington, so we keep busy and have a bit extra coming in . . .'

Vogel felt his eyes beginning to glaze over. Martha Kivel's words came pouring out in a torrent with barely a pause for breath and little or no opportunity for interruption. She certainly had more to say for herself than her husband. It seemed she was not an unobservant woman though.

'I'm sorry, Mr Vogel, you didn't come here to listen to all that, did you,' she said eventually.

Vogel blinked rapidly behind his spectacles. He didn't often lose control of an interview. He really needed to get this one back on course. Local gossip and background information were always useful of course, but there was a limit.

'So, when did you hear that the Greys had moved in and taken over?' asked Vogel.

'Oh, only a couple of days after we left,' said Jack Kivel.

'We moved out on the Wednesday and they moved in on the Thursday,' Martha interrupted, not for the first time. 'That was the final straw really. Sir John must have had it planned well in advance, must have done. Colin the postie saw all the comings and goings. That hurt as much as anything. Like we was disposable. All that time being told we was family, living like family, we thought, with the Fairbrothers, and then we was out on our ear and this couple from London shunted in almost before we'd shut the door to our home behind us. Outsiders, they were. But then, that's what we must always have been, really, we reckoned. The way we was treated.'

'Did you ever hear anything about how the Greys were appointed?' asked Saslow. 'Whether or not Sir John knew them before he hired them, perhaps, or anything like that?'

'Nope, us don't know nothing about them Greys. Nor do us want to,' said Martha vehemently.

'So, when did you hear about Sir John's illness?' continued Saslow.

'Well, I'm not sure us can tell 'ee that exactly,' said Martha. 'Must have been a couple of months or so after us was chucked out, I suppose. Obviously, Sir John was keeping it quiet. But that's hard to do round here, very hard. There was nothing, then the word got out, and it just went around everywhere locally. Someone said there'd been a story in one of the papers. But we never saw it. Seemed to come on quite suddenly, his illness. We thought so, anyway. There was a few local tradesmen still went up there at first. And they saw him shuffling around on sticks, apparently. Didn't speak to anybody and kept out the way. Proud man, Sir John. We could understand that. Course we could. But it hurt all the more, you see. We'd have taken care of him. And we wouldn't have told nobody nothing. We never gossiped about the Fairbrothers, not even when Sir John suddenly decided to get rid of his first wife, Caroline, and move in that Italian trollop, Antonia.'

'I take it you didn't approve?' said Vogel, this time unable to suppress his smile. Martha Kivel and Bella Fairbrother clearly had very similar opinions of Sir John's second wife.

'No, us didn't,' said Martha. 'We thought Sir John had taken leave of his senses, to tell the truth. Brains in his trousers. We stuck by him, of course, and tried to make Antonia welcome. Never liked her though. And she didn't last, thank God. They married as soon as he could get a divorce from Caroline, then she walked out on him four or five years later and took him for a pretty penny by all accounts. We never got to the bottom of exactly what happened. We were just glad to see the back of her to tell the truth. I think Sir John would have liked Caroline back, but she'd found someone new and didn't want anything more to do with him. He treated her very badly. Sad for the children though.'

'But they stayed with Sir John at the manor, didn't they?' queried Saslow.

'Yes, Sir John had somehow managed to arrange to have principle custody, which surprised us,' Martha continued. 'We'd never have thought Caroline would have let them go. I mean they spent a lot of time with their mum, of course, but it wasn't like living with her. They didn't just have to put up with the trollop, there

was all this shuffling between their mum and dad. There were
constant rows about it, too. Freddie was fifteen at the time, and
Bella was thirteen. Difficult ages. I don't think Freddie ever got
over it. Reckon that's what pushed him off the rails. I expect you
knows about him being the wild one?'

'Yes, although we might like to hear more about that another
time,' asked Vogel. 'Meanwhile, can I ask, did you ever have any
contact at all with Sir John after you were asked to leave? A phone
call, or a letter perhaps?'

'Nope,' said Jack. 'We were in touch with his solicitor for a
bit, of course. But once we'd agreed to the settlement and signed
all the papers to get this cottage made over to us and that, we
never heard from any of 'em again. When we learned that Sir John
was ill we tried to phone him. We thought, well, if he was poorly,
maybe that explained things a bit. But his mobile didn't even go
to answer service any more. And when we called the house, the
number had been changed. All the time we was living there we
had the same number at Blackdown, but suddenly that had
gone along with everything else.'

'Did either of you have any idea if there was anything else that
might have caused Sir John to cut himself off like that, apart from
his illness?' asked Vogel.

Martha chimed in again, shaking her head. 'Not really,' she
said. 'We wondered if it had affected his brain in some way, to
tell the truth. Otherwise it just didn't make sense to us, really, for
him to behave how he did. I mean, if you'm ill you want your
family and close friends around you, don't you?'

Vogel agreed that most people did want that. He finished his
tea and a second piece of cake while Saslow tucked into a second
bacon roll. Then the two officers thanked the Kivels and left.

In the car Saslow turned to Vogel as she started the engine.

'Bit of a riddle, isn't it, boss?' she commented.

'It certainly is, Saslow,' said Vogel.

'I mean none of it adds up really, does it?'

Vogel took off his spectacles and wiped them with his handkerchief. He was a man who still always carried a linen handkerchief.
He didn't like paper tissues. They left little bits all over your glasses.

'Oh, it adds up all right,' he replied. 'These things always do. It's
just that we haven't worked out the mathematics yet. That's all.'

TEN

A sun-tanned man with sun-bleached hair, still handsome in a dissipated sort of way, sat outside a bar in Brisbane gazing out to sea. He had just lunched on Brisbane Bay bugs, a crustacean some thought every bit as delicious as lobster, and which Brisbanites, of course, thought even better. The man drew deeply on a cigarette. He'd decided some time ago that he was never going to give up now, so he might as well stop fretting about it and just enjoy. However, on that particular afternoon, he derived little pleasure from the sensation of acrid smoke filling his lungs.

He had a freshly filled glass of pale Aussie beer, the amber nectar of his chosen country of residence, on the table before him. The beer was also giving him little pleasure. His mobile phone, switched to silent, was on the table next to the glass. He hoped the call he was expecting would come soon. And sure enough, before he was halfway through his beer, the phone buzzed and vibrated.

He picked it up, hoping for an explanation that would put his mind at rest.

'Yes,' he said.

'Do you know what's happened?' asked his caller.

'I know,' replied the man. 'I saw it online. Not made our papers yet. It was an accident surely? I mean, we only had to wait . . .'

'Of course it was an accident. Nothing has changed. We can still go ahead with our plan.'

'OK, what happens now?'

'Well, we need you back here obviously, assuming you still want to be involved?'

'Of course I do. I don't have much choice, do I, if I'm going to protect my inheritance.'

'Right, you should call your sister and tell her you're on the way. Then you should contact the police where you are. They will put you in touch with the investigating team in the UK. As you are the heir, they will want to talk to you—'

'Investigating team?' interrupted the man. 'I thought you said it was an accident. Why are the police involved? And why do they want to talk to me? I wasn't even in the country.'

'It's just routine. You have nothing to worry about.'

The voice was both confident and soothing.

'Are you sure?'

'Yes, quite sure. But everything needs to be done properly, and with apparent transparency. We cannot afford any mistakes. I hope you understand that.'

'Yes, I understand,' said the man.

'I must stress that you need to be disciplined and vigilant in everything you do,' said the disembodied voice. 'You have made many mistakes in the past.'

'That's as may be,' said the man. 'But not anymore. I have too much to lose.'

'We all do,' said the voice, ending the call.

Freddie Fairbrother wasn't entirely reassured, but he was certainly not going to back out now. In any case, he had a history of believing what he wanted to believe, rather than facing up to any potentially undesirable reality.

Freddie had led a fairly indolent life in Australia for almost two decades, enjoying the sun and the sea. And the beer. He didn't do drugs any more, although he undoubtedly drank far too much. He had an easy smile and bright blue eyes. He was attractive to women and had enjoyed the company of a succession of girlfriends over the years. But none of his relationships ever lasted. In spite of the beer, he was muscularly slim and more than averagely fit for a man of his age, because he swam regularly, sailed, and scuba-dived. Freddie loved anything to do with the sea, but scuba diving was his true passion, largely because he had long ago been seduced by the Great Barrier Reef, that unique complex of almost 3,000 individual reefs and 900 islands stretching for an extraordinary 1,400 miles just a short boat ride from the coast of Queensland.

Freddie was going to miss the Barrier Reef. Diving regularly into the depths of this massive coral paradise had sparked in him more genuine emotion than anything else he had ever experienced. When coral bleaching had struck, Freddie had found himself weeping into his mask. People, including family and such friends as he had, rarely aroused any sort of emotion in Freddie. His father had once accused him of being a sociopath.

Certainly, whilst on the surface appearing to be likeable and funny, he was extraordinarily selfish. All Freddie had ever really cared about was Freddie. And that would never change.

His streak of irresponsibility remained. Freddie had enjoyed a good life in Australia, financed by a relatively modest but more than adequate allowance from the family business. His home was a small wooden bungalow right on the beach. He drove a jeep. He had a little boat he used for fishing and diving trips. He had enough money to drink himself into a stupor whenever he liked. And he didn't need to work. That for Freddie had, at first, been more or less the perfect package. He hadn't hankered after great riches. Until recently, when he had come to dwell on what he saw as the unfairness of having been deprived for so long of his birthright. He still had no desire to work to attain either money or the position in life which he felt should already be his. But a course of action, or rather very little action, had been presented on a plate to Freddie, which would allow him to enjoy the privileges of his birth without actively doing anything to achieve them.

All Freddie had to do, he had been assured, was to be Freddie. To play out the role for which he had been born, and for which he had been extensively educated and groomed as a boy and a young man.

Freddie's birthright awaited him. And, as his forty-first birthday approached, somewhat to his surprise, he found he wanted it back. Rather badly.

He took a sip of his beer and gazed out to sea, to where he knew the corals of the greatest reef in the world lurked just a few feet below the surface.

His lips curved into an involuntary smile. The reef wasn't going anywhere. But from now on diving it would be, as for the majority of people, only a holiday pastime for Freddie Fairbrother. That was just fine, he told himself. Freddie was going to be able to afford as many holidays as he liked. Five-star hotels. Private jets. Helicopters. Constant VIP treatment. He couldn't quite explain himself, but perhaps it was because he had been born a Fairbrother, and, deep inside, had never been able to fully dismiss his heritage, that he now lusted after all

those seductive trappings of wealth and power which he had so
casually cast aside as a young man.

Vogel and Saslow were together in Wellington police station
attempting to collate all the varied strands of information, when
Vogel received a call from Bella Fairbrother to tell him her brother
had been in touch, that he had contacted the police in Australia,
and that he would be flying home as soon as possible.

Vogel was intrigued. This was not quite what Bella had led
him to expect. And he had already tried several times, without
success, to call the number she had given him for her brother.

'Were you surprised to hear from him, Miss Fairbrother?' he
asked.

Vogel thought there was the briefest of pauses.

'Of course not, detective inspector,' Bella replied. 'You said it,
he was sure to hear the news sooner or later. And he is family.
In spite of everything.'

'You told me you wouldn't bet on your brother getting in touch,
even when he learned of your father's death. That he was not like
other men. Those were your words, Miss Fairbrother.'

This time there was definitely a pause.

'Yes, well, that still holds good, Mr Vogel. My brother clearly
is, and always has been, totally unpredictable.'

'I see. And did he perhaps express an interest in what the situation is concerning the bank and the family trust, following the
death of your father?' queried Vogel.

'Well yes, of course he did. I was not able to give him a
sensible answer, though. I am still desperately trying to unravel
everything.'

'Is the number he called from the same one that you gave me?'

'I think so, yes. But Freddie told me he was going to be on the
next available flight. I gave him your details, and he said he would
call as soon as he landed.'

Vogel grunted unenthusiastically as he ended the call. He
still had that sense of not being properly in control of this
investigation.

Saslow glanced at him enquiringly.

'Looks like the prodigal son is returning,' Vogel muttered.

'Freddie Fairbrother?'

Vogel nodded.

'That's a bit of a turn up for the books, after being estranged for all this time, isn't it?'

'Not when a share in one of the most famous banks in the world and the possibility of inheriting billions is at stake.'

'But isn't he supposed to be a sort of a hippy character, not interested in possessions or personal wealth and all that sort of stuff?'

'Have you never noticed what happens to hippies as they get older, Saslow?' asked Vogel, adjusting his glasses on the bridge of his nose. 'They turn into everybody else.'

ELEVEN

As soon as she had finished her telephone conversation with Vogel, Bella Fairbrother set off for Blackdown Manor in her metallic grey Mercedes sports car.

On the way, using her hands-free system, she tried, for the umpteenth time since learning of the terrible fire, to call a certain phone number. There was one person she really needed to talk to concerning what had happened. Yet again there was no reply. She hadn't really expected there to be. She was, it seemed, for the time being at any rate, on her own.

She headed onto the M5, coming off at the Wellington turning, and drove for a few miles along the A38 towards Exeter before swinging a left and meandering her way through a network of country lanes up into the Blackdown Hills towards the old manor where she and her brother had been brought up.

Even the drive felt strangely uncomfortable that day. Bella Fairbrother was not by any stretch of the imagination a sentimental woman. But as she swung the little Merc carefully around a succession of blind corners screened on either side by the prohibitively tall banks topped with hedges, which lined the vast majority of the rural roads and lanes of Devon and West Somerset, she felt that sinking feeling in her stomach which always came when she was apprehensive about something.

Not only was her father no longer going to be at the manor to greet her, as he'd always been before their mutually agreed estrangement the previous year, nor the Kivel family, of whom she had only the happiest of memories, but even the house was not going to be there anymore.

The old manor had been built in a commanding position and stood high amongst the hills from which it got its name, almost level with Culmstock Beacon, one of the line of ancient fire beacons, dating back to Tudor England, which were lit to send news of the arrival of the Spanish Armada all the way from the tip of Cornwall to London. Although its immediate privacy was, by and large, well-protected by the high banks and hedges, Blackdown could be seen in the distance from more than one vantage point, if you knew where they were. Bella wanted to prepare herself before actually approaching the house. So she pulled her little car to a halt in a gateway, set back from a section of narrow road, a mile or so from the house as the crow flies.

She stepped out, made her way to the gate, and looked out across the fields. She had, of course, known what to expect. She had even seen some TV news coverage. Nonetheless the spectacle before her came as a terrible shock. It was a long time since she'd gazed across the hills from this gateway, probably dating back to childhood days when she and her brother, and sometimes the Kivel boys, had ridden their ponies along the country lanes and across the fields that her father had owned.

At first, she thought she may have stopped in the wrong place. But she hadn't, of course. It was just that the tall chimneys and the towering Tudor façade of Blackdown Manor simply no longer existed. All she could see was a near flattened ruin, from this distance just a pile of rubble with only the occasional piece of wall still standing.

She gasped. To her annoyance she felt tears forming in her eyes. She wiped them briskly away. Bella Fairbrother had spent her entire adult life, and most of her childhood come to that, refusing to display any sign of weakness. After all, surely one of the latest crop of Fairbrother siblings had to have inherited at least a little of the grit and determination of their much-lauded ancestors, who had created and nurtured one of the greatest private banks in the world? It had never, from early childhood, looked as if that sibling might be Freddie; although Bella had loved her brother dearly back then, and for years just hadn't noticed. But one of the things that had made her eventually come close to despising him, was the weakness she had seen develop in him as he grew from a likeable happy-go-lucky child into a deeply disturbed and self-indulgent young man. A weakness, in her opinion both then and now, that had led to his problems with drugs and drink and taken him along a path ultimately making it impossible for him to remain the heir apparent to his father and a future chairman of Fairbrother International.

Yet Bella and her big brother had been close. They'd been great chums as children. And for a moment she could see a picture flashing before her of the young Bella and Freddie cantering across the fields which stretched in front of her, on their childhood ponies, she totally fearless and in the lead as usual, even though she was the youngest, Freddie bringing up the rear, quite content to hold back and merely follow. Her pony had been a feisty little grey and his a bigger, but gentler, roan. Both of them splendid equine specimens, of course. The Fairbrother children always had the best that money could buy. However during their teenage years they also had a mother who'd been more or less forced to live miles away from them, whom they saw only intermittently; a father who was absent from their lives more often than he was present; and a fiery stepmother who regarded both her stepchildren as an inconvenience and made no secret of it. Until, of course, Freddie had become a devastatingly handsome twenty-year-old. But she preferred not to think about that.

Bella didn't know exactly what had turned her brother into the man he was, barely like any Fairbrother she had known or heard of, nor herself into the woman she was, once described by the *Financial Times* as 'arguably the most ruthless and able woman the City has ever known'. And, like most high-achieving women, she somewhat resented such descriptions on the grounds that men in the same kind of roles were unlikely ever to be described in that way. Their ability would be taken for granted because of the positions they held; as would their capacity to operate with whatever ruthlessness might be required in order for them to fulfil their professional obligations. She did know that she had felt obliged to take on a role in life which, when she'd been that child galloping without a care in the world over her family's land, she could not have imagined becoming her destiny.

Throughout the history of their famous bank there had always been a male Fairbrother at the helm. Indeed, rather the way the British royal family had historically been obliged to always produce an heir and a spare in order to ensure the continuation of the line of succession, so Fairbrother men had always been obliged to continue their line in order to maintain control of the family bank. Only the Fairbrother traditions remained rather more archaic than that of the royals. England had a proud history of great queens, and, since changes to the law in 2013, even the order of succession to the throne was no longer gender dependent. The Fairbrothers, on the other hand, had never allowed a woman chairman, nor had Bella's father ever seemed able to grasp the concept of her becoming the first, regardless of her ultimately showing herself more than capable – in stark contrast to her low-achieving brother.

Bella sighed. After just a few seconds more, she shook herself out of her reverie, climbed back into her car, switched on the engine and proceeded on the last short leg of her journey to view close up the devastation of her family home. It had to be done. Bella Fairbrother considered it her responsibility to evaluate the damage, then take whatever action might be required. And Bella never shirked responsibility.

However, it was starkly apparent that virtually nothing could possibly remain of the treasures she had taken for granted as a child. The Chippendale furniture, the collection of nineteenth-century watercolours, the family portraits and, of course, above all, the Gainsborough. Tough and disciplined as she undoubtedly was, Bella found herself that morning almost overwhelmed by an immense sense of loss. The home she had known as a child, and the father she had known and loved throughout her growing up there, could never be retrieved.

A huge part of her life was over. All she could do was move on to the next stage. And she knew what her mission was now. She had no doubt at all. She must save the bank. At all costs. The bank could not, and would not, be lost. The financial stability of Fairbrother International must be restored. Nothing else really mattered.

Meanwhile, as Bella had assured Vogel, Freddie Fairbrother was on his way to the UK. He had booked himself onto a British Airways flight to London Heathrow, straight after presenting himself at an Australian police station.

Freddie settled into his first-class pod and accepted the glass of champagne and dish of nibbles offered promptly by attentive cabin crew. He was determined to enjoy the journey, whatever difficulties he might have to face upon arrival.

Freddie still had a considerable cash flow problem. His allowance from the family business certainly wouldn't stretch to first-class air travel. But that was all going to change soon. He'd raked up every dollar he had to make this trip, and paid for the first-class fair on a credit card taken right up to the limit. But he wasn't worried about any of that. Why should he be?

He had begun to feel a certain resentment that he couldn't afford to travel whenever, and in whatever style, he desired, drive a better motor car, and maybe, just maybe, live in a house that wasn't made of wood. Now all that was going to change.

Those feelings had developed within him gradually. Had that fateful telephone call making a series of quite extraordinary suggestions come to him ten, or maybe even six or seven years ago, instead of six months, Freddie would just have laughed. He genuinely wouldn't have considered it to be anything other than a joke. It was, in fact, only relatively recently that Freddie had started giving anything at all much attention. Of course, through almost all of his late teens and his twenties, and into his thirties, he had existed in a foggy cloud comprised more or less equally of marijuana smoke and alcohol fumes.

It was only as he entered his forties that Freddie had, albeit only occasionally, started to ponder not only his future but also the futility of his present.

Clearly there could be no going back, and Freddie hadn't been able to see any way of moving forward which might offer the kind of change he wanted. If he wanted it. Indeed, he'd had no idea really what he wanted. That had always been Freddie's biggest problem. So, he'd stayed just how he was. An ageing beach bum idling and drinking his days away. He'd rarely been actively unhappy. But he had come to wonder, just occasionally, what might have been.

Then the call had come, bringing with it his destiny. Or that's how Freddie saw it. A whole new future lay before him. He'd seen at once what it could be, and for perhaps the first time in his life found that he knew what he wanted. He'd been given a quite unexpected, and rather extraordinary, second chance to regain the life he had been born for. All he had to do was reach out and grab it. And that was exactly what Freddie had done. He was going to be a Fairbrother again.

The aircraft took off and a male flight attendant, almost certainly gay, refilled his glass and treated him to a beaming smile. Freddie smiled back, his charming smile, the lazy one which started merely as a twitch of the lips and grew wider, narrowing the dimples at either side of his mouth until they were just creases.

Freddie had once woken from a drink and drug-induced stupor to find himself in bed with two men. It had always annoyed him that he could remember virtually nothing of what had actually happened. He wasn't gay, of course. A little bit, maybe, because there had been one or two other men. Maybe more. Freddie supposed it would seem stupid to most people if he told them that by the time it got to going to bed time, he had sometimes barely known the difference. In any case, there had been many occasions when he had chosen a chunk of good Colombian black and a decent bottle of brandy over either sex.

But those days were well behind him now. Freddie had changed, just as, ironically under the circumstances, his father had told him he would.

'It happens to us all,' Sir John had said, despairingly sending him off on his travels. 'You'll want what everyone else has, eventually. Maybe even a wife and family.'

Freddie had laughed in his face. Particularly in view of the conduct of Sir John's own dissolute second wife. He had despised his father in those days. Many young men and women, in their teens and maybe early twenties, turn against the values of their parents. For Freddie, it had been far more than that. Sir John Fairbrother ran one of the world's most important private banks. As had his father, grandfather and great-grandfather before him. The young Freddie had loathed everything Sir John stood for, and everything Fairbrother's represented. The gulf between father and son was about as great as it could be. Freddie was embarrassed by Sir John. Sir John was embarrassed by Freddie. And appalled by his wanton behaviour.

Freddie could hardly remember, now, whether he walked out on his father to live his hippy lifestyle, or whether his father insisted that he go. In any case the past didn't matter anymore. Only the future.

He ate a delicious steak washed down with a fine claret, and contemplated, as airline travellers unused to regular first-class travel are inclined to, on the extraordinary difference between first and pig class. There couldn't be many greater contrasts in life, Freddie thought. Heaven and hell were contained within one improbable piece of human engineering hurtling through the skies at 600 miles an hour.

After a couple of decent brandies, enjoyed whilst he watched a movie, he stretched out on his comfortable flat bed and slept through the rest of the first leg of his journey, all the way to Singapore.

After another meal, more champagne and more brandy, he slept through most of the next leg too, and arrived at Heathrow feeling remarkably fresh.

It was almost two decades since he had stepped foot on British soil. More than nineteen years since his father had effectively disowned him and denied him his inheritance, telling him he'd allocate him an adequate and permanent living allowance, but would be cutting him out of his will.

However, Freddie remained his father's eldest child and his only son. He thought he might even consider marrying himself, and producing a son. It would, after all, be expected of him now.

He walked tall through Heathrow airport. He was unshaven, and his hair was uncombed. His eyes looked a tad bleary, the only-to-be expected result of a heavy alcohol-induced sleep combined with the inevitable jet lag of trans-continental travel. He was dressed in his customary faded blue jeans, a well-worn bomber jacket over an unironed shirt.

None the less, he was a Fairbrother. The oldest surviving male of the line. And he was back to claim his inheritance.

TWELVE

B ella drove slowly along the driveway towards the ruins of the big old house, trying to put her memories back in their box. Bella Fairbrother was not one to dwell upon the past, or indeed upon anything she could do nothing about. Today was somehow different. She hadn't expected to feel the way she did.

A uniformed constable on scene-guard stopped her from driving right up to the house, instructing her to park at the road end of the drive along with several other vehicles. Blackdown Manor was a crime scene, and it looked as if it might remain so for some time, Bella thought.

She was told she could walk a little closer towards the burned-down remains of her childhood home, but must not cross the cordon of blue and white tape stretching around the remains of the house. Just as she was approaching, two fire officers emerged from the ruins of Blackdown Manor carrying between them on a stretcher what appeared to be a body bag containing human remains. They were followed by another two officers also carrying a stretcher and a body bag.

There was something quite chilling about witnessing this scene, about seeing dead people being carried about in, what were more or less, sacks. Particularly in view of the identity of those people. DI Vogel had told Bella that it was more or less certain that the two victims of the fire could only be Sir John Fairbrother and his nurse, but that it was possible they may never be formally identified.

The body bags did not look very substantially filled either. Bella remembered from the shocking reports of the Grenfell Tower disaster that in the event of a truly major fire sometimes virtually no remains at all are found of the deceased.

None of this did anything to lessen the shock of what she found herself witnessing.

Bella was tough as old boots. All the same, she felt her knees wobble. She was standing next to a Crime Scenes Investigators' van. She leaned against it for support, and fleetingly closed her eyes to shut out the spectacle unfolding before her. Therefore, she heard the voice before seeing the woman walking towards her.

'Are you OK?'

Bella opened her eyes. A tall woman, probably in her late fifties, wearing the obligatory white plastic Tyvek suit in order to protect the integrity of the crime scene, was regarding her with some anxiety.

'Uh yes,' Bella answered automatically.

Her eyes travelled to the far side of the gravelled area where it seemed the two bodies were now about to be loaded into an unmarked transit van by two men also wearing Tyvek suits.

'Wasn't expecting to see any of this, I suppose,' said Bella. 'Given me a bit of a turn.' She moved away from the CSI vehicle and drew herself up to her full five feet, five-and-a-half inches, 'I'm fine now,' she said.

The other woman pulled back the hood of her suit, revealing an abundance of curly reddish hair not unattractively streaked with grey.

'May I ask who you are, and what you are doing here?' she said, her courteous and concerned approach belying the directness of her words.

Bella introduced herself. 'I just wanted to see the place for myself,' she explained. 'I grew up here, you see. And the whole thing has been, well . . . It's too terrible to take in. I guess we all have to get used to death, particularly as we get older, but this . . .'

Bella waved an arm at the burned-out house, taking in the anonymous van with its tinted windows into which the two victims were now being unceremoniously loaded.

'It's all so violent, so horrible.' She lowered her voice to a slightly distracted whisper. 'I never expected this,' she said again.

'Who would?' responded the woman gently. 'It's a terrible way to die, and almost as terrible for those left behind. I'm Karen Crow. Home Office Pathologist. I'm sorry about what you've witnessed, Miss Fairbrother.'

Bella was still staring at the transit van. The men who had loaded the remains of the two dead were now shutting and locking the rear doors.

'It looks, so, so anonymous,' murmured Bella. 'So undignified.'

'I do understand how you feel,' said Karen Crow. 'In cases of death by fire in particular it is very difficult to maintain dignity, at this stage anyway. Those men are employed by the coroner's office to collect dead bodies in situations like this, and anywhere foul play might be suspected. They will be taken to the nearest police mortuary where I and my colleagues will conduct as much of a post-mortem as possible, which in cases of a fire is often not terribly constructive. And I promise you, Miss Fairbrother, we will show your father and the other deceased person as much respect throughout as we possibly can.'

Bella turned her head slightly to look directly at Karen Crow for the first time. The pathologist had very clear, pale-blue eyes. Bella doubted neither her honesty nor her compassion.

'Thank you,' she said.

The van containing the remains of the dead was about to pass the spot where the two women were standing. Bella watched its back end proceeding up the drive to the road beyond.

'I don't know what I expected, but I didn't think it would be like this, or that I would feel how I do,' she said. 'I really didn't.'

'I can understand that,' replied the pathologist. 'Nobody ever does. It's my job to deal with death, particularly violent death. I've been doing this job for a lot of years, and you can imagine what I have seen, so much that I wish I hadn't seen. I still don't think there's anything worse than fire. I am so sorry for your loss.'

'Thank you,' said Bella again.

She was surprised at how much she appreciated, not just the human contact, but also the comfort the other woman was clearly trying to offer.

She made a conscious effort again to pull herself together, and reminded herself that the purpose of her visit was not just what she had told Karen Crow. She had reasons beyond merely surveying the scene of the crime and indulging in nostalgic reflection concerning her family and the splendid house which had been the family home for centuries. Until two nights previously.

'There are some papers, private papers, important for the business, I was wondering when I might be allowed access,' she said. 'Can you help?'

Karen Crow looked mildly surprised. 'I'm not sure I am the right person to ask,' she said.

Bella realised that her switch from stunned grief to business-like practical must have seemed excessively quick.

'I just thought, well, whilst I was here . . .' she began, in a lame attempt at explanation.

'But, in there?' Dr Crow queried, turning to look again at the crumbling ruins which were all that remained of Blackdown Manor. 'Papers? I'm no expert on that sort of thing, but I don't see how anything like that could have survived the fire which consumed this place.'

'Blackdown has, or rather it had, a huge cellar,' Bella began to explain. 'My father, many years ago, further excavated it and installed an underground indoor swimming pool complex. He turned the other part of the cellar into a specialised storage room. Blackdown held many irreplaceable treasures, and whilst I am sure almost all will have been tragically lost, there is just a chance there could be some pieces, perhaps paintings, in that storeroom which may be retrievable. Also, the papers I mentioned. You know about the family bank, I'm sure, Miss Crow. Well, can you imagine the records that have been accumulated over the years? Much has no bearing at all on the modern Fairbrother's, but it almost all has tremendous historical value, and then there are the papers which we do really need. I am trying to help the board continue to run the bank in the manner that my father would have done were he still alive.'

'And you really think this storage room could have survived?'

'I'm hoping so,' replied Bella Fairbrother. 'It was lead lined, and all the storage containers were made of protective materials. The idea was that the room and its precious contents would be protected against any eventuality, including, and perhaps particularly fire. My father also said that it would survive a nuclear attack.'

Bella laughed briefly, an almost involuntary half-strangled little sound. She had no idea why. There wasn't anything very funny about the prospect of a nuclear attack, nor the grim reality of the terrible scene which lay before her.

'Well, you'll need to speak to CSI and the fire investigators about that,' said Karen Crow. 'But whatever they tell you and whatever the condition of the papers in that storeroom, you can only be given permission for access by the police investigation team. The place is a crime scene and I personally have no idea how long it is likely to remain so . . .' She stopped abruptly. 'There's John Michaels, he's the head honcho fire investigator.'

Karen waved to attract the man's attention, then made a beckoning motion with her fingers. Obediently Michaels approached. The pathologist made the necessary introductions, and Bella explained about the storeroom and her desire to gain access to its contents.

'Ah yes, I think we've found the storeroom, or what's left of it,' he said. 'But in spite of its construction there is substantial damage. After all, the entire underground area, the pool complex and the storeroom had thousands of tons of burning rubble collapse onto it and then the fire boys blasted it with thousands of gallons of water. The pool area is completely destroyed, the roof caved in, you wouldn't even know there'd ever been a pool there if you hadn't been told. As for the storeroom, I assume you know it was lead lined and bolstered by heavy duty steel beams . . .?'

Bells nodded quickly in agreement.

'Well, because of its construction it has not been completely destroyed,' Michaels continued. 'But the roof has partially caved in, pretty inevitable under these circumstances, and there must be considerable water damage inside, so if it's paperwork you're looking for, well, I wouldn't be too optimistic—'

'My father said his storeroom would withstand a nuclear attack,' interrupted Bella, repeating what she had just told Karen Crow. 'All my father's papers, both personal, and the bank records which I am particularly interested in, were stored within that room. He had moved almost everything here, where he was convinced it would be safe in almost any eventuality.'

'Well, we shall have to see,' said John Michaels.

'But it looks like he got it wrong,' Bella continued in little more than a mutter.

John Michaels raised his eyebrows.

'Look,' he said. 'Now I know of the importance of that area I'll see if we can't achieve access as soon as possible. But I am a little puzzled, Miss Fairbrother. I mean, I would have expected in the modern world that certainly the business records you have referred to would be stored on computer, and backed up in the usual way. Is that not the case?'

Bella shook her head.

'My father was an old-fashioned man, Mr Michaels,' she replied, by way of explanation. It sounded pretty lame, even to her own ears. 'He always did things his way, and he didn't entirely trust computers.'

Nor anyone he worked with, including his daughter and his entire board of directors, she thought to herself. She said no more.

John Michaels still looked puzzled. As well, he might, Bella reckoned.

'I see,' he said eventually. 'Of course, you certainly wouldn't be allowed on the premises at the moment. There's a major safety risk, obviously. Even if we find that any of the contents of the basement storage room have remained substantially intact, there is no possibility of you being allowed to enter it until its construction has been fully assessed. With fire parts of a damaged premises may appear to have remained undamaged, but the reality is they could collapse at any moment. Also, you do know, don't you, we still have a crime scene here, and may well do for two or three more days, I'd say.'

'So I understand,' said Bella, glancing at Karen Crow. 'And even after you guys may have declared the area safe, it's the police who have to give permission for me or anyone else to go inside. Is that right?'

'It is,' said John Michaels.

'Or to have anything that remains inside removed, I assume?' queried Bella.

'Indeed,' said Michaels.

'So, who specifically do I need to contact?' asked Bella.

'DI David Vogel,' replied the chief fire investigatory officer. 'He's in charge.'

'Ah,' said Bella Fairbrother.

It seemed that she was going to need Vogel on her side before she could do anything. She was not overly optimistic, but she reckoned she may as well contact the DI again as soon as possible.

At that moment her phone rang.

*   *   *

'Miss Fairbrother, I think I'm going to need another word with you,' said Vogel.

'Yes, of course, Mr Vogel,' replied Bella. 'I was just thinking the same about you.'

Were you indeed, thought Vogel, reflecting again that this young woman was going to be a force to be reckoned with.

'Might I ask where you are at the moment, Miss Fairbrother?' asked Vogel.

'I'm just leaving Blackdown Manor. I came out to have a look for myself. It . . .' The young woman paused.

Vogel waited.

'It was more of a shock than I expected. I mean there is virtually nothing left . . . and they were bringing out bodies, well, remains . . .'

Vogel couldn't be sure, but he thought there was a catch in Bella Fairbrother's throat. That was a turn up for the books.

'It must be very upsetting for you, Miss Fairbrother, I'm sure,' he said levelly.

'It is yes, quite upsetting.'

Vogel thought Bella sounded rather taken aback by her own reaction. He pressed on.

'Miss Fairbrother, I wondered if I could ask you to come to the incident room we've set up at Wellington police station?' he asked. 'There is somewhere here we can talk privately. And we do need to take a statement from you.'

There was another brief pause.

'All right, Mr Vogel,' said Bella. 'I'll leave straight away.'

'Thank you very much,' said Vogel. 'That would be most helpful.'

He meant it too. Although the privacy he had promised Bella Fairbrother comprised only the rather austere station interview room.

Wellington police station, an unprepossessing concrete building dating back to the 1950s, was now the on-the-spot headquarters of the investigation, and thirty or so of the fifty officers promised by Hemmings, under the MCIT umbrella, were now working out of the station. They were never all there at the same time, of course, but there was still not a lot of room. And the station's regular staff, three uniformed constables and five police community service officers, were not impressed at being effectively squeezed

out of their usual work space. Half the time there wasn't room
for them to park their cars in the station's small car park, or even
in the road outside.

Photographs and charts continued to be collated and arranged
on every available wall, but the main work was undertaken by the
officers working on their own laptops, linked to the Police National
Computer. It was a full-time job for the officer in charge to keep
up with it all. And much as Vogel was a hands-on copper who
liked to get out and about far more than most of his rank, it was
indeed a great help that Bella Fairbrother was coming to him that
morning and he did not have to go to her.

He was studying the various reports and interviews recorded
by other members of the team when Karen Crow called.

'I know it's only a formality, but I thought you might like to
know that we have now officially identified Sir John Fairbrother
through his dental records,' the pathologist told him. 'We're just
waiting now for the nurse's dental records to come through from
the Philippines, and then, from our point of view, the case will
be closed. The condition of the bodies is such that there really is
nothing more we can do.'

Vogel thanked her and returned his attention to his laptop. It
was a shame, but everything Karen Crow had said was only what
he had already assumed. There was no way pathology could be
expected to offer any further help to the investigation from the
examination of the victims of such a catastrophic fire.

Bella Fairbrother was as good as her word. She pulled her little
Mercedes to a halt in the road outside less than forty minutes after
she and Vogel had spoken on the phone.

Vogel happened to glance out of a convenient window just as
she arrived. He watched her climb out of the car and walk briskly
towards the station door. She still had the confident swagger about
her which he'd noticed when he first met her at the Mount Somerset.
In Vogel's experience that was almost inevitable in those who
enjoyed both considerable wealth and extensive power.

The front office was not manned that day. Vogel walked swiftly
through and opened the station door for her. She looked mildly
surprised. Vogel liked surprising people.

He ushered her straight into the interview room, gesturing for her to sit down to the side of the desk which was the main piece of furniture. There was recording equipment in the little room, but Vogel would not be using it as this wasn't a formal interview. Vogel sat down opposite her. They were quickly joined by Dawn Saslow, who took the third chair.

Vogel politely thanked Bella for coming.

'I really need to go over a few things with you, and then Dawn will take that statement,' he began.

Bella nodded her assent.

'There have been some developments which you may or may not know about,' Vogel continued. 'Are you aware that George Grey, your father's employee who was injured on the night of the fire, has walked out of the Musgrove hospital where he was being treated and that we have so far been unable to locate him?'

'Yes, I do know about that,' assented Bella. 'I saw it on the regional news last night. He was described as someone the police believe could help them with their enquiries. I took it to mean you thought he might have started the fire, or at least been involved in some way. Is that so, DI Vogel?'

'It is far too early to make any such assumption, Miss Fair-brother,' replied Vogel. 'We are still investigating and accumulating evidence. But we certainly regard George Grey as a person of interest, and we need to find him and talk to him as a matter of some urgency. I wondered what you could tell me about Mr Grey and his wife?'

'Me?' queried Bella, sounding surprised. 'Why would I know anything about them? I've never even met the Greys.'

'Never?' queried Vogel.

'Never. I told you, DI Vogel, I've been estranged from my father for over a year. And whilst I have encountered him once or twice in the City, which would be almost inevitable, I haven't been back to Blackdown during that time. I doubt he'd have let me through the door if I had turned up here. And, actually, it was some months before that when I was last here. The Kivels were still employed then, still living in The Gatehouse. Everything seemed normal and appeared to be how it had always been. I had no idea that my father was planning to get rid of them after all those years and move in the Greys. If indeed he was planning it. It could have been some spur of the moment thing. It was just like my father to make some sort of snap decision for reasons which he would probably not disclose to anyone. He wasn't a man who thought he had to give reasons for anything he did. He always did exactly what he wanted, and hang the rest of the world.'

Vogel found himself blinking away behind his spectacles. Bella Fairbrother's apparent display of emotion over the phone earlier had clearly been temporary. Her attitude to her father had definitely not softened.

'So, you had no idea why he sacked the Kivels?' he continued doggedly.

'No idea at all.'

'People locally seem to think the sacking was in some way connected with his illness,' said Vogel. 'Do you think that might be the case?'

'Like I told you, I really wouldn't know. You may find this hard to believe, but I didn't even know he was ill until after the board had been told. They naturally assumed I knew, of course. My father eventually got his solicitor to tell me. His solicitor! Even harder to believe, don't you think?'

'Did you not then try to get in touch with him directly?'

'Yes. I phoned several times. Each time I got his message service, and he never called back.'

'Did you ever consider just coming to see him?'

'Mr Vogel, I didn't even know for sure where my father was. And in any case, he had made it quite clear he wanted nothing more to do with me. I wasn't going to beg.'

Vogel certainly believed that last remark. He could not imagine Bella Fairbrother begging anyone for anything.

'Were you told what your father was suffering from, and just how ill he was?' Vogel asked.

'Oh yes,' replied Bella. 'I was also told that my father was hoping to live for at least a year or two more, and that the drugs he was taking were making it possible for him to continue to function in business. But that he wanted me to know that he had made every provision for the continuation of the bank, and a private provision for me from his personal fortune.'

'What did you make of that?'

'What I made of that, Mr Vogel, was that my father had decided to cut me out of the bank and do his best to make sure I had nothing more to do with it. A private provision from his personal fortune, indeed. I have never wanted his damned money, detective inspector. Nor have I ever needed it. I have demonstrated again and again that I can succeed at the highest level in the world of commerce, without him or anyone else propping me up.'

Vogel stared at her in silence for a few seconds. This was a formidable woman, all right. Even when she was sitting down Bella Fairbrother sat up so straight that she looked tall. Everyone understood about walking tall. Bella Fairbrother, although of average height, sat tall. And she had a way of making everyone around her feel rather on the small side. Even Vogel, who was comfortably over six foot.

'I take it from this that your father made a new will, perhaps quite recently, is that so?'

Bella Fairbrother shrugged her shoulders. 'I don't know,' she said. 'But it wouldn't have occurred to me that he hadn't left an up-to-date will clearly representing his wishes. My father would never have put himself in a position where he died intestate. Not with the bank at stake. Not to mention his personal wealth. My father lived and breathed money, DI Vogel. It was his every reason for being. And everything he did in his life was motivated either by financial gain or to protect the interests of Fairbrother's bank, which, when you think about it, amount to one and the same thing. Even to marrying, when he was a very young man, a woman who came from the right sort of breeding stock to produce the right sort of children to take control of the bank when the time came. Unfortunately for my father that didn't go quite according to plan. His second child was a girl, me, therefore, however clever and able I proved myself to be, I would never be good enough because I was the wrong gender. And he had yet to learn that his only son was a wastrel quite incapable of running any sort of business, when his eye was taken by a woman little better than a common whore, albeit doubtless excellent at her job, and he ditched my mother without a backward glance.'

Vogel was having a blinking fit again. He was never comfortable with overt talk of sexual matters, particularly when a woman was doing the talking. He glanced away, hoping Bella Fairbrother would not notice his discomfiture. He was almost sure she didn't. She was frowning slightly as she continued her reverie. Her body language indicated that she was wound up like a spring. Vogel had learned to be cautious to the point of cynicism concerning anyone involved, however remotely, in a murder investigation. But he would have bet six month's salary that this part, at least, of what Bella was saying was the truth. And that telling the story caused her genuine pain.

'My mother's father was a stockbroker and she had a degree in economics which she never used because my father would not countenance even the possibility of allowing his wife to work,' Bella continued. 'Her position on the board was merely token, as such appointments have always had been with all the Fairbrother women. Until me. I was never prepared to be merely the token Fairbrother woman on the board, and that is primarily what caused the rift between my father and me. That, and my tendency to question his leadership. Now I have reason to believe that the board might turn to me to take, at the very least, shall we say, a prominent position again at Fairbrothers. It's already been indicated that most of them feel they need me back on the board because I know more than anyone else about my father's affairs and his way of running things.'

Bella stopped talking at last. Vogel, thankfully had stopped blinking.

'So what made you drive straight down here, Miss Fairbrother? I mean, you knew that your father was dead and that there were probably going to be serious repercussions concerning the future of the bank, something that is clearly very dear to your heart. Also, presumably, with so much at stake, you need to see his will as soon as possible. Wouldn't it have been more constructive for you to stay on in London?'

'Look, Mr Vogel, I spoke yesterday to Peter Prentis, the solicitor who has handled my father's affairs for years and who informed me of my father's illness. He told me that he was no longer in possession of the will my father had drawn up with him about a year previously, soon after we became estranged. At around the same time my father arranged to have almost all of the business and personal files, until then mostly archived with Peter Prentis, removed and transported to Somerset.

'It also seems that my father then appointed a solicitor here in Somerset, in Taunton, with whom he conducted a lot of private business. Peter Prentis told me he'd had very little contact with my father in the year or so preceding his death, and that the last time had been the telephone conversation in which he had told Prentis of his illness, and asked him to pass on the information to me. Clearly, I needed to see this Taunton solicitor, Mr Vogel, as a matter of urgency, to find out what I can of my father's dealings with him. And I have an appointment this afternoon. Also, I have to find those files. Some may be lodged with this solicitor, of course, but I believe that the majority of my father's papers, including those removed from Peter Prentis' office, may be in a specially strengthened storeroom which my father constructed in the basement of Blackdown Manor. I am also hoping, although it may be just a vain hope, that some of the valuable family paintings, and perhaps some other pieces, may be there and have survived the fire. And that's why I wanted to see you every bit as much as you wanted to see me, Mr Vogel. I really need to be allowed access to the manor very soon, to gain entry to what's left of the storeroom, see the damage for myself, and evaluate what may be salvaged. I understand only you can give permission?'

'Me and the fire service,' said Vogel. 'We will do our best to assist, but safety is the first priority, and preserving the authenticity of the crime scene a close second.'

'I see.'

Bella Fairbrother looked as if she were about to argue, but didn't. This is a woman used to getting her own way, thought Vogel

'Is it really that urgent, Miss Fairbrother?' asked Vogel.

'Almost certainly, detective inspector,' responded Bella Fairbrother. 'Almost certainly.'

Vogel left Saslow to take the necessary formal statement from Bella. But when he heard her leaving the police station he made his way to an appropriately positioned window to watch. She had managed to find a parking space almost directly outside, and she drove away with a squeal of wheels, accelerating quickly along Victoria Street. She was clearly one of those who did not really consider that speed limits applied to her. Even right outside a police station. And probably not many other limits, either.

Vogel was thoughtful. He took what he considered to be a

healthily cynical attitude to anything involving big business and big money. Miss Bella Fairbrother did not seem unduly concerned about preserving her father's reputation. But he suspected that her mission to save Fairbrother International might also involve a considerable intent to save her own skin. After all, she had been deputy chairman of Fairbrother's until little more than a year ago. Sir John Fairbrother may have been a maverick, but Bella herself had admitted that she'd worked more closely with him than anyone else.

Vogel suspected that Sir John's death, and the fire which had brought it about, along with the destruction of Blackdown Manor, were all attributable to an intrigue reaching deep into the darker extremes of international finance. And it was surely impossible to believe that his daughter had not been complicit to some degree.

THIRTEEN

Police Sergeant Leon Knott was one of the safer neighbourhood team covering Brentford. When the call came in he was on patrol with PC Neil Faraday.

A body had been discovered in the lock at the Thames end of the Grand Union Canal.

Knott and Faraday were in their squad car heading back to Chiswick police station along the Great West Road. Faraday was driving. He turned the squad car around at the first opportunity and headed back into Brentford.

The town sits alongside the River Thames, opposite Kew Gardens, where the Grand Union and the River Brent merge and flow into London's principal waterway. Brentford Dock, now the site of a 1970s housing development, once provided a gateway to the rest of England for international trading vessels which chugged up the Thames and transferred their goods onto canal barges there. The dock, eighteen miles from the coast, was Britain's furthest inland shipping port, and its location had been chosen because of the huge 28 feet rise and fall of the Thames just outside. Once the canal barges had been loaded, they would enter the Grand Union, the backbone of Britain's canal system, via the lower part of the River Brent, and a large tidal lock known as Thames Lock.

This lock could be crossed by a road bridge, and a footbridge, leading to another more precarious footbridge, then Catherine Wheel Road and the Brewery Tap pub. Thames Lock itself, still in effect the gateway to the British canal system, actually comprised of a pair of locks separated by a narrow strip of land upon which sat the lock-keeper's hut.

And it was in the lock nearest to the Brewery Tap side of the canal that the body had been discovered by part-time volunteer lock-keeper Bill Cox.

Knott and Faraday parked in Catherine Wheel Road and walked over the footbridge to where they could see Cox, wearing his distinctive yellow high-vis jacket, standing at the lock-side amongst a small group of people. A narrow boat was moored just outside the lower gates which stood half open.

Brentford still retained a lot of the characteristics of a small town, in spite of having been swallowed up in recent years by extensive redevelopment causing it to be labelled West London's latest property hotspot, and Leon Knott was a local man, who himself owned a pleasure boat which he kept in Brentford Dock marina, as did Bill Cox. So Leon knew Bill, and was fully aware of the operating procedure of Thames Lock. Being tidal, access was restricted to just under two hours either side of high tide, and no vessel could pass through without the presence of a lock-keeper, which in October, and throughout the winter and early spring, was by appointment only.

Bill Cox hurried towards the two police officers.

'We got a body in the lock,' he said unnecessarily, and continued with a kind of nervous verbal diarrhoea. 'Am I glad to see you two. I got hold of it with me boat hook. And a nasty turn it gave me too, I can tell you. Almost an occasion to have a vessel come through nowadays, at this time of year. They either stay up in the canals or stay out in the Thames, the pleasure boaters anyway, get the odd work boat, of course, we still have the one working yard, but I'll tell you one thing, Leon, you know me and canals and boats, what I wouldn't have given to have been here in Brentford in the days when the big ships was unloading their cargoes into the barges, the traffic, can you imagine what it must have been like—'

'Bill,' interrupted Leon Knott loudly.

'Oh, I'm sorry,' said Bill Cox at once.

Leon noticed that the lock-keeper's voice was high-pitched and shaky. 'I've had a bit of a shock. You know what, all my years on the river, and doing this job, never come across a body before . . .'

He stopped himself this time. 'Sorry,' he said again.

'That's fine, Bill,' said Sergeant Knott. 'Perfectly understandable.'

'It's upset me a bit, to tell the truth,' continued Bill. 'I mean, it's just an ordinary day and you just don't expect, I mean do you . . .?'

'No, of course not,' said Leon Knott. Then he continued in an encouraging fashion, 'Just tell me exactly what happened, Bill. How did you find the body?'

'Well, like I said, we had this narrow boat come through, heading out onto the river. The *Hilda May*. Going upstream to Maidenhead. The tide was right, gotta catch the tide right with a narrow boat, as you know, Leon, they've not the power or the steerage to cope with the Thames, unless you've got the tide behind you . . .'

'I know, Bill,' interrupted Leon Knott, a note of warning in his voice again.

'Oh yes. Well, she came into the lock all right. No trouble at all. Then when I tried to open the lower gates to let her out the other side, I had the devil of a job, I can tell you. There was obviously something stuck. I got my long boat hook and poked about a bit, and eventually the gate opened enough to let her through. Of course, this lock was built to accommodate vessels wider than a narrow boat, if it had been a standard canal lock she'd have been stuck there, for certain.'

Bill paused, as if realising he was digressing again. 'Well, as soon as she was through I got the boat hook again and it snagged onto something pretty quickly, so I just pulled. And up it floated. I let go, straight away, and down it went again. I shouted out, couldn't help myself, so the skipper of the *Hilda May* moored up and came back to see if I needed help. But I just dialled 999. Didn't want to mess with it without the police here. There's not much more I can tell you, Leon.'

'All right, Bill, so you didn't see this body very clearly then?'

'No, not really. I was that shocked, you see,' he added again.

Leon had one last question.

'You're sure it was a dead body, aren't you, Bill?' he asked. 'I mean, it could have been a bundle of rubbish or old clothes, or even a guy or something. We're coming up to Guy Fawkes night, after all, aren't we?'

'It's a body, Leon,' said Bill, a trifle indignantly. 'A man, and he didn't look as if he'd been in the water for long. Couldn't have been that long, anyway, or we'd have found 'im floating on the surface. As it was, he sank right down again when I let go of . . .'

'Now, you didn't touch anything, did you, Bill?' interrupted Knott.

'Touch anything? The poor bastard sunk down to the bottom again. What do you think I did? Jump in along with him?'

'OK, Bill, take it easy,' responded Leon Knott. 'Let's have a closer look, shall we?'

He approached the lock side, at the same time asking the small group of people standing around to vacate the immediate area.

Knott and Faraday both lent over the lock and peered into the murky water. Knott knew that the lock was about twelve feet deep, and the water level was probably halfway up the sides. He couldn't see anything below the surface.

'Right then,' he said. 'Let's get your body out of there, shall we, Bill? How many boat hooks have you got?'

Bill produced three long boat hooks and agreed to help the two policemen locate and remove the body from the lock. Bill was well built and fit for a man in his early sixties, but Neil Faraday was a rugby-playing thirty-something, an exceptionally big strong lad, and he took the brunt of the dead weight when it came to hauling the body out, and laying it, face up, on the ground.

Sergeant Knott looked down at the dead man with some reluctance. In spite of Bill's almost certainly correct assertion that he had not been in the water for long, one of his open eyes appeared to have been eaten by something already. It was not a pretty sight.

Knott also immediately noticed the state of the man's upper left leg, which appeared to have suffered several wounds that had clearly been stitched up by medical professionals. His trousers, blue jeans, had fallen down, revealing the extent of his injuries, and were rolled around his lower legs, something which could presumably have been caused either when he entered the water or during the operation to recover his body. In spite of the time of year the man was not wearing a jacket, although this also could have been removed in a similar fashion.

There appeared to be bloodstains on his shirt, around the area of his right shoulder and on his jeans, another indication that he could not have been in the water very long. In cool British waters a dead body might remain below the surface for a week or even two, Sergeant Knott reckoned, but, as Bill had so long-windedly pointed out, vessels did pass through Thames Lock at all times of year, albeit not as frequently as they once did. It was possible that the body may have lain at the very bottom of the lock for a couple of days, perhaps, without discovery, but certainly unlikely that it had been there much longer than that.

Bill Cox, in spite of looking slightly nauseous, was also studying the corpse.

'Poor bastard fell in, I suppose,' he commented. 'How we don't get more accidents with folk winding their way back into the Dock estate from the Brewery Tap, is beyond me. I've never known a fatality before, though. Not in my time. Never.'

Leon Knott was only vaguely listening. He suspected Bill Cox might well be right in his assumption. Between eighty and 100 people were found dead in the River Thames every year, mostly suicides, and almost all of the rest accidents. Cases of murder or manslaughter were rare, extremely rare. And it was, of course, unlikely that anyone would attempt to commit suicide by jumping into a lock. Not unknown. But unlikely. Most river suicides took the form of the poor unfortunates throwing themselves off one of the 214 bridges which cross periodically along the length of the Thames.

Leon leaned over and checked the dead man's trouser pockets looking for any signs of identification. He was already wearing the gloves, which, like all modern police officers, he always carried. He knew better than to touch the corpse with his bare hands even though the chances of much forensic evidence remaining on a body pulled from the murky depths of Thames Lock were pretty slim.

There was nothing.

Neil Faraday was still poking about in the lock with his boat hook.

'I've got something,' he called out, and brought his hook up with a beige coloured jacket on the end of it, which he let fall to the ground.

Eagerly Leon stepped forwards and with his gloved hands went through the pockets. Still no wallet, or anything else for that matter. Every pocket was completely empty.

Leon stared at the man's face, then let his gaze wander again over the bloodstains on his shirt and the wounds to his legs that had so clearly been stitched up by a professional.

Leon was a methodical policeman, a stickler for detail. He always liked to begin a spell on duty, if he could, particularly if he was going out on patrol, by quickly checking the latest notifications on the PNC, the police national computer. And every police station in the country received missing person alerts, which would be flagged as being of special interest if the subject of that alert was suspected of involvement in a crime, and even more especially if that crime was murder.

'That's it!' Leon Knott shouted, causing Bill Cox, who still looked as if he might be sick at any moment, to jump half out of his skin.

'That's it,' the sergeant repeated. 'I think I know who this is.'

He stared at the face again. He couldn't say for sure that he recognised the dead man from the picture he'd been looking at the previous day, but people always looked different when they were dead in Leon Knott's opinion. And Sergeant Knott had witnessed more than his fair share of death. Before joining the force he'd been a squaddie, and he'd seen a fair bit of action too. More than he'd ever wished for.

'I can't say for certain,' he said. 'But I think this is a runaway the Avon and Somerset are looking for. They want him in connection with suspected arson. And not just arson. Two people died in a fire in a country house down west somewhere, and I reckon this is their suspect. Can't quite remember his name. Greg, Gary . . . no, I think it was George something or other.'

Leon stood up. Even Bill Cox was looking a tad interested, and not just plain sick any more.

'I think we may have found ourselves a murderer, boys,' said the sergeant.

He immediately made a call back to his Chiswick base, and was patched through to the HQ of the Met's Major Incident Team.

The young DC he spoke to quickly recognised the possible importance of Leon Knott's report. If the dead man found in the canal really was the character wanted by the Avon and Somerset on suspicion of involvement in double murder, then his death took on immediate significance, and would more or less automatically be regarded as suspicious.

'Hang on,' said the DC. 'I'll put you through to the boss.'

Detective Superintendent Nobby Clarke was just leaving her office when her desk phone rang. She had a meeting with the deputy chief constable that she really shouldn't miss. But she never could walk away from a ringing phone.

She returned to her desk and answered the call. She listened intently to all that Leon could tell her. And whilst doing so she logged into her computer and launched a search for the missing persons order put out by the Avon and Somerset.

'George Grey,' she said, as soon as there was an appropriate pause in Leon's narrative. 'Suffered stab wounds at the time of the fire which destroyed Blackdown Manor, home of Sir John Fairbrother who was killed in the fire along with his nurse. Suspected of possible involvement in the fire which is believed to be arson. But walked out of Taunton's Musgrove hospital whilst police were still investigating him. Is that your man, Sergeant Knott?'

'I think so, ma'am,' replied Knott. 'I can't be sure, of course. And he was carrying no identification, or none that we've found so far anyway. But he has recently stitched wounds to his leg and one shoulder, which I thought was a bit of a clincher. And he looks pretty much like the photo I saw in Chiswick nick – as far as I remember anyway.'

'OK, I'll send the pic to you straight away, so you can have another look,' said Clarke. 'Right. I've texted it. What do you think?'

'Give me a second, ma'am,' said Knott, holding the phone away from his mouth and manoeuvring his screen into text mode.

He studied the photo for a few seconds, looked again at the body lying on the canal bank before him, and back at the picture on the screen one more time.

'It's him, boss, I'm almost certain of it.'

'Right. Any immediate indication of what may have happened?'

'Nothing obvious, boss.'

'So, he could have just fallen in,' continued Clarke.

'Maybe, but why here? Why was he in Brentford? He must have had a reason for coming here, walking out of a hospital like that. If it's just an accident, well boss, there aren't half a lot of questions need answering . . .'

'You are absolutely right, sergeant,' responded the super. 'Have you contacted CSI and pathology yet?'

'Yes, of course, boss. Did that first, just in case.'

He paused looking up across the canal to Dock Road. A car had just been parked as close as possible to the lock. He could see Patricia Fitzwarren, the regional Home Office pathologist, stepping out of it. And, just beyond, a Crime Scene Investigators' van was approaching from off the high street.

'Actually, Dr Fitzwarren has just arrived, and so have CSI,' he continued.

'OK, they'll make sure the scene is secure, and that's the main thing right now,' said Nobby Clarke. 'I'll get a team together, and we'll be with you as soon as we can.' She paused. 'Oh, and good work Sergeant Knott,' she added, as she ended the call.

Dr Fitzwarren was still at work when Nobby Clarke arrived at Thames Lock with DC Lloyd Springer. According to protocol, as a superintendent with overall responsibility for a number of MIT teams, Clarke was far too senior to take part in a first-response call like this. However, Nobby didn't really do protocol, as everyone who worked for her, or with her, knew only too well.

The CSI boys had already cordoned off the area around Thames Lock, and blocked off Dock Road – which in any case had a semi-permanent barrier across it, providing only alternative access to Brentford Dock if the main access road, Augustus Close, were for any reason impassable. DC Springer parked as close as he could to the scene of the crime, and the two officers approached the nearest CSI vehicle in order to equip themselves with Tyvek suits and protective shoes.

Det. Supt Clarke knew the place a little. She had a friend who lived in the Dock whom she occasionally visited. Thames Wharf – the basin behind it where a number of river and canal boats had residential mooring, the remains of what had once been a major London boatyard – and Johnson Island, home to a community of artists, were all linked by a little network of paths and bridges. The existence of all of this was effectively screened from the nearest through road, Brentford High Street, and anyone shopping on the high street or visiting a pub or restaurant – other than perhaps the Brewery Tap, which in any case was very much a local – would be totally unaware of the existence of what was, surely, in the modern world, a most improbable convergence of people and place. If this were indeed a murder, considered Nobby Clarke, then it seemed likely that the perpetrator was someone with local knowledge.

The CSI team, assisted by local police, were scouring the area for any further evidence. A sergeant, probably the officer she had spoken to earlier, Clarke thought, was standing just outside the cordon, still in his unprotected blue uniform.

Dr Fitzwarren, also clad in the compulsory Tyvek suit, was crouched alongside the body. She looked up as Nobby Clarke and DC Springer approached.

Patricia Fitzwarren was relatively young for her job, in her mid-thirties. She was an attractive young woman, but, certainly when she was at work, her somewhat elfin features clearly bore the mark of what she had already seen in her life. She was also pretty acerbic when dealing with police officers, or anyone else who might feasibly hinder her at a crime scene. Nobby thought this sort of attitude was almost obligatory for pathologists. Sometimes she wondered if they were born that way.

'Good afternoon, Pat,' said the super.

'Nothing very good about it for this fella,' muttered Pat Fitzwarren, swiftly returning her attention to the dead man.

Here we go, thought Nobby.

She had brought with her a print-out of the photograph the Avon and Somerset had circulated of the man they were looking for, and carefully compared it with the dead man lying before her. Sergeant Knott was quite right. This was almost certainly George Grey. He would have to be formally identified, of course, but there wasn't much doubt. And there was the evidence of the freshly stitched-up stab wounds to add to the obvious visual resemblance.

'What can you tell me, Pat?' she asked.

Patricia Fitzwarren stood up and took a step away from the body. 'It's more what I can't tell you, I'm afraid,' she said.

'Sorry?' queried Nobby.

'Well, I know what you want to know,' continued the doctor. 'Did he jump, did he fall, or was he pushed?'

'Something like that,' Clarke replied.

'Ummm. And that's what I can't tell you, not at this stage anyway. There are no overt signs of any injury, except the cuts to his shoulder and leg which had clearly been sustained prior to the incident which caused his death and had already received medical attention. No immediate evidence of a bang on the head or anything like that, but I can't be sure until I get him back to the mortuary. I can't even tell you whether he was dead or alive when he entered the water. From the look of him I suspect he was alive and that he drowned. But that's only a guess at this stage. I'll be able to ascertain that, of course, from whether or not there is water in his lungs when I cut him open.'

Clarke nodded. She had a strong stomach. The picture created of the man before her being sliced and sawn open by the diminutive Dr Fitzwarren did not unduly disturb her. Unlike DI Vogel, she reflected fleetingly and not unaffectionately. Many times, she had seen him turn vaguely green and walk away from a post-mortem examination in order not to throw up over the evidence.

'What about time of death?' she asked. 'Or should I say date of death. Any idea how long he has been in the water? If this is the man Avon and Somerset are looking for, and I am now pretty certain it is, then it can't have been more than twenty-four hours or thereabouts.'

The pathologist nodded. 'Certainly not more than twenty-four hours, I wouldn't think,' she said. 'There is no real sign of decomposition yet, but something's been nibbling at him already. So probably not much less than that.'

Det. Supt. Clarke averted her glance from George Grey's rather gruesome left eye, thanked the pathologist and stepped back. She wasn't going to learn much more from this scene, or from standing looking at the dead man. Any secrets he may yet be able to share would, as Dr Fitzwarren had doubtless correctly indicated, not be revealed until the post-mortem operation.

She looked around her again, at the housing complex beyond the lock, the lock itself, its steep drop unprotected by any kind of fencing, and the narrow bridge leading to Catherine Wheel Road. A well-built man wearing a high-vis jacket, the logo of the Canal and River Trust just visible beneath his lifejacket, was now standing next to the sergeant she presumed to be Leon Knott. With Lloyd Springer at her side, Nobby Clarke stepped over the cordon protecting the crime scene and approached the two men.

'You must be the lock-keeper,' she said, addressing the man in the high-vis coat.

The man nodded.

'And Leon Knott?' she queried, turning to the uniformed sergeant.

'Yes, ma'am,' said Knott. 'And this is Bill Cox.'

Nobby Clarke noticed that, in spite of his heavy clothing and the coolness of the day, beads of sweat were visible on the lock-keeper's forehead.

'Had a bit of a shock, I expect,' she commented, not unsympathetically.

Bill nodded. 'It's the first body I've ever found in my lock,' he said. 'Or anywhere else, come to that,' he added, almost as an afterthought.

'How long have you been lock-keeper here?' asked Clarke.

'I've been doing it for nearly five years now, ever since I retired from BA. Ground staff at Heathrow. I'm a volunteer, of course, they don't pay us nowadays. One of a team who work in shifts. I'm just lucky I've got enough of a pension that I can do it. I love it, being outdoors, watching the river craft pass . . .'

He paused. 'Well, most days I do.'

Nobby Clarke nodded her understanding. 'And do you live locally, Bill?'

'Yes. Almost on site. Got a flat in the Dock, right on the river, and a little Shetland two-berth moored in the marina. After I retired we sold up the family home in Boston Manor and moved down here. Bit of a dream for me, to tell the truth . . .'

'So, you know it well around here then. That pub over there,' she said, pointing across and beyond the lock. 'The Brewery Tap isn't it . . .?'

'Yes, it is,' responded Cox.

'Good little boozer too,' interrupted Sergeant Knott. 'Popular with a lot of people who live in the Dock.'

The sergeant gestured towards the housing estate which sprawled across a triangle of land flanked on each of its three sides by the Grand Union Canal and the River Brent, The Thames, and Syon Park.

'Bit of a precarious walk home, isn't it?' continued Det. Supt. Clarke.

'Bill thinks a miracle more of 'em who use The Tap as their local don't end up in the drink around here,' agreed Knott. 'And I'm inclined to agree with him. I mean, look at that bridge.'

Nobby Clarke looked. 'I see what you're getting at,' she said. 'And our friend wasn't a local. He would have been unfamiliar with the layout here. The steps. The bridge. All of it. And if it was after dark, well, he could easily have fallen in, I suppose. Particularly having just walked out of hospital, and with those wounds. He would have been heavily sedated before they were stitched up too, I reckon.'

'Yes, but he fell in the lock where the ground is level, and there aren't any obstacles,' said Knott.

'Indeed, but neither is there any kind of fence or safety barrier,' responded Clarke. She paused. Thinking. Knott voiced her thoughts before she quite got to them.

'Pretty easy to push someone in there, though, ma'am,' he said. 'Particularly if that someone is already injured and a bit groggy.'

The super smiled. 'That's as may be, Sergeant Knott,' she said. 'But we have no evidence at all yet to indicate such a thing, do we?'

'Of course not, ma'am,' replied Knott. 'But we do know who he is and where he came from, and that he was already wanted by Somerset police in connection with arson, don't we, ma'am?'

'We almost certainly do, Knott.'

'So I can't help wondering what he was doing wandering along by the lock side. We don't even have any idea what he was doing in Brentford, do we, boss? Not yet, anyway.'

'No, we don't,' said Clarke. 'But we know he must have come more or less straight here after he walked out of that hospital in Taunton. He's been in the water getting on for twenty-four hours, Dr Fitzwarren thinks. That means he must have headed up here pretty much as soon as he legged it from the hospital. So why would he come here so quickly? And make quite a long journey when he must have been in significant discomfort, at the very least.'

'To meet someone, ma'am?'

'That was my first thought.'

'Or maybe he has family here.'

'Ah yes, good thinking, Knott,' said Nobby Clarke. 'OK, I'm going to get my team on door-to-door work. The pub obviously. The Brentford Dock estate. The shops and all the various businesses in the high street. Find out if anyone saw George Grey or knows anything about him. Indeed, if anyone around here knew him at all before whatever happened here.'

She paused for just a few seconds. 'Any hotels hereabouts?'

'There's a new Premier Inn, just a couple of hundred yards away, a Holiday Inn up at Brentford Lock, and a Travelodge a bit further off towards Kew Bridge.'

'Right, we'll make them a priority too. If Grey wasn't staying in one of those, maybe he was meeting someone that was.'

She turned to DC Springer. 'OK, Lloyd, over to you,' she said. 'Let's call in the troops and get on with it. And we'll need all the help you local lads can give us too, Sergeant Knott.'

'Yes, ma'am,' said Knott.

He'd heard of Nobby Clarke, of course. Her reputation, and the stories about her somewhat unusual name, went before her. The truth was he was more than a little tickled to find himself given the opportunity to work with her.

FOURTEEN

It was late afternoon when Vogel received the call.

His caller's opening words were: 'How are you, you old devil? Still boring the arse off everyone you work with.'

He recognised the voice at once, of course. And as ever, he felt his pulse quicken.

'I'm well, thank you very much for asking, boss,' he said. 'How are you?'

He found that he was smiling. Det. Supt. Nobby Clarke always seemed to make him smile. And he still missed working with her on a day-to-day basis, as he had in the Met. Clarke had headed an MIT team and he had been her number two. When it came to his fellow officers, Vogel didn't care whether they were men, women, transgender, or giraffes. All that mattered to him was that they were good at their jobs. And Nobby Clarke was almost certainly the best he had ever worked with.

'I've got a bit of news for you, and when I want you to know how I am, I'll tell you,' reposted Clarke.

Vogel felt his smile widening. 'Whatever you say, boss,' he said.

'Good. I think we've found that missing person you're after, George Grey, re the Blackdown Manor fire. They tell me you're SIO.'

'Deputy SIO—'

'Really?' interrupted Clarke. 'Since when have you been able to tell the difference?'

Vogel ignored the interruption. He couldn't wait to hear the rest of Clarke's news.

'That's great, boss,' he said. 'I really think Grey might be the key to it all. We certainly need to give him the tenth degree. Where is he? I hope you've got the slippery bastard somewhere safe?'

'Oh yes, Vogel, we've got him somewhere safe, all right. In the morgue. I'm afraid your Mr Grey is dead. He's not going to be doing any more talking, and if he proves to be the key to anything it'll have to be posthumously.'

'You're kidding, boss.'

'Don't be ridiculous, Vogel. Of course, I'm not kidding. And what else have I told you repeatedly?'

'Not to call you boss, boss.'

'Well done, detective inspector. And I told you that when I was your boss. It's even worse now.'

'Sorry . . .'

Vogel paused. Why did she always have to do this? The woman seemed to take a perverse pleasure in teasing him. Or he assumed that's what it was. He found it particularly frustrating on this occasion as she was making him wait for information she knew he was extremely eager for.

'I'm still here, Vogel.'

'Sorry, Nobby,' he said.

He was sure he heard the DS chuckle. He would never be comfortable with calling a female senior detective, who was tall, blonde, and rather elegant, Nobby. Vogel couldn't help it. That was just the way he was. Everybody else seemed able to deal with it well enough. Not Vogel. But he did his best.

'So, what happened, and where did you find him, b–Nobby?' he asked.

'We don't know what happened. Not yet, anyway. We found him earlier this afternoon at the bottom of Thames Lock at Brentford. His body caused the lock gates to snag.'

'Oh, for God's sake,' said Vogel. 'Do you know how long he'd been in there?'

'Not exactly, but it seems likely it was approaching twenty-four hours, which means he must have made his way to Brentford straight after walking out of hospital.'

The DS briefly went over what Pat Fitzwarren had said concerning George Grey's condition, and the time and possible cause of death.

'So, we don't know a lot, Vogel,' she said. 'But we've launched a major investigation, obviously. It's possible that your man's death could be an accident, and if the deceased had been almost anyone except someone already wanted in connection with a major murder investigation, indeed a possible suspect, then accidental death would probably have been our first thought. Particularly as the whole area is a health and safety nightmare.

There's a pub just across the way, via a couple of bridges, a narrow walkway, and an unguarded stretch along the lockside, which is almost certainly where he entered the water. There's a big housing estate, Brentford Dock, on the other side of the lock, and a lot of the residents use that pub as their local. The general consensus of opinion is that it's a miracle more people, half-pissed, don't end up in the drink here. It's not easy walking. But as far as your George Grey's untimely demise is concerned, there are far too many coincidences and unanswered questions for us to regard it as likely to be an accident. I am treating this as a suspicious death, Vogel, and the investigation will proceed accordingly.'

'Too right, boss,' said Vogel.

'Yes. Now this is your case. Or that's the way I see it, anyway. And we seem to have found your major lead, who may not be much use to you himself, but there must be someone around here who knows your man and a heck of a lot else besides, I shouldn't wonder. I think you should get yourself up here, Vogel, first thing tomorrow at the latest, unless you've got something more important to do down there in the sticks?'

'No,' said Vogel. 'I haven't.'

'OK, do you want me to clear it with your super?'

'Yes, please, boss, I mean . . . N-Nobby,' said Vogel, as usual hesitating over the name.

Clarke let that one pass.

'I'd better go visit Mrs Grey now, though,' said Vogel. 'Somebody's got to make the death call, and I'd like to see how she reacts. I was pretty sure she wasn't telling us half what she knew when we interviewed her before. Maybe the death of her husband might jog her memory. Then I've got some stuff I need to finish up. So first thing in the morning it is, if that's all right with you.'

'As you wish, Vogel,' said Clarke. 'How will you get here? Don't suppose you've passed your driving test yet, have you?'

Vogel winced. Nobby Clarke knew him rather too well.

He dodged the question. In any case, Det. Supt. Clarke was clearly well aware of what the answer would be.

'Saslow will be driving me,' he said.

'Ah good, you're still working with her then,' commented Clarke, letting Vogel get away with his bit of prevarication. 'Sharp cookie that one. Is she OK?'

They both knew what Clarke was referring to; that last case which neither Vogel nor Dawn Saslow were ever likely to be able to put totally behind them.

'She's fine,' Vogel replied shortly.

'Good. Call me when you're getting close.'

'Yes, boss,' said Vogel. 'Sorry, yes Nobby.'

He winced as he said the name. He would never get used to it, never.

He was still in Wellington police station, sitting with his laptop open in front of him at a desk in the station's biggest room, which wasn't nearly big enough. He glanced across at Saslow, who was standing at the far end, studying something on one of the wall charts.

He walked over. 'Do you fancy a trip to London tomorrow?' he asked her.

Then he explained about his call from Det. Supt. Clarke and the discovery of George Grey's body.

Saslow's face lit up. Which might have seemed rather odd to anyone except another police officer. This was at the very least an intriguing development. Of course; she was pleased to know she would be actively involved, thought Vogel. Any young officer would be. Particularly one who was clearly determined to overcome experiences which might have brought down a lesser person. And he had reason to believe that Saslow welcomed the opportunity of working with Clarke just as much as he did.

'But right now, I'm afraid we have to visit Janice Grey,' Vogel continued.

He saw Saslow's expression change. The light went out of her eyes. She'd guessed, he thought. All police officers hated breaking the news that a loved one had died. More than once in his career he'd had to break the news of the death of a child to distraught parents, and many times the death of a much loved, husband, wife, partner, or even dear friend. It never got any easier. Although, Vogel had to admit to himself, he didn't feel quite the same about it this time as he usually did.

After all, George Grey had been, and remained, the only suspect so far in a case of double murder by arson, and Vogel was not at all convinced that his widow wasn't also involved. Certainly, it was hard to believe that she had known nothing of whatever it was that her husband had been up to on the night of that terrible fire.

'The death call,' muttered Saslow, resignedly, breaking into his reverie.

'Yes, but it's much more than that this time, isn't it, Dawn?'

Her face brightened just a little. Vogel had known he wouldn't have to explain.

'Well yes, Janice Grey surely has to be up to her ears in whatever's going on, hasn't she boss?' Saslow volunteered. 'Just like her husband.'

'Quite probably,' agreed Vogel. 'At the very least I suspect that she knew what George was up to, or at least had a fair idea.'

'I'll get my coat,' said Saslow.

'Yep. Oh, and ask Margot Hartley to get a family liaison officer on board, will you?'

Saslow nodded, jumped to her feet, and began to move at speed, coat in one hand, phone in the other.

Janice Grey might be a suspect in her own right, but she was also the wife of a man who had died suddenly and possibly violently. So, Vogel had done what he would always do as part of the death call routine, made arrangements for a family liaison officer to be allocated to her.

This also had another purpose, of course. Particularly in circumstances where the bereaved might be under some kind of suspicion, family liaison doubled as on-the-spot eyes and ears for the investigating officers, in this case keeping a close watch on Mrs Grey, everything she did and everyone she might be in contact with. A good FLO could be an invaluable source of information.

Mrs Grey opened the door of The Gatehouse before Vogel or Saslow had even knocked on it. This was in stark contrast to their earlier visit.

She looked even more unkempt than when they had first met. Again Vogel reckoned the woman had been crying. Her eyes were red-rimmed and slightly swollen. Perhaps she'd had a fair idea that something would happen to her husband after he'd walked out of hospital. Maybe she'd expected to hear from him and feared the worst when she didn't. Or maybe she had merely shed tears of self-pity.

As soon as she saw the two police officers she seemed to know what they were there for. But didn't they always, thought Vogel.

'What is it, what is it?' she asked, her voice high-pitched with apprehension. 'Has something happened to my Georgie? It has, hasn't it? That what you're here for, just tell me, tell me . . .'

She sounded near hysterical.

Vogel interrupted her calmly, and as kindly as he could. 'Look, can we come in Mrs Grey, please?' he asked. 'We do have some news. But why don't we all go inside and sit down. Then we will tell you everything.'

The woman's shoulders dropped. Suddenly she looked even smaller than she actually was.

She knew all right.

Without uttering another word, she led Vogel and Saslow into the sitting room. Vogel perched on one of the chintzy chairs, gesturing for Mrs Grey also to sit. She did so. On the sofa. Saslow sat down next to her.

'Mrs Grey, I'm afraid I have some very bad news for you,' he began. 'It would seem that—'

Janice Grey didn't need him to finish. She seemed calmer. Her expression had changed to one of glum resignation. 'He's dead, he's dead, isn't he?' she interrupted. 'My Georgie's dead, isn't he?'

'I fear he almost certainly is,' Vogel continued. 'We need him to be formally identified, of course, but there seems little doubt. The police officers who have seen the body of the man we believe to be your husband have identified him to their own satisfaction from the photograph you gave us, which we circulated nationwide. Also, of course, there are wounds present on the deceased which are similar to those sustained by Mr Grey on the night of the fire, and these are an additional aid to identification.'

Mrs Grey stared at Vogel. 'What happened to him, what have those bastards done to my George?'

Vogel explained where and how George was found, in Brentford at the bottom of Thames Lock.

'What was he doing in Brentford?' asked Mrs Grey, and Vogel had little doubt that her surprise was genuine.

'We don't know, not yet anyway,' replied Vogel. 'In fact, we were rather hoping you might be able to tell us.'

'I haven't got any idea,' said Janice Grey.

'Do you have friends, or relatives perhaps, in the area?'

Janice shook her head. 'What the hell was he doing in Brentford?' she muttered, repeating herself. 'I told him no good would come of any of this. I told him. He never listened, my Georgie, not to me anyway, never . . .'

'What do you mean by that?' Vogel asked. 'No good would come of any of what?'

'Nothing,' Janice Grey replied quickly.

'Mrs Grey, you also asked "what have those bastards done to my Georgie?" I need to know what you mean by that too?'

With what appeared to be a huge effort of will, Vogel thought, Janice Grey struggled to regain control of herself.

'I don't know what I'm saying,' she said. 'Really I don't. I just meant . . .'

She paused, as if seeking the right words. 'I just meant, well, the bastards who've done for my George. Whoever they are. That's all.'

'Mrs Grey, I did not at any stage tell you that anybody had "done for your George". I have not mentioned murder. Indeed, at this stage we are not entirely sure what happened to your husband.'

'Well, it's pretty obvious, isn't it,' Mrs Grey blustered. 'You found him at the bottom of a canal lock. What are you saying? He fell in? He's not stupid you know . . .'

She paused again, this time in order to correct herself. 'He wasn't stupid. What was he doing by a canal anyway? He wouldn't have just fallen in. I took that for granted.'

'People do, Mrs Grey,' said Vogel. 'Your husband would have been very weak, it's reasonable to assume, after what he went through on the night of the fire. We have reason to believe that he died within hours of walking out of The Musgrove. He'd been heavily sedated in order for the surgeon to effectively stitch his wounds. He could still have been affected by that. He would probably have been taking pain killers. And I understand there is a pub close to where his body was found. He might have been drinking. We just don't know yet.'

Janice Grey looked distinctly unimpressed. 'My Georgie hardly ever drank, always said he didn't like being out of control,' she said.

'Well, if he was in pain, he may have made an exception.'

Mrs Grey grunted, clearly unconvinced. 'Some bastard did for him,' she muttered almost to herself, looking down at her lap.

Then she looked up and met Vogel's eye. 'Look, as far as I know, Georgie's never even been to bloody Brentford. Not before. And I certainly haven't. Maybe somebody abducted him. Yes, that's it, someone went into that hospital and abducted my Georgie.'

'And why would anyone do that, Mrs Grey?' asked Vogel patiently.

The veil came down over Janice Grey's eyes again. 'I don't know, do I? Isn't that your job? To find out.'

'Yes, and so we will, Mrs Grey. One way or another. You need have no doubt about that. But if you know anything that might assist us, and I must say I believe you probably do, we would be most grateful for your help.'

'I don't know nothing about nothing,' Janice Grey responded quickly. 'I've told you that before.'

'Yes, you did, Mrs Grey. But your husband is dead now. He won't be coming back to you. And he will never be able to tell us the truth about what happened to him on the night of the fire, and exactly how he received those injuries. Because I am pretty sure that he didn't tell us the truth when we interviewed him at the Musgrove. Nor will he now ever be able to tell us why he felt it necessary to leave hospital so suddenly, when still weak from his injuries, and travel straight away to West London. I think you know far more than you are admitting to, Mrs Grey. And if you do have information which might shed light on any of this, then you really should share it with us. Before you find yourself in a great deal of trouble.'

Janice Grey shook her head yet again. 'I don't know nothing,' she said stubbornly. 'Except he was attacked by armed intruders. He told me all about it in hospital.'

'What did he tell you exactly, Mrs Grey?'

The woman looked as if she felt she'd allowed herself to be caught out, Vogel thought.

'Nothing you don't already know,' she said quickly.

'Mrs Grey, your husband did indeed tell me this cock and bull story about unknown armed intruders attacking him, but I don't believe a word of it, and I very much doubt that you do either.'

Mrs Grey took a deep breath. 'Of course, I believe what my Georgie told me,' she insisted. 'He was attacked by men with guns, the same men who probably set fire to the house.'

'Yes. Men with guns. Your husband was stabbed. Wouldn't you expect him to have been shot if these intruders were armed with guns?'

Mrs Grey shrugged. 'How would I know?' she said. 'Maybe they didn't want to make a noise.'

'All right, did your husband indicate to you exactly how he was attacked, and whether or not he knew who these alleged intruders were?'

'What do you mean alleged intruders?' asked Janice Grey.

'Will you please answer the question,' instructed Vogel curtly.

'He said they came up behind him. He had no idea who they were. Why would he?'

'And you, too, have no idea who his mystery assailant or assailants might be?'

'Of course not. I keep telling you, I don't know anything about any of it.'

'Mrs Grey, I believe there are things that you do know that, for whatever reason, you are keeping to yourself; quite possibly vital information. If that is the case, and I strongly suspect that it is, then I must warn you against failing to reveal such information in very serious circumstances. Three people have now died, Mrs Grey. There is little doubt that the fire here at the manor, which killed two of these people, was started deliberately, and we strongly suspect that the third, your husband, was murdered. You really must tell us what you know, Mrs Grey, not only for the sake of your dead husband, but also for your own sake.'

Mrs Grey raised a hand to her mouth. Another flicker passed her eyes. This time Vogel could see fear in her eyes. For a moment, he thought she was going to open up.

Then the shutter came down again.

'I don't know nothing,' she said.

FIFTEEN

Meanwhile Bella Fairbrother had been fully occupied throughout the day. In the afternoon she kept her appointment with William Watkins, the Taunton solicitor her father had been using for the past year or so, at his office in Hammett Street, Taunton's premier location for legal and financial professionals.

It turned out, however, that he was rather different to most in his profession. He was well past usual retirement age, for a start. Bella had been told by Peter Prentis, her father's London solicitor, that this was down to the cost of a number of failed marriages and an even greater number of children.

Prentis had been somewhat scathing about Willian Watkins, and had even indicated that, because of his precarious financial situation, the Taunton solicitor might not be beyond bending the law when it best suited him or his clients. Bella suspected that Prentis had no way of knowing that, and was merely jealous of the man who seemed to have virtually stolen his number-one client. But she certainly would not put it past her father to employ a solicitor he could bend to his will.

Watkins came out into the corridor and greeted Bella at the lift she had taken to his fourth floor office. He was a handsome man, with a full head of silver hair, belying the age Bella knew him to be. He had a gentle smile, and a quiet manner about him.

He ushered Bella in, and gestured for her to sit on an upright chair in front of his desk whilst he sat down behind it facing her. The first thing she noticed was that the west-facing windows had no curtains. Instead, pieces of old newspaper had been stuck over the windows, presumably in order to prevent William Watkins and his clients being blinded by the afternoon sun.

'I am not sure how I can help you, Miss Fairbrother,' said Watkins straightaway, placing the tips of his fingers together so that they formed a point upon which he propped his chin.

'Well, I do understand, and I realise this may be difficult because of client confidentiality and that it's probably against legal protocol for you to discuss in detail my father's affairs with me, Mr Watkins, even though he has passed on,' said Bella. 'But I am hoping you may at least be able to tell me what papers he has lodged with you here, in particular whether or not there is a will—'

'No, it's not that, Miss Fairbrother, it's not about client confidentiality or anything like that,' interrupted Watkins. 'You see, I don't have anything at all archived for your father here. He took away all the papers I did have almost a year ago, and I haven't seen them, or your father since.'

'Did he go to another solicitor?'

'I couldn't say, Miss Fairbrother. Although I have a feeling your father employed a number of solicitors over the years – in different parts of the United Kingdom, and probably overseas, and that he deliberately limited what each of us dealt with so that none of us knew the full picture concerning either his business or personal affairs.'

William Watkins paused. 'Or am I being far too Machiavellian?' he asked.

'It is not possible to be too Machiavellian concerning my father,' replied Bella, who was thinking that this was pretty much the way Sir John had run the whole of his life. 'He was a remarkable man, of course. He had been ill for some time, but I always believed he would make it possible, before he died, for those who would have to take over his affairs to do so. The fire and his sudden death have changed all that, and I am left, quite bluntly, with trying to clear up a fearful mess. Have you really no idea what he did with the papers he took from you?'

'Oh yes, he made that clear enough. He told me he wanted to store everything in the storeroom he had built at Blackdown Manor, which he reckoned was safe in any eventuality, including nuclear warfare.'

Bella never wanted to hear that description again, and would certainly never repeat it again, not now that she had seen the ruins of Blackdown. So, he'd moved everything to the storeroom – which meant, if the contents of that storeroom had been destroyed, or even substantially destroyed, the complex financial riddle she was about to try to unravel was going to be even more difficult.

She said none of that, of course, only responding mildly with a smile that was more of a grimace: 'Yes, he always said that.'

'Well, the one thing I do know is that your father's affairs were very complicated,' Watkins continued. 'So, I hope for your sake, and for the sake of all of his family and his business, that the storeroom has proved to be as safe as he considered it to be.'

Bella didn't bother to answer that. Clearly the man didn't know the half.

'Could I ask you, without asking you to divulge the content at all, did the work you undertook for my father involve the making of a will?' she asked.

Watkins appeared to ponder for a moment. 'Not exactly,' he said at last.

'I'm sorry?' queried Bella. 'What do you mean by that?'

'He asked me to write an addendum to his will,' replied Watkins. 'I never saw the will itself.'

'Isn't that unusual?'

'It is indeed. Then again, your father was a most unusual man, wasn't he? But there was no real reason why it shouldn't be done, so I complied with him. It is an effective legal document, I can assure you.'

'But, of course, you are not at liberty to tell me what this addendum was?'

'To be frank, it referred throughout to trust funds, overseas accounts and investments, insurance policies, and so on, and meant little without access to the original will. Or, certainly, it meant little to me. Which I assume was your father's intention. Of course, if references had been made to specific beneficiaries . . .' William Watkins paused again, looking down at the table. 'To specific family members, for example,' he continued, looking up once more and meeting Bella's eye, 'I couldn't possibly tell you. Primarily, it seemed to be a matter of ensuring that, after his death, certain of his funds and assets would be distributed throughout his business empire in the way he wished, and similarly concerning the management of his personal wealth, the details of which he did not confide in me.'

'I see,' said Bella, thinking just how typical of her father that was.

She thanked the man and left.

She glanced at her watch. It was just gone four p.m. She thought that she might pay another visit to Blackdown Manor a little later. She wondered for how long a police presence would be maintained there after the initial fire investigation and CSI work had been completed. She suspected not for long, considering the police cuts enforced in the UK over recent years by successive governments. It could just be possible that she might be able to sneak into the remains of the ruined manor and see for herself the condition of the storeroom which offered the only hope, it seemed, of anything surviving the fire. After all, if health and safety and all the rest of them held back for much longer, any remotely retrievable contents would be destroyed by the elements.

Bella glanced up at a dull heavy sky. It might be only early October but this was more like a November day. The weather was horrible. Vast quantities of water had already been poured onto the manor by the fire service. Now it looked as if the heavens were about to drop another load over the poor old place at any moment. Almost certainly before the night was out.

As she climbed into her car she began to formulate a plan. It had to be carefully worked out. Her wardrobe needed some attention too. She was wearing suede fashion boots with heels, tiger print leggings and a fitted leather jacket over a lightweight sweater.

She needed work boots and warm protective clothing. She also needed a powerful torch, and a crow bar. Maybe other tools. A hammer perhaps. And she knew just the place to go to fulfil her needs.

She was more than familiar with the market town of Wellington. It was, and always had been, a proper country town and she was confident that she would acquire all that she wanted there. She parked in the car park off Fore Street.

Her first stop, right on the corner, was Perry's, an old-fashioned ironmongery store which she had been brought up to believe sold everything in its field. Or maybe just everything!

'If Perry's 'aven't got it, it doesn't exist,' Jack Kivel used to say.

Visits to Perry's with Kivel were amongst Bella's foremost childhood memories. She remembered standing alongside Jack while old Mr Perry, who had even seemed old to her then and yet was still about the place, had rifled through drawers and tins looking for exactly the right screw, clip, or whatever obscure gizmo might be required.

All the memories came flooding back as she stepped through the doors. The shop had changed shape a little since she'd last visited. The counter was longer, the layout not quite the same. But it was still Perry's, and she suspected that there weren't many shops like it left anywhere in the world.

Not for the first time in the past couple of days, she had to make an effort to shake herself out of her reverie. This would never do. Life had moved on. The task ahead of her was not going to be a pleasant one. And nobody, it seemed, was going to come to her rescue. She just had to get on with it alone.

'Why, hello Miss Fairbrother,' said a familiar voice. It was Guy. Also still there, then.

A thought occurred to her. A bit late, she admonished herself. She was still well known in Wellington. Purchase of the items she had on her mental shopping list was bound to attract attention. If she wanted to go ahead, she would have to explain herself — or at least appear to.

'Hello Guy, nice to see you again,' she said, smiling brightly.

'Indeed, Miss Fairbrother, but under such terrible circumstances. We are all so sorry, about your father, and the old manor.'

'Thank you, Guy.' Bella adjusted her smile.

She told him the things she wanted to buy and watched the surprise flit across his eyes.

'Trying to salvage what we can out at the house,' she said. 'There's not much, but there are some metal boxes and such like which were in storage that I'm hoping may not have been entirely destroyed. I want to go and have a good poke about. Once the police give me the go ahead of course.'

Bizarrely, it was more or less the truth. Nonetheless, Bella was rather surprised by how plausible she sounded. The last bit was a blatant lie of course. She had no intention of waiting any longer for anybody to give her permission to enter her own family home.

After Guy had supplied her with all that Perry's could provide, she made her way along Mantle Street to the new country shop where she bought over-trousers, a Barbour jacket and a woolly hat. The shop had not been there when she had last been in Wellington, and she didn't recognise the owner. Neither did he show any sign of recognising her. So she was not required to explain anything.

Her final call was to the local shoe shop, the aptly named Wellington Boots, where she duly bought herself a pair of wellies. Owner Anne Brummett recognised her at once, of course, greeted her warmly, and, like Guy, offered condolences about her father's death, and the loss of the great old house that was Blackdown Manor.

Once again though, no explanation of her purchase was required. In the west of England you never have to explain why you need a pair of wellington boots. The exceptionally high rainfall level of the south-west peninsular takes care of that, in addition to the rural nature of much of the area.

Bella loaded her purchases into her car and considered what she should do next.

Clearly, it made more sense to make her foray into the ruins of the manor after dark, thus giving herself the best possible chance of doing so undetected. And there was still a good hour of daylight remaining. However, there was something she might do to kill the time, that she probably should have done already. She would pay Mrs George Grey a visit. Like everyone else, including the police and the fire service, Bella Fairbrother was not at all clear about exactly what had happened to cause Blackdown Manor to be burned to the ground and bring about the death of two people. So much didn't make sense. She knew that arson was strongly suspected, and that George Grey was wanted by the police. But beyond that everything was mere conjecture. And she wondered, as indeed Vogel had, exactly what Janice Grey might know. She'd truthfully told Vogel that she had never met either of the Greys. Now she thought, was the time to change that.

And whilst she was about it, she could also check out whatever police presence there might still be at the manor.

She headed out of Wellington on the A38 in the direction of Exeter, then off over the Blackdown Hills along those so familiar country lanes. This time she did not stop to gaze nostalgically across the hills at the burned-out house that had been her home for so long. She already knew all too well what those ruins looked like, and the image would be emblazoned in her memory for ever more.

She approached Blackdown Manor only minutes after Vogel

and Saslow had left, although Bella had no way of knowing that. The family liaison officer had yet to arrive. A special constable was still on scene-guard at the gates, but allowed her through when she explained who she was and that she wished to visit Janice Grey, merely warning her not to cross the tapes cordoning off the ruined house itself.

As she parked outside The Gatehouse she noticed a twitch of a curtain. Was somebody, presumably Janice Grey, sitting inside watching the driveway?

Bella walked up the garden path and was about to knock on the door when it opened before she had a chance to do so. Just as it had for Vogel and Saslow. The woman who stood before her looked dishevelled and unkempt. Straggling greying hair framed a pale face. She may recently have been crying.

'Yes,' she said rather aggressively.

'Mrs Grey?' enquired Bella, trying to sound as pleasant and unthreatening as she could.

'Who are you?' countered the woman, equally aggressively.

'I'm Sir John's daughter—' Bella began.

'Are you indeed? Well, you're a bit late then, aren't you?'

Bella was puzzled. 'I don't quite know what you mean, Mrs Grey,' she said. 'It is Mrs Grey, isn't it?'

The woman just stared at her belligerently.

Bella carried on regardless. Who else was the woman likely to be? 'I just stopped by to say how sorry I was to hear that your husband had been injured. I'm sure you are aware the police are looking for him, that they want to talk to him about the fire. But I know my father trusted George totally.'

She tried a bit of flattery. 'And you too, of course.'

Mrs Grey's gaze did not flicker.

Bella battled on. 'I just wondered if you knew what happened that night? I mean, you and your husband worked together, didn't you? You'd have known if he were planning to do anything like start a fire, wouldn't you?'

Bella stopped, mentally kicking herself. She hadn't meant to be quite so blunt.

Mrs Grey's eyes narrowed. 'Well, if he was so trustworthy, why would he do that, then?' she asked sharply. 'You're worse than the coppers.'

'No, I didn't mean, look I'm sorry,' Bella stumbled. 'I just wanted to talk to you—'

'I don't know nothing,' Janice Grey interrupted. 'George never told me what went on with Sir John, said it was all confidential. I know he'd never have done anything to hurt him, I know that.'

'May I come in?' asked Bella somewhat hopefully.

'No, I've said all I'm going to,' replied the woman. 'Too much already.'

Bella considered putting her foot in the door but didn't. She'd probably seen too many movies. More than likely she still wouldn't gain entry to the Grey home and would just end up with a squashed foot.

'Well, perhaps another day,' she said lamely, turning to walk away.

'It wasn't supposed to happen, you know,' Mrs Grey suddenly called out.

'Sorry, what?' queried Bella over her shoulder.

'It wasn't supposed to happen,' Janice Grey said again. 'Nobody was supposed to have got hurt. My George would never have hurt Sir John. Nor anybody else come to that.'

Bella turned and took a step back towards the house.

'Mrs Grey, you know all about it, don't you? You know what your husband did that night, and you probably know why, don't you?'

Janice Grey stood full square in the doorway, just in case, it seemed, Bella might try to push her way into the house.

'I'll tell you what I do know,' said the woman. 'My George is dead. So, he's not going to be no good to the police now, is he?'

Her voice was loud and clear, but held just the very slightest tremor.

Bella took an involuntary step backwards. 'He's dead?' she queried feebly.

'They done for him, didn't they?' continued Janice Grey. 'And who knows who might be next before this is over. It could be me. They could be after me now.'

Bella was battling to get over her shock. 'W-what do you mean, it could be you?' she asked.

Janice Grey looked Bella up and down. 'Or it could be you,' she said. 'You're a Fairbrother after all. Oh yes, it could be you.'

Bella was stunned into silence.

Janice Grey began to laugh, almost hysterically.

With a huge effort Bella pulled herself together and managed to speak again. 'M-Mrs Grey, won't you tell me what you mean?' she asked. 'Who is the "they" you say did for your George? How, exactly, did he die? I, uh, I don't understand . . .'

Bella had moved forward onto the doorstep. Suddenly, and without warning, Janice Grey slammed the door shut in her face. As it closed Bella heard the unmistakable sound of a bolt being shot.

Bella did not bother to call after the woman. In any case she was too busy trying to recover from the shock of what Janice had told her. George Grey was dead, and his widow clearly appeared to think he had been murdered. She'd also indicated that she knew who those responsible were, and that she felt she was in danger, and that Bella might also be in danger.

It was a lot to take in. Bella was thoughtful as she returned to her car. Mrs Grey had more to tell, if she wished to, that was for sure. But Bella wasn't going to get any further with her, certainly not at the moment. She, at least, had another way of finding out what had happened to George Grey. She reached for her mobile and called Vogel. The DI, on his way back to Kenneth Steele House, answered at once. Bella wasn't surprised. After all, he had told her to call at any time, and she was, she supposed, one of the key figures in a murder investigation.

After the briefest of pleasantries, Bella cut straight to the chase. 'Look, Mr Vogel, I understand that George Grey is dead. I hope you don't mind me calling, however, I know Mr Grey was a suspect, but as he worked for my father and this is another death following the fire at Blackdown, I do feel a kind of responsibility. I wondered if you would tell me what happened to him, how he died?'

There was a pause on the other end of the line, as if Vogel was considering how to respond to Bella's question. 'Miss Fairbrother, no information of that nature concerning Mr Grey has been made public yet,' said the DI eventually. 'I have to ask you why and how you have come to believe that Mr Grey is dead?'

'His wife told me,' said Bella bluntly. 'I've just left The Gatehouse.'

'Miss Fairbrother, we have a very serious ongoing investigation here. Clearly you have an involvement, if only by default, as does Mrs Grey. But I must ask you not to interfere again.'

'I only visited Mrs Grey because I thought it was my duty as my father's daughter, to say how sorry I was that her husband had been injured,' lied Bella. 'Then she told me he was dead. It is right, isn't it? George Grey is dead.'

There was another pause before Vogel answered. 'I cannot officially confirm that George Grey is dead because he has yet to be formally identified,' he said.

'But you know, don't you? I want to know what happened to him. Did he die of his injuries?'

Again, she had to wait for the answer.

'All right, Miss Fairbrother, I can tell you that the body of a man we believe to be George Grey was found earlier today in a West London canal. And that it does not appear that he died from the injuries he received on the night of the fire at Blackdown.'

'My God,' uttered Bella. 'What happened? Did he drown? I mean are you saying he jumped in? Killed himself? Could he just have fallen? Or . . . or—'

This time Vogel spoke quickly, interrupting her. 'I can only say that investigations are continuing,' he said. 'I cannot tell you more. I'm sorry.'

After ending the call Bella sat for a moment wondering what to do next. The news of George Grey's death and the manner of it was yet another shock. One half of her just wanted to go back to her hotel room and bury her head in the pillows. But she was a Fairbrother. And she was on a mission. Nothing she had heard should deter her from that. After all she was seeking knowledge, and she had been brought up to believe that knowledge was strength. Knowledge was power. She would carry on with the task she had set herself.

The special constable was not in sight. Presumably sitting in his car outside the gates. She started the engine and drove slowly down the drive towards the manor in order to check out the crime scene security arrangements there. It was almost quarter past six. As she had suspected there appeared to be no further presence. The fire investigators and the CSIs had probably not finished altogether yet, but certainly packed up for the day. Nonetheless

she didn't stop. For whatever reason, and even under the circumstances of having so recently heard that her husband was dead,
or maybe because of that, Janice Grey seemed to be keeping a
close watch on the comings and goings along the drive that led
to the ruins of Blackdown Manor. Then there was the special
constable. And Bella didn't want to arouse his suspicions. She
turned the car in a tight circle and left the estate along the main
drive by which she had entered, shooting a last glance at The
Gatehouse as she passed.

The special constable was no longer outside the gate, neither
standing nor sitting in his vehicle. Bella assumed that it had been
considered unnecessary to keep a night-time scene-guard on duty,
not when the crime scene was so remote, and also little more than
a pile of cinders and charcoal. There was still Janice Grey to
consider, however, and it was possible that patrol cars would stop
by during the night. She would take no chances. She decided
to stick to the plan she had already formulated.

Bella knew the territory well. She had, after all, been born
in the old manor, and spent a substantial part of her growing up
there. Instead of turning left towards the road back to Taunton,
she swung right along a winding lane leading deeper into the
Blackdowns, and after three miles or so took another right along
what was little more than a track through a wood, first checking
ahead and in her rear-view mirror to ensure that not only were
there no other cars about, but nobody at all who might notice
her leaving the main drag.

The track was not made for low-slung sports cars; indeed, it
was the track which the firemen had dismissed as a possible
route to Blackdown Manor when their way along the drive had
been blocked by that fallen oak. But Bella Fairbrother knew what
she was doing. She proceeded slowly only a couple of hundred
yards along the first and more accessible part of the track until
turning into a partially cleared area where her car would not be
seen, even in the unlikely event of anyone else making their way
along the track at that time of day. She parked and switched off
the ignition. Silence engulfed her. Bella had always rather liked
woodlands. Dusk was falling. She sat in the little car for a few
minutes drinking in the atmosphere, allowing the heavy still
greenness to bring her some peace, or as much peace as was

possible that day. In spite of Mrs Grey's warnings of danger, which may have been hysterically delivered, but none the less, could not be casually dismissed, Bella felt no fear. Not even a sense of unease. This was her land.

She stepped out onto the leafy soil and manoeuvred herself into the over-trousers she had bought, slipping them on over her designer jeans. Then she swapped the suede fashion boots for her newly acquired wellies, her light leather jacket for the Barbour, pulled on the newly bought woolly hat, and slung over her shoulder a bag containing the tools she had acquired at Perry's. By then it was almost totally dark. With her torch trained carefully down on the track, just a couple of feet ahead of her, she set off along a path through the woods which she remembered quite clearly from her childhood. It led directly to the manor house. There was a hedge or two to scramble through and a locked gate to climb over, but Bella Fairbrother was fit and agile.

She arrived at the ruined house within twenty minutes. Then came the difficult bit. Most of the house had collapsed and was little more than charred rubble. It was difficult at first even to recognise the layout of the old place, although portions of wall remained jutting up into the night sky, and she just hoped there were no hot spots remaining.

Still keeping the beam of her torch low, she made her way with difficulty towards the area of the house where the storeroom had been located. The swimming pool appeared to no longer exist. It looked as if much of the structure of the old house had collapsed on top of it. None the less she skirted around it in case of a further structural collapse.

Everywhere there were piles of blackened rubble, and puddles of water. She picked her way carefully through. Now that she was inside the remains of the manor, she could see what the fire investigator had meant. But she had one advantage over him, the CSI, and all the rest of the experts. She knew Blackdown Manor like the back of her hand. She shone her torch around to where she thought the stone steps leading down to the basement area must be. And there they were clearly illuminated in the beam, just off to her right. Or rather, there were the remains of them, leading merely into a pile of collapsed stone and charred wood where, she was quite sure, the storeroom had once been located. If the door still stood, which Bella thought highly unlikely, it was buried. And clearly, the storeroom no longer had a roof.

Almost involuntarily Bella sat down on a pile of wet rubble, shocked by what lay before her.

She wondered what on earth she had expected after such a catastrophic fire? But, in spite of what she had been told, she certainly hadn't expected anything as extreme as this. If any part of the storeroom and its contents still existed, it would probably require a bulldozer to remove what lay on top. Her father had clearly been wrong in his prediction that the basement room would withstand a nuclear explosion. And it appeared, from William Watkins' account, that he had relied even more on the invincibility of the storeroom than Bella had realised.

She lowered her face into her hands. There was nothing more to see here, and nothing that could be done. She was just about to stand up and begin her return journey when she heard a slight noise behind her. Was it the sound of a footstep, or just a further movement of the ruins?

Before she could turn she felt strong hands around her throat and a knee in her back.

'Don't move, don't even think about moving, or I'll bleddy kill you,' said a male voice.

Bella tried to scream, but no sound came out of her. She could barely breathe. The fingers pressing against her windpipe were like steel. It seemed like Janice Grey had been right about one thing. She was in danger now, that was for sure. Danger of dying perhaps, in the ruins of what had once been her home.

'Right,' said the voice. 'Now don't do nothing stupid. I'm going to relax my grip, because I want you to tell me who you are, and what the hell you're doing here?'

One hand was removed from Bella's throat. An arm now encased her upper body. The knee was still in her back. As promised, the grip of the second hand, still around her throat, slackened. Bella struggled to catch her breath.

'OK,' said the voice. 'That's it. Just take it easy, and answer my questions. Who are you, and what are you doing here?'

Bella no longer thought she was going to die. Not at that very second anyway. As her lungs became able to work normally again, so did her brain. She knew that voice. Surely, she knew that voice.

'Come on, get on with it.'

Yes, she knew the voice all right. She had grown up with it, after all. But it didn't make sense. What would he be doing here?

'Jack?' she queried tremulously. 'Jack, never mind me, what are *you* doing here?'

The second hand was removed at once from around her throat, and the knee dropped away from her back. She was aware of sudden movement. Then the beam of a flashlight shone straight into her eyes, blinding her.

'Miss Bella, it's you. For God's sake.'

The beam was shifted away from her eyes. The man holding it diverted it fleetingly to shine at his own face. 'Yes, it's me, Miss Bella,' said Jack Kivel.

'You frightened the life out of me,' said Bella, managing a nervous laugh.

'I'm sorry about that,' said Jack. 'I wanted to know who you were and what you were up to, didn't I?' He paused. 'And what are you up to?' he asked.

'It seems that my father had ultimately stored almost everything of real importance, to the bank, and so much else, here, in his blessed storeroom. It's all such a mess. I thought if I could salvage stuff, get to his papers, maybe it would help . . . and I might even find some of the paintings intact . . . I can see now there's fat chance of that . . .'

'But why the sneaky stuff, creeping in after dark. You'm Bella Fairbrother. This is, or rather was, your home.'

'The place is still a crime scene, Jack, and considered unsafe, could be days before they let me in officially, and I couldn't wait, I don't have time to waste.'

She peered at Jack through the gloom. 'But, come on, what the hell are you doing here?'

'I was lamping up the four acre.' Jack gestured towards a rifle propped against a length of crumbling black wall. 'Somebody's got to keep they rabbits down. There's a new copse up there on the edge of Top Wood. Young saplings. Treat for bleddy rabbits, they be. I was just about to switch me lamp on when I caught a glimpse of torchlight. Only a few feet away. I hunkered down to let you pass, then I followed you here.'

'Jack, why would you care about the rabbits and the trees,

or what I or anyone else was doing up here? My father sacked you. He treated you appallingly. Turned you and Martha out of your home.'

'To tell the truth, Miss Bella, coming up here after dark with me rifle calms me down, makes me feel better about things. More than ever tonight, after what's happened. None of what you've just said makes any difference, you see. I love this land, and I never stopped being your father's man. He still looked after us, me and my Martha, didn't he? He gave us a place of our own, Miss Bella. Just a small cottage, but it's a home, a real home, that nobody will ever be able to take from us. We'll always have to thank him for that.'

'I suppose that's one way of looking at it. But, oh Jack, I was afraid you were going to kill me.'

'To tell the truth, I thought you was one of the armed intruders come back, didn't I? I had no idea it was you, Miss Bella. How could I 'ave done. In all that gear you've got on.'

'You terrified me, Jack.'

'I'm that sorry, Miss Bella.'

'I know, Jack. Anyway, it's been a wasted journey as far as I'm concerned. Are you going back to your lamping?'

'Perhaps. Seeing the state this place is in has put me off doing anything much, that's for certain.'

'I know how you feel.'

'Yep. I may just go home. My Land Rover's up by the four acre. How did you get here, Miss Bella, I don't like you being out here on your own.'

'I've got my car parked as far as I could up the farm track. We can walk back up that way together, if you like. But Jack, for God's sake, why am I suddenly "Miss"? You were part of my growing up. Call me Bella, will you, like you always used to.'

'Ah, I did, didn't I?' Jack smiled, suddenly the gentle kindly man Bella remembered. 'Those were the days. It seems like a lifetime ago, though, doesn't it? Me and Martha, we haven't seen nor heard of you in so long. And now, ah well, it's all gone. All of it.'

Bella took a last lingering look around the ruins of the grand old house that had been her family home, fleetingly allowing herself to remember again the best times, before her mother had left, when she and her brother had not had a care in the world.

'Yes, Jack, it's all gone,' she said. 'Gone for good.'

The walk back to the car seemed quicker to Bella than the walk to the manor had done. But the territory was even more familiar now, and she had Jack by her side. He had always made her feel at ease and given her confidence.

Ever since she'd learned of the fire, Bella had been battling her own anger and frustration. They still lurked just beneath the surface. But it was only after parting company with Jack, and manoeuvring her car back along the farm track onto the road, that she gave in to her feelings. She pulled into the side and allowed her tears to flow. Tears of near rage. She had been horrified by the fire and the resulting deaths. She was now almost equally horrified by the aftermath. In both practical and emotional terms everything that had happened was a total disaster. A disaster, which, at that moment, she felt quite incapable of dealing with.

Her rage was directed at her father for his obduracy, at the extent of the fire damage which had exceeded her worst expectations, and at her own sense of helplessness and terrible foreboding.

Still struggling to control her tears she reached for her mobile. Then she thought better of it and put the phone away, started the motor, swung the car and began the drive back towards Taunton, still wondering exactly what she should do next.

At the top of Whiteball Hill, on the A38, she turned right into the lane that led down to Sampford Arundel, where she knew there was still a telephone kiosk. She parked up, and fished around for some coins in her pocket. The ever-threatening rain of the past couple of days was finally falling heavily again. She hurried to the phone box and dialled a number which she read off her mobile. It was the number she had consistently been trying to reach.

This time a man's voice answered.

'At last,' said Bella.

'OK. Before we start, no names, not mine, not yours, not anybody's, agreed?'

'I'm in a bloody call box.'

'I know, that's why I answered.'

'I've been trying to call you for two days.'

'Yes, from your mobile. Not only did I tell you never to do that, I also thought we had agreed we would not be in touch until this was all over.'

'I think a fire that claimed two lives has rather changed that, don't you?' riposted Bella, the sarcasm heavy in her voice.

'Oh, I don't know,' said the voice. 'It's all the same, it's what we wanted. A timely accident really. Things have just happened more quickly, that's all. Probably exactly what we needed.'

'It's not the bloody same, and it's not what I bloody needed.'

Bella knew she was shouting down the phone. She couldn't help it.

'Blackdown has been burned to the ground, and the police and the fire service are already pretty damned sure the fire was started deliberately—'

'Accidents do happen, my dear,' the voice interrupted calmly. 'Please try not to worry. Everything's going to be all right. I have it all under control.'

'How? How on earth could you have anything under control? People have been killed. And for nothing. Everything we need has been destroyed. The Taunton solicitor, he didn't have the will. He said he thought it was in that bloody storeroom. I've just been to the house, inside the place, or inside what's left of it. It's just rubble, the storeroom isn't there any more, I can't see how the will or any of those papers could possibly have survived, let alone all the beautiful things that were in the house, even the Gainsborough must have been destroyed for God's sake. And without those papers I don't know what we are going to do . . .'

'Not everything.'

'What do you mean, not everything?'

'Trust me, dear girl. There are still people who will do whatever is needed. The most important of the stored papers and, uh, certain other items, were removed before the fire. They will be forwarded to you in due course, so that you can get on with your job. The business is all that matters . . .'

Bella barely heard the last few words. She was still struggling to take in the import of what had been said first.

'That means you did know, you did know about the fire,' she blurted out. 'That it really wasn't an accident.'

'Does it?'

'Yes it bloody does. I wondered. Of course I did. I didn't want it to be true, but I feared it. And I was right. It's pretty damned obvious. You started it, didn't you? Or more likely you got . . .' Bella paused, remembering the instruction not to use names, and accepting she should obey it. For the time being, anyway. '. . . got a certain person to do it for you. Why don't you just admit it?'

The man on the other end of the line emitted an audible sigh. 'Well, clearly, if anyone started that fire deliberately it probably was the person you are referring to. The police seem to think so. He presumably had his own motives, totally unrelated to ours. He was always a dodgy character, wasn't he? And it really doesn't matter either way. It's all the better for our plans, that's what matters.'

'Not my bloody plans.'

'Oh yes, your bloody plans too. You are in on this, my dear. And you have been throughout. Aren't you forgetting that?'

It was true. Absolutely true. But not like this, never like this. Why had she allowed herself to become involved in this crazy plan? Bella realised she was trembling.

'I didn't know the half of it, did I?' she shouted into the phone. 'I didn't know anybody was going to die. There wasn't supposed to be a fire that would take two lives. That's double murder – which I did not sign up for . . .'

'Casualties of war,' said the voice calmly.

'We're not at bloody war,' stormed Bella. 'Never mind saving the company, never mind the money, we're going to jail, all of us . . .'

Bella's words came tumbling out in a torrent. It wasn't like her, but she was in shock and she knew that she sounded hysterical.

The voice that interrupted her was calm.

'We are not going to jail. None of us can ever be proven guilty of anything.'

'Really. I've just learned about the third death. This whole thing is going from bad to worse.'

'What do you mean?'

'As if you don't know, the body of a certain person was found in a canal in West London this morning. His death is being treated by the police as suspicious.'

'I didn't know that. So, what do you think I had to do with it? Do you think I pushed him in?'

'I wouldn't put it past you.'

'Thanks for the vote of confidence.'

'Yes, well, I'll tell you something you really may not be aware of. I don't know how much this man knew about the whole operation, and I don't know exactly what he did, or what he meant to do. But I can tell you one thing, I'm pretty sure his wife does.'

There was a brief silence.

'I'm not sure I understand what you're trying to say.'

'I'm trying to say that if you killed him because of what he did and what he knew, then you're probably going to have to kill his poor bloody wife, too,' Bella stormed.

'Really. I still don't understand you.'

'Oh, I think you do. But let me spell it out. I've seen the wife this evening. Her last words to me were "this wasn't supposed to happen". Then she clammed up. And she looked pretty damned terrified, as well she might, I suspect.'

'I see.'

The voice on the other end of the line sounded relaxed and non-committal.

'Do you?' Bella wasn't hysterical any more, just plain furious. 'Well, I wish I damned well did. You seem to have tricked everyone around you, including me. Situation normal, in fact.'

'I have tricked no one. You did sign up for this. Half of it was your idea.'

'Half of it maybe. Not the half that involved three murders.'

'I think you may be exaggerating, my dear.'

'Exaggerating? How the hell do you exaggerate death? I've had enough. I'm not sure I can carry on with any of this, and I can't continue this conversation, either—'

Bella was interrupted yet again by the still calm voice. 'Please don't do anything rash, dear, will you? Remember you're in this as deeply as anyone.'

Maybe it was the continuing calmness of that voice that finally did it. Bella just hung up.

SIXTEEN

Detective Sergeant Ted Dawson was in bed at his Wellington home and had just dropped off to sleep when the call came a few minutes after midnight.

It was control at Taunton police station.

'We've just had a 999 call from Janice Grey, out at Blackdown Manor, widow of that feller they pulled from a lock off the Thames, says there are armed intruders out there.'

Ted Dawson was suddenly wide awake.

'Right,' he said. 'What do you want me to do?'

'We wondered if you could take a run out there, have a look, as you're close. We're taking it seriously, obviously, we're sending a patrol car around and armed response are on their way. So, don't do anything rash. Just have a bit of a reccy. The woman's in quite a state. We haven't been able to get much sense out of her. But it could well be nothing. Apparently there were reports of armed intruders on the night of the fire, but nobody could find any evidence of that.'

'That's right,' said Ted Dawson. 'All part of the mystery.'

'Yes, and this could be another false alarm. But the boss says be careful.'

'Of course,' said Ted Dawson.

He left the house almost immediately. There was very little traffic. It took him a scant half hour to reach Blackdown Manor. As he approached he switched off his headlights. There was a watery moon giving a faint but indispensable light.

He continued to motor slowly toward the start of the drive, and The Gatehouse. The engine was barely ticking over. He just hoped he would be neither heard nor seen, if indeed there were intruders about.

When he reached the point in the road from which he could see The Gatehouse he slowed to a halt, switched off the engine, and wound down the driver's window to give himself a better view. The curtains were drawn but he could see chinks of light in at least a couple of rooms. At a glance, everything seemed normal. There did not seem to be a parked vehicle anywhere, other than the Range Rover in the driveway which he was pretty sure belonged to the Greys. But then, he reflected, if he were planning an uninvited entry into somebody else's home under cover of darkness, he would not park his vehicle right outside.

Just as he was pondering whether to risk approaching the house, the front door opened. Quite suddenly. A shadowy figure, clad in either black or very dark clothes, hurried out into the garden. Was this one of the reported intruders? It seemed likely, but was he armed? He was definitely clutching something that could be a handgun. Ted couldn't quite see, and was really only assuming that the shadowy figure was a man. A man who seemed to be looking for something. Or someone. Mrs Grey, perhaps?

The man pulled open the door of a shed to the left of the house, and seemed to look inside. Then he scooted around to the right of the house, briefly disappearing from sight. After a minute or so he reappeared and began to run towards the road – directly at Ted Dawson.

It was inevitable that he would see Ted's vehicle. And if he was armed, then Ted would be a sitting duck. Ted quickly switched on his engine and his headlights and leaned on the horn. The black-clad figure, face concealed by a balaclava of some sort, froze for just a second or two in the glare of the lights. To Ted's alarm, he definitely was carrying a hand gun, which he suddenly levelled at the windscreen of Ted's vehicle. Moving faster than he had in years, Ted stepped on the accelerator and drove straight at the armed man, who leapt to the left, ran back into the garden of The Gatehouse, and then along the path that led around to the back of the house.

Ted pulled to a halt, but kept his engine running and his headlights on for a minute or two. Then, when the man failed to reappear, he switched off his engine, and sat listening. The intruder – or intruders Mrs Grey had said – must have a vehicle parked somewhere, surely. Blackdown Manor was quite remote. Nobody would have walked there.

He was listening for an engine to start. At first he heard only silence. Then the sound of an engine, but not one being started up. Instead what Ted could hear was a vehicle approaching along the road outside the manor, possibly more than one. The palms of his hands were sweaty, as was the back of his neck. Ted Dawson wasn't armed. If this was the intruders' vehicle approaching, he was in no way prepared or able to deal with them. But surely they wouldn't come back, would they? After all, they didn't know he was alone and unarmed, he tried to reassure himself. Nonetheless he was worried. He wondered if he had time to turn his car around and take off in the opposite direction. But he could now see headlights approaching, and they were very close. He had no time at all. He switched his own headlights off. At least he wouldn't be quite such an easy target. The vehicle drew to a halt just the other side of The Gatehouse. It was a police Range Rover, almost certainly an Armed Response Vehicle.

Ted heaved a huge sigh of relief, stepped out of his car and walked towards the ARV, holding up his warrant card in one hand.

'Police,' he called. 'DC Ted Dawson.'

He was half blinded by the beam of a powerful torch.

'Over here,' called a voice from somewhere behind it.

Ted hurried over. He didn't think he'd ever been quite so glad to see anyone in his entire life before as this AR team.

He gave the team leader, who introduced himself as Sergeant Phil Phillips, a rundown of the events he had witnessed.

'Any sign of the woman?' asked Phillips. 'The woman who called this in?'

'No,' said Ted Dawson. 'Not that I've seen anyway.'

Ted knew that Phillips must be thinking what he was thinking. Would they find Janice Grey alive? And might there still be armed men in the house? Ted had only seen one man. It seemed that Janice Grey had indicated that there had been more than one. But she had, understandably, been in a panic.

'OK, you stay here, with our vehicle,' said Phillips.

He turned to his team.

'Mark, you stay with DC Dawson, and watch our backs. Ray, Johnno, you two with me.'

And with that he led the two officers, at a crouched run, towards The Gatehouse. The door was still ajar. Phillips kicked it wide open with one foot.

'Armed police,' he called loudly. Then again: 'Armed police. If there is anyone in the house come out now. If you are armed, put down your arms. Come out with your hands up.'

No one emerged. There continued to appear to be no sign of life inside the house. No sound. No movement.

Almost immediately Phil Phillips led his little team inside.

Ted was full of apprehension as he watched and waited. It seemed like a very long time before the AR team emerged from the house, but was probably only four or five minutes.

They were alone. No armed men, and no Janice Grey. But that did not necessarily mean she wasn't still inside. And if she was, she was likely to be either dead or seriously injured, Ted suspected.

'Have you found the woman, have you found Mrs Grey?' he blurted out anxiously.

'No, the house is empty,' replied Phillips. 'There's nobody there at all.'

They found Janice Grey at dawn the next morning. She was alive. Although suffering from exposure and nervous exhaustion.

A preliminary search had been launched as soon as AR had declared the immediate area clear, but after a couple of hours or so had been called off until daylight. Constable Joe Curry, twenty-two and fresh from police college, was one of those assigned to search the ruins of the manor house.

They found Mrs Grey cowering in an exposed part of the basement area of the old house, hiding beneath a tepee of half collapsed beams. She was in a state of total terror.

'Police, we're the police,' shouted Constable Curry. 'It's all right you're safe now. We're here.'

It took several minutes and the help of two other officers to quieten the woman. She was quite hysterical. At first, she seemed unable to grasp that the danger she had faced during the preceding night was no longer present.

'You're safe, really, you're quite safe,' said Joe Curry, for the umpteenth time.

Janice Grey looked at him with frightened eyes, but eyes which did at least appear to be finally seeing the young constable. It seemed, however, that she remained unconvinced.

'Safe?' she queried. 'I'm not safe. And I never will be again.'

'We're going to look after you,' continued Joe, oblivious to the somewhat amused looks he was receiving from his more seasoned colleagues. 'We're going to get you to hospital and have you checked out, then we'll take it from there.'

Janice Grey was barely listening. 'They'll get me,' she said. 'I escaped this time, I won't again.'

A paramedic team was approaching.

Suddenly the woman stood up, finding strength which totally took young Joe aback.

'I don't want them,' she said, pointing at the paramedics. 'They can't help me. I want Detective Inspector Vogel. I want to tell him everything.'

Vogel had already arrived at Blackdown by the time Janice Grey was found. He and Saslow had been awoken in the early hours, and had delayed their trip to London once they learned of the night's events at Blackdown. They were standing outside The Gatehouse, drinking welcome paper cups of coffee poured from huge thermos flasks provided for the search team, when they learned that Janice had been located. And that she was alive.

'She wants to talk to you,' the team leader told him. 'Now.'

'C'mon, Saslow,' said Vogel at once, abandoning his coffee. 'Let's get to her before she changes her mind.'

The two officers hurried to their car and Saslow drove as fast as she dared down the driveway, which had at least now been cleared of all remaining debris from the storm.

Mrs Grey, wrapped in a thermal blanket, was being helped from the ruins of the old manor by two women paramedics. She spotted Vogel as soon as he stepped out of his car, and at once attempted to shake herself free of her supporters.

'Let me go,' she cried. 'Let me go. I have to speak to Mr Vogel. Right away.'

The paramedics tried to restrain her. 'We need to get you to hospital first,' said the taller of the two women.

'No, no,' shouted Janice, who appeared close to hysteria again. 'I'm not going anywhere until I've spoken to Mr Vogel,' she repeated.

By then, Vogel was at the woman's side. 'It's all right, Mrs Grey,' he said. 'I'm here.'

He placed a calming hand on the woman's arms, then turned

slightly to address the paramedics. 'Why don't you just give us ten minutes before you take Mrs Grey away?' he said. 'In your ambulance or our car. And somebody get her a hot drink or something.'

The paramedics exchanged glances. 'I don't like it,' said the taller one.

Both women looked doubtful.

'Your car,' interjected Janice Grey, addressing Vogel with surprising assertiveness. 'Just you and me.'

This time she successfully shook herself free of the paramedics, and Vogel proceeded to escort her to the vehicle whilst the medics looked uncertainly on.

'So, what exactly is it you want to tell me, Mrs Grey?' asked Vogel, once the pair of them were safely ensconced on the back seat.

The woman no longer seemed quite so sure of herself.

'I'm frightened half out of my wits, I'll tell you that,' she said. 'It's all gone wrong, you see. The fire, none of it, none of it was supposed to happen. Not like this. And then my George . . .'

Her voice tailed off.

'Mrs Grey, you said that before, what exactly do you mean by "none of it was supposed to happen"?' asked Vogel.

Janice Grey shook her head, very slowly, from side to side. Her voice was quiet when she spoke again, barely more than a whisper. 'It wasn't,' she said. 'It really wasn't. Nobody was meant to be harmed. My George wouldn't hurt a fly, not my George. And now he's gone. They've killed him. Killed my George, that's what they've done.'

'Who, Mrs Grey? Who has killed George?'

'I don't know, I really don't know. That's the trouble. But they tried to do me in 'an all last night. I'm damned sure of that.'

'Mrs Grey, why don't you try to tell me what you do know,' encouraged Vogel.

The woman looked confused. 'Yes,' she said. 'Yes. That's what I want to do. It's just, well, it's all such a mess. And I don't know where to begin.'

'You could try to begin at the beginning, Mrs Grey,' said Vogel.

The woman nodded. 'I must, I must,' she said, almost as if she was addressing herself.

'It began just over a year ago. My George, well, he knows people, doesn't he? You know, people who do thing others can't. Or won't.'

Vogel got the picture. After all, George Grey was a petty criminal with a considerable record of minor offences. Additionally, over the years he had probably been involved in all kinds of nefarious activities which had never come to the attention of the law. He almost certainly did know people able and willing to perform all kinds of undesirable services.

'I understand,' said Vogel.

And he did. Only too well.

'Yes,' murmured Janice Grey. 'Anyway, my George knew a man who knew a man who knew Sir John. George was asked if he might be prepared to look after Sir John. That meant coming down here and setting up home here. Driving, working around the place, gardening, odd jobs, that sort of thing, and a bit of security. But the inference was that George may be asked to do things above and beyond the usual call of duty. However, the pay would more than compensate. And I would be employed too. We didn't know as what exactly at first. We didn't know Sir John was ill. That was what this was all about. That and the money.'

'The money?' queried Vogel.

'Yes. The money. It's always about money with people like that, isn't it? Anyway, George and I talked it over. And it didn't take much talking about. Things was pretty bad for us, well, my bit of trouble didn't help . . .'

The woman paused. 'It was lies all of it. Like I told you before. And so the court found. But my work, my real work, was gone for good. It's true enough what they say too. Mud sticks. We managed to get a little house in Stepney, when we got together, but we couldn't keep up the payments. I still had legal fees to pay, and then George lost 'is market stall. We'd 'ad some good times, as well as the bad, mind. Never a lot of in-between, though, and latterly there'd been only bad times.

'So, we both agreed, if the deal was as good as was being promised we'd have to go for it. We knew it was a bit dodgy, of course, but we reckoned a man like Sir John Fairbrother would know what he was about, that we wouldn't be at too much risk. And George, well, he was always a bit of a chancer.

'It was arranged that George would meet Sir John, and when he came back, well, I could tell he'd been shocked by something, but he never did tell me what it was. He just said he couldn't believe his luck. The deal was good all right. We'd have The Gatehouse to live in, rent free, and we'd be paid £1,000 a week each. There'd be opportunity for bonuses too. Big bonuses. "What will we have to do for them," I asked. "You won't have to do anything," George said. "It'll be all down to me." Of course, it didn't work out like that. But George said that's how it would be, and they wanted me too, because I was a nurse, Sir John had Parkinson's, and he was determined to keep his condition as quiet as possible. So the bank wouldn't be harmed. "That was all," said George.

'Well, I should have realised, even if George didn't, if something looks too good to be true, it usually is. But when we got here, everything did seem all right for a while. Albeit a bit odd. We didn't see Sir John for a long time. Or I didn't anyway. By the time I met him for the first time it was obvious he was a very sick man, badly affected by his illness. He needed me then, didn't he? His speech was the worst. He'd taken the decision to shut himself off from the world, and our job, George and mine, was to look after him and keep the world out.

'Then one day George came in, looking a bit shaken, and he said Sir John had told him he wanted him to burn the house down.'

At first Vogel thought he must have misheard.

'Sir John told George what?'

'That he wanted him to burn the house down.' Janice Grey sounded quite matter of fact.

'With him in it?' queried Vogel, trying to sound just a matter of fact.

'Well yes, apparently that's what Sir John wanted so it wouldn't look like he could have had anything to do with it.'

'Ummm. Rather a high-risk strategy then, as it turned out,' said Vogel mildly.

'I told you, Mr Vogel, none of that was supposed to have happened. Nobody was supposed to get hurt.'

'Right. And did George tell you why Sir John wanted him to burn down his house with him in it?'

'Yes. It was because he had money troubles. Big financial

problems. His own, personal like, and the bank. He wanted the insurance money. That's what he was after.'

'Mrs Grey, there's no doubt Blackdown Manor was a valuable property and would have been substantially insured, but in terms of bailing out an international bank the amount involved would be little more than a drop in the ocean, don't you think?'

'I wouldn't know about that, would I? There was a Gainsborough portrait, wasn't there, worth millions? George said it was all about cash flow. Sir John just needed to keep all his balls in the air for a few more months.' Janice Grey managed a small smile. 'He always talked like that, did my George,' she commented.

'So, it was George who set fire to the house?'

'Well yes, but only because Sir John wanted him to. He told George there was going to be an enormous bonus for him. A six-figure sum, George said.'

'And do I assume then, that there were no armed intruders?' Vogel asked.

Janice Grey coloured slightly. She shook her head.

'So how did your husband suffer those stab wounds?'

Janice looked away from Vogel, avoiding his steady gaze. 'I really couldn't say.'

'They were rather unusual injuries, as I am sure you know,' Vogel said. 'There was a great deal of blood, but your husband suffered only relatively superficial damage to his body. Extra-ordinarily fortunate placement, the doctor said at the Musgrove.'

Janice Grey remained silent and continued to look away from Vogel.

'C'mon, Mrs Grey,' persisted Vogel. 'You know perfectly well where I am going with this, don't you?'

'I do not. I have no idea at all.'

'I think you have, Janice. I believe your husband's wounds were inflicted in such a way that as little damage as possible was caused by them. You are an experienced nurse. You would have been able to do that. You would have known how to execute stab wounds so that they actually did far less harm than at first would have appeared. You could do that, couldn't you?'

'What?'

Janice Grey's face was already very pale, her eyes sharply defined in dark wells. She seemed to grow even paler. Just as her husband had done in hospital earlier when Vogel had cross-examined him about his part in the fatal fire.

'I couldn't stab anyone, I just couldn't,' she insisted. 'Not under any circumstances. And certainly not Georgie. My poor Georgie.'

She appeared to be choking back tears. Vogel had neither the time nor the inclination to be sympathetic. This was a woman who had already stood trial for murder. In spite of her protestations, who knew what she was really capable of? It was certainly now beginning to look as if both the Greys had been involved to some degree or another in the fire which had razed Blackdown Manor to the ground and taken the lives of two people.

He ploughed on.

'All right then, Mrs Grey. It's time you started telling me what did happen that night instead of what you claim didn't. If you didn't stab your husband, either in complicity with him or not, and you have admitted there weren't any intruders, armed or otherwise, then who did?'

Janice Grey stifled another sob. 'He did,' she said.

'I'm sorry,' responded Vogel. 'Who is "he"?'

'George. My Georgie stabbed himself.'

'Your husband stabbed himself?' queried Vogel.

He couldn't keep the surprise from his voice. That was something he hadn't considered. He could hardly believe it was possible.

The woman nodded.

'That's hard to believe, Mrs Grey.'

Janice Grey narrowed her eyes. 'Yes, well, that's as may be,' she said. 'But that's what happened.'

She shot out the last words with a certain amount of latent aggression.

'Could you perhaps explain exactly how it happened, Mrs Grey?'

The woman stared blankly ahead. She was clearly very weak. Vogel wondered if he should call the paramedics, but at once dismissed the thought. He needed her story. And he needed it now.

'Were you there, Mrs Grey?' he asked. 'Were you with George when he stabbed himself?'

'Yes.'

The woman's voice was small.

'So, what happened? C'mon, Mrs Grey!'

Vogel was a patient man. But he had his limits.

'C'mon,' he repeated, more loudly. 'Tell me what happened.'

Janice Grey turned her head slightly, and looked Vogel in the eye.

'I told George what to do,' she said.

'What? You told your husband to stab himself?'

'No, no, not that.' The woman sounded impatient. 'I'd never have done that. George insisted that I showed him where to stab himself. So that there would be a lot of blood, but not a lot of serious damage. That was the plan. To make it look as if he'd been attacked. George said Sir John was going to make all the pain worthwhile, that the bonus he was going to get would be enough for us to buy our own place again.'

'Didn't either of you think that setting the house on fire with your employer in it was just a little bit dangerous? Unless you meant for him to die, of course.'

'We didn't, I swear we didn't. George knew what he was doing, you see. He trained to be a fireman years ago. He said it was a piece of cake to start a fire which would undermine the structure of the building, but not endanger Sir John in his bedroom. George was careful, he started the fire at the front of the house. Sir John and his nurse were in his bedroom at the back, and it was supposed to be fire-proofed, that's what George said anyway.'

'But Sir John was endangered, Mrs Grey. About as endangered as you can get. His bedroom may have had fire-proofing, but once that gas tank went off and pretty much lifted the roof from the place, it would have been worse than useless. Sir John died in the fire. Along with his nurse. So what went wrong?'

'I don't know. It all went according to plan at first. George lit the fire at the front, blocking the main entrance. He piled up some furniture and poured on petrol. I mean, it was always going to look like arson, he suspected that the firefighters would guess that early on, but he didn't need to hide anything because he was blaming all of it on armed intruders. We knew Sir John and the nurse were going to tell the police there were armed intruders. So, we just thought that would be accepted, and if nobody had died it probably would have been. Anyway, I went over to the house and helped George, helped him stab himself. Then I went back to The Gatehouse, leaving George outside the front of the house on his own. George was sure that the fact that he appeared to be so badly stabbed would shift suspicion away from him. And it would have done, surely, if, if . . .'

'If the gas tank hadn't exploded and two people hadn't died? Is that what you are trying to say, Mrs Grey?'

The woman nodded. 'I was in The Gatehouse, looking out through a window. I'd just seen the first fire engine arrive, everything seemed to be going to plan, and then there was this enormous explosion. The entire house just turned into a fireball, instantly. It was pretty obvious it would be a miracle if anyone came out of that alive. I couldn't believe it. Nothing like that was supposed to happen, you see.'

'Mrs Grey, domestic gas tanks do not readily explode. The fire investigators suspect that the tank had been tampered with. Was your husband responsible for that too?'

'No. Of course not.'

The woman was clearly agitated, and indignant, somewhat bizarrely so under the circumstances, thought Vogel.

'No. My Georgie wouldn't have done that. Everybody knows what happens when gas explodes. He just lit a little fire at the front of the house. Just enough for Sir John to be able to claim his insurance. That's all my Georgie did.'

Vogel was not at all sure that George Grey hadn't been responsible for everything which led to the catastrophic fire, but he decided not to push the point. He wanted as much information as he could glean from Janice Grey, whilst her defences were down.

'Did you see your husband again that night, after you'd helped him to stab himself?'

'No, well not here, not at the manor. None of the emergency vehicles could get through at first, could they? So they were all at the end of the drive, right by The Gatehouse. There were armed policemen everywhere too. I stayed indoors, out of the way, only went outside the once, when the house exploded. I couldn't help myself. But after that, I went back in, like the fireman told me. I didn't have any choice. It was hours before the fire engines moved down towards the house, and the ambulances.'

'But weren't you worried about George? You knew he must be lying there injured? You'd been instrumental in that, after all.'

'Only because he made me. And, of course, I was worried. I knew he must have lost a lot of blood. It was terrible, terrible, just sitting there waiting and doing nothing. But George had told me to go home and keep my head down, so that's what I did. I saw an ambulance leave, and then this police officer came and knocked on the door. He told me George had been injured. He asked me some questions, which I avoided as best I could, then eventually he told me where George had been taken, and I drove in to Taunton hospital after him.'

'Yes, you went to the hospital. You saw George there, and spoke to him, I presume? Because I am told your husband never totally lost consciousness, in spite of his injuries.'

'Yes. I hadn't been back from The Musgrove long when you and that woman police officer arrived.'

'So, what did your husband tell you that he wouldn't have told me?'

'Well I don't know what he told you, do I—'

'C'mon, Mrs Grey, you know exactly what I mean,' interrupted Vogel.

'All right, all right. Well, George was a bit woozy, they'd sedated him so they could stitch up his wounds. And he was shocked and frightened, frightened he might get done for murder. He said he couldn't understand what had happened. The gas tank was right at the back of the house, and several metres away from the house. George said they don't explode easily either, those tanks.'

Vogel was intrigued. Could it really be possible that George Grey was as puzzled by the exact cause of the explosion as everybody else?

'What did your husband think might have happened, Mrs Grey?' he asked.

'George thought somebody must have tampered with the tank, so that it leaked, or something like that. That's what he told me anyway.'

'And who did he think that somebody might have been?'

'He had no idea, no idea at all.'

'Are you quite sure that your husband wasn't the person who tampered with the tank?'

'Of course he wasn't,' said Janice Grey firmly. 'My George wasn't a murderer. And he knew how dangerous that would have been, to have gas leaking into the house. He wouldn't have done anything like that.'

'But, Mrs Grey, you have admitted that it was your husband who set the house on fire. And you were both aware that he intended to do that, and that he had carried out his intention. Wasn't that dangerous enough in itself?'

'Look, George was quite sure the fire services would get there and put the fire out before any harm came to Sir John or his nurse. And that's what would have happened if somebody hadn't interfered. He was sure of that. Told me in the hospital he still believed that.'

'Who do you think did interfere, Mrs Grey?'

'I don't know, do I? No more than George did. But I'll bet it's the same people who did for my George, and then came looking for mc last night. They're ruthless murdering scum, it's because of them Sir John and his nurse died in the fire. Not because of my George.'

'And yet your George chose to execute this plan on a night when the only means of access to Blackdown Manor for fire appliances was blocked by a fallen tree, did he not?'

'Well yes.'

'If he didn't wish Sir John to come to any harm, why would he do that?'

'He'd been afraid the fire services might get here too quickly and put out the blaze before enough damage was done to the place for Sir John to make sufficient money out of his insurance claim. When the tree came down that seemed to be the perfect opportunity. He and Sir John agreed that would be the night. George said it would still be all right because the firemen would be able to carry some sort of hand-held pump through. But it would all take just that bit longer—'

Janice Grey was interrupted then by a hovering paramedic who knocked on the car window. 'I'm sorry, detective inspector, we really must get Mrs Grey to hospital,' she said.

Vogel nodded his assent, and watched in silence as Janice Grey was helped from the MCIT pool car and led to the waiting ambulance.

SEVENTEEN

That same morning Bella Fairbrother had been woken in her Mount Somerset hotel room by the ring of her mobile phone. She was still half asleep when she answered. She had, after all, been awake half the night fretting about what her next course of action should be, and had only finally dropped off a couple of hours earlier.

'It's Jimmy,' said her caller.

Jimmy. Jimmy Martins, the recently appointed acting chairman of Fairbrother's. Bella could see the time at the top of her screen. It was just before seven a.m.

'I'm sorry to call so early,' he continued. 'But I'm afraid this can't wait. I've been up all night going through the figures. It's even worse than we thought . . .'

Bella tried to shake herself into full wakefulness. It wasn't worse than *she* thought, that was for sure. But Jimmy Martins didn't know the half of it. He had always been her father's stooge. He was still a stooge, which was why Bella had pressed the board to offer him the chair, and him to take it, if only on a temporary basis. Bella did feel at least a tad guilty about that, unlike her father, to whom guilt had always been a stranger. She let Martins carry on talking.

'The bank seems to be operating by osmosis,' he went on. 'There is just no substance to anything. I had no idea how bad things were. And I spent most of yesterday dodging the financial press, Bella. They're on to it.'

'I've told you, Jimmy, once I've got hold of the will and all the paperwork, we can start unravelling the various trusts that will now come into fruition following my father's death. You know how it works. How it's always worked. Upon the death of the oldest surviving Fairbrother these trusts automatically yield huge bonuses, but remain ongoing for future generations—'

'My God, you mean you aren't even in possession of the will yet, nor all those other papers?' interrupted Martins.

He sounded as desperate as Bella was beginning to feel. But, on a kind of autopilot, she behaved as she always did, doing her best both to sound assertive and to conceal her own feelings.

'Everything is in hand, Jimmy,' she said, knowing only too well how far that was from the truth.

'We don't have much time,' replied Martins. 'The bank is a mirage. And the news is clearly out. The shares are going through the floor. Look, Bella, your father died in a fire. How long will it be before he is officially declared dead, before a death certificate is issued? It could be weeks. Months even. I don't know if we can hold on that long.'

'Of course, we can. Fairbrother's has gone through worse than this in three centuries of trading. You just have to hold your nerve, Jimmy.'

'You sound disconcertingly like your father at times,' responded Martins. 'Look, there's more. There are all sorts of irregularities in the figures. Particularly concerning pensions. I've been looking into not only the Fairbrother International pension funds, but also those of some of the subsidiaries. All too often the sums just don't add up. Did you know about this, Bella?'

'Of course not. I came off the board of Fairbrother's over a year ago, remember, Jimmy . . .'

'If I'm right about this, something has been going on for a lot longer than a year, Bella. These funds have been tampered with, I'm almost sure of it.'

'Jimmy, you must be mistaken,' said Bella, hoping she sounded more convincing than she felt. 'My father would never countenance anything untoward concerning pension funds. Apart from the terrible betrayal of trust, he would have known just how catastrophic it could prove, not just for the bank but right across all the Fairbrother business interests. I think everyone involved with administering pensions learned that from the Robert Maxwell debacle.'

'It depends how desperate someone is, and I am beginning to suspect that your father was very desperate indeed,' said Martins.

Bella leaned back against the pillows, and briefly closed her eyes, so wishing that the entire scenario in which she had, she now realised, so unwisely allowed herself to become embroiled, would just disappear. And that included, at that moment, Jimmy

Martins, who had absolutely no idea of the true extent of her
father's desperation. For a moment, she had no words. Neither
did he have any idea that the whole lot of them, including the
board, might be indirectly involved in crimes far greater than
embezzlement.

Mercifully she didn't have to say anything. Martins was
continuing to speak.

'Look, to be frank, all of us on the board knew things weren't
quite how they should be, and obviously it was public knowledge
that our share prices were well below par. But that is the case
with many big companies nowadays, and I think we all believed
that your father would find a way through, as he always had. I
suppose we could be accused of having had our heads in the sand.
But Sir John was a brilliant businessman, of course. Quite exceptional. Even after he became ill, and ultimately ceased to come
into the offices, he continued to run the show. Well, you know
what he was like.'

'I certainly do,' said Bella, with more than a little feeling.

'Yes. Of course, you do.'

He paused, and Bella thought she could hear him taking a deep
breath before he spoke again.

'The thing is, Bella, and I've been considering this all night, in
view of everything I have now learned, I do not feel I can continue
as acting chairman of Fairbrother's. I intend to offer my resignation to the board later today. Out of respect for both you and your
father, I wanted you to be the first to know—'

Bella sat bolt upright in bed. She no longer felt sleepy.

'For God's sake, Jimmy, you mustn't do that,' she said, aware
that her voice was much louder than she had intended, but unable
to do anything about it. 'You can't do that. You really can't. It
was only two days ago that you accepted the appointment. Nothing
has changed since then.'

'Actually Bella, everything has changed. I now know so much
more about the dire state the business is in, and also, I have a
fair idea of the extent of highly dubious business practice which
has led to this. There are other concerns too, of course, the fire
which killed your father could be arson, and the man the police
were looking for in connection with it has died in suspicious
circumstances. I really cannot continue—'

Bella interrupted there, deliberately ignoring the last part of what Jimmy Martins had been trying to say.

'Jimmy, look, once the trust funds have been realised we should be able to effectively settle any financial irregularities,' she began. 'I can assure you that would always be my intention. And there are billions involved here.'

'I'm not prepared to wait, Bella. The risk is too great. As chairman, albeit recently elected acting chairman, I am technically responsible for the whole awful mess. But it was not of my doing, and I am not prepared to carry that responsibility now that I have learned the extent of the—'

Bella tried again. 'All right, Jimmy,' she said. 'I do understand. But will you at least wait until I have collated all the information I have gathered over the last couple of days, and until we can have a face-to-face meeting.'

'Well, I don't know . . .'

'Jimmy, I am sure you don't wish to be seen to have presided over the fall of Fairbrother's. Look, I'm planning to come back to London today. Can we meet early tomorrow morning?'

'I'm not sure I can afford to wait that long. Can't you make it this afternoon?'

'Well, late afternoon perhaps. I could come to the office at, say, five? I have other meetings first which could have a really positive bearing on the situation.'

'I just don't know, Bella—' responded Jimmy.

'Yes, you do,' Bella interrupted. 'Please trust me. You owe it to this family, surely, after all these years.'

Jimmy Martins seemed to take a very long time to answer. 'All right,' he said eventually. 'Five p.m. this afternoon it is. But I have to tell you, Bella, I really do not think there is anything you could possibly say that might make me change my mind.'

'Look, at this stage I just want to thank you for the opportunity to attempt to do so,' said Bella, before ending the call.

She climbed out of bed, reached for her hotel issue towelling dressing gown, and sat down on the couch by the window, holding her aching head in both hands.

She had once read some words of wisdom that would stay with her always, and indeed had often comforted her in bad times. If you feel like committing suicide, wait until tomorrow.

Part of the thinking behind that, she'd always assumed, was that tomorrow never came.

Her tomorrow, however, had arrived with a vengeance. She was in a corner she could see no way out of. The events of the previous night had shocked her to the core.

She hadn't exactly lied to Jimmy Martins. There were no meetings in her diary for that day, but she was seriously considering arranging at least one. Although that certainly was unlikely to have the positive influence she had promised the acting chairman. She'd merely said the first thing that came into her head in order to stall the man – perhaps only delaying the inevitable, but at least giving herself time to think. If she took the course of action she was considering, it would be she who would prematurely pull the plug on Fairbrother's, not Jimmy Martins.

Bella was no saint, nor had she ever been. She was probably one of the toughest businesswomen in the world, certainly one of the toughest in international banking.

Even the remotest possibility of suicide had never crossed her mind before. But it might have been a serious consideration on that awful morning, were it not for her daughter. Kim had been brought up without a father, in the lap of luxury, yes, but by a mother who was all too often preoccupied with her career. Nonetheless Bella loved her daughter dearly, and one thing she could not do was leave her alone. Neither was she at all sure that she could allow Kim to grow up without having a mother whom she could respect. A mother who, ultimately, had tried to do the right thing. Albeit probably too little too late.

However, she might still be wrong in her judgement of the situation she found herself in. And she could end up putting her own future and that of the bank in jeopardy for no good reason. It was the kind of dilemma she had never, in her most nightmarish dreams, imagined having to face.

In spite of everything that had happened, including the events of the last few days, Bella had an intense pride in, and loyalty to, her family and the family business. She had often made it clear she would do anything to protect Fairbrother's and ensure the future of the bank. She had also always retained huge professional respect, if nothing else, for her father. And it was all of those factors which had combined to lead her to her present lamentable circumstances.

It seemed not to be true, after all, that she would do anything for Fairbrother's. She had a limit. And she suspected she had reached it. Actually, she may have progressed beyond it. She believed she was partially responsible for three deaths. Three murders. She did not know for certain that there had been three murders, of course, neither did she know if she could be held legally responsible – and in fact she suspected that she could not be, not yet anyway. But her involvement in the complex sequence of events which had led to the fire at Blackdown, and to those three deaths, could surely be proven. In any case, even if she faced neither prosecution nor any other form of restitution, she would have to live with that possibility.

She checked her watch. It was still only 7.30 a.m.. Too early to reasonably make the phone call she found herself pondering. In any case, once she had made that call, she would be setting in motion a chain of unstoppable procedures which could lead irrevocably to her own downfall and that of the bank. She decided to have a long hot shower in an attempt to clear her beleaguered head.

An hour and a half later, showered, dressed, and sitting again on the couch by the window, this time drinking strong coffee and picking at a room-service breakfast, she found that, whilst her head was a little clearer, she remained no less troubled. Should she make that phone call, or not? If she did, there would be no going back. That was for certain.

She switched on the TV, the regional news programme. The lead item was a break in at The Gatehouse at Blackdown Manor. Armed intruders had been seen on the premises. Police were anxious to locate the householder, Mrs Janice Grey, who was missing.

Bella recoiled in shock. The bulletin indicated that the incident had occurred during the night, just a few hours after she had made her phone call from the public box on Whiteball Hill.

Without giving herself any more time to think she picked up her phone and dialled David Vogel's mobile number.

He answered at once, as seemed to be his wont, in spite of the early hour, for which Bella apologised.

'Don't apologise, Miss Fairbrother,' responded Vogel. 'I'm running a murder inquiry. There is no early.'

'Uh right,' continued Bella. 'Look, I've just seen a news bulletin about a break-in at the Gatehouse. It says Mrs Grey is missing, I was wondering—'

'She's safe, Miss Fairbrother,' said Vogel. 'She was found soon after daybreak. I believe a media statement is being prepared.'

Bella found herself overcome with relief. She wasn't sure if she could deal with another death, whoever was responsible.

'I'm very glad, Mr Vogel,' she said. 'Look, I was hoping you might have time to meet up today. I have some information for you, something I would like to discuss with you which I feel I can no longer keep to myself. It's quite important.'

'Well, of course,' replied Vogel. 'Can you give me any indication of what it might be about?'

'No, no I can't,' said Bella quickly. 'I need to see you. Face to face. It's all too, too . . .' She paused, searching for the right words. 'Delicate,' she finished, rather lamely, she thought.

'And I sense that it's urgent?'

'Yes. It is. Most urgent, I suspect.'

'I see. Where are you, Miss Fairbrother? Are you still in Somerset?'

Bella replied that she was.

Vogel and Saslow were by then well on their way to London, just ten minutes or so from the junction between the M5 and the M4. Their journey had already been delayed by The Gatehouse incident. Vogel was eager to meet up with Nobby Clarke at Brentford and share details of their investigations.

'Right, well that's a tad tricky,' continued Vogel. 'Unfortunately, I am on my way to London. There are inquiries I need to conduct in the city, primarily concerning the Greys, and what has happened to both of them. And there is also the post-mortem on George Grey later today. Are you sure you couldn't at least give me the gist of what you have to say now, on the phone?'

'No. No, I really can't. But I'm also travelling back to London today. Indeed, I shall leave quite soon. I could meet you anywhere you like, after about one-ish probably.'

'Or, I could get another MCIT detective over to you from Wellington straight away—'

'No, Mr Vogel, I really want to see you,' interrupted Bella.

She couldn't quite explain why it had to be David Vogel that she talked to, but she had noticed his intelligent eyes and his thoughtful sensitive manner. She could not bear the thought of confiding in some clumsy plod.

'OK, the post-mortem is at 1.30 p.m. We could meet as soon as I've seen all I need to. That should certainly be by about three, I would have thought, possibly earlier.'

'Right. Where?'

'Well, I shall be at the morgue at the West Middlesex hospital. Let me think. You won't want to come there—'

'Can you come to me?' interrupted Bella. 'I live in Chelsea Harbour. It's the right side of town from Brentford. We could meet at my flat, then it won't matter if you are unsure of the time.'

'All right,' said Vogel. 'I shall try to make it by 3.30, but thank you for bearing with me.'

Bella was aware that would probably make her late for her meeting with Jimmy Martins. But, that appointment remained one she might ultimately not wish to keep. She gave Vogel her address and ended the call.

She then tried to return her attention to her breakfast, but had little appetite. Bella Fairbrother was extremely worried. She had no idea whether she was doing the right thing or not. But more and more, it seemed the only course of action she would be able to live with.

She abandoned her breakfast tray and headed for the bathroom to complete her morning routine. She hadn't yet put on her make-up. Bella never liked to face the world without her make-up, and she had also come to believe over the years that her brain worked better once she was fully made up. On this occasion she didn't think it would help, but she could only go through the motions.

She'd just opened the bathroom door when her room phone rang. She assumed it was room service or reception calling. Nonetheless, out of habit, she hurried to answer the call.

'Hello, sis,' said the still familiar voice of her only brother. 'Fancy a visitor?'

'Ah, so you *are* in the country . . .' she began, then a thought occurred to her. 'You're calling on the hotel phone. How did you know I was here?'

'How do you think,' replied Freddie Fairbrother laconically. 'Can I come up?'

'What do you mean, come up? Where are you?'

'I'm downstairs, Bella, speaking from the phone at reception.'

'I don't believe it. You've got a cheek after all this time. You could at least have let me know you were coming. OK. C'mon up. Room twenty-four.'

'Trust me, you're going to be pleased to see me.'

'I'm sure,' said Bella, who couldn't actually have been less sure. She remained in some trepidation for the two or three minutes until Freddie knocked on her room door.

The man who stood in the corridor was older and, if anything, thinner. His sun-bleached white-blonde hair was certainly thinner, and he had a tan like old leather. He was wearing faded jeans, a slightly crumpled shirt beneath a well-worn leather bomber jacket; the same clothes, in fact, that he had worn for the flight from Australia. And they looked like that, too. All the same Freddie managed to remain vaguely attractive, in a frazzled sort of way.

He smiled his laconic smile. Familiar even after so long. It was the same old Freddie.

'Christ, you look rough, sis,' he said, by way of greeting.

She smiled back, a strained little smile. As children they had always indulged in rough banter, casually throwing insults at each other. But there had been a great affection between them all those years ago, until it had been pretty much destroyed by their massively bitter falling out. And Bella would never forget that awful time, as she was quite sure her brother wouldn't, in spite of what she had always regarded as his carefully cultivated air of laissez faire.

That was history, of course. But could there now be any sort of future for either of them? In the last twenty-four hours Bella had more or less decided there could not be.

Nonetheless she stood back to usher her brother into her room.

'I haven't got my war-paint on, and, of course, there's the little matter of twenty years having passed since we last saw each other,' she said. 'Oh, and you don't look so hot yourself, by the way.'

Freddie was still smiling. 'I came more or less straight here from the airport,' he said. 'But I did stop to be given this. By a courier.'

He held up the calfskin briefcase he was carrying, offering

it to Bella. She took it from him, glancing at him question-
ingly. Although she had a pretty good idea what he was going
to tell her.

'It contains, amongst other things, our father's will,' said Freddie.

'I see. And, I assume you already know the crux of that will?'

'Of course.'

'Well, go on then.'

'Pretty much as was agreed beforehand. Our father's share-
holding is split between us, sixty per cent to you and forty per
cent to me, with the proviso that neither of us can sell those
shares for a minimum of a twenty-year period. There are letters
in there—' he waved a hand at the briefcase – 'from our father
expressing his wish to the board that you are appointed chairman
and chief executive. His wish, as you know, was that I should
take no real active part, but that I should be appointed to the
board more or less to enhance the Fairbrother presence and ensure
Fairbrother family interests. There is also, I was told, everything
in that briefcase that you will need to sort out the trust funds
and rescue the bank.'

Bella shook her head in amazement, already beginning to
feel as despairing of her brother's lack of grasp of reality as
she always had.

'Just like that?' she queried.

'Well, it was always the plan, wasn't it?'

'It may have been better had our father trusted me a little more
when he was running the bank, don't you think?' she asked. 'And,
the plan, Freddie, seems to have gone a little array, do you not
think?'

'I don't know what you mean.'

'Freddie, three people have died, all of them probably murdered,
that wasn't part of any plan I agreed to. I assume you have some
conception of that.'

'Yes, but Bella, the old man only had months to live anyway,
at the most. And George Grey had his own reasons for starting the
fire. If he did start it . . .'

'Of course, he bloody started it. And you really think that was
his own idea, do you?'

'Yes, I do. Of course, I do. It certainly had nothing to do
with me, that was for sure.'

Bella found she was beginning to feel angry. She had to make a real effort to keep her voice level.

'Freddie, I should have expected this from you,' she said. 'You always have believed only what you want to believe, and behaved exactly how you wanted to behave. Nothing has ever had anything to do with you, and nothing is ever your fault. You may have spent twenty years lotus eating, but you haven't changed a bit, have you?'

Freddie shrugged. 'Look, you get what you want, Bella, you get to run the show, and I get what I want, to live as if I run the show. I won't interfere. You know that. I don't see what the problem is.'

'You never did, Freddie. Not even when you shagged your own father's wife. Your stepmother, for God's sake. You saw no problem, at all, did you?'

'Ah, I might have guessed you'd bring that up. I was stoned. She was drunk. Shit happens. And Pa would probably never even have known about it if you hadn't told him.'

'That wasn't the bloody point, Freddie. You were always stoned. And Antonia was always a slag. I didn't care about her, but I cared a lot about you, whether you believe that or not. I did it for your own good, Freddie. I wanted you to get cleaned up.'

'Yes, but it didn't turn out that way, did it. Pa chucked us both out, me and Antonia. And he threatened to shop me to the police for dealing drugs unless I agreed to be banished to the Antipodean. But now, Bella, I am the prodigal son. Pa wanted me back in the fold. And you need me to help carry the board. You're the whiz kid businesswoman. You know I'm speaking the truth.'

'What I know, Freddie, is that this whole wretched scheme has spiralled out of control. I'm not countenancing murder. Triple murder. I just can't. I have my daughter to consider.'

'Oh come on, Bella, don't claim the moral high ground, not with me. You've never been bloody Mother Theresa, that's for sure. Now you have everything you've ever wanted within your grasp. All you need do is reach out for it. Just let's stick to the plan, and we'll all come out of it smelling of roses, you'll see.'

'Freddie, I'm not sure that I can stick to the plan. And you should listen to me. We're already in very big trouble. I don't intend to let it get any worse.'

'What do you mean?'

'You'll thank me for it one day.'

'Like I thanked you for shopping me to our father?'

'I know we used to ship our convicts to Australia, but I think modern Australia was probably preferable to jail, however modern, don't you?'

Freddie was studying her anxiously. 'I don't like what you're saying, sis. What are you up to? What are you going to do?'

'I have an appointment later today to meet the detective inspector in charge of the police investigation. The murder investigation, Freddie. That is what I'm up to. He's in London. I'm driving back to my place and meeting him there. Why don't you come with me? If we leave now, you'd have time to have a shower and even grab some sleep before he comes. Freddie, we need to get out of this. None of it was our idea. You and I may both be able to avoid prosecution if we speak up now.'

'Bella, we aren't going to be prosecuted. We haven't done anything wrong.'

'Oh, I think we have, Freddie. We may not be guilty of murder, but we are certainly guilty of a conspiracy which has led to murder.'

'I don't see it like that, at all, sis.'

'No more would you, Freddie.'

'Look, don't do it. Please. You'll ruin everything.'

'You sound like a schoolboy, Freddie. Everything is already ruined. Until the fire, yes, we were involved in a conspiracy to save our family business, but in terms of human life we were just letting nature take its course. I'm not only being altruistic here. Once murder is suspected, a police investigation goes onto another level. A bit of business skulduggery, even pretty high-level fraud, is one thing. Murder is entirely another.'

Freddie sat down with a bump on the edge of the bed.

'I didn't think of it like that,' he said. 'I mean, the fire was caused by George Grey. That's not down to us in any way. And he could have just fallen into the canal.'

'So, you know the details, then, do you?'

'Some of them.'

'Come with me, Freddie.'

'I dunno, sis. I've always been a coward. I don't think I'm up to dealing with the police. I thought everything was going to be straightforward.'

'Which is pretty naive, Freddie.'

'That's me then, I suppose, a naive schoolboy.'

'I'm sorry, Freddie, I didn't mean to have a go at you. I don't want either of us to get any further embroiled in this, that's all. It's gone way beyond what we agreed to. You must see that.'

'Yes, I do. Of course, I do.'

Freddie looked unusually thoughtful. 'You really don't think we're going to get away with it, do you?' he said glumly. 'Not any of it. Not now. Not with three deaths.'

'No, and anyone who thinks we will is barking mad. Which of course, I have always suspected to be the case . . .'

Bella thought of her phone call the previous evening. She was speaking the truth. The man who had been so casually dismissive of those three deaths, the man who had sent Freddie, armed with his briefcase full of vital papers, to find her, was surely mad.

'You're right,' said Freddie suddenly. 'You have to be.' He sounded totally deflated. 'I guess I was kidding myself.'

'I guess we were all kidding ourselves. Look, I'm still extremely fond of you, Freddie. Come with me, now. Before it's too late for us both.'

'I can't, Bella. I just can't.'

Bella studied her brother with care, weighing up the man behind the easy charm. The eyes that rarely met yours, the weak mouth. Just like the boy she had once known so well.

'OK. Well, I intend to leave soon. If you are not going to come with me, what are you going to do? I think at this stage you must be either with me or against me, Freddie.'

'I'm with you, of course I'm with you,' said Freddie. 'You've totally convinced me. The whole thing is a disaster. Like I said, I was kidding myself as usual. So I guess there's only one thing I can do. I've got a hire car outside. I'll head straight back to Heathrow and catch the first available flight back to where I've just come from.'

'You may not have your allowance for much longer. If you stay here I'll make sure you're provided for. You can move in with me in London, for as long as you like. Until we've sorted something out, anyway.'

'You may be in jail, we may both be in jail.'

'Perhaps. But if we speak up now, perhaps not. Neither of us expected anything like this to happen, after all. And we certainly didn't have anything to do with it.'

'No, I'll go back,' said Freddie quickly. 'I have my house in Australia, well, more of a shack, but right on the beach. I like the life well enough. And I did get a welcome home present.' He reached into the pocket of his jacket and produced a thick wad of fifty pound notes. 'Fifty grand, a down payment apparently.'

'Well, that's about the only welcome you're getting, I'm afraid,' said Bella. 'If you want to go, then go. All you've done is make a very fleeting visit back to the UK after learning of your father's death. I will tell the police that. And if you go now, your involvement will surely appear to be so slight it's quite likely nobody will come after you. Not to the other side of the world, anyway. And even if they do, I don't see how anything can be proven against you.'

'Which leaves you taking the rap, sis.'

'Not me alone. And I intend to make quite sure of that. I'm going to tell the police everything. I don't see that I have any choice. That any of us have any choice. I thought there was nothing I wouldn't do for Fairbrother's. But I didn't even consider murder might be on the agenda. I mean, that's for gangsters and secret service agents. Not people like us.'

'Are you sure we really are talking murder here, though?'

'Honestly, Freddie, "talking murder here"? What sort of language is that? Anyway, the answer is yes. I thought we'd clarified that. Or are you still just being naïve?'

'No. OK, sis. I told you. I realise you are right. Quite right. I don't know what I was thinking about.'

'Nothing new there then.'

The words were potentially harsh, but Bella softened them with a gentle smile. And she reached with one hand to lightly touch her brother's cheek.

'I have missed you, Freddie,' she said.

'And you're going to have to miss me again,' Freddie responded. 'I'm heading for the airport. But I have a room booked here, so first I'm going to use it to clean up and have a kip for a couple of hours.'

'Goodbye again, then,' said Bella.

Freddie glanced at the briefcase, which lay, still unopened, on the sofa. 'I should take that,' he said. 'Return it.'

Bella shook her head. 'No, I'll make sure it gets to the right people. The new acting chairman of the bank, and our father's solicitor. They may still be able to salvage something.'

'OK, whatever you say.' Freddie stepped forward then, and enveloped her in a hug. 'I've been wanting to do that ever since you opened the door,' he said, smiling at her.

'Me too,' said Bella, realising, rather to her surprise, that she meant it. After all, Freddie was still the brother she had once so adored.

She found she was fighting back tears. Over the years she had occasionally dreamed of a reunion with him. But this reunion, in circumstances so shocking and potentially dangerous that they would almost certainly destroy both the Fairbrother family and the Fairbrother family business, was the stuff of nightmares.

'See you in another couple of decades, then,' said Freddie.

He stepped back. He wasn't smiling any more. He looked sad, and vulnerable. Frightened even.

Well that was understandable. Bella was frightened too. Both of what she had already done, and what she was about to do.

Freddie took the lift down to reception and headed straight out to his car. He intended to fetch his bag and then try for an early check-in. He really did need to get some sleep before he did anything else. That part of what he had told his sister was the truth. There was, however, very little truth in any of the rest of it.

First he had a phone call to make. And he needed to make it immediately, before he had time to think about it any further. Freddie had never been able to carry the burden of responsibility. Any sort of responsibility. Unlike most of the rest of his family, past and present, he was a follower, not a leader. But he was not prepared to follow his sister along the path she had now chosen. He'd come home to England to retrieve his birthright. And now that the opportunity to do so was in reach, he found that it meant more to him than he'd ever realised.

He walked to a secluded corner of the car park. The hotel's grounds stretched before him. He wasn't quite sure, but he thought he could just see the beginning of the Blackdown Hills in the distance, the hills where he had grown up. He and his sister had been so close then. And Bella was right, of course, neither of them had ever agreed to the sequence of events which had now engulfed them. But, in Freddie's opinion, there could be no going back. He wanted the future that he now felt was so nearly his. And, as far as he was concerned, people may have died, but there was no proof at all of deliberate intent to kill. Murder was something he preferred not to even think about. And Freddie Fairbrother had always been extremely good at dismissing from his mind almost anything which might concern or offend him.

He reached into the pocket of his jeans for his phone and called up a contact number. The recipient answered almost at once.

'Make this quick, I told you not to call again on your own phone.'

'I know. I'm sorry. I had to speak to you right away.'

'Is something wrong?'

'Yes, It's Bella,' Freddie began.

EIGHTEEN

V ogel called Det. Supt Clarke just as Saslow turned off the M4 onto the slip road leading towards Hounslow and Brentford. He checked his watch. The time was 10.40 a.m. The traffic had been heavy around Heathrow, heading into central London, as Vogel had expected, it nearly always was nowadays, even past what would normally be regarded as the rush hour.

'I reckon we're about twenty minutes away,' he said. 'Where are you?'

'I'm at the scene,' replied Nobby Clarke. 'Come to the Brewery Tap, in Catherine Wheel Road. It's right by the canal. The postcode is TW8 8BD. Your satnav should take you straight there. You'll want to meet the landlord. I'll get him to open up for us. Seems almost certain he saw George Grey very shortly before he died. May well be the last person to have done so, apart from his murderer – assuming he was murdered, of course.'

Vogel sat up straight in the car seat.

'Well, that sounds interesting,' he said.

'Indeed. And it appears that Grey wasn't alone either. Look, I'll tell you when I see you.'

By the time Vogel and Saslow arrived at the Brewery Tap, Nobby Clarke, accompanied by a young black man Vogel did not recognise, was already at a table by the window.

She waved to Vogel and Saslow who made their way to join her. Nobby greeted Saslow warmly. Vogel was glad that there was clearly such mutual liking and respect between the two women. Saslow could only be helped by the support and friendship of a senior officer like Clarke. Vogel was well aware that the events of the previous year, which had had such a profound effect on both he and Saslow, had made the young DC wonder if she would, or even could, remain on the force. He was extremely glad that she had decided to stay on, and now seemed so determined to overcome any disquiet she might still be experiencing.

'Nice to see you again, DC Saslow,' said the detective

superintendent at once. She didn't mention that case. But then she
wouldn't. Vogel knew that Nobby Clarke's philosophy of policing
was very simple. The only way to effectively proceed was to move
on after every setback. And then move on again.

She greeted Vogel with casual affection, introduced the two
officers to DC Lloyd Springer, then turned to Saslow again.

'What are you drinking?' she asked. Adding with a grimace and
gesturing towards two cups on the table: 'We're on the coffee.'

Vogel smiled. Nobby Clarke liked a drink. Malt whisky for
preference. But eleven a.m. in the morning was just a tad too
early, even for her, it seemed.

He and Saslow also both asked for coffee. Clarke led them to
the bar, ordered, then introduced them to the landlord, Peter Forest.

'Peter, I'm sorry to ask you this,' she said. 'But do you think
you could go over again with DI Vogel here what you told my
DC last night. We believe the deceased man found in the canal
was one George Grey, whom Mr Vogel was seeking in connection
with a very serious case of arson in the west of England. I think
you know that?'

Peter Forest nodded his assent. 'I do,' he said. 'No problem.
I'm happy to help. Shall we sit down?'

He gestured to the table where DC Springer remained sitting,
then led the way over.

Vogel opened the proceedings. 'So, I understand Mr Forest,
that you think you may have seen the deceased on the day that
he died. Indeed, quite possibly very shortly before he died. Is
that so?'

'Yes, I'm pretty sure I did. I've seen a photograph of him, and
if it wasn't him it was his double. He came in here about eight
o'clock, or thereabouts, the night before last. The football had just
started, you see . . .'

'Mr Forest, this is a busy pub. What makes you so sure? Was
there something that made you particularly notice the man you
believe to have been George Grey?'

'Yes, when he came in I thought he might be already drunk.
Or on drugs. I'm careful about that sort of thing. So, I watched
him, studied his face. Then I realised it probably wasn't drink or
drugs. Not recreational, anyway. He was ashen. He walked with
a limp. He looked ill. I wondered what he was doing out visiting

a pub, but that was none of my business. As long as he didn't die
on the premises of course—'

Peter Forest stopped himself abruptly. 'Sorry, I didn't mean . . .'

'That's quite all right, Mr Forest, I know what you meant. What
else can you tell me? How long did George Grey stay? What was
he drinking, that sort of thing?'

'He stayed about an hour I think, maybe more. He was drinking whisky, large ones. But the chap he was with was doing all the
buying. George Grey just sat there, same table we're at now . . .'

'Ah yes, the chap he was with?' queried Vogel, glancing sideways
at Clarke.

'Don't worry we're on it,' said the superintendent quietly. 'I'll
fill you in later.'

'So, will you tell me about this other man?' continued Vogel,
looking back at Peter Forest.

'Yeah, I didn't take so much notice of him to tell the truth,'
said the landlord. 'I remember he was bearded and wearing a
baseball cap, so I couldn't see his hair, or his face properly really.
Anyway, I was more interested in your George Grey. Didn't like
the look of him at all. Although the other man did seem to be
taking care of him. Seemed quite solicitous, and like I said, did
all the drink buying. Except the first one. Grey ordered that himself
when he came in.'

'So, you did speak to him?'

'Barely,' said Forest. 'All he said was, large whisky, please.
Then he went and sat down over here. So he wasn't any trouble.
I did ask the other man if he was all right. Said I was a bit
concerned.'

Forest didn't look as if he was going to say anything more.

'What was the reply to that?' Vogel prompted.

'Oh, he said your George Grey had just been to the dentist and
was a bit wobbly, that he'd be all right after a few drinks.'

'Didn't you think that was a bit strange, Mr Forest?'

'No, not really.'

'Mr Forest,' Vogel continued. 'If someone is a bit wobbly after
a visit to the dentist they don't normally go to a pub and down
large whiskies, do they?'

'Oh, I don't know, you get all sorts in here.'

'How many whiskies do you think he had?'

'At least three. Maybe four.'

'In an hour or so?' queried Vogel. 'Enough to make most people woozy, don't you think, even someone who didn't already look ill and unsteady on their feet.'

'Yes,' Forest agreed a little reluctantly, 'I suppose so.'

'Do you know what time he left the pub?'

'Well, no, not exactly. Sometime after nine, I would think. But I had to change a barrel, and the connector was playing up. Then my brother phoned me, I was out of the bar for about fifteen minutes or so.'

'And I take it you didn't recognise either of the men when they came in to the pub.'

'Well no, I didn't. I mean, they certainly weren't regulars. And they certainly hadn't been in recently. But, there was this niggle, I did have the feeling I had seen them before. I just couldn't place them, that's all. I do have a pretty good memory for faces. Helps in my line of work. Particularly if you have to ban someone.'

Forest grinned. Vogel smiled politely back. Although he was really not interested in amusing asides. He took the conversation straight back to the point.

'If you had seen them before, do you think it was here, in this pub?'

'More than likely. I don't get out much.'

He grinned again. This time Vogel didn't bother to smile back.

'Would you say most of your trade is local, Mr Forest?' he asked. 'The pub is tucked away a bit.'

'About fifty-fifty probably. But there's quite a big rental market in Brentford, in the Dock, in the new developments in the high street and along towards Kew Bridge, and up by Brentford Lock. People come and go hereabouts. Just as you've got to know someone, they're moving on.'

Vogel glanced at Saslow and Clarke. 'Either of you anything else to ask?' he enquired.

The two women both said they hadn't.

Vogel glanced towards Lloyd Springer.

'Just one thing, did you or anyone else hear what the two men were talking about?' asked the young DC.

'They were talking quietly. Most of the time. But your George Grey, he seemed to be asking for something. Asking where something was. I think I heard him say "why haven't you brought it?" He raised his voice, seemed angry.'

Vogel thanked Peter Forest, and the landlord returned to the bar.

'So, what about the second man?' asked Vogel as soon as he'd gone, addressing Clarke. 'You said you were on it.'

'Well, yes. We've been making door-to-door inquiries. Just to the left of Thames Lock, as you walk toward the Dock, there's a basin with several residential moorings. Thames Wharf. Houseboats, couple of narrowboats. Seems there's a barge there which was bought about eighteen months or so ago by a man who could match Forest's description of George Grey's companion on the night of his death. Tall, bearded, and bald, but usually seen wearing a baseball cap. We got this from the chap who looks after the wharf. And that's about it. Not even a guess at age. He said all bald men look the same age.'

Clarke chuckled. 'He might be right, too,' she said.

'What about a name?' asked Saslow.

Clarke nodded. 'Yep. Called himself Richard Jones. Not quite as bad as John Smith, but getting there. Anyway, it seems he paid cash for the barge and for two years' mooring fees in advance. Surprisingly enough, nobody asked too many questions, and all our efforts so far to trace this Richard Jones have come to a dead end.'

'So, he could well be using a false name and that really does make him suspicious,' commented Springer.

'Yes,' agreed Vogel. 'We need to find him, that's for sure. Do I assume there's been no sign of him around here over the past couple of days since Grey was last seen in the pub?'

'Absolutely not. In fact, it seems he's only very rarely been seen since he bought the boat. Nobody got the chance to get to know him or anything about him. Also not surprising. We've put out a national alert for him. But there's not a lot to go on, unfortunately.'

'No, I don't suppose there is,' said Vogel thoughtfully, as he finished his coffee. 'Wouldn't mind a look around, before the inquest. Crime scene first perhaps?'

'I was going to suggest that,' said Clarke. 'Let's get over there shall we.'

Vogel stood up and headed for the door, Saslow at his heels and Nobby Clarke just a step or two behind. Vogel thought he saw her casting a wistful look at the optics behind the bar which seemed to include an extensive range of malts, but he couldn't be sure.

Clarke then led the way to Thames Lock, which was, of course, still cordoned off, pointing out en route Town Wharf, and the bridge which health and safety didn't seem to have discovered yet.

'I see what everyone means about this place,' muttered Vogel.

Pat Fitzwarren was long gone, along with the corpse. CSI were still at work and a pair of uniforms were protecting the crime scene. There were no barriers on either side of the murkily deep Thames Lock, which, thought the DI, was an accident waiting to happen. Or alternatively, an eerily likely location for a murder.

'If it wasn't for George Grey's recent history, and the fact that we suspect him of arson leading to the death of two people, you'd easily believe he fell in here, wouldn't you?' Vogel mused. 'Certainly, after four large whiskies and the state he was already in. It would have been dark too, and I wouldn't think the lighting around here would be all that.'

'Indeed, but this is a possible double murderer, who was with a mysterious companion who seems to have already disappeared on us,' commented Clarke. 'We also don't know why he turned right toward the lock when he left the Brewery Tap, instead of left towards Brentford High Street. The hotels, the station, buses, taxis – all those things are in the other direction. This footpath leads only to the Dock housing estate. Even the entrance to Town Wharf is in the other direction.'

'So, if his bearded drinking mate was the equally mysterious boat owner, do we assume he wasn't going back with him, then?' asked Saslow.

'Who knows, he could have been so disorientated he didn't have a clue where he was going,' said Clarke.

'Or, perhaps he knew someone who lived in the Dock,' offered Saslow. 'Someone who might put him up for the night. Perhaps that's where he was heading, and he did just fall in the lock. It has to still be a possibility.'

'Yes,' agreed Vogel with a certain reluctance. 'But what about the bearded drinking companion? If he was with him, why didn't he raise the alarm when George fell? Unless, of course, he pushed him in, which is the theory we all favour, I think. The truth is, though, we don't even know whether or not the two men left the pub together?'

DS Clarke nodded. 'No, we don't. But it would have been so easy; not taken much of a push, from what we hear of George's condition.'

'Surely he'd have cried out, screamed or something,' commented Saslow. 'Wouldn't someone have heard something?'

Vogel looked around him. Although more or less surrounded by buildings of one sort or another, Thames Lock was peculiarly isolated. Some of the Dock flats overlooked the canal, but Vogel thought the residents would have had to be either looking out of their windows or standing on their balconies, on a cold wet October evening, in order to have a chance of noticing anything. Even then, in the dark, and with aircraft passing overhead intermittently, it was, he considered, probably unlikely. And the lock in which George Grey's body had been found was the one furthest away from the flats.

'You know, I reckon only someone actually walking by would have seen or heard anything,' he replied, after a moment's reflection.

He stared into the lock. Deep water. Tall sides. There was just one vertical ladder which would be difficult for anyone to reach and climb in the dark, even if they had been in good condition physically and mentally when they had entered the water, which George Grey reportedly had not.

'Whether he fell or was pushed he wouldn't have had much chance of getting out of there, even if he hadn't been half off his head with booze and medication,' Vogel commented.

It was starting to rain yet again. Nasty weather in London as well as Somerset. Clarke shivered as she muttered her agreement.

Vogel leaned forward and took a last lingering look into the lock; deep, black and oily.

'What a truly horrible way to die,' he murmured, half to himself.

NINETEEN

Bella took rather longer than usual applying her make-up and drying and styling her hair. She always thought that appearance was important, today it seemed even more so.

Her father had had a saying which, many years ago, she'd taken on board as a kind of mantra. Never let the act drop.

Even now she would try to live up to that for as long as possible, but she was well aware that if she went ahead with her avowed intention to reveal all to DI Vogel, that might become increasingly more difficult.

Once satisfied with her appearance, Bella quickly packed her bag, then sat down with more room service coffee to make some phone calls – mostly to continue to rearrange her London life – and to text her daughter. Her message merely sent love and asked Kim to call her mother as soon as possible. It was lesson time, and pupils at Kim's boarding school were not allowed to take phones into the classroom. However, Bella knew that her daughter checked her phone as frequently as she could, in free periods and during lunch and other breaks, and confidently expected to hear from her before the day was out. She didn't know yet exactly what she was going to say to Kim. She did know how much she needed to hear her daughter's voice.

Bella eventually left the hotel just after ten thirty a.m. She had a fair run along the M5 and M4, and into London, arriving at her Chelsea Harbour apartment just under three hours later. Her phone rang as she was about to pull into the underground car park. The caller was her daughter. Bella pulled to a halt by the car park entrance in order to maintain a signal.

'Is something wrong, Mum?' asked Kim almost straight away. 'You sound funny.'

Bella smiled to herself. That was the trouble with daughters. And sons too, she suspected. They knew you too well.

'No, nothing's wrong,' she lied. 'Well, except for dealing with the aftermath of the fire. And your grandfather, and everything. I've just got back from Somerset. It's not been easy . . .'

'Of course not, Mum, I'm sorry. I wasn't thinking. I've been upset, too. But it must be really horrid for you.'

Not for the first time Bella wondered how she had managed to produce such a kind and sensitive daughter. These were not known Fairbrother attributes.

'It's all right, darling,' she replied. 'Just a lot to sort out, that's all.'

'And, well, I know you and Grandad didn't get on, and all that, and we hadn't seen him in yonks, but the fire was such a shock, wasn't it?' Kim continued. 'An awful way for anyone to die. Are you sure you don't want me to come home for a few days? Miss Jackson's already said I could, any time I want. I can go and see her straightaway . . .'

'No, Kim. You stay where you are. For the time being, anyway. I just wanted to hear your voice, that's all.'

That, at least, was the truth. Unlike much of the rest of what she had said, thought Bella.

After a brief further chat Bella ended the call, having promised that the two would speak again that evening. She knew she might only be delaying the inevitable, but she had chosen to decide then, after her meeting with DI Vogel, exactly what she should tell her daughter.

She carried on into the car park, then made her way up to her penthouse apartment. The river view normally brought her almost instant peace and contentment, to a certain degree, even on a bad day. But there had never been a day as bad as this.

She made herself a mug of tea, sat down at the table by the window, and opened the briefcase Freddie had given her. Their father's will was on top. She removed it and opened the buff envelope. The will seemed to be exactly as Freddie had described it. The other papers were all neatly stacked below. It would be, as she had always known, a complex job to unravel the tangle of trust funds and investments which she had been led to believe would allow a vast input of cash into the bank once her father's death had been registered. Then there were the hedge funds. A nightmare in themselves.

But it was a task she had been prepared to undertake, with the help of some of Fairbrother International's most experienced and able employees. Until the fire. Until three people had died. Until she had, she believed, been made complicit in murder.

She pushed the papers to one side. Their content really made no difference. She'd made up her mind what she must do. Rather to her surprise, perhaps, her conscience would let her take no other course of action. She checked her watch. It was only twenty minutes past two. From what he had said, DI Vogel would be another hour or so at least. She wanted to get their meeting over with as quickly as possible. The idea of waiting more than an hour seemed interminable.

Then the entry phone rang. It seemed she would not have to wait so long after all.

She spoke into it. 'You're early,' she said.

'Are you expecting someone?' replied a familiar male voice. A voice she recognised at once.

It was not the voice she was expecting.

'You?' she responded in surprise. 'What are you doing here?'

'I have a message for you.'

'Who from?' asked Bella.

It was an inane question. She suddenly knew only too well who the message must be from. And so much was suddenly explained. Her caller did not even grace the question with an answer.

'It's a very important message,' he continued. 'A message that could change everything. Can I come up?'

A message that could change everything? Bella didn't think so. But this was a caller she could not turn away, even though she had been taken completely by surprise. And she was, of course, curious. At the very least. What was his involvement exactly?

She pushed the entry button, then walked across her flat and opened the door into the outer lobby to wait the arrival of the lift. Her caller was wearing a dark grey raincoat, its hood loose on his shoulders, boots, and gloves. He looked both out of place in the smart modern apartment block, and as ill at ease as she felt. However, the heavy rain, which seemed to be as much of a permanent feature in London this October as it had been in Somerset, was still falling heavily.

She stood back to let him into the flat, and closed the door behind them.

'So what is it? What is this very important message which has brought you all the way to London then?'

'I have to ask you a question first,' said her caller. 'I believe you have a meeting with DI Vogel?'

'How the hell do you know that?' asked Bella.

Then she answered her own question. 'Of course. Freddie. As weak and untrustworthy as ever. But why did he contact you?'

'He didn't. Not directly.'

'Not directly? So . . .' Bella paused, trying to make sense of it all. 'So, you're in on everything, are you?' she asked. 'Am I to assume that things have not been at all how they seemed, and that you have been involved all along? That's it, isn't it?'

Again, her caller ignored the question.

'I have been instructed to ask you if there is any chance that you can be persuaded to cancel that meeting?' he said.

'Have you indeed, well, the answer is no, I cannot,' said Bella forcibly.

'Is there nothing that could be said which might persuade you to change your mind?'

'After what has already happened? After three people have died? Been murdered? No. There isn't.'

'And you are absolutely sure of that?'

'Yes, I most certainly am. And you can report back that I will not be bullied.'

'Of course not,' said the caller mildly. 'In that case I have no choice. My orders are to give you this message.'

He slipped a gloved hand into his raincoat pocket and withdrew a hand-gun. Ironically a Glock 17, the revolver which is standard issue to arms-authorised officers throughout the UK police force. Only Bella didn't know that. Neither would she have much cared.

She was numb with shock and disbelief. Yet at the same time her brain was buzzing, as she registered what was happening. She was starkly aware that she had made a catastrophic error of judgement – not for the first time in recent months, but, it seemed, quite probably for the last.

She hadn't even considered that morning, when she had told Freddie of her intentions to confess all to DI Vogel, that her brother might report back in the way that he clearly had. Indeed, she'd believed him totally when he'd told her that he would cut his losses and run. After all, he'd done it before. But in any case, even had she considered it, had she suspected that he might have other plans, it still would not have occurred to her that she might be in any danger. And certainly not in danger of her life.

Even when her unexpected caller had arrived she had not, in any way, been alarmed. Why should she have been? This was not a man she had ever previously had cause to fear.

She was afraid now. Dreadfully afraid.

A part of her still could not quite believe what was happening. There she was, in her own apartment, in the middle of London, literally staring down the barrel of a gun. It was levelled at her now, pointed at her head. And there appeared to be some sort of extension fitted to the barrel. A silencer. She registered that in a detached sort of way. After all, this couldn't be real, could it? If it was, if she was about to die, she knew, without any doubt who was responsible for ordering her death. It couldn't be, could it?

'No, there must be a mistake,' she said, in a voice she did not quite recognise as her own. 'Why are you doing this? Stop. Please. Don't—'

But there had, it appeared, been no mistake. These were to be Bella Fairbrother's last words. Her visitor held the gun steadily, professionally, and his aim was deadly. He pulled the trigger. There followed a dull pop.

Bella fell backwards onto the floor. She was dead before she hit the ground.

Her visitor stood for a moment looking down at the body. He stood very still, almost as if he were paying his last respects. Perhaps even regretting, for a moment, the course of action he had presumably agreed to take. Then, being careful not to touch anything, he moved across the room to the window where the briefcase Bella had been given by her brother earlier that day still lay open on the table. Using one gloved hand he replaced the papers Bella had removed from the case, closed it, picked it up, and left the apartment.

As he pushed the front door shut behind him he could hear Bella Fairbrother's phone ringing. She would never answer it again.

TWENTY

Vogel and Saslow arrived at Chelsea Harbour at 3.23 p.m. Patricia Fitzwarren was still completing her examination of George Grey's body in the post-mortem examination room at the West Middlesex hospital's mortuary. But her initial findings had been inconclusive, and, by the time Vogel had decided to leave her to it, she'd already confessed that she could not see much chance of that changing.

Considerable quantities of alcohol, heavy-duty pain killers and other medication had been found in the stomach of the deceased, more than enough to have caused him to be dazed and unsteady on his feet as he made his way, for whatever reason, along the side of Thames Lock. In addition to the wounds received on the night of the fire, it became apparent that George Grey had more recently received a blow to the side of the head, probably simultaneous with falling into the lock. But Dr Fitzwarren was unable to ascertain whether this blow had been caused by George hitting his head as he entered the lock, or whether the blow had been the cause of him falling, executed by a third party hitting him on the side of the head with a blunt object.

There would naturally be a coroner's inquest. But unless new evidence presented itself, both Dr Fitzwarren and Vogel assumed that the coroner would have little choice but to deliver an open verdict.

On the drive in from Brentford, Vogel had made several attempts to call Bella Fairbrother in order to confirm his estimated arrival time.

He did not, of course, receive any reply.

It was Saslow who attempted to use the entry phone system of the apartment block. When there was repeatedly no response, Vogel again called Bella's mobile, to no avail.

After an abortive couple of minutes the two officers began to discuss what they should do next.

'I don't understand it,' said Vogel. 'Bella Fairbrother doesn't strike me as the sort of person who would fail to keep an appointment. And certainly not one she had been so eager to make in the first place.'

'Could she have been summoned in to Fairbrother's head office?' asked Saslow. 'She made it quite clear to you that there was a considerable crisis.'

'Yes. Maybe. But I would have expected her to at least call to cancel. Anyway, she's not even on the board is she?'

'Well, no but . . .'

'Look this place must have some sort of concierge service. There have been three deaths already, Saslow, connected with the Fairbrothers and the fire at the manor, I think we should try to gain entry.'

'Right, boss . . .' Saslow began.

At that moment the front door of the apartment block opened, and a woman resident emerged. Vogel stepped forwards, but Saslow was faster. She grabbed the door just in time to stop it closing. The woman, her face registering alarm, looked as if she didn't know whether to block the doorway or get out of the way.

'Police, on an urgent inquiry,' Vogel said by way of explanation, flashing his warrant card at the woman, who nodded nervously and stepped aside.

The two officers took the lift to the penthouse.

'We could be wasting our time,' commented Vogel. 'We have no way of gaining entry to the flat if Bella doesn't open the door, whether she's inside or not.'

'You could shoulder it, boss,' commented Saslow, deadpan.

'You've been watching too much TV,' said Vogel.

'No way, boss, not with the hours you make me keep,' replied Saslow.

They were both smiling as they stepped out of the lift into the small lobby area which served Bella's penthouse apartment. In spite of the entry phone system, there was a second doorbell.

Saslow pushed it. Three times. No reply.

'What now, boss?' asked Saslow.

Vogel glanced around him. There was clearly no sign of a forced entry or any sort of disturbance. He really wasn't sure now what he had expected to achieve by pushing his way into the building.

'We'll have another go at tracking Bella down, and if we can't find her then we should consider seeking out a key holder and having a look around,' he said.

However, Vogel had learned never to overlook the obvious, when, as a young bobby, he'd been entrusted to seek out a deposed European royal, by then a UK resident, whom his superiors had wanted to interview in connection with a quite serious fraud. The Princess of somewhere or other. He'd spent two fruitless days looking for the woman, until an older and wiser colleague asked him if he'd checked the phone book. He hadn't. And there she'd been, fully listed. Not even ex-D.

So, before walking away, Vogel leaned forward and tried the door handle. It turned easily. He pushed the door open gently, automatically noticing as he did so that it was fitted with the kind of lock which is operated by a flick switch from the inside, but requires a key from the outside.

He stepped into the inner lobby, Saslow at his heels. The door to the big open-plan living room was open.

'It's David Vogel, Miss Fairbrother, are you there?' the DI called out. 'Your door was unlocked. We are just making sure you are all right—'

He stopped abruptly. Saslow was at his elbow by then. He heard her gasp, and out of the corner of his eyes saw her sway slightly. Saslow was still not back to her best. This was the kind of shock she didn't need.

'Hold on, Dawn,' muttered Vogel.

The body of Bella Fairbrother lay almost exactly in the middle of the room. She had fallen flat on her back with her head pointing towards the big picture windows at the river end of the room, and her feet pointing towards the door.

It seemed most likely to Vogel that she had been facing some-body standing just inside the room, somebody who had probably only recently entered the apartment.

There was no doubt at all that she was dead. She appeared to have been shot in the centre of her forehead, just above her eyes, and part of the top of her head had been blown away exposing grey matter. Her brain. Her eyes were wide open and staring sight-lessly at the ceiling.

Death was never pretty. The sight of Bella Fairbrother, who had always seemed so exceptionally alive to Vogel, after such a sudden and violent death, was particularly disturbing. It had been only that morning that the DI had spoken to her on the phone. She had told him she was still in Somerset and would drive back a little later. She couldn't have been in her flat for long before she was killed. Vogel wondered, of course, if she would still be alive had he somehow or other arranged to meet her earlier, as she'd clearly wanted.

He was vaguely aware of a choking sound from Saslow. He turned in time to see her hurrying out of the apartment. He hoped she wouldn't be sick in the lobby, there might be evidence there, but he wouldn't blame her if she was.

He made himself return his attention to the dead woman. A woman he had not entirely trusted in life, but nonetheless a bright and vibrant human being. And she was the mother of a teenage girl. Now there was a death call Vogel hoped he didn't get to make.

He looked again at the entry point of the bullet. It would undoubtedly have killed Bella instantly. The human brain will normally continue to function for ten to fifteen seconds after a direct shot to the heart. But a direct shot to the brain destroys the nervous system at once, and the body shuts down straightaway. Death is immediate.

Vogel was glad that Bella would have had no time in which to suffer. But there was something disturbingly clinical about such an accurate shot, through the central forehead and into the brain. It smacked of assassination, military style. Either the perpetrator had been exceedingly lucky, or he was some kind of professional. Vogel favoured the latter.

He would have liked to check out the body himself, and have a look around the flat for any further indication of what had occurred, and any clues that might suggest a possible motive, or even point to the identity of the perpetrator – although that would probably be hoping for far too much – but, like all modern police officers, Vogel didn't dare do or touch anything which might muddy the crime scene. He must wait for CSI to do their job.

He stood looking at Bella Fairbrother's body for a few seconds more. He regarded her death as primarily his responsibility. No logical argument would ever change his mind on that. And, whilst suspecting that Bella was far from innocent of at least a certain degree of nefarious involvement in the sequence of events which had led to her own passing, Vogel was overwhelmed with a sense of deep sadness. And guilt. Vogel's wife always said that, in that regard, he was better suited to being a Roman Catholic than a Jew; at least he would be able to say a few Hail Mary's and gain some absolution. As it was, Vogel carried his guilt around with him like notches etched into his soul. The wanton murder of Bella Fairbrother – which, taking into account the logistics of her journey from Somerset, must have occurred within a maximum of a couple of hours before his and Saslow's arrival at her apartment, probably less – threatened to carve a very deep notch indeed.

Vogel's expression was grim as he stepped out into the lobby and prepared to call in the crime.

A case which had started off as quite possibly no more than a tragic accidental fire had now led, directly or indirectly, to the death of four people. And with this fourth death, the murder of a young woman, a mother, whom he believed may well have been trying to put herself under his protection, the case had just got personal for Vogel. It was as if a metaphorical gauntlet had been thrown down before him.

Vogel felt as if he was accepting a challenge to combat, from which he would not back away until everyone responsible for this series of terrible violent crimes had been brought to justice.

TWENTY-ONE

I t was an MIT case, of course. Nobby Clarke arrived at Chelsea Harbour little more than an hour after the first response team. The crime scene had been cordoned off and a smattering of uniformed officers were making sure that nobody contaminated the scene. CSI and Dr Patricia Fitzwarren were already there. As was an MIT unit under the command of DCI James Pearson, who was also leading the London end of the investigation into the death of George Grey, and already familiar with the various strings to the Blackdown Manor case.

He didn't look overjoyed at the arrival of his detective super-intendent. Nobby was quite sure he felt that she should be safely behind her desk, where she belonged. And she sympathised abso lutely with him. That was exactly how she'd always felt about MIT brass interfering when she'd been a detective chief inspector leading her own team.

'It's all right, Pearson,' she said curtly. 'Only a fleeting visit. I'll be out of your way soon enough.'

Pearson coloured slightly. He had reddish hair and that sort of pale pink-white skin which tended to turn a deeper shade of pink very easily. Nobby might have felt sympathy for him if he hadn't been a senior police officer. As it was, she was vaguely amused. But she tried not to show it. This was hardly the occasion.

'I want to see Vogel,' she continued. 'This case is beginning to have huge ramifications. We need to work out a strategy between our two forces. As far as I'm concerned, this murder is an MIT job, and you are the senior investigating officer, but clearly it's entangled with the cases Vogel and his Avon and Somerset MCIT team are already investigating. So I'm putting myself up as liaison, all right?'

'Of course, Nobby,' Pearson replied smartly.

Unlike Vogel, Pearson didn't have a problem addressing Clarke in the informal manner that she preferred. He still looked as if he would have preferred her not to be there, though.

'And don't worry,' added Clarke, knowing full well she was accurately putting his thoughts into words. 'I'll soon be back where I belong.'

After the arrival of Pearson and his team, Vogel had taken Saslow to a nearby coffee shop. She'd managed to refrain from being sick, as far as he knew. She'd certainly avoided vomiting in public. But only with difficulty, Vogel suspected. She still looked shaken.

Nonetheless Saslow stood up at once when Det. Supt. Clarke entered the coffee shop. With a mildly impatient wave, Nobby gestured for her to sit.

'Well, this is turning into a right old mess, isn't it, Vogel?' she commented by way of greeting.

'That's one way of putting it,' the DI muttered.

'Right,' continued Clarke, pausing only to order a double espresso. 'This is Pearson's case, right? It's MIT. Unlike George Grey, Bella Fairbrother was neither an Avon and Somerset suspect, nor on the run . . .'

'Well, I don't know about that, boss, I mean Nobby—' began Vogel.

'Oh, don't be ridiculous, Vogel,' interrupted Clarke. 'My boys and girls are already on the case. It would be hours before you could set up your lot here, even in the unlikely event of your brass letting you even attempt to run a murder investigation in Met territory.'

Vogel knew she was totally correct about that. But he said nothing.

'However, this is clearly going to overlap with the investigation you are already running,' Nobby Clarke continued. 'So, you obviously should continue to handle the West Country end concerning this latest murder too. I've told Pearson that. And you'll both liaise through me. Four people, all connected in some way, have died following your fire, Vogel. I know one of those deaths is not yet proven to be murder, but I damned well suspect it was, as I'm sure you do. So, I'm not having any inter-force rivalry from anybody, is that clear?'

Vogel nodded. 'Yes, boss,' he said.

He actually quite liked it when Nobby Clarke was in full flow, although, of course, he would never admit it to her.

'Right, so we have a team on door-to-door, and we're getting the closed-circuit TV footage. The security here is pretty good, as you would expect. It would be damned difficult to break in, and, in any case, there is no indication of forced entry. Almost certainly Bella Fairbrother let her murderer into her apartment of her own free will, which indicates that she knew him – or her.'

Vogel nodded, a tad impatiently. He had worked that out straight away.

'Now, concerning the CCTV, as soon as we've found any shots of our man, or woman, I'll let you know,' Clarke continued. 'There must surely be something, and we should get to it fairly quickly. We already have a fix on the time Bella Fairbrother entered the underground car park here, and we know what time you and Saslow arrived, so that narrows things down nicely. We have only a relatively short window during which our killer must have made his appearance.'

'How short?' asked Vogel abruptly.

'Ah yes,' responded the superintendent. 'Bella arrived in the car park at 1.37 p.m., less than two hours before you and Saslow got there, so—'

Clarke was interrupted by the ring of her phone. She took the call at once, without apology.

'Right,' she said. 'Ummm. Well, I would have expected that. But at least we've got him on film. Yes, please send the footage to my phone straightaway.'

She turned her attention back to Vogel and Saslow. 'We have footage of a male who used the intercom system to gain entry to Bella Fairbrother's flat at 2.25 p.m.,' she said.

Vogel felt his stomach lurch. That almost certainly meant that Bella was still alive less than an hour before he and Saslow arrived at her apartment, and only fifteen minutes or so before he first called her to say they were on the way. His assessment of the situation, whilst still standing in her apartment looking down at her dead body, had been quite correct. If he had somehow managed to arrange his meeting with Bella earlier in the day he may well have saved her life. But he hadn't done so. Bella Fairbrother was dead. And he might never know now what she had been planning to tell him. That could easily have died with her.

Nobby Clarke glanced up at Vogel. 'You weren't to know, David, you couldn't possibly have known,' she said, seemingly aware of his thoughts without him even having to voice them.

'No, of course not, boss,' Vogel replied quickly.

But they were empty words. He felt he had let Bella Fairbrother down, and he knew that he always would. The likelihood of Bella herself being involved in whatever skulduggery had now led to four deaths, including her own, made no difference at all to his feelings on the matter.

'Right,' Clarke continued, as if that brief exchange hadn't happened. 'That's the good news. The bad news is that he's made sure its damned near impossible to identify him. No surprise there, though . . .'

Nobby's phone pinged.

'That'll be the CCTV footage,' she said.

The three of them poured over the screen. A figure wearing a dark-coloured, hooded raincoat stood in the doorway of Bella's apartment block. The hood was up, and he kept his head down. He was wearing gloves. There was no clear shot of his face. He'd made sure of that. He had clearly worked out where the cameras were situated and ensured that his face was turned away throughout.

Nobby played the thirty seconds or so of film twice. It was Saslow who spoke first.

'You know what,' she said. 'We can't even be absolutely sure it's a man. Not from that.'

'Well, if it's a woman she's unusually broadly built,' said Nobby. 'Anyway, it just looks like a man, doesn't it? I can't quite explain . . .'

'I know, I agree absolutely,' said Saslow. 'Moves like a man, too. I only meant, well, the footage is so inconclusive—'

'Would you play it one more time, Nobby?' Vogel interrupted, remembering for once to address the superintendent in her preferred way, even though she'd so far been too focused on the case that afternoon to correct him.

Clarke played it.

Vogel watched carefully. There was something familiar about the body language of the visitor who had almost certainly been Bella Fairbrother's killer, but Vogel couldn't quite place it.

'I'll send it on to you, Vogel,' said Nobby. 'And unless there's anything else you want to do here, I reckon you should get back to Somerset and follow up on any leads from down there.'

'I've been trying to get in touch with Bella's brother, Freddie Fairbrother, he was supposed to be calling me, but he hasn't, and no answer from his mobile,' said Vogel. 'I'm pretty sure he's in the country by now. He has to be told, obviously. But he also needs to be interviewed, which is something I would like to do personally, wherever he is. I don't even know if he and Bella have met at all since their father's death. He could have all kinds of relevant information. And he might or might not know that he does.'

'Yes, I'd go along with that,' said Clarke. 'We can't take anything at face value right now. Certainly not if the name Fairbrother is involved.'

She downed the remains of her double espresso in one.

'OK. I'll let Pearson know that's your line of inquiry. Now, I've got to get back to base. But I'm your liaison, yes?'

'Yes, boss,' agreed Vogel, who actually always wanted to pursue every line of inquiry himself. But then, so did Nobby Clarke, in spite of her seniority. Which was probably one of the reasons they understood each other so well.

TWENTY-TWO

F reddie Fairbrother had not booked himself on the next available flight to Australia, as he'd told his sister he would. After all, he'd decided that he wouldn't go along with her planned course of action, and once he'd made that call to the one person who could stop Bella, everything changed. Obviously.

He had, however, hedged his bets – something of a habit with Freddie – driven to Heathrow, and checked himself into an airport hotel.

He didn't really like to think about what might happen to Bella now. He told himself she would just be brought back into line, made to realise what she and the whole of what remained of the Fairbrother family stood to lose if she carried out her threat, as Freddie saw it, to tell the police what she knew.

But then, ever since hearing of the fatal fire at Blackdown Manor, he had been intent on convincing himself that there was a relatively innocent explanation for everything; and most certainly no conspiracy to murder. Freddie remained extremely adept at pulling the wool over his own eyes. He was actually very anxious about Bella, fearing the fate that might now befall her. But, at the same time, he told himself that he was being ridiculous. Whatever happened to Bella now, she had brought it upon herself by stepping out of line. And in any case, his sister was not an errant double agent who had fallen foul of the Russian state. Putin wasn't out to get her. There was no question of Freddie having put her life at risk. Bella would be fine.

However, the truth was that Freddie wasn't sure of that, nor anything else. In fact, he had dodged several calls that afternoon from DI David Vogel – the detective his sister had told him was heading the investigation into the fire at Blackdown and the subsequent deaths, the detective he had promised to call upon his arrival in the UK – partly because he was afraid of what the policeman might have to tell him.

Finally he picked up. After all, he told himself, presumably his sister had given Vogel his number, and the detective's call could well be just routine.

'Good afternoon, Mr Fairbrother,' said the DI formally. 'I have been trying to contact you as a matter of urgency, because, well, there is no easy way of saying this, but I am afraid I have some very bad news for you.'

Freddie was standing by his room's triple-glazed picture window, idly watching a 747 coast in to land on the runway nearest to his viewpoint. He felt his knees buckle. There were two armchairs by the window. He sank quickly into one of them. Vogel was still talking.

'Normally, Mr Fairbrother, in situations like this, we would not deliver such news over the telephone. But as we do not know where you are, there seemed little choice—'

'It's Bella, isn't it?' Freddie interrupted. 'Something's happened to my sister. Just tell me, for God's sake, tell me.'

Freddie had difficulty getting the words out. His throat felt as if it were closing up. He couldn't swallow. He wasn't even sure he could breathe properly. He was gasping for air.

'I'm afraid so, Mr Fairbrother. I am extremely sorry to have to tell you that your sister is dead.'

'How?' asked Freddie, his voice little more than a croak. 'How did Bella die?'

'I am afraid she has been shot, Mr Fairbrother.'

'Shot? Murdered?'

'Yes, sir. I fear so.'

'Oh my God! Where? Who? Do you know who did it?'

'Not yet,' said Vogel quietly. 'But we will find out, you can trust me on that, Mr Fairbrother. She was killed in her home, in her London flat.'

'Oh my God,' said Freddie again.

'Look sir, I realise you have had a terrible shock, but we do need to interview you as soon as possible. Perhaps you would be kind enough to tell me where you are, and we could make an appointment.'

'I don't know. I mean, why do you want to see me? I didn't have anything to do with it.'

'I wasn't suggesting that you did, Mr Fairbrother,' said Vogel. 'But you are Bella's brother and she is now the second member of your family to have died in, at the very least, suspicious circumstances, in under a week. I assume you are in the UK now, sir?'

'Uh, yes.'

'So, may I ask if you have seen your sister since your arrival here?'

'Uh, yes,' said Freddie again.

He was in too great a state of shock to lie. In any case, he feared he would only further incriminate himself.

'And when was that, sir?'

'This morning. I saw her this morning.'

'In Somerset?'

'Yes.'

'Are you still there?'

'No.'

'So where are you, sir?'

Freddie was well aware that Vogel's manner was one of somewhat exaggerated patience. He didn't entirely blame him.

'I'm at the Heathrow Sofitel,' he said.

Again, Freddie felt that lying would probably cause more trouble than telling the truth. He didn't want to put himself in a position where he was on the run from the British police, not if he could help it anyway.

Vogel continued to speak. 'Mr Fairbrother, it is quite possible that you are the last person to have seen your sister alive. Apart from her killer. Or certainly the last person to have spoken to her. I need to meet up with you as quickly as possible. I'm in London myself. I will come to your hotel and, traffic permitting, I should be with you in just over an hour.'

'I don't think there's anything I can tell you . . .'

'You may well have important information without even realising it, Mr Fairbrother. Please stay exactly where you are, and I shall be with you as soon as possible.'

With that Vogel ended the call.

Freddie's heart seemed to be beating twice as fast as usual. The back of his neck felt sweaty and his hands were trembling.

Bella was dead. She had been murdered. He felt sure he knew very well who had killed her, or, more probably, arranged her killing. And Freddie himself had been instrumental in his sister's death. It was the call he had made that morning which had led to this. He had little doubt about that.

Freddie may have been close to his sister once, but he had not seen her in twenty years. And he had always blamed her for the irrevocable rift with his father. After all, she was the one who had blabbed. So, he had felt little love for his sister, seeing her again after all that time. Unlike Bella, the other way around. However, Freddie had probably never really loved anyone in his life. Not since his childhood, anyway. But Bella was his flesh and blood. Not only that, she was the one who, armed with the contents of the briefcase he had handed over to her that morning, had been supposed to oversee the rescue and revitalisation of the family bank. And Freddie had continued to hope that Bella would merely be made to see sense, and that the rescue operation would continue as planned.

The news that she was dead, murdered, was therefore a shock in more ways than one. Not only was Freddie quite terrified by the prospect of an impending police interview that, unless he was very careful indeed, might lead to him being suspected of complicity in his sister's death; but he did not see how the greater plan he was part of could possibly now proceed. Not without Bella.

Freddie wasn't good at coping with difficult or stressful situations, which was why he had been more or less content to live the life of a lotus eater for so long. The situation he now found himself in was beyond difficult and stressful. It was a catastrophic debacle. Far from reclaiming his position as leader, if only nominally, of the Fairbrother clan, he could end up in jail. And he had absolutely no idea what to do about it.

Then his phone rang again.

'Good afternoon, dear boy,' said the voice of the man he had long ago learned to fear. The man he now quite believed could be capable of anything. But Bella's murder? Surely not that.

'Did you do it?' he asked, his voice still little more than a croak. 'You couldn't have done, could you? Did you really kill Bella?'

The reply was swift and uncompromising. 'Please be very careful what you say. Do not use names. Do you understand me?'

'Yes,' croaked Freddie.

'Right. How do you know she is dead?'

'The police called me. David Vogel.'

'How did he have your number? You've only just arrived in the country.'

'I don't know. I suppose B . . . uh . . . she gave it to him. But you haven't answered me. Did you do it? Did you kill her?'

'I did what had to be done. She was about to blow the whole thing wide open, and it was you who told me that. Remember? She was out of our control. It was the last thing I wanted to happen. But she brought it on herself. You must see that. She had to be removed, for all our sakes and for the sake of the business, however hurtful you, or I, might find that. We must move on now. And we can move on together. As long as you do what I say, dear boy.'

'Yes, yes of course,' croaked Freddie again.

He was now trembling so much so that he had difficulty holding his phone. He suspected that he might have cause to fear for his own life. But he just hoped that he was indispensable, now that Bella was gone.

In any case, he had always been an unlikely rebel. On the one hand so wanting to go his own way, and on the other almost invariably needing to be told what to do if faced with anything remotely difficult or challenging. He knew he shouldn't be 'so bloody weak', as his sister had told him, not for the first time, that very morning. But he'd never been able to help his weakness, Bella wasn't there anymore. And that was largely down to him. So now all he could do was listen, obey, and hope that his caller still knew what he was doing and had a way out of this mess. He usually did, after all.

'Right,' came the reply. 'I am going to arrange for a package to be brought to you. The same package that you unfortunately handed over this morning. You will take that to head office straight away. Its contents will almost certainly encourage the board to believe that the business can be saved, and that all they have to do is keep things going until the will and the trust fund papers the briefcase contains can be put into operation . . .'

'But B . . ., I mean, she, said it could take weeks for a death certificate to be issued—'

Freddie wasn't allowed to finish.

'The family business has survived for centuries, I think it can survive for a few more weeks, as long as the board can be convinced of the ultimate result. That will be your job. And following the regrettable absence now of any other family member to take over the reins, you must make yourself available to chair the board. It is what will be expected.'

Freddie's jaw dropped. Quite literally.

'I can't chair the board,' he blurted out. 'I wouldn't have a clue. I don't know how to run an international company.'

'No. Of course not. But I do. And I shall run the company with you as a mere figurehead. Which, by the way, was all that the person who regrettably is no longer able to fulfil the position was ever going to be. Only, unlike you, she didn't know it.'

'B-but, you're going to be in hiding for the rest of your days, that's what you said, wasn't it?'

'The Internet makes the world a very small place. I have always intended to remain in control. To be, quite literally, the power behind the throne.'

For the first time it occurred to Freddie that his caller had gone mad. Quite mad. But he still felt he had no choice but to rely on him.

'Look, I'll try, I'll try to do as you ask. But it's going to be way past office hours before I get to head office. There might not be anybody there.'

Freddie could hear a dry chuckle.

'You needn't worry about that,' said the voice. 'Under these circumstances I reckon the lot of 'em will be working all night.'

'All right,' said Freddie. 'There's something else, though. Vogel's on his way to see me. He insisted. I don't know what to say. I'm terrified of saying the wrong thing. You must help me. You must tell me what to do—'

Freddie was by then in a total panic. His words came tumbling out, until he was finally interrupted by that almost irritatingly calm voice. What would it take to make that man panic, Freddie wondered obliquely.

'Of course, I will tell you what to do. You will have to speak to the police eventually, but not now. You need to calm down, and we should have a meeting so that I can brief you thoroughly. Meanwhile, when we have finished this conversation I want you to destroy your phone, and purchase a pay-as-you-go one as soon as you can. You mustn't use it again to call anyone. The police have probably put a track on you. We can't be too careful. You should check out of the Sofitel immediately. Take the Heathrow Express into town, and book yourself into the Paddington Hilton. I will get the briefcase delivered there. It should be waiting for you when you arrive. Then you should take it to head office, as I've already told you. And you must pull yourself together. The board have to believe that you are capable of running the show, because they need a figurehead as much as I do . . .'

'But I can't. I can't run the show. I can't run anything . . .'

'I just told you. I will be with you every step of the way. You don't have to run anything, just pretend that you are. You were a promising actor, once, weren't you?'

'I don't know. People said so . . .'

'Yes, they did. You still have the talent, I'm sure. Now what are you wearing?'

'W-what . . .?'

Freddie actually had to look at himself in order to answer. He had finally showered, shaved, and changed into fresh clothes for the first time since his flight over. But he was still similarly clad.

'Jeans, and a shirt, but everything's clean,' he said.

'Do you have a suit with you?'

Freddie did. The only one he owned. His funeral suit. He had, after all, been expecting to attend a funeral, his father's funeral. Now, with Bella's death, it looked as if he might be attending two funerals. At least.

'Yes,' he said.

'OK, put it on. And a tie?'

'Yes.'

It was a black tie. His funeral tie.

'Put that on too. We need you to look like a businessman. If you look the part you will be all the better equipped to play it, right?'

'I suppose so,' said Freddie.

'Good. Now all you have to do is to believe that we can still pull this off. We can, you do believe that, don't you?'

'Can we?'

'Yes. Without any doubt at all. And you know what, dear boy? I think we're both probably going to be better off without her. Really I do.'

'Right,' said Freddie. And then to himself, after the call ended, he muttered, 'You really are quite mad, aren't you? Quite mad. Why on earth didn't I see that before?'

Nonetheless, he proceeded to do exactly what he had been told. He could see no alternative.

TWENTY-THREE

U ltimately Freddie checked out of the Sofitel whilst Vogel and Saslow were still ploughing through the heavy late-afternoon traffic on the M4 made even worse than usual by equally heavy rainfall.

What he didn't know, however, was that Vogel had put a contingency plan into operation as soon as he'd ended his earlier phone conversation with Freddie. There had been four murders, almost certainly, whatever could or could not be proven in a court of law. Not only did Vogel mistrust everyone who was remotely involved with this case, he mistrusted the perennially illusive Freddie Fairbrother more than most. So he'd taken no chances.

He'd asked Nobby Clarke to divert a couple of her people from Brentford, less than half an hour away from Heathrow, where they were still conducting door-to-door and other inquiries into the George Grey affair, and dispatch them to the Sofitel on a watching brief.

They had seen Freddie leave, and followed him onto the Heathrow Express. Vogel and Saslow were still a good twenty minutes away from the Sofitel when Nobby Clarke called with the news.

'Your bird has flown his nest,' she said. 'But don't worry, Vogel. We're on his scent. Right up his arse actually.'

'That's good,' said Vogel. 'Only, don't let your guys approach him, will you? I'd like to see where he leads us and what he gets up to without alerting him, if that's possible.'

'Teach your grandmother,' said Clarke, ending the call.

Vogel was smiling as he related the exchange to Saslow, albeit without including Nobby's last remark.

'So what do we do now, boss?' asked Saslow.

'I'm not sure, Saslow,' replied Vogel. 'Just give me a moment, will you.'

He now had the footage on his phone of the mystery man arriving at Bella Fairbrother's apartment block. Almost certainly her killer. And he'd been playing it repeatedly ever since leaving Chelsea.

The niggle at the back of his mind was growing more and more insistent. There really was something, something about the mystery man's body language which was sending him a signal, a signal that this was somebody he knew, or at the very least had met. He just couldn't quite get there. Vogel, however, was the most dogged and determined of policemen. His mild manner and equable personality gave little indication of just how stubborn and intractable he could be. He was like a Canadian Mounty, or the Canadian Mounty legend, anyway. He worked on the principle that he would always get his man. And, eventually, he nearly always did. Because no case was ever closed without a result, as far as Vogel was concerned, whatever his superiors might say.

He played the short piece of film again and again. Each time telling himself it would be for the last time. Then he played it again.

And suddenly, suddenly, he remembered what had been bugging him.

'Oh my God, Saslow,' he said. 'I think I've got it.'

'Got what, boss.'

'I think I know who Bella Fairbrother's mystery caller was. I may just have identified her killer. And, I have to tell you, Saslow, it defies belief.'

He paused. 'I could still be wrong. I've finally realised what was bothering me. But it could be coincidence, or my memory might be playing tricks on me. Either way, Saslow, we have people to see and questions to ask. Nobby and her lot are all over Freddie Fairbrother. I think we can safely leave that end to them now. You and I need to get ourselves back to West Somerset, smartish.'

'C'mon boss, put me out of my misery,' said Saslow. 'Where exactly are we going and why?'

'We're going to the home of the man we saw in that CCTV footage,' said Vogel. 'At least, I hope we are.'

'But he was unidentifiable, boss. You couldn't see anything really except a shape in a bloody great hooded raincoat. You couldn't even see his hands because he was wearing gloves. Even the Met's tech boys have already said there's little or nothing they can do to make him identifiable.'

'I'm sure that's true. Thing is, though, from the start there was something that was bugging me about his body language, something that made me feel he was familiar to me. Did you notice what he was doing with his hands in that CCTV footage?'

'Not really, boss. They were just loose in front of him, most of the time, from what I recall.'

'Absolutely spot on, Saslow. But when he was speaking into the entry phone he began to repeatedly rub his hands together, palm to palm. It looked like a kind of nervous mannerism. You know, some people, when they're under stress rub their chin, or bite their lip, or tap their fingers on something. Whatever. This character, even with gloves on, rubs his hands together. And I reckon he probably always does it. I was sure from the start that I had seen someone do that recently, exactly the same way. But I couldn't remember who, or under what circumstances. And now, finally, it's come to me.'

Vogel treated Saslow to a big, somewhat self-satisfied, grin.

'Oh come on, for God's sake, boss,' said Saslow.

'I think it's Jack Kivel,' said Vogel. 'Kivel rubbed his hands together that way when we first went to his house and quizzed him about the fire and Sir John. Exactly that way. I'm sure of it. I think Jack Kivel killed Bella Fairbrother.'

Saslow whistled long and low. 'Wow, boss, that's a heck of a big assumption to make based on someone rubbing their hands together.'

'Yes. Which is why we're heading to the Kivel home before alerting anyone else. If Jack's there, and can prove beyond any reasonable doubt that he's not been out of the area all day, then he's in the clear and I'm wrong. But, well, I can just see him in my mind's eye, at his cottage, rubbing his hands together, perhaps a tad nervously, uncomfortable anyway. I didn't think anything of it at the time, because clearly the loss of Blackdown Manor and Sir John's death had been a big shock to the Kivels, even after the way they'd apparently been treated. But our Joe in the CCTV footage does exactly the same thing. And you know how pedantic I am about those sort of details, Saslow.'

Saslow knew. 'I'd call it anal, boss,' she said.

TWENTY-FOUR

F reddie destroyed his phone straight away, as instructed. He took out the SIM card and put it in his pocket. Then he drowned the phone in the washbasin in his hotel bathroom and wrapped its remains in an old newspaper which he dropped into a bin in the hotel lobby.

He checked out and took the walkway to the Heathrow Express terminal five station, where he boarded the next train to Paddington.

All the time he was fighting to remain calm and in control, and not entirely succeeding. He was certainly in no state to notice the two MCIT officers, DCs Jarvis Jones and Pamela Bright, who took photographs of him in the hotel lobby and then followed him onto the train, even if they had not been highly trained architects of surveillance.

Jones and Bright boarded the same carriage as Freddie. They were both in their twenties, each dressed in their personal choice of the anonymous uniform of modern youth: hoody, tracksuit bottoms and trainers for Jones; leather jacket, torn skinny jeans and boots for Bright.

They sat holding hands and appeared to have eyes only for each other. They were the epitome of a young couple in love. If it had occurred to Freddie that he might be followed, he would have been highly unlikely to have them as his most probable tail from amongst the diverse group of passengers on the Express.

At Paddington Freddie went straight to the Vodafone shop where, as instructed, he acquired a new pay-as-you-go phone. Jones and Bright disappeared into the entrance of the Tube station. Not that Freddie had noticed. Their part of the surveillance operation was over.

A second team was waiting on the station, also male and female DCs, Ali Patel and Marsha McKay, this time dressed and behaving like city business colleagues. As soon as Freddie exited the Vodafone shop, Ali Patel made his way in. Patel showed his warrant card and was able to obtain details of Freddie's transaction, including the number of the new phone he had acquired, thus allowing his future movements to be tracked should he at any stage give those following him the slip, which, as yet, he displayed no signs of attempting. It was abundantly clear that Freddie Fairbrother remained blissfully unaware of the surveillance operation focused on him.

Meanwhile DC McKay, pretending all the while to be speaking into her mobile, followed Freddie into the Paddington Hilton, through its entrance on the station concourse. In the lobby she sat down at once on a conveniently situated couch, and whilst continuing to appear to be talking into her phone, watched Freddie check in. Freddie was then directed across the lobby to the concierge's desk, where he was handed a brown leather briefcase, which he carried with him to the elevator leading to the rooms.

As soon as the elevator doors closed behind him, McKay approached reception, showed her warrant card, confirmed that Freddie had indeed checked in for the night, and obtained the number of his room. She sat down again on one of the lobby couches and prepared to wait.

A few minutes later a black cab pulled up outside. It was actually a police surveillance vehicle, with another MIT officer, DC Joe Parker, at the wheel. Almost immediately Ali Patel appeared and climbed into the back. The cab did not move.

A few minutes after that Freddie Fairbrother stepped out of the elevator and into the lobby. He was carrying the same brown leather briefcase, but other than that he was a man transformed. Indeed, McKay wondered if she might almost have missed him, were it not for the briefcase.

His unruly bleached blond hair had been slicked straight back. He was wearing a slightly stiff looking, but well-tailored, charcoal grey suit, a bright white shirt and a carefully knotted black tie.

He dropped off his room key at reception and left through the revolving doors onto Praed Street. McKay made no attempt to follow him. Her job was also done, for the time being, although she might be asked to wait at the Hilton for Fairbrother's return; or take part in a room search, should her superiors request this and succeed in obtaining a warrant.

Patel and Parker spotted Freddie as soon as he stepped onto the pavement. He hailed a cab from the rank right outside the hotel.

Parker immediately took off in cautious pursuit. Following another vehicle through congested London streets is never easy, and even though Parker was something of an expert – and the apparently properly registered cab he was driving gave him not only a certain invisibility, but also access to bus lanes and other restricted areas – he was reassured by the knowledge that the tech boys would soon be tracking Freddie Fairbrother's shiny new phone, if they weren't already.

As it happened, tailing Freddie's cab as it headed east along the Marylebone Road, with its bus and taxi lane, was relatively easy to begin with. But when they reached the City, the build-up of evening traffic in the narrower streets made Parker's job far more difficult.

Ultimately the inevitable happened. Freddie's cab slipped through traffic lights at a road junction, the lights changed, and Parker was forced to stop. He might well have risked jumping the lights, but a double decker bus was blocking his way.

'Shit,' said Parker.

'Don't worry, I think our man's reaching his destination,' said Patel. 'Look what's ahead.'

Parker did so. Less than half a mile or so in front, slightly off to the right, he could see a towering, distinctively angled shape, a building so tall it stood several storeys above the others in that part of the City.

'Fort Fairbrother,' said Patel, using the popular colloquial name for the head office of Fairbrother International. 'And I'll bet that's where Freddie's going. He's dressed for the part, isn't he?'

'I guess so,' said Parker, who took it as a personal insult when a mark escaped him, however close the probable destination.

Both men noticed that the next set of lights were changing to red.

'I'm off,' said Patel opening the door. 'I reckon I can get there quicker on foot. Let Pearson know.'

And he took off at a run down the street.

Freddie was indeed heading for Fort Fairbrother. His advisor had been quite correct concerning the apparent extension of normal working hours. There were lights on throughout the building, and the front office remained open.

His arrival caused quite a stir. The news of Bella Fairbrother's death had preceded him to the headquarters of his family's business empire by only an hour or so. And by osmosis had leaked to most of the rest of the City soon after that, even though a public announcement of her death had yet to be made.

The shares of Fairbrother International threatened to fall to a whole new low.

Acting chairman Jimmy Martins, who had still been anxiously waiting for Bella to arrive for a meeting crucial to the future of the bank when he heard that she'd been killed, was locked away in his office with the company secretary, Ben Travis. Both men were already in shock, and more than anything else, although neither admitted it to the other, they were determining how to save their own skins. Should they jump ship? If so, that might hasten what now seemed to be the inevitable collapse of Fairbrother's. But if they stayed on, would they be seen as continuing to be complicit in the undoubtedly dubious activities of their late boss, the company's former chairman and chief executive officer Sir John Fairbrother.

Each had more or less come to the conclusion that the lesser of the evils confronting them would be to cut their losses and run, when the front-office receptionist called to say that Mr Freddie Fairbrother was in the lobby and was requesting to see Mr Martins as a matter of urgency.

An astonished Martins told her to send Freddie up at once.

'What on earth can he want?' asked Ben Travis, when Prentis told him who was about to join them. 'I thought he was devoted to lotus eating on an Aussie beach.'

'I have no idea,' muttered Martins, whose peptic ulcer was playing up almost unbearably. Whatever the modern theory about ulcers, he was in little doubt that the burning gnawing sensation which engulfed his abdomen occurred most frequently and most extremely in direct relation to the degree of stress he was under.

'You don't think he's come to claim his inheritance, do you?' Travis continued. 'If so, he's damned well welcome to it, as far as I'm concerned anyway—'

He was interrupted by a brief tap on the chairman's office door. In walked Freddie. He'd been a teenager when Martins had last seen him. Ben Travis, a newer Fairbrother's executive, had clearly heard the stories but never actually met Freddie before.

Just as DC Patel had remarked to DC Parker, Jimmy Martin's first impression was that, all of a sudden, Freddie at least looked the part of a banker.

Pleasantries and introductions between the three men were cursory. Martins did not move from behind his desk. Instead he sat back in his chair and waited for Freddie to explain the purpose of his visit.

Freddie looked totally at ease. He stepped forward, set down the brown briefcase on the acting chairman's desk, and opened it.

'My father's will is in there,' he announced.

His voice was firm and surprisingly authoritative, not entirely unlike his father's, thought Martins.

'The case also contains papers concerning the various trust funds and investments which will, as I am sure you know, release substantial funds into the bank, following my father's death.'

Freddie paused. He smiled confidently at Martins and Travis.

It seemed crazy, thought Martins, but he almost looked as if he were milking the moment. Martins remembered then, Freddie had been a budding actor when he'd gone off the rails all those years ago.

'And as you will see, my father left his shares in Fairbrother International, and indeed the whole of his estate, to be divided between my sister and me,' Freddie continued. 'With the news of my sister's untimely death, which I am sure has already reached you, I am the sole beneficiary. In addition, it was my father's wish, that subject to the approval of the board, my sister should take over as chair and CEO of Fairbrother's International, because of her boardroom experience, with myself, the sole surviving male Fairbrother, as her deputy. So, again, following my sister's death, I feel it incumbent on me to step forward and offer myself to the board to take over that role.'

Martins was amazed. Freddie Fairbrother might not be an entirely useless erstwhile hippy after all. But, in any case, it really didn't matter whether he was or not.

He and Travis exchanged glances. Could this be the way out they had been seeking? It was not possible, surely, that Freddie Fairbrother would be capable of effectively running a major international company under any circumstances, let alone that he could have the expertise to steer the Fairbrother ship through extremely troubled waters.

However, did they care?

There surely could not be a better scapegoat, in a situation which was becoming increasingly more precarious, than Sir John Fairbrother's only son.

At first, as he marched across the marbled lobby floor of Fairbrother Fort, Freddie felt curiously elated. It would seem that he had pulled it off. Well, so far anyway. Certainly Martins and Travis appeared to have accepted everything he'd said at face value. Ultimately, they had merely told him that they would study the will and the other papers and get back to him.

But that was a result, wasn't it?

He'd been asked to perform a certain task, which could be instrumental in saving Fairbrother's, and it would seem that he had been successful.

It was only when he stepped outside that he realised he had absolutely no idea what to do next. And if his bid to take over as chair and CEO of Fairbrother's was successful, then he would be even more lost. How could he even begin to imagine that he could run the company? It was one thing being told that he was only ever going to be a puppet, but Freddie would need his strings pulled twenty-four-seven.

He thought he would walk for a bit to clear his head.

Freddie hadn't noticed Ali Patel hovering in the lobby and approach reception as he left the building. Nor did he notice the cab which was keeping behind him by virtue of a kind of stop-start manoeuvre in and out of the line of traffic.

However, neither did Parker, driving that cab, notice the broadly-built middle-aged man who was attempting to keep both the cab and Freddie Fairbrother in his eyeline.

After a while Freddie used his new pay-as-you-go phone to call the only number on it. He needed help. Fast.

The number rang, but there was no reply. And no message service. He tried again. Same result. Another two attempts also failed, as he had, by then, expected.

Freddie's hands were trembling again, and the back of his neck felt clammy again. It seemed crazy that only a few minutes earlier he had been on something of a high.

What did this mean? Had he been abandoned? But that would surely serve no purpose. Surely he had been right to consider himself indispensable now. He must try to think. Which wasn't something he was good at. But he knew he must keep calm and attempt to sort himself out, even if only temporarily. There was, of course, an argument for just giving up and going to the police. As his sister had told him that morning, was it really only that morning, his connection with all that had happened was fleeting. It was likely nothing could be proven against him, and possible that even Bella's death hadn't changed that.

For once in his life Freddie felt he had to make a decision. But, perhaps, not straightaway. He looked around him. There was a pub just across the road. What he needed, before he did anything, was a drink, he decided. And that was a decision he had often made before.

He ordered himself a pint of Fosters, his beer of choice, and a whisky chaser.

Outside in the street Parker pulled the surveillance cab to a halt, ignoring the hoots of impatient motorists. He contemplated abandoning the vehicle and following Fairbrother into the pub. But he was pretty sure there was no other entrance to the boozer, and considered he would be better off waiting for Freddie to emerge, ready to follow him to his next port of call. In any case, hopefully Ali Patel would not be too long making his inquiries at Fairbrother Fort, and he could go inside the pub.

The broad-shouldered man attempting solo surveillance faced no such dilemma. He knew exactly what he was going to do, and quickly, whilst Parker was still contemplating his next move, he marched straight into the pub and approached Freddie Fairbrother.

'Evening, Freddie,' he said. 'It's been a long time.'

Freddie Fairbrother's eyes opened wide in astonishment. It may have been a long time, but he recognised the other man at once. After all, he'd been a major part of his childhood.

'You,' he said. 'You. What are you doing here?'

'I've been sent to look after you.'

'But . . . but, why would . . . I mean, they told me you'd been sacked . . .' Freddie paused as a shocking revelation occurred to him. 'You haven't been sacked, have you?' he said. 'You've been doing his dirty work all the time. Did you kn—'

Jack Kivel put a firm hand on Freddie's right arm and squeezed with hard sinewy fingers.

'No, don't say it,' he ordered. 'Don't say anything we both might regret.'

Freddie stopped talking.

'I'm going to take you to him,' he said. 'That's what you want, isn't it?'

Freddie was no longer sure it was at all what he wanted. He was beginning to wish with all his heart that he hadn't made that phone call in the morning, and that he'd boarded the first possible flight back to Australia, as he had told his sister he would. He'd treated his visit to Fairbrother Fort as a performance, and had almost enjoyed it. He knew he had shown talent as an actor once, long ago. Possibly the only talent he'd ever had for anything. Reality was now beginning to hit with a vengeance. His sister had been murdered. More than likely by the man standing before him, a man he thought he had once known well, but whom he clearly had never known at all. Again he wondered if he might also be in danger. He couldn't be, though, could he? He was indispensable now, after all, wasn't he? He just had to do what he was told. That was where Bella had gone wrong.

'Of course,' said Freddie.

'Right,' replied Jack Kivel. 'Now, I don't suppose for one moment you've noticed, but you are being followed.'

'Oh my God,' said Freddie.

'So, before we go anywhere, we have to shake off your tail. Can you run?' Kivel eyed Freddie up and down. 'You look pretty fit considering your track record.'

Kivel grinned, as if trying to make himself appear likeable. It didn't work.

'I can run,' said Freddie nervously.

'Good. Now, there's a cab outside that's been tracking you, there's a second man, too, but he was still in Fairbrother House when you came out. I'm hoping he hasn't caught up yet—'

'Hang on, I don't understand why I have to run,' interrupted Freddie. 'Half an hour ago I was putting myself up to chair the board.'

'Yes, and that will happen. We need things to settle a bit, one or two things need to be arranged first, and we can't risk being followed to where I'm taking you now, can we? Look, I'll cause a diversion, get in the cab's way. You turn right out of the boozer, and walk normally for the first block or so, then leg it as fast as you can. St Paul's is about three quarters of a mile away. Tuck yourself in a doorway or something. I'll get in a taxi and come and pick you up. Just make absolutely sure you see it's me before you get in, OK?'

'OK.'

'But first, give me your phone.'

Freddie did so.

Kivel slipped it down the side of the seat of his chair.

'What are you doing now?' asked Freddie.

'You are being followed, Freddie, and it would seem almost certain that you were picked up at your hotel at Heathrow,' Jack Kivel explained patiently. 'Therefore, there would have been people on your tail when you bought your new phone. These are top cops, for certain. Professionals. Ten to a penny they have your new number, and they've already pinged it. Your trail will end here.'

'Oh my God,' said Freddie for the second time.

He then found himself watching in amazement as Kivel reached for Freddie's virtually untouched whisky, took a quick mouthful, and tipped the rest casually down his chin and over the front of his jacket.

'I will leave first, be right behind me, then take off, fast as you can, yes?' commanded Kivel, as if nothing untoward had happened.

'Yes,' said Freddie.

DC Parker, at the wheel of his surveillance cab, had his eyes fixed on the pub door when it swung open. Out rolled a drunk, who staggered across the pavement and into the road directly in front of the cab. In almost the same instance Parker saw Freddie Fairbrother leave the pub and walk briskly west.

Parker started his engine and prepared to move forwards in gentle pursuit. But the drunk was blocking the way. Parker blew his horn. No response. He wound down the driver's window and stuck his head out.

'Get out of the fucking way,' he yelled.

The drunk was either beyond understanding or didn't care. He certainly didn't move. Instead he stared at Parker in a puzzled sort of way, and asked, 'Are you for hire, my good man?'

'Move before I fucking make you!' yelled Parker.

Light seemed to dawn. The drunk took a step back towards the pavement, then fell over. Unless he was prepared to drive over the man, Parker's cab was going nowhere.

Instead he climbed out and ran to try to help the drunk to his feet, or just drag him out of the way, if that proved to be all that was possible. A cloud of whisky fumes hit him in the face. The drunk seemed comatose. Like a dead weight. And he was not a small man. Parker could not move him. Not easily anyway.

Parker was almost never indecisive, but he really wasn't sure what course of action he should take. Maybe he should just abandon his cab and try to catch up with Fairbrother on foot. He looked along the pavement. He could no longer see Freddie. But it was after dark, although the street was well lit, and there were pedestrians blocking his view. He decided to take off at a run, and weaved his way along the pavement for 100 yards or so. There was still no sign of Freddie Fairbrother. He gave up, and ran back to his cab. The drunk had gone. Disappeared.

'Shit,' muttered Joe Parker to himself. 'I think I've just been had.'

TWENTY-FIVE

From the moment of Vogel's road to Damascus moment concerning Jack Kivel, it took just over two and a half hours for Saslow and Vogel to reach the Kivels' Wrangway cottage. The heavy rain which had hindered their progress along the M4, from the moment they joined the motorway heading out of London, followed them all the way west, but on the M5 the traffic was relatively light.

It was not a pleasant journey, Vogel had been impatient and unusually anxious, and his mood was not improved by receiving a phone call from Nobby Clarke in which she confessed that MIT had lost Freddie Fairbrother. He chose not to share with her his suspicions about Jack Kivel, preferring to wait until he had at least some evidence to back up what was little more than a hunch. He knew only too well what Clarke thought about hunches. And it remained possible that he and Saslow were about to learn that Jack had not been anywhere that day. Let alone popped up to London to commit a murder.

The two officers hurried from their vehicle and stood outside the front door of Moorview Cottage, huddling beneath the inadequate porch in a bid to find shelter, whilst waiting for an answer to their knock. Vogel noticed the Kivel Land Rover was parked outside, but that didn't necessarily mean Jack was at home, he could be using another form of transport.

'Who is it?' called Martha, after what seemed a very long time, from behind the closed, and almost certainly locked, door.

'Police,' called back Vogel. 'DI Vogel and DC Saslow. Sorry to arrive unannounced. Just something we need to check with you and your husband, Mrs Kivel.'

The door was promptly unlocked. Martha Kivel stood silhouetted in a dimly lit hall, the bright lights of the kitchen, which the Kivels' clearly used as their main living area, behind her.

'Jack's not here,' said Martha. 'I never answer the door after dark if he's away. Not without checking who's there, first.'

'Uh yes, quite right, Mrs Kivel,' began Vogel. 'I wonder, could we just . . .?'

Martha Kivel stepped back out of the doorway. 'You must come in, of course,' she said. 'Come on in, the pair of 'ee. Get out of this terrible weather we'm having. Come into the kitchen where 'tis warm.'

Vogel and Saslow did so gratefully. Martha proved to be as hospitable as ever, offering tea and, once again, home-made sponge cake before even asking what the two officers wanted.

'You said your husband isn't here, Mrs Kivel?' queried Vogel.

'No. E's away with some of 'is army buddies. They meet up every so often and relive old times, drink more than's good for 'em, too, I shouldn't wonder. But I don't begrudge my Jack. He's worked hard all 'is life, and he's a good man.'

Vogel and Saslow involuntarily exchanged glances.

'I'm sure he is,' commented Vogel levelly. 'Might I ask when he left, Mrs Kivel, and when you are expecting him back?'

'Oh, he went this morning. He got a call from one of his mates. Short notice, but a couple of them had met by chance, somewhere up London way, wanted him to join them, if he could. I drove him to the railway station, and off he went. He won't be back til tomorrow. They'll make a night of it, that's for certain. He asked me if I minded, like, and I said course I didn't, you go and enjoy yourself.'

Martha Kivel stopped abruptly, her expression suddenly concerned. 'Why are you asking?' she enquired somewhat nervously. 'Has something happened? Has something happened to my Jack—'

'No, no, nothing like that,' Vogel interrupted.

'Is Jack in some sort of trouble?' Martha Kivel persisted.

Vogel didn't answer that question directly.

'I'm sure everything's fine, Mrs Kivel,' he said obliquely. 'We'd just like to talk to Jack, that's all. I don't suppose you know the names of any of the chaps he was meeting?'

Mrs Kivel shook her head. 'Well no, just 'is army mates, I don't know them, you see . . .'

She looked puzzled now.

'Do you know exactly where they were meeting up?' asked Saslow.

Mrs Kivel shook her head again.

'Did Jack tell you where he would be staying overnight?'

'Well no, a B &B, I expect. That's what they usually do. I mean, I can always get 'old of 'im if I want to, can't I? I only have to ring his mobile . . .'

She paused. Her face brightening. 'Why don't I do that? Then you can speak to him straightaway. Now . . .' She looked around the kitchen. 'Where did I put my phone? It's got to be yer somewhere . . .'

'No, don't do that, Mrs Kivel,' said Vogel quickly. Too quickly, he suspected. He immediately sought to soften his words. He wanted to see what more information he could glean from Martha Kivel before her husband was alerted.

'I mean, it can wait. We'll pop back and see him tomorrow. No need to ruin his night out by interrupting him now.'

'Oh, all right then, if that suits you . . .'

'It suits me very well,' said Vogel. 'Perhaps you'd give me his mobile number before we go, though, Mrs Kivel. I don't think we took it the last time we were here. I might call him in the morning to make an appointment.'

He took a mouthful of sponge cake. 'Even better than last time, Mrs Kivel,' he gushed. 'You must give me the recipe for my wife.'

'Oh, I'll write it out for you, Mr Vogel,' said Martha, beaming. 'I'd be delighted to. Handed down to me from my grandmother, it was.'

'Well, it's delicious,' commented Vogel, trying not to think about what Mary might say to him if he brought her home a cake recipe.

'I didn't know Jack had been in the army, Mrs Kivel,' he added, trying to sound as casual as possible.

'Oh yes, he went in as a boy. The Parachute Regiment. Sir John was already in. Jack followed him, really. The Kivels have worked for the Fairbrothers for generations. And Sir John and Jack was kids together, you see. Just like our kids and his two. They saw some action too. Northern Ireland, The Falklands. Goodness knows how long they'd have stayed in, but then Sir John's father died suddenly. And that was that. Sir John had to take over the bank. That's what Fairbrother men do. Jack followed him out like he'd followed him in, and Sir John employed him

straightaway, up the manor. Course, men bond through all that
sort of thing, don't 'em?'

'Yes, I believe they do,' agreed Vogel.

'That was what was so terrible, you see,' Martha Kivel continued.
'They was that close. My Jack worshipped Sir John. And then he
dumped us, Jack and me, just like that, without a word of explanation. Jack's never said much, he doesn't, but I don't reckon he'll
ever get over it, not ever.'

'I see,' said Vogel.

'So what do you know about their army careers?' he continued,
trying to sound conversational.

'Oh that's men's stuff, isn't it?' replied Martha Kivel. 'That's
what my Jack always says. He did tell me Sir John saved his life,
and he owed him everything. He said that when the old bugger
chucked us out. Still wouldn't hear a word against him.'

'Sir John saved his life? Has he ever said where? In the Falklands
perhaps?'

'No, I don't think so. I think it was Germany. They were posted
in Germany for quite a while.'

'Not in action, then?'

'What? Oh. I see what you mean. No, I don't suppose it could
'ave been in action. Not in Germany.'

'But he's never told you any more about it?'

'No. Only how grateful he was. You see, my Jack, he says
real soldiers never talk about stuff. Well you can understand that,
can't you?'

Martha paused. 'But why are you asking me all these questions?
You've still not told me.'

'Oh, I'm sorry, Mrs Kivel. I'm interested, that's all. Your Jack's
clearly had a very varied life.'

'You didn't come all this way to talk to me because you'm
interested in Jack's varied life,' said Martha. 'I'm not saying
anything else until you tell me what's going on.'

Martha's voice was suddenly quite sharp. Her eyes bright with
indignation. Vogel cursed himself. He'd been treating the woman
like a fool, largely because of her homely manner and her regional
accent. He should know better. Martha Kivel was clearly no fool.
And there was still a chance that she was aware of her husband's
covert activities. Assuming of course that there were any such

covert activities. But the circumstantial evidence, at least, was growing nicely. He needed to rebuild relations with Martha. He just hoped it were still possible.

'I'm so sorry, Mrs Kivel,' he said. 'I've allowed myself to be diverted. I really wanted to ask you and your husband some more questions about George Grey, and what you both know about goings on at the manor after Sir John became ill and removed you and Jack from your positions. I'm not even sure which came first, are you?'

Martha didn't look totally convinced, but she was, perhaps, a little mollified. Certainly, she answered Vogel in a more normal tone of voice.

'We've never been sure either,' she began. 'If he was ill when 'e sacked us, we didn't know about it.'

Saslow joined in, asking questions neither officer really wanted or needed to know the answer to, or in some cases already did, about Sir John's behaviour, the nurse who died in the fire, and any other employees.

In fact, by then neither of them could wait to leave Martha Kivel and put the next stage of their investigation into operation. The suddenly executed absence of Jack Kivel from his home made him a far more viable suspect. Either that, or there had been a huge coincidence. And David Vogel, in common with most serving police officers, did not believe in coincidences.

'Right, Saslow, we need to find Jack Kivel soonest, get his phone pinged straight away, make sure he doesn't disappear on us,' he said, once they were outside.

'You think Martha's probably already calling him to tell him about our visit, don't you?' said Saslow.

'You're damned right I do,' said Vogel.

'So does that mean she's in on it, assuming we're right about Jack?'

'That he's at the very least a cold-blooded murderer, and probably some kind of trained assassin?' queried Vogel. 'It seems that he may have the military credentials. Fairbrother too. As for Martha, I don't damned well know. But I'm taking no chances. Get onto district HQ in Taunton. I want surveillance on this cottage right through the night and into tomorrow, until I say so. And then get hold of Micky Palmer. And Polly Jenkins. I need them both back in. Tonight.'

'Right, boss,' replied Saslow.

'I'm going to call Nobby Clarke,' Vogel continued. 'Seems likely Kivel's still in her patch. And I'd very much like the full details of Freddie Fairbrother's activities, as monitored by her boys and girls before he gave them the slip, on my desk by the time I get back.'

'Yes, boss,' said Saslow, who was beginning to look and behave rather more like her old self.

Kivel picked up Freddie without incident, in the genuine black cab he'd hailed as soon as he'd finished so effectively diverting DC Parker. He asked the driver to take them to Victoria Station. There he led Freddie to the Hertz office and hired a car using his own credit card and driving licence. Nobody was looking for Jack Kivel. As far as Jack knew. Not yet anyway.

They were just about to drive away, in a suitably inconspicuous grey Toyota Prius, when Jack's mobile rang. It was Martha. She had called as soon as Vogel and Saslow left Moorview Cottage, just as Vogel had predicted she would.

'All right, maid,' said Jack by way of greeting.

As well as the use of West Country vernacular, Freddie noticed a subtle change in Kivel's voice, his regional accent just a little stronger, his diction less pronounced.

Jack Kivel's facial expression changed too as he listened to his wife. For the first time since he had met up with him that day, Freddie could see that Kivel was anxious. He didn't sound it, though, when he spoke again to his wife.

'Oh, don't fret, maid,' he said. 'It'll be some nonsense or other. Nothing to worry about, for sure. Look, I'll be back in the morning.'

He listened again. 'No. They 'aven't phoned me. Not yet anyway. There, that proves it, doesn't it? Nothing important.'

He exchanged a few more pleasantries with Martha and ended the call, at first without comment.

'What's happened?' asked Freddie nervously. 'I can tell something's happened.'

'It appears the police are taking an interest in my activities,' said Jack.

'What does that mean? What happens now?'

'I'm not entirely sure,' said Jack. 'But we both know someone who will know exactly what to do, don't we?'

Freddie sincerely hoped so.

Jack put his phone in his pocket, and removed a second, pay-as-you go phone to make a call. He quickly related the crux of his conversation with Martha.

'Look, there's nothing to incriminate you, is there?' came the response, soothingly. 'Nobody can prove anything.'

'No, I suppose not,' said Jack. 'But the police do seem to be closing in a bit.'

'They've still got no idea. I can't see any reason why the plan shouldn't go ahead. Although, I may need to disappear off the radar for a bit. As long as they don't find me, we're all pretty much OK. We do need Freddie on side, though. How does he seem?'

Kivel glanced sideways. 'Not one hundred per cent.'

'No, I thought not. He's always needed constant guidance and reassurance, that one. You must get him to me as quickly as possible.'

'Well, we've just picked up a fresh hire car. We're more or less on our way.'

'Not here,' came the swift reply. 'Let me think a minute.'

There was a brief pause. Then he gave another destination, and suggested a time.

'I'll have made arrangements for my disappearance by then. But, don't worry, I'll sort Freddie out first. He's going to be my puppet. I just have to make sure he's prepared to jump when I pull his strings.'

'OK,' said Kivel. 'See you there.'

'And don't forget to ditch your other phone. They'll be putting a track on it, for sure.'

'I won't,' said Kivel.

Freddie, of course, could only hear one side of the conversation. But he got the gist. And he was, by now, a very frightened man. However, he knew he was in far too deep to do anything other than go along with whatever the new plan might be.

TWENTY-SIX

Vogel asked Saslow to drive straight to Kenneth Steele House. On the way he went over the day's events again and again in his mind; the shock of Bella Fairbrother's death, and the almost equally great shock of suspecting that Jack Kivel might be responsible for it.

'I can't believe we all missed the possible significance of the military connection,' he commented to Saslow. 'It's not like Micky Palmer, that's for sure.'

'Well, we simply didn't know about Jack Kivel, it isn't something that ever came up, and he and his background have no Internet presence at all,' replied the DC reasonably. 'Also, as far as Sir John's military career is concerned, there was nothing to flag it. Eton then Sandhurst and the army seem just so predictable for the kind of young man he must have been when he joined up.'

Like Vogel, and presumably Micky, she had known that much about Sir John, it was part of his Wikipedia entry for a start, but not considered it important.

'I mean, in his sort of family it's the obvious alternative to Oxford or Cambridge, isn't it?' Saslow continued. 'Often for the not so bright. Although every indication is that Sir John was a very bright man indeed.'

'Yes, perhaps too bright,' responded Vogel. 'Too much of a maverick anyway. And overconfident, probably. We know he played the banking game pretty fast and loose, and that the Fairbrother ship is lying in very troubled waters. Yet his daughter seemed to believe that without him at the helm it would be an even bigger ask to steer it back on course.'

'She was prepared to take the job on, though, wasn't she, boss?' commented Saslow. 'Almost eager.'

'Yes, in spite of having walked out of the bank a year or so previously following a row with her father,' Vogel mused. 'Or allegedly.'

He was still thoughtful when they arrived at Kenneth Steele.

Micky Palmer hurried towards the DI as soon as he and Saslow entered the incident room.

'Boss, the tech boys have been on. They got a fix on Kivel's phone. Somewhere around London Victoria Station.'

Vogel whistled long and low. Victoria Station. From there Kivel could be heading almost anywhere, home or abroad.

'Just the one fix?' he queried, already pretty sure what the reply would be.

'Yes. The phone's not been live since.'

And neither will it be, thought Vogel. He considered Micky Palmer's choice of words.

'You said around Victoria Station,' he queried. 'Not the station itself?'

'Apparently not on the concourse, no. Somewhere just outside. They couldn't be precise. He took a call from Martha's number, she called just like you said she would, and he was on the phone for a few minutes.'

'Right, that's something, but how on earth can we find out where he went next? Assuming he ditched his phone, which he almost certainly would have done after Martha's call. We know he doesn't have his own vehicle. He travelled to London by train, according to Martha. Trains from Victoria don't come this way, but they do go all over, including Gatwick airport, and then there's the Victoria bus terminus.'

'If he wasn't located actually in the station, perhaps he's hired a vehicle, boss,' suggested Saslow.

Vogel took a deep breath. 'Dawn, you're a genius,' he said. 'There aren't that many hire car pick-up places actually in central London, but most of the big boys operate out of Victoria. It's worth checking anyway.'

'Well, yes boss, but even if he has hired a car, would he have used his own driving licence and credit card?' asked Saslow.

'I'm hoping he may have done just that, before Martha called him, before he knew we were on to him. Get Polly to check it out straightaway.'

Vogel turned back to Palmer. 'So, have you got anything else, Micky?' he asked.

'Yes, boss. I've been focusing on Sir John and Jack Kivel's military careers. It seems they didn't just become Paras at the same time, they joined the SAS together in 1982, just before the Falklands War. Kivel was twenty-three, already an NCO, Sir John was a bit older, twenty-six, and a captain. He was promoted to major four years later, aged thirty, young for the rank, in peace-time anyway.

'Wherever Sir John went, he made sure Kivel did too. The SAS is for elite soldiers, everybody knows that. But apparently Kivel and Fairbrother stood out, even in that company, as shit hot. Tough as old boots, the pair of 'em. They specialised in undercover operations, the least said about the better, which often even other SAS men wouldn't touch. They quit together too, when Sir John left to take over Fairbrother International, and Kivel's been in Sir John's employ ever since. Or he was until a year ago . . . you know that though, boss.'

'Yes, but maybe his alleged sacking was camouflage,' volunteered Saslow, who had returned from briefing Polly Jenkins. 'Looks like it now, doesn't it? Kivel was always Fairbrother's man, and George Grey was hired to take the fall. How's that for a theory?'

'It would be a better one if Sir John wasn't dead,' commented Micky Palmer.

'Yes, it would, wouldn't it,' responded Vogel. 'Excuse me a moment. I have a couple of calls to make.'

The first call was to Karen Crow.

The pathologist answered at once. 'Don't you ever stop working, Vogel?' she remarked by way of greeting.

'Not when I have four murders to solve,' replied Vogel. 'Look, you told me you'd formally identified Sir John through his dental records, right?'

'Yes. There wasn't enough left of the poor bastard to effectively test for DNA. Not unusual with fire victims, as you know.'

'But just as indisputable, isn't that so?'

'Absolutely. Yes.'

'OK. All the same, I wouldn't mind a word with his dentist. Do you have his details handy? A mobile number would be good if you've got one. I'd like to talk to him right now, if I can.'

'Would you indeed? What are you up to, Vogel?'

'Karen, I'm in a hurry.'

'All right, all right, I'm pretty sure he called me back from his mobile when I originally contacted him, so it should be in my phone. I'll text you.'

Two minutes later Vogel was speaking to a rather surprised Mark Rowland, Sir John Fairbrother's Exeter-based dentist, who confirmed that he had seen Sir John just three weeks before his death, and that he had been able to supply a full set of dental records to Karen Crow.

'His teeth were in a very bad state,' said Rowland. 'He was in the advanced stages of Parkinson's, which can have an extremely damaging effect on a patient's teeth. We're not entirely sure whether it's the drugs or the disease which does the most damage. Several of Sir John's teeth were crumbling away, and he was suffering quite severe pain. To be honest, there wasn't a lot that could be done. I just tried to make him as comfortable as possible.'

'I don't suppose there could be any doubt about these records, could there, Mr Rowland?' asked Vogel.

'Doubt? Certainly not. I'd completed the usual charts, and there were also X-rays.' The dentist paused. 'Are you suggesting this surgery may have made some sort of mistake, Mr Vogel?' he asked sharply.

'No, no, of course not,' replied Vogel, quickly changing tack. 'I just wondered, how long had Sir John been your patient?'

'Oh, not long. Nine or ten months, I think. If that. I understood he had used a London dentist until he became ill. If you want the exact date he registered with us, my receptionist could check for you in the morning—'

'No, that won't be necessary, Mr Rowland,' interrupted Vogel. 'One more thing, though, had you ever met Sir John Fairbrother before he became your patient?'

'No. Never.'

Vogel leaned back in his chair. He was following a train of thought which was surely far too wild to seriously consider. Nonetheless, he wasn't going to stop until he had fully explored it.

He called up the records of data so far gathered, including interviews made by the team temporarily based at Wellington police station, both door-to-door locally and with any persons of interest who may have been in contact with either Sir John or his nurse Sophia Santos.

An interview with Santos' sister in the Philippines, conducted by local police, ascertained that Sophia had reported that the demands made of her, particularly in terms of working hours, were exceptionally high. But she had taken the post because the salary offered had also been exceptionally high, apparently two to three times what the nurse would have expected in the UK. In addition, there was promise of a bonus, to be paid after Sir John's death, on condition that she continued to care for him until that eventuality.

Santos had, of course, been the only live-in nurse, assisted by Janice Grey. Three agency nurses who had been occasionally employed, were also interviewed. Each gave an almost identical account. They had been called only to work night shift, and Sir John, on high levels of medication, had been asleep most of the time and uncommunicative for the rest.

Paul Preston Evans, the swimming pool man DC Dawson had told Vogel about, had been interviewed as it seemed he'd been one of the last people, outside of those directly caring for Sir John, to see him alive.

Preston Evans had confirmed that he'd caught Sir John unawares in his swimming pool about a month before the fire and been immediately ushered out by Janice Grey.

'Sir John looked terrible, I was quite shocked by his appearance,' Preston Evans had said. 'He'd always been a strong fit man for his age, and I couldn't believe how he'd deteriorated. It was as if he'd shrunk. And he looked so weak. A shadow of his former self.'

The interviewing DC had then asked how long it had been since Paul Preston Evans had previously seen Sir John.

'Oh, it was months, maybe a year, I suppose,' said Preston Evans.

And yes, he confirmed, Sir John had then looked perfectly well and the same as always.

Vogel recalled that Sir John had been treated privately by Bristol neurologist James Timson, a Parkinson's specialist, who had also been interviewed early in the proceedings. Vogel called up the interview. It seemed that Sir John's condition had at first improved slightly under the care of Mr Timson, and his estimated life expectancy had increased accordingly.

The neurologist was unsure exactly how long his patient had suffered from the disease. Then came the information Vogel was looking for. It seemed that Mr Timson had only treated Sir John

Fairbrother for about eleven months, and had not seen any earlier medical records.

'They were always on the way, but never seemed to turn up,' he said.

Vogel sat for a moment deep in thought. He had so far found nobody who was in any sort of close contact with Sir John at the time of his death who had known him for more than a year. Anyone who did had been sacked, or simply avoided, or in the case of his immediate family, allegedly become estranged.

Vogel was still trying to make sense of what all this might mean, when Polly Jenkins came running across the incident room.

'I've got it, boss,' she said triumphantly. 'Jack Kivel hired a car from Hertz at Victoria about two and a half hours ago. It's a metallic grey Toyota Prius. They're sending over all the details.'

'Well done, Polly,' said Vogel. 'Put out an alert for that car. Get onto traffic right away. Tell them to forget about speeding violations. I want every traffic officer on the major highways out of London on the lookout for this vehicle. Particularly focusing on the motorways and arterials heading west and south. Kivel didn't hire a car to stay in the city, and I'm gambling that as he picked it up in Victoria, he wouldn't be heading north or east out of London. Right, Polly, move.'

Polly moved.

Vogel could feel the adrenalin rushing through him. The news of Kivel had somehow triggered him into action. He'd made his decision.

'Saslow, with me,' he called.

Saslow followed briskly. As Vogel strode through the incident room with the young DC hard on his heels, he called out to Micky Palmer.

'Micky, get Hemmings on the phone. Tell him Saslow and I are on the way over to his house, and there's been a possible development in the Fairbrother case which I must tell him about face to face.'

Palmer looked slightly askance. Vogel knew what the DC was thinking. It was getting on for midnight. Hemmings was going to be absolutely thrilled to receive the news that Vogel and Saslow were about to arrive at his home.

TWENTY-SEVEN

V ogel filled Saslow in on his latest theory as she drove.
The young DC didn't seem to quite know what to say.
Vogel knew how she felt. His phone rang just as they
pulled up outside Hemmings' large mock Tudor semi, which
neither of them had ever visited before, in Clifton on the south
side of the city.

'Traffic just picked up Jack Kivel's hire car on the M5,' said
Polly Jenkins. 'Just past the Bristol intersection.'

'Well, well, so is he coming home, I wonder? That would be
pretty damned cool behaviour.'

'I dunno boss, but it seems he has a passenger. More than likely
Freddie Fairbrother, from what Nobby Clarke's lot have said. Their
full report's come through. It seems Freddie had help giving 'em
the slip. From a drunk, a burly broad-shouldered man, probably in
his late fifties. Or more than likely our Jack pretending to be drunk,
they think now. Traffic are covering every junction as the vehicle
passes, tracking but making no approach, like you said, boss.'

'Good,' said Vogel. 'Just keep me posted.'

Hemmings opened his front door before either Vogel or Saslow
had the chance to ring the bell. He was wearing pyjamas and a
velvet dressing gown that was more like an old-fashioned smoking
jacket. Vogel didn't dare look at Saslow.

'This had better be good, Vogel,' the superintendent growled.

'Well, that's one word for it, I suppose,' said Vogel.

'I do wish you wouldn't talk in riddles, Vogel,' said Hemmings.
'Right, as you're here you'd better come in.'

He led the way into a plushly carpeted sitting room. Even under
such taxing circumstances Vogel could not fail to notice an
abundance of velvet. Almost certainly down to Mrs Hemmings,
he suspected.

Hemmings gestured for his visitors to sit, side by side on an
expansive, gold, velvet-covered sofa. He did not look happy.
Somewhat pointedly he did not offer them any hospitality.

Vogel began to speak, reporting on the day's events and doggedly explaining his theory, which, he felt, began to sound more far-fetched the more he tried to rationalise it.

Hemmings listened in silence until he came to a natural end. Vogel waited patiently for his superior officer's response, which seemed an inordinately long time in coming.

'You are something else, Vogel,' Hemmings said eventually, his tone no longer indicating whether or not he remained irritated by the presence of the two detectives. 'You really are. And you have just presented to me what is probably the most outlandish scenario I have encountered in my entire career.'

'Sorry sir,' said Vogel lamely, largely because he could think of nothing else to say.

'Yes, well, the thing is, I think you might well be right,' the superintendent continued, to Vogel's relief. 'So, the only question is, what exactly are we going to do about it?'

He paused. 'Kivel, and Freddie Fairbrother, we think, are some-where on the M5 in a hire car. I don't suppose we have any idea where they are going?'

'No sir, I'm afraid not,' replied Vogel. 'I thought Kivel might be playing it cool and heading for home when I first heard where his car had been spotted. After all, we haven't got any hard evidence against him. Not yet anyway. But I don't think he'd take Freddie back to his cottage, unless his wife is in on it all too, of course—'

Vogel was interrupted by the ring of his phone.

He muttered his excuses and glanced at the screen. The caller was Polly Jenkins again. He answered at once.

'Boss, traffic say Kivel has just turned off the M5 at Junction eighteen,' Polly reported. 'He's heading south on the A4.'

Vogel was a new boy in the west of England, and his know-ledge of road configurations anywhere was not as good as it should be, because he didn't drive. But even he knew what lay in that direction.

'My God,' he muttered, with sudden certainty. 'The airport. They're heading for Bristol Airport. Hold on a minute, Polly.'

He turned to Hemmings. His senior officer was on his feet, his own phone in his hand, every iota of his body language positive and decisive. Vogel was not surprised. Hemmings wasn't the boss of MIT for nothing. Clearly the superintendent was already right up to speed.

'Tell Polly to make sure traffic continue to monitor the situation,' he instructed. 'You and Saslow, get to the airport. I'll liaise with the airport police and arrange backup. Armed backup. Please be careful, Vogel. If you catch up with our man first, don't do anything until you have backup. Is that clear?'

'Of course, sir,' said Vogel.

He was already halfway out of the house, Saslow hard on his heels.

Bristol Airport was quiet. More or less closed. Although the airport was licensed for night take-offs, in reality these were few and far between, particularly out of the holiday season.

Vogel was aware of this. He also knew that Bristol Airport was something of a centre for those who did not have to rely on the services of commercial airlines. Multi billionaire Sir James Dyson, one of the south west's most successful businessmen ever, kept his own personal jet, a forty million pound Gulfstream, parked at the airport in its own two million pound hangar. Sir John Fairbrother, perhaps sensitive to the scrutiny of his company's shareholders, had preferred, when necessary, to charter private aircraft capable of intercontinental travel. Or travel on somebody else's.

During the drive to the airport Vogel had called Micky Palmer and asked him to check if any flights were booked in or out of Bristol airport that night.

Micky had returned the call just as Vogel and Saslow were turning into the airport complex. The airport authorities had reported that a private jet, registered to a Saudi Arabian sheik, had landed within the last few minutes. The jet, a Gulfstream like Dyson's, with a range of 7000 nautical miles, had also been booked to fly out of Bristol within the hour.

Saslow pulled into the short-term car park as Vogel had instructed. He didn't want to attract attention by parking their car anywhere that it shouldn't be. As the two officers walked across the access road to the terminal building, just the one at Bristol, Vogel's phone rang again. It was Polly Jenkins to tell him traffic had reported that Kivel's vehicle had just been spotted turning into the airport. It seemed Vogel and Saslow had got there first.

'Let's get back into the car park, keep out of the way,' said Vogel, mindful both of Hemmings' instructions and Saslow's confrontation with violence the previous year, from which he did not believe the young officer had yet fully recovered.

The grey Prius appeared almost immediately and pulled up right outside the terminal in a restricted parking area. Clearly Jack Kivel was in a hurry, and with the terrible crimes Vogel now believed he had almost certainly committed, a parking violation, even at an airport, would be unlikely to bother him.

Two men emerged from the Prius. The lights from the terminal building were bright enough for Vogel to be able to identify one of them as Jack Kivel, and the second, from photographs provided by the MIT surveillance team, as Freddie Fairbrother.

They quickly entered the terminal building, Kivel leading the way.

Vogel glanced around, there was no sign of any other police presence. No airport police, although they must surely be around somewhere. No armed response. Nobody.

He turned to Saslow. 'Look Dawn, I'm going over for a closer look, see what's going on. I want you to stay here, wait for backup, OK?'

'No boss, if you're going over there. I'm going too.'

'I'm not putting you in danger, Saslow, not again.'

'Sir, it might not be Heathrow but that terminal building is a big place. We can keep out of sight, I'm sure, just check nobody gets away. Keep a watching brief. Maybe alert airport personnel. Much easier with two of us.'

Vogel knew there wasn't time to argue.

'Stay with me,' he commanded, as he hurried across the road.

The two officers entered the terminal cautiously. At first, they couldn't see Kivel or Fairbrother or anyone else who might be of interest to them. All the check-in desks and the bars and cafes seemed to be closed.

Then they caught sight of three figures at the far end of the building, close to departures. One was a tall bearded man wearing a baseball hat. The second was Jack Kivel. The third almost certainly Freddie Fairbrother.

'We mustn't get too close, Saslow,' instructed Vogel. 'Kivel might still be armed.'

'In an airport, boss?' queried Saslow.

'They're not airside,' responded Vogel. 'You don't go through security until you go airside. For all we know they could all be armed.'

The three men seemed to be in deep conversation. And thankfully, they appeared to remain unaware that they were being watched. In order to make themselves less visible Vogel and Saslow sat down on two of a row of plastic seats.

After about five minutes a female airport official came and spoke to the tall bearded man, who then seemed to start taking his leave, in an apologetic sort of way.

'What on earth is that woman doing?' muttered Vogel. 'Airport staff should have been warned not to approach.'

'Seems like the word hasn't got through,' responded Saslow. 'Wires crossed somewhere. She doesn't look as if she's aware of any sort of danger.'

After a brief further exchange, the other two men, Fairbrother and Kivel, turned to walk towards the exit to the car park. The bearded man followed the airport official towards departures. It was probably his imagination, but Vogel reckoned he could hear the revving of a Gulfstream's engines outside on the runway.

Vogel looked anxiously around him. There was still no sign of the promised backup.

'Shit,' he said. 'That bastard's going to get away. I'm not having it.'

He turned to Saslow. 'Stay here. Do you hear me. Stay here.'

Then he took off at a run across the terminal building, passing close to Kivel and Fairbrother, but moving so quickly that they did not begin to react until he'd reached the bearded man and the airport official.

'Sir John, Sir John Fairbrother,' he shouted, holding out his warrant card at arm's length. 'Stop. Police.'

The bearded man turned at once, probably involuntarily, Vogel thought later.

'I'm sorry I think you must be mistaken, officer,' he said calmly. 'My name is Jeremy Carter. You can see my passport if you wish.'

Vogel placed one hand firmly on the man's arm, and with the other took a set of handcuffs from his pocket.

'You are Sir John Fairbrother,' he said. 'And I am arresting you on suspicion of four counts of murder and conspiracy to murder, and on suspicion of an as yet unspecified number of counts of fraud. You do not have to say anything. But it may harm your defence if you do not mention when questioned something which you later rely on in court. Anything you do say may be given in evidence—'

Vogel didn't get to quite finish the caution. Moving with considerable speed for a burly man, Jack Kivel had arrived at his side.

'Back off, DI Vogel,' he said. 'You don't understand what you are dealing with here. Just back off.'

Vogel was momentarily distracted. And before he could attach the cuffs, Fairbrother wrenched himself free.

Vogel turned to look at Kivel, and found he was staring down the barrel of a Glock handgun fitted with a silencer. A gun that had probably already killed once that day. Vogel no longer had much doubt about that.

'Jack, don't make things any worse for yourself,' he said lamely, looking hopefully back across the terminal. He could see that Saslow had arrested Freddie Fairbrother, who, predictably, appeared to have made little fuss. There was still no sign of any further police presence. Where the hell was that backup?

Meanwhile Fairbrother Senior had grabbed the stunned-looking airport official and was holding a pocket knife to her throat.

Vogel could barely believe what was going on. It all seemed to be happening in slow motion. It was surreal.

'C'mon, Jack,' said Fairbrother suddenly. 'You'll have to come with me. There's no choice now. You've been seen with me. You can't bluff your way out of this one, and neither can I. We can still get away. The bank might be history, but we needn't be.'

The Glock wavered in Jack Kivel's hand. 'But we did all this for the bank,' said Kivel. 'That and your damned family name!'

'Well that's over now, but we can still escape to somewhere no one will be able to get at us and live a new life. In luxury. It's all been arranged. You know that.'

Vogel was surprised at how calm Sir John Fairbrother seemed to have remained. This was some piece of work. How could he be that way, under these circumstances? There was, of course, only one possible conclusion. The conclusion which Kivel had finally reached on the drive from London.

Sir John Fairbrother had gone quite mad. Raving mad. Stark staring bonkers. Off his rocker.

Kivel was talking. 'I have a wife, boss – children, grandchildren . . .'

'C'mon Jack, I'll get them to you whenever you want,' said Fairbrother as he dragged the terrified airport official closer to the departure gate. 'We can do this.'

Kivel turned a little to watch. His broad shoulders had slumped. Vogel wondered if he dared grab the gun.

'I always go where you go, don't I, boss?' he said. 'And do what you say. Always.'

'Yes, well, you owe me, don't you, Jack. You'd have been locked up years ago if it wasn't for me.'

'At least I would have been my own man.'

'Oh c'mon, Jack, don't I always look after you? I will now. I promise you.'

'And you think they're just going to let us fly out of here, do you?' Jack asked. 'To live this new life with your fancy Arab friend?'

'You've got the gun, Jack,' said Fairbrother. 'And God knows, you know how to use it.'

'Yes, like I did earlier today. Something I already regret with all my heart.'

'C'mon, Jack,' said Fairbrother yet again. 'She was a loose cannon. I did love my daughter, you know, but she had to go. She was about to bring us down.'

'We are down, boss, down as low as you can get.'

Vogel heard a noise behind him. They'd arrived at last. Numerous black-clad armed police officers were storming the terminal.

Kivel saw it too. If Fairbrother had noticed, he gave no indication. He seemed locked in his own crazy world.

'It's finished, boss,' said Kivel quietly. 'This time we've gone too far.'

Kivel turned towards Vogel. 'Tell Martha, I'm sorry, will you,' he said.

And with that he turned the handgun around, pointed it at his own face, and shot himself through the mouth. The back of his head exploded, and he crashed instantly to the ground.

Vogel was momentarily transfixed. Sir John Fairbrother immediately let go of the airport official and lurched toward the fallen Kivel. Vogel grabbed him, this time managing to attach and fasten the handcuffs in one swift motion. But Sir John did not resist. Instead he stood quite still looking down at Jack Kivel.

Then, and Vogel could hardly believe his own eyes, this man who had behaved with such wanton mindless cruelty, who had committed such terrible evil, and shown a total disregard of the lives of other human beings to the extent that he had arranged the murder of his own daughter, began to weep.

TWENTY-EIGHT

The next day, or technically later that same day, Vogel interviewed Freddie Fairbrother at Bristol's Lockleaze police station.

There remained a lot of unanswered questions, and Freddie was now probably the only person able or likely to provide answers to any of them.

Vogel had promised Freddie, before the formal interview began, that he almost certainly would face no charges if he told the truth and revealed all that he knew about his father's extraordinary plan of deception. Freddie had, after all, been out of the country until less than forty-eight hours previously, and his direct involvement was slight. Vogel told Freddie that he was confident he would be free to leave the UK within a few days and return to Australia, which was now all he wanted to do.

In return, Freddie – to use a phrase which had been a favourite of Vogel's first sergeant – had begun singing like a bird.

'My father knew that Fairbrother International was close to collapse, and that because of his irregular business practices he would probably end up in jail, possibly, at his age, for the rest of his life,' Freddie began. 'He had attracted the attention of fraud investigators more than once over the years, but nothing had ever been proven. If he failed to keep Fairbrother's afloat, and he knew that he was about to fail, there would be an investigation on a whole new level. He feared that not only was he going to lose the bank, but his reputation, and that of the family, would be ruined for ever. Which to him was of massive importance, overshadowing even the probability of a jail sentence.'

'And so, in your own words, Mr Fairbrother, will you please tell me the details of this plan your father concocted which was supposed to save the bank and keep his reputation intact?' asked Vogel.

'Well, I don't know it all . . .'

'Just everything you do know, Mr Fairbrother.'

'Well, as you would be aware, Mr Vogel, the bank is a family affair, a family business, and it has survived many centuries of trading. One of the reasons for this is that continuity has always been maintained, largely by a unique system of trust funds, and other investments, which can only be released back into the bank following the death of the incumbent chairman, which is an appointment for life, you understand. Like being a monarch.'

Freddie managed a small smile. 'A despot monarch, usually, and certainly in my father's case,' he continued. 'The chairman traditionally retires from active participation at a certain age, if he lives that long, and appoints a chief executive to actually run the company, but he remains chairman until his death. These moneys are then realised when the next chair, always another Fairbrother, takes office, ensuring a fresh influx of funds with every generation, and more or less copper bottoming the future of the bank even if the previous chair has left it with problems. My father, I suppose, wanted to have his cake and eat it, as they say.

'By faking his own death he could maintain his reputation, and at the same time ensure the future of the bank. That's what he thought anyway. He also thought he could carry on running things from behind the scenes. The bank, in particular, had always been his toy after all. Crazy really. Now you come to think of it.'

Yes, thought Vogel. Beyond crazy.

Aloud he said, 'Your father actually found someone to, in effect, die in his place. Do you know how he managed to do that? Why would anybody agree to that?'

Fairbrother shrugged. 'Well, Pa didn't actually seek someone out to do that. It happened by chance. He told me he was coming out of a restaurant in Covent Garden, with friends, when he damned near fell over this homeless guy lying on the pavement. The two of them just stared at each other. Pa said the man was his double, a slightly smaller, weaker, version of himself – even the same thick white hair – and about the same age. He could also see that this man was ill. The idea came to him that night, and he went back to Covent Garden the next day to try to find the man, which he did quite easily, and learned that he had Parkinson's and a very limited life expectancy. So, basically, Pa offered him care for the rest of his days, a luxurious home, all the medical attention he needed and so on, if he would take Father's place. The man wouldn't have to do anything, he would be protected from difficult contact with outsiders, anything he wanted would be provided for him without question, and so on.'

Vogel tried not to show too much astonishment. He supposed he shouldn't be that amazed. Sir John Fairbrother had clearly thought he was near immortal and could get away with anything. He also, equally clearly, had immense powers of persuasion.

'And the homeless man agreed to all of this, just like that?'

Fairbrother shrugged. 'You're living rough, out in the cold, drinking meths and cider. Somebody offers you warmth and comfort, champagne and fine brandy. Bit of a no brainer, some might say.'

Vogel supposed Freddie Fairbrother had a point.

'When did your father tell you all this?' he asked.

'He came to see me about seven or eight months ago. Just turned up in Brisbane, complete with beard and bald head. A simple but excellent disguise. I almost didn't recognise him at first. But, of course, I hadn't seen him in eighteen years.

'The substitute Sir John was already installed at Blackdown. Bella knew all about it from the beginning. She and my father had staged their fall-out, you've probably guessed that, and she quit the board of Fairbrother's so that she would be able to disassociate herself from the mess the company was in. Pa told me he wanted me back in the fold because he was afraid the board still wouldn't accept Bella without the presence of a male Fairbrother. I was going to be the prodigal son. The thing is, Mr Vogel, I found that I rather wanted my birthright back. I really did. And it seemed like the perfect plan, in which everyone would be a winner.

'The bank would be saved. As far as the world was concerned my father would die with his blessed reputation still intact, but actually he would be living on this exotic island he secretly owned in the Middle East, under the protection of his chum Sheik Abdul whose family fortune has been greatly enhanced by many years of involvement in Pa's dubious international financial dealings. Pa was totally confident he would never be found there, and that he would be able to continue pulling the strings at Fairbrother International. Bella and I would each get exactly what we wanted, the top job at Fairbrother's, or more or less, for her; all the trappings that come with being head of the Fairbrother clan for me, without doing the work, and the homeless man got a standard of living and a level of care he could never have dreamed of.'

'But then it all went wrong. What happened, Freddie?'

'Well, Pa's poor sap responded rather too well to the care he was receiving. Pa had told me in Brisbane that he would be dead in weeks. Eight months later he was still going strong. Or reasonably strong. Meanwhile the affairs of the bank were becoming more desperate, critical in fact. My father realised something had to be done, things had to be speeded up or the whole plan would fail.'

'And your father told you that, did he? That he had decided to speed up his impersonator's death?'

Fairbrother looked furtive, as if realising he may have inadvertently revealed rather too much about his own involvement. 'Uh no, he didn't tell me anything like that,' he said quickly. 'I thought the fire was an accident. I still thought that when I arrived in the UK. I knew it was being investigated, but I was confident that no evidence of arson would be found.'

I'll bet you were, thought Vogel, who already realised that Freddie's capacity for self-deception was probably greater than his capacity for deceiving others. Unlike his father.

'Do you know who this man was, the man who, in effect, died in your father's place?'

'No idea,' said Freddie casually.

'Do you not even know his name?'

'No, why would I? He was just some homeless jerk. Pa used to refer to him as Johnny Two.'

Freddie laughed humourlessly.

'I see,' said Vogel, who was fighting an almost overwhelming urge to slap Freddie Fairbrother across the face. Instead he stood up, keeping his hands loose at his sides, and asked Freddie to do the same.

'Frederick John Fairbrother, I am charging you with conspiracy to murder your sister, Christabella Ann Fairbrother, and also conspiracy to fraud. You do not have to say anything. But it may harm your defence . . .'

Freddie did not seem to hear the caution. He stood with his mouth slightly open and an expression of disbelief on his face. He'd heard the first bit all right.

'You're charging me?' he asked ingenuously. 'But you told me you weren't going to. You told me I could go home. Home to Australia . . .' His voice tailed away.

'I have absolutely no recollection of that,' responded Vogel deadpan.

'But I've only been in the country for forty-eight hours,' Freddie continued.

'Yes, and look what you've achieved,' said Vogel, equally deadpan.

'And you said yourself, I'm barely involved, never have been, not with any of it,' Freddie continued. 'These charges are nonsense. No court will convict me.'

'Mr Fairbrother, I feel confident we shall be able to prove that you phoned your father yesterday morning, straight after Bella had undoubtedly told you she had arranged to meet me at her home. You knowingly sent your sister to her death. Oh, and you have just confessed that you were fully aware of your father's fraudulent attempt to fake his own death for both personal and professional gain. I am quite confident that we will gain convictions against you.'

'You've tricked me, you bastard,' said Freddie.

'Not at all, Mr Fairbrother,' said Vogel.

A small satisfied smile twitched at the corners of his mouth.

EPILOGUE

Sir John Fairbrother was made of stronger stuff. He pleaded that he had been suffering from amnesia and could remember next to nothing since disappearing from his home. He knew nothing of the imposter who had taken his place at Blackdown Manor. He knew nothing of the catastrophic fire at the manor. He knew nothing about the death of George Grey, nor of his dear daughter, Bella. Jack Kivel was clearly responsible for all of it, and Sir John had no idea why.

His solicitor Peter Prentis arrived from London and, although not entirely able to hide his shock at the events which had been brought to his attention, went through the motions of taking control of the situation. His client, he said, would answer no more questions, and would be pleading not guilty to all charges.

A second search of the grounds of Blackdown Manor and the immediate area, following the break-in at The Gatehouse, revealed signs of recent habitation in an old keeper's cottage, on Fairbrother land, which had previously been dismissed as derelict. A camp bed, tinned food supplies, and a small portable generator were found in an upstairs room with boarded-up windows.

It seemed incredible that Fairbrother would have chosen as a hiding place somewhere actually on his own property, but he was clearly a man conditioned to thinking outside the box. A man not only without morals, scruples, conscience or almost any normal human emotions, but also without a great deal of fear. Vogel reckoned that is exactly what he had done, that he had vacated his barge in Brentford and high-tailed it there right after killing George Grey. The one murder Fairbrother had surely committed himself, whether or not that could ever be proven. It therefore appeared likely that it had been Sir John himself, with or without the assistance of Jack Kivel, who had broken into The Gatehouse, presumably with the intention of silencing Janice Grey. He had, after all, almost certainly been more or less on the spot, camping out in the old keeper's cottage less than a mile away. And he had once been an elite soldier – of an age, but doubtless still more than capable of dealing with a small frightened woman.

Vogel was determined that Fairbrother would pay for his truly horrific series of crimes. He considered the man to be every bit as much of an evil monster as any violent criminal he had encountered in his career, and there had been a few of those.

There was considerable evidence against Sir John, albeit much of it circumstantial. But Vogel was aware that the key to it all might be the evidence of his own son.

Vogel had thoroughly enjoyed charging Freddie Fairbrother and watching the man's somewhat smug and confident demeanour change to one of shocked and fearful disbelief. However, a little plea bargaining might eventually be called for, because it was imperative that Freddie should be prepared to give evidence against his father in court.

Martha Kivel claimed to have been totally ignorant of all her husband's nefarious activities, in spite of a number of items of value from Blackdown Manor, including, somewhat incredibly, the Gainsborough worth millions, being found in Jack's shed in the Kivels' back garden. Vogel found it difficult to believe that Martha hadn't had at least an inkling over the years of the lengths to which Jack was prepared to go on behalf of his employer and boyhood and army friend. However, he had little choice but to give her the benefit of the doubt.

Further inquiries into the military careers of both Kivel and Fairbrother revealed that, whilst stationed in Germany, Kivel had been suspected of killing a taxi driver during an argument over the fare following a drunken night out. Fairbrother had given Kivel an alibi, which the military police had been obliged to accept even though they'd believed it to be false. Fairbrother had saved Kivel's life, in a way, but only in facilitating him to continue to live in freedom. And, as Vogel had half guessed following the brief exchange between the two men which he had witnessed at Bristol airport, it seemed that Fairbrother's hold over Kivel might have been down as much to a kind of blackmail as comradely love and loyalty.

The response of airport police and the apparent lack of communication at Bristol Airport on the night Kivel took his own life there and the two Fairbrother's were arrested, was the subject of a Civil Aviation Authority Inquiry.

Janice Grey was charged with conspiracy to commit arson. She steadfastly maintained that, whilst she now realised that her husband must have been hired by the real Sir John and been fully aware of the whole intrigue, she'd had no idea that the man she had cared for to the best of her ability had been an imposter. And that whilst she had been aware of the plan for George to set fire to Blackdown Manor, she'd believed, as she thought George had too, that this was merely in order to obtain insurance money, and that there had been no intention to harm anyone. Except, of course, George! Vogel thought the woman was probably telling the truth, also that George had been ultimately little more than a scapegoat, and that it had almost certainly been Jack Kivel who had tampered with the gas tank and caused the explosion at the manor. But this was now unlikely ever to be known for sure.

Nobby Clarke pulled all the strings she could in the Met and at the Palace of Westminster in order to bring some sort of retribution against Sheik Abdul. It was of course a lost cause. The sheik's lawyers asserted that his private jet had been made ready at Bristol Airport to transport a very important passenger who could not be named for diplomatic reasons. When this VIP had failed to turn up it had returned empty to the Middle East.

Sophia Santos' remains were flown back to her distraught family in the Philippines, where she would be buried with due Catholic honours. Vogel hated it when foreign nationals died violent deaths on British soil. He always considered that the British forces of law and order, if not the whole country, had let them down.

Another innocent victim of the whole debacle was Bella Fairbrother's fourteen-year-old daughter Kim. Victim support and social services were involved in assisting the understandably devastated girl. But it transpired that Kim had for a couple of years, and unbeknown to her mother, been seeing the father who had played no part in her upbringing. Sean Reardon had been her mother's fitness instructor when he and Bella had had a brief affair. It seemed there'd been no question of Bella wanting him in either her or her daughter's lives. But Reardon had been delighted to later have the chance to get to know Kim, and upon learning of her mother's death and all the horrors surrounding it, had promptly offered the girl a home.

Vogel asked Nobby to launch a major inquiry in London to try to discover the identity of the man Sir John Fairbrother had so cynically plucked from the streets of the city in order to take his place. Johnny Two was eventually identified as Roland North, originally from Chelmsford, Essex, who had ended up on the streets following a series of broken relationships and an inability to hold down any sort of employment, possibly due to a drink problem. It turned out that he had a son, Wayne, who spoke with rather a distinctive accent which Vogel believed was known as estuary English, a blend of Cockney and Essex. It seemed likely that Wayne's father had probably had much the same accent, and been advised to talk as little as possible, blaming the ravages of Parkinson's for his poor speech. Wayne had apparently over the years made a number of attempts, albeit ineffectual, to find his errant father, and at least wanted to give Roland North, or what remained of him, a proper funeral. This was duly arranged in Sampford Arundel Church, not far from the manor house which had been home to Roland for the last months of his life. The only home he'd had in years.

Janice Grey, on bail, asked if she could attend. Vogel, Nobby, Ted Dawson and Saslow also attended. Tom Withey, not totally able to fight back a tear or two, and Bob Parsons were there, representing Wellington Fire Service. A small wake was held at the Blue Ball. Fiona, the landlady, provided some complimentary food. Nobby bought the first round of drinks.

Vogel offered to join in. Nobby glanced scathingly at his ginger ale, the DI's favourite tipple.

'Never, ever, will I let you near a bar,' she said. 'We could all end up drinking that stuff.'

'It might do you good, boss,' said Vogel.

'When I want you to tell me what will do me good, Vogel, I'll let you know,' said Nobby, downing her usual double malt in one.

Vogel grinned.

'Decent of you to come, boss,' he said quietly.

'Poor sod,' commented Nobby Clarke. 'He had a bloody awful life and a bloody awful death.'

'Yes, well, at least we've got that bastard Fairbrother banged up where he belongs.'

'On remand, Vogel. He's not been convicted yet.'

'If this one walks, I shall personally burn down the court he stands trial in,' said Vogel.

'Fighting talk, DI Vogel.'

Vogel grunted.

'Don't worry, I'll provide the petrol,' said Nobby.